ALSO BY OMAR TYREE

Single Mom
A Do Right Man
Flyy Girl
Capital City
BattleZone

Omar Tyree

Sweet St. Louis

A NOVEL

Scribner Paperback Fiction
Published by Simon & Schuster
New York London Toronto Sydney Singapore

SCRIBNER PAPERBACK FICTION
Simon & Schuster, Inc.
Rockefeller Center
1230 Avenue of the Americas
New York, NY 10020

First Scribner Paperback Fiction edition 2000

Designed by Karolina Harris

Manufactured in the United States of America

10 9 8 7 6 5 4 3 2 1

The Library of Congress has catalogued the Simon & Schuster edition as follows:
Tyree, Omar.
Sweet St. Louis : a novel / Omar Tyree.
p. cm.
1. African-Americans Fiction. I. Title.
PS3570.Y59S94 1999
813'.54—dc21 99-36604
CIP

ISBN 0-684-85610-7
0-684-85611-5 (Pbk)

For my wife, Karintha
and my two boys
Ameer & Canoy
so that they'll know
that love
is a must
and is not
an option!

If love was ever explainable
mankind would have found a way
of controlling its grip
a *lonnng* time ago!

But love is God
uncontrollable
unpredictable
the undeniable link of humanity
the nucleus of creation
and the soul of the universe!

THE GREATEST SCIENCE
by Omar Tyree

St. Louis, Missouri, placed right smack in the heart of America and left of the Mississippi River that flows from north to south and through the midwestern region like a major artery, was sizzling hot in the month of May 1999. So hot was the city of St. Louis in the springtime that younger women were already wearing suffocating shorts with pockets so tight you could barely stick a dime in them. They wore thigh-high skirts and stomach-length shirts with those look-at-me-right-now colors: bright greens, luscious oranges, cool blues, bleached whites, bumblebee yellows, and whatnot. And these young women were showing *far* too much skin for the guys in St. Louis to handle, too much, in fact, for young men *anywhere!* Especially in the springtime when the hormones jumped Double Dutch on the brain. Maybe it was the heat of those outfits that drove the young guys insane. Then again, they were not supposed to notice, I guess. Or maybe not *acknowledge* that they noticed. At least not with their immature whistling, X-ray-vision stares, verbal expressions of rawness, and plenty of other things they felt so desperate to scream from their slow-moving cars, or from the well-worn corners that they loved to stand on from sunup to sundown.

"Haaay, sweet lady! Whoooweee!" some of the men shouted as the midday sun forced them to routinely check the sweat on the back of their roasting necks.

Ant and Tone fit right in with that overzealous crowd. Both young, shiny brown, and male, they were just as eager to peel off those two layers of clothing and get naked with the young brown women who walked the hot, springtime streets of St. Louis as the much *older* men admitted to. But at ages twenty-seven and twenty-eight, respectively, a separation of philosophy was apparent. Ant, while letting Tone drive his 1979 cranberry-colored Chevy, was becoming more creative in his approach to the mating game. In his field of work as an auto mechanic, he had enough thinking time on his hands to come up with a few new lines. Lines that would stop a curious woman in her tracks. Or at least he *hoped* that they would. So he practiced them. Sometimes to his partner Tone, but mainly to himself, to figure out a perfect rhythm of entrapment, like a young lion in training, leaping through the high grasses of Africa, over and over again.

"Man, I *love* the springtime!" Tone expressed to his partner, watching everything as they cruised the forever busy Kingshighway Boulevard with the windows rolled down. It was lunch hour, and shapely women were *everywhere*! Tone was in heaven as he drove, decked out in a bright red St. Louis Cardinals baseball jersey.

Ant, still in his work clothes, a short sleeved denim jumpsuit, didn't allow Tone to drive his car every day. He wanted to make certain he wouldn't look back on the experience as a big mistake.

"Yeah, well, just make sure you pay attention to the road," he warned, protective of his car.

Tone said, "Look, man, your car is in good hands. Aw'ight? Damn! You act like this ride is alive or something."

Ant looked at Tone's dark brown hands on his wood-and-chrome steering wheel and smiled. "She *is* alive. And her name is Bernadette."

Tone chuckled. "Yeah, that sounds like an old-ass name for her, too. She about twenty years old. That might as well be *sixty* in human years."

"She in good shape though," Ant countered. "That's why everybody be ridin' me to get in."

"You spent about a million dollars on her," Tone said. "She done had a face lift, lippo-suction, and every damn thing."

"That's *ly-po*-suction."

"Whatever."

Tone grinned and considered his friend crazy, while catching something interesting on the sidewalk to his right.

"Go 'head, Ant. Say that line you been workin' on to this one?"

Tone was smiling for miles. But he just didn't get it. Ant didn't want to waste his choice words and creativity on just any two legs walking by. He had big plans for his new material. The way he looked at it, it was like having one bullet left inside a six-shooter with a murderer in hot pursuit of his warm body.

Ant was shaking his head before he even looked at the woman.

"Naw, man, you just don't say it to anybody."

Then he looked her over, as she walked down the sidewalk to his right. She was just as shiny brown as he was, and tall. Ant never liked tall women. It was something about the way they walked, almost as if they were falling over; uncoordinated. On the other hand, if they walked tall and straight, they seemed like giants to him, like those Russian and German women in the Olympics of the seventies and eighties that he had watched with his older brothers and uncles. Those extra-long superwomen. Yet, this brown sister walking down Kingshighway was nowhere near *that* tall! Ant just didn't want to use any of his lines on her. She wasn't climactic enough on the Johnson scale. He didn't feel it for her down low. Or not as strong as he wanted to.

"She too tall anyway," he complained to his partner.

Ant was only five ten, and Tone was even shorter at five nine. But Tone *loved* tall women! It was all in the long brown legs, feeding his freaky visions of tree climbing.

"Man, go 'head and say it, and stop making excuses. She right there. Look at her," he challenged.

Ant took another peek at her. She *was* right there; he could probably reach out and touch her arm with his right hand, which rested atop his passenger-side door. She was even close to their age, a young working woman. They could see it in her face and in her outfit: a conservative blue knee-high dress with soft leather shoes and flesh-tone stockings. Even her hairstyle was conservative, straightened and curled at the edges with no artificial coloring. She had class and full maturity. However, she was walking as if she had a schedule to hold but was trying her best to ignore it. In fact, her pace was too calculated, almost as if she was *expecting* someone to stop her. That was the only thing that made Ant want to talk to her. She seemed ripe for practice.

Before he realized it, he opened his mouth in her direction while his Chevy eased alongside her with his friend Tone, full of expectations, at the wheel.

"Hey, miss?" Ant waited to catch her eyes, like a fish to the worm. Only then would he finish his precious line. "You wanna make a trade with me?"

That's when his heart rate increased. He had done his part, and now she had to do hers, while Tone prepared to burst in half from all of the tension involved.

First she looked at the car, which had a brand-new paint job and shiny chrome rims. She just *knew* he wasn't referring to trading that *car* for something. It looked as if they had put a lot of work into it. Yet, she was curious. Game bait.

"A trade? Trade for what?" she asked him.

"A piece of me for a piece of you."

The world just stopped and stood still for a second, like a dancer on freeze. Then she smiled, shook her head, and decided that it was time to cross the street.

Tone looked into Ant's dejected face and burst into laughter.

"I told you that shit wasn't gon' work!"

"Aw, man, first you said it was genius."

"*Genius?* I don't even use that word. So you *know I* didn't say that. You told yourself that shit."

Ant was disappointed. It was the wrong woman for his line. But at least he got her attention long enough to say it. And she smiled. What did that mean? Was she at least impressed, or simply amused? Nevertheless, she had walked away, and his originality was wasted.

"Take me back to work," he pouted. "I'll drop you off on Grand."

Tone continued to laugh and went on to tease him. "Awww, the little girl mad now 'cause his line didn't work."

Ant shook his head, denying it. "Whatever, man. I gotta get back to work. Make a left on Delmar." Then he added with a smile, "I got way more girls than you anyway," just for ego purposes.

Tone studied his friend's smooth brown face and low-cut hair for a second. He always wished that his own face could be so smooth, or that his own hair could look so neat. Even Ant's trimmed mustache was right on the money. Tone realized there was nothing he could say about his friend's comment, because it was true. Ant had more numerous *and,* more importantly, *willing* companions.

Ever since they first met in Jennings, Missouri, just outside of northern St. Louis, they had competed for the opposite sex, athletic bragging rights, and even for the use of their name. With the same birth name of Anthony, Anthony Wallace, a year older, quickly secured the more desirable title of "Tone," while for a short period of time, the younger, Anthony Poole, was known as "Little Tone." The younger Anthony was never able to swallow that humble piece of pie, so he informed everyone to call him "Ant" instead. And ever since the girls began to notice and to pass out home phone numbers on small pieces of paper, they almost unanimously preferred to give them to "Ant" rather than to "Tone." Then the younger Anthony went on to outgrow his older friend anyway, physically as well as mentally.

Tone contemplated it all, and came up with the only weak response that he could offer. "Yeah, well, you didn't get *that* girl." Then he began to smile, realizing full well that Ant's ego had always gotten the best of him. He just had to have *everything* his way.

Ant said, "Man, that girl wasn't all that. I got plenty of girls who look better than her."

"You don't have her though."

"I don't need that girl! I only talked to her 'cause you kept ridin' me about it."

"Yeah, 'cause you thought your line was all that. I told you it wasn't gon' work."

Tone was loving it! Egging Ant on was how he managed to keep their friendship in equilibrium. And if his partner was such a greater man, Tone figured he would have moved on to higher ground a long time ago.

"Look, man, I don't *need* no line to get *that* girl!"

"You wanna ride back there and talk to her again?"

If Ant were ever a violent guy like Tone could be, it was times like these where he would have punched Tone in his sometimes-gold-tooth-wearing mouth.

He shook his head instead, planning on ignoring it all. "Look, man, just pull over on Grand Boulevard so I can get back to work."

Tone nodded, knowing his fun had come to an end. Ant was still a good partner to him, and one of the few trusted friends that he still had from the old neighborhood who hadn't moved on, moved away, gotten married, been locked up for a number of years, or been killed in the street life.

Ant had always managed to keep his nose clean with a lifelong passion for cars that he had acquired from his well-schooled family of uncles and older brothers. They had all loved, repaired, and remodeled cars. His second brother even did time in jail for proving that he could steal them. Ant thought that was rather ridiculous. Sure, he loved cars like the rest of the men in his family, but he damn sure wasn't willing to go to jail for one!

Tone, on the other hand, had a long record of petty everything: theft, assault, drug selling, and even a few sex charges that he was fortunate to escape doing any hard time for. He seemed to know just when to stop to avoid a real prison bid. He had never dedicated himself one way or the other, negative or positive. He couldn't keep a job *or* a hustle long enough to make progress. In a word, he was a slacker, one who lacked the desire and dedication to become all that he could be.

But the two of them were partners, through thick and thin, long and short, high and low, and rough and smooth.

"So, what's up for later on, man?" Tone asked, holding on to the wheel as if he owned it. "You wanna head down to the casinos and see who down there?" As usual, Tone didn't have much of anything on his schedule, so driving around during Ant's lunch hour only served as a tease.

Ant shook his head. He was getting rather tired of doing the same things day in, day out for what seemed like twenty years. "Naw, man, it ain't nothin' new going on down there. I get tired of them places."

"What do you want to do then, go to East Boogie tonight, and see what's going on over there?"

Ant frowned. "East St. Louis looks plain depressing, man. Last time I was over there, I almost got in a shoot-out. That city needs a real makeover."

Tone looked surprised as he pulled over on Grand Boulevard to return the wheel to its owner.

"You was almost in a shoot-out? When?"

"Two weeks ago."

Tone still looked surprised. "You got a gun now?"

"Naw, man, I was with my cousin. He had *his* gun."

"Rico?"

"Yeah."

Tone started to laugh again as he climbed out of the car. "Yeah, I ain't *think* ya' ass had no gun."

Ant slid over into the driver's seat. "I don't need no gun. The only gun I need is right here," he bragged, grabbing his crotch under the wheel.

"Yeah, well, you better stay away from all these microwaves while you out here chasing miniskirts. Or that gun'll be burnin' ya' ass up."

"Naw, boy, that's *your* style, not mine. I deal with only clean toasters. And *you* need to stay *your* behind out of them rusty parks."

Tone grinned and said, "Yeah, whatever, dawg. Just get wit' me later on."

"Aw'ight, I'll see what I can do."

Tone stopped and looked back at the car, knowing better. "You not gon' front on me tonight, are you?"

Ant didn't want to promise him anything. "I told you, I'll see what I can do, man."

Tone stood frozen and began to doubt. "Look, man, if you wanna go solo tonight and drive around, wandering the streets like a damn cat, then let me know, and I won't bother you. 'Cause you be actin' like a damn girl when you get in them moods."

"Or, I might just have plans to get with one tonight," Ant responded, grinning.

"Not with that line you used earlier," his friend started up again. "'Hey, girl, you wanna make a trade wit' me?'"

Ant turned his head, disgusted, and drove off. Tone continued to laugh from the sidewalk, heading straight for the open parks of St. Louis, and to his favorite benches under the shade of tall trees. And once he got there, he planned to shoot the breeze and possibly share some good weed with whoever was out and willing.

While driving south on Grand Boulevard, Ant headed back to Paul's Fix It Shop on Gravois Avenue, the far south side of St. Louis, where he worked from Monday through Saturday. As he drove, he thought deeply about all of the seemingly wasted moments of his life. What was it all for? What was he heading toward? And where did he really want to be? It damn sure wasn't hanging out on the streets every night with Tone. There *had* to be more to life than *that!*

Then he thought about the tall brown sister on Kingshighway, and exactly what her smile meant. Maybe she *was* interested. Then again, maybe not. After all, she did shake her head and cross the street. How interested could she be?

"If I offered her a million dollars, she wouldn't have crossed the street," he fretted to himself. "Then again, I ain't got a million dollars to offer her."

Then he wondered if she would tell all of her girlfriends, cousins, and her mother about his line. Women would always run their mouths about a good line. He had been with enough of them to know. They almost seemed to *brag* about the lines that different guys used. That's how he knew, for sure, that creativity, delivery, and timing were all-important necessities in picking up a woman. A well-executed line and a truckload of money seemed to go a long way.

"Yeah, she gon' tell people," he convinced himself. "And once she tells about five people, and they run their mouths to about five more, my damn line'll be ruined forever."

The more he thought about it, the more annoyed he became.

"Shit! I knew I shouldn't have listened to Tone. He don't know the first thing about women. He just made me waste a damn good line for nothing. That girl wasn't even all that good lookin'."

So Ant headed on back to work with plenty on his mind, in search of some kind of fulfillment and the real meaning of life, something that Tone didn't seem to give two shits about. In the meantime, they were both just counting the days as they slipped on by. However, for Tone, those days seemed filled with any and every thing. But for Ant, they were more like a glass jar of emptiness.

Emptiness described the feeling that Sharron Francis had on her day off from work at the St. Louis International Airport. She had far too much time on her hands. And misguided idle time can be a sure invitation to entertaining preconceived notions of naughtiness. Had she visited the man she planned to see downtown at the Hampton Inn, that naughtiness would have been filled to the rim with sweaty twisting, twirling, and running out of breath to hotel sheet music. Nevertheless, she considered it pointless. Pointless and cheap, like the plain white sheets that they did it on. Besides, she *knew* better. The man was married. And in her right mind, it was wrong. But *girrrl* did it *feeel* so right!

RRRIIINNNNGGG! . . .

. . . RRRIIINNNNGGG! . . .

. . . RRRIIINNNNGGG! . . .

It was probably Mr. Married Man himself, calling from a hotel pay phone, and covering his tracks as usual, just in case his wife would question the phone calls made from his room. But Sharron refused to answer.

For what? she quizzed herself. *I can find good sex anywhere.*

What she *really* wanted was reliable companionship. Not a long-distance married man. The fact that he treated her so well and offered her money was not a substitute for the closeness that she wanted. In fact, the money made her feel more like a whore. A paid-for mistress. A sex toy. So she had never taken a dime from him.

. . . RRRIIINNNNGGG! . . .

. . . RRRIIINNNNGGG! . . .

She sat on the sofa and shook her head, disappointed with herself, and disappointed with the fate of her gender, as the phone continued its tempting and desperate rings.

But she fought it off. She fought it off. She fought it . . . *OFF* while continuing to shake her head and ponder the relations between men and women.

No matter what we do, it always seems like we're on the bottom of things whether we're married or *single,* she thought to herself. *So I guess Celena was right: You use them like they use you.*

Thinking of the advice from her best friend and roommate, who also worked at the St. Louis airport, Sharron decided to go ahead and page her as soon as Mr. Married Man would get the message and leave her the hell alone. After all, he didn't want *her* to get attached, right? So why should *he* be?

Find yourself some other mistress *to play with, because I have feelings, needs, desires, and everything else that real people have. Real people like your wife and your kids.*

When the phone stopped ringing, Sharron paged Celena immediately and took the first call following, praying to be right.

"What's up now, girl?" Celena's tempered tone rushed over the line from the pay phone at the airport. "You know when my break is. I'm busy as hell right now. And why you wait so long to answer the damn phone? You decided not to go, didn't you?"

Sharron smiled, relieved that it was her girl. "Yeah, I decided not to go. I mean, what's the point?"

"Mmm-hmm, I knew you couldn't do it," Celena hummed.

"Do what?"

"Parade around with a married man."

Sharron smiled even wider, an honest girl caught sneaking her way out through the back door.

"You wasn't raised that way," her friend told her. "You was just trying your best to be like me."

"I wasn't trying to be like you. It just happened."

"Yeah, sure it did, after you asked me a million questions about it. 'Do married men really do it better?'" she teased.

"I did *not* ask you that," Sharron responded, appalled by the insinuation.

"Yes you *did* ask me. Girl, you ask me shit, then you just up and forget about it. Maybe it's that Memphis air that you grew up in," Celena suggested. "You think you're such a damn saint. You screwed this married man, didn't you?"

"Why you gotta be all loud about it?" Sharron asked her. "Where are you calling me from? People might be listening to you."

"Girl, they don't know who the hell I'm talkin' to, Sharron Francis."

All Sharron could do was shake her head and grin it off. "You are so foul. You know that, right? And why do you keep comparing everything that *I do* to Memphis? I am my *own* person. If you took the time to *visit* Memphis with me, you would see that."

Celena snapped, "I got *no time* for playing horseshoes in Tennessee. Okay?"

They broke out laughing, thinking of the fifteen-minutes-of-fame group Arrested Development and their popular song and references to Sharron's home state.

Sharron decided to change the subject, right as Celena was announcing her need, and *desire,* to return to work. There was a young man involved in Sharron's day who had inadvertently helped her make the final decision not to be naughty with Mr. Married Man.

"Do you know what this guy said to me today?"

"What?" Celena asked. She was all ears and anxious. "Hurry up. I gotta go."

"Don't rush me."

"Well, come on. I gotta go already."

"If you're all in a rush, I'll tell you later then."

Celena became hesitant and annoyed. "How are you gonna start to tell me something and not finish? God, I hate when people do that! Just tell me what he said already!"

"Please deposit ten cents for the next two minutes!"

"See that? Damn! Hold on, girl."

Celena slid another quarter into the pay phone.

"You have to get back to work, remember," Sharron reminded her.

"Sharron, if you don't tell me what you started, I'm gonna ring your damn *neck* when I get home! Don't you know you could mess up my whole day like that?"

Sharron couldn't believe it. Everything was so urgent to Celena; so right now, right here, right this minute or I'll die!

"Do you need to know *that* bad? Dag!" Sharron changed her mind, deciding to keep it to herself. Celena didn't need to know *all* of her business. She sure didn't know *all* of Celena's. It was nowhere near being a two-way street. It was more like a free-flowing one-way street on Sharron's end, but a jam-packed four-lane expressway on Celena's.

"You should have never started to tell me then," her friend pouted.

Sharron thought quickly of a believable lie, just to get off the phone with her.

"I was walking down Kingshighway to catch the bus, and this guy rides up next to me and asks, 'Are you Naomi Campbell's cousin? You got the same high cheekbones and long legs.'"

Celena waited for more. *That can't be it!* Then she complained. "Is that it? Girl, you made me waste my damn quarter! You don't look *nothing* like Naomi Campbell. What, you're both chocolate brown and tall? I think she's five nine anyway. You're only five six and a half. Call me when you got something better than that. Okay? *God!*

"Maybe I *do* need to visit Memphis," she continued. "Because the things that impress you are so . . . so average. I can't believe you."

"Well, bye," Sharron said, faking offense.

"Well, *bye* to you, too!"

When they hung up, Sharron thought of the real line that was expressed to her on Kingshighway that afternoon, and wondered how Celena would have responded to that one.

"A piece of me for a piece of you," she repeated to herself with a grin.

She couldn't help but chuckle out loud, tickled by it, like a feather stroking the romantic side of her mind. Was it because she was from Memphis? Or was it simply a good line? One thing was for sure, it made her reconsider her date with Mr. Married Man. Was she really getting a piece of *him,* or just a piece, period? What exactly did "a piece of yourself" mean anyway? Was it all physical? Or could it also be mental, spiritual, and emotional?

It was a perfect line. And he probably had no idea how perfect it was. "A piece of me for a piece of you." Or maybe he needed to make a major adjustment and change it to "All of me for all of you." Because she needed *more* than just a piece. Humans *all* needed more. Then again, maybe humans had somehow gotten greedy, and pieces of one another were all that we could realistically get, because we were *all* connected to other important parts: extended family, business associates, and longtime friends. Nevertheless, all of those thoughts running through Sharron's mind made her wonder about the man. By the way:

"He wasn't no ugly fish out the water, either. Maybe I *would* like a piece," she told herself.

As for Celena, the girl thought she was the living definition of "hip" just because she was born and raised in St. Louis, Missouri, while Sharron was born and raised in Memphis, Tennessee. Celena acted as if St. Louis was Chicago, New York, and L.A. all rolled up into one. But who could blame her with all of the attention that she created for herself. Maybe it was because she was the middle sister of the three Myers girls. And not having the distinctive recognition of being the oldest or the baby, Celena made do as a rough-and-tumble tomboy and a real dynamo when it came to enjoying herself, especially while with men. *Any* man!

Yet she was still a tomboy to Sharron. Celena even worked as an airline caterer instead of at the gift shop, a food stand, or as a luggage monitor like most of the other women who worked at St. Louis International. And although she made more money as a caterer, you could hardly tell with the way that she spent it. You would think that the word "sale" had been erased, or had never been part of her vocabulary. So she was always broke; broke and borrowing to pay off steadily increasing credit card bills.

Sharron, through the hands of fate, had been forced to live as an only child, losing an older brother to crib death and a younger sister to a stillborn birth. At age nineteen, Sharron lost her mother to breast cancer. Yet, she never seemed glum about it, or at least not on the outside. She just learned to take life as it was given to her, while adding whatever she could along the way to make it better. Like the addition of Celena as her friend, a friend whom Sharron had met just six years ago when she had first moved to St. Louis, a wide-eyed teen, attending college away from home, "to grow up and experience the world," her mother had told her, less than two years before dying. "And never let *my* health stop you."

But her mother's health and death *did* stop her. It stopped Sharron from having faith in her own future. It stopped her from focusing on school. And it often stopped her from finishing what she started, school included. Sharron would go cold turkey and just quit, tired of it all. Tired of struggling *for* or *against* something as uncontrollable as life, and as uncontrollable as love.

She loved Celena Myers though. Loved her like a sister. A sister who had helped her to reach for a new day and for new adventures to liven each day. And as misguided as she could be in her attempts to make life hold more substance than work, food, sleep, and sex, Celena was the truth. She was real, as real as they were opposites as friends, like so many other sister friends of the world. They were opposite but complementary. For as much as Sharron needed Celena for adventure, hope, and energy, Celena needed Sharron for stability, morality, and warmth. They were soul sisters like Ant and Tone were soul brothers, all just finding their way, however they could, to make it in life.

RRRIIINNNNGGG! . . .

. . . RRRIIINNNNGGG! . . .

. . . RRRIIINNNNGGG! . . .

As tempting as he still was, Mr. Married Man that is, the truth was that there was much more out there. There was always something, or some*one* who would be more fulfilling than naughty candy that eventually rotted you.

Convinced of it, Sharron simply walked away from the phone and returned to her room. She kicked off her shoes, plopped down on her perfect orthopedic bed, and picked up on page 132 of Lolita Files's *Scenes from a Sistah,* where she had left off the night before. She realized that there were real meals out there. Pieces of something else to hold on to. And pieces of something else to love.

Hate was the opposite of love. And Anthony Poole *hated* standing in lines! He hated the entire institution of it. Mainly he hated standing in lines because some people never had to go through the humiliation. However, he and Tone usually did. Yet, Ant refused to think of himself as unimportant. He was simply unconnected. *Who said these ugly muscleheads are better than me just because they play for the Rams anyway?* he posed to himself.

He and his friend Tone watched as the beefy, well-dressed football players waltzed right into the club ahead of them and the chatty, scantily dressed women, who all waited patiently on Martin Luther King Drive as the line moved ahead slower than a bottle of Heinz ketchup.

"That's Derek Rand and Steve Tinsley," Tone noted with a smile. He was pleased—gold-toothed, green leather shoes, and all—to even enter the same club with the Rams players. Tone considered it a pleasure. That's why he spent nearly two hundred dollars on his shoes, to make sure he could hold up against important people, whether those dark green shoes matched the majority of his multicolored wardrobe or not.

Ant was dressed in all black, like an unmasked ninja, right on down to his Giorgio Brutini shoes. He could care the hell less who was in the club with him, as long as he was able to receive the respect that he felt he deserved.

"Who are all those other guys?" he asked rhetorically. He knew the answer to that before he even asked.

Tone hunched his shoulders and guessed. "Bodyguards, friends, cousins. You know how that shit goes; everybody they know gets in."

"You think they paying?"

Tone had to think a little harder for that one. "I'on know. But if they ain't, that's a whole lot of people to be gettin' in for free." Then he got a little pissed at the idea. "Matter of fact, if they ain't paying, then I'm keepin' my ten dollars, too. Shit, I need these ten dollars *much* more than *they* need it!"

Ant just smiled, knowing damn well that Tone was blowing a bunch of hot-ass air. He knew like the bulge in his pants that his boy Tone was going to cough up those ten dollars faster than an eight-year-old at the corner store for candy. It was ladies-get-in-free-before-eleven night. That meant there would be plenty of cheap women inside. Cheap women were easier to handle. But at those twenty-dollar, limited-space clubs, with the snotty women in those places, Tone sometimes felt as if he'd tossed his money to a street junkie who was feigning for that next hit. Wasted. But Ant? Ant loved that kind of challenge.

"IDs," the security asked them as they reached the front door.

I bet they didn't ask for their *IDs,* Ant thought to himself, still ranting at the disrespect. It was thoughts like those that ruined his nights out before he even tried to enjoy them.

"What's wrong with you?" Tone asked his partner. He could feel the hesitation. No words were needed. He frowned and said, "Look, man, if you're in one of them damn moods of yours again, then as soon as we get in this club, you do your thing, and I'll do mine."

"I don't want girls asking me why you got a gold tooth in your damn mouth anyway," Ant cracked, attempting to lighten his posture.

"You tell 'em 'cause it makes 'em *feel* like gold when I'm eatin' 'em," Tone countered.

Ant's smile was more a cringe of distaste. "You tell 'em that shit your damn self."

"Aw, man, you know you wit' it. You just embarrassed to talk about it," Tone suggested with a wide-open smile of his own. "You can talk about it with me, dawg. I'm your boy."

Ant couldn't wait to get the hell away from him. He walked clear across the blue-lit dance floor like a man on a mission, and headed straight for the men's room to check himself out, and to prepare himself for the competition.

Ain't nobody in here *got shit on me! I don't care if they play for the Rams, the St. Louis Cardinals, or the Dallas* Cowboys *for that matter! My game is tight!* he told himself, while staring *through* himself in the mirror. He was looking more inside of himself then *at* himself. He knew that the real deal was how strong each man *felt,* regardless of what he had, how he dressed, or how many people knew him. Ant felt that he could rule the world if ever given a chance. A chance would be all the help he needed to shine, like the gold around his neck and around his wrist.

"You got the time, brother?" he asked a lesser competitor in a purple suit. *What is it, Prince and the Revolution night up in here?* he asked himself, with an inside chuckle. *This guy looks like the Black Joker.*

The oversized brother flipped his wrist and said, "It's eleven thirty-five."

Ant looked down at his own gold-plated watch that read eleven-forty, five minutes ahead, just like he liked it. "Thanks, man. I was just checking." *By the way, lay off them barbecue ribs for a minute. Or do some push-ups or* something! *Damn!*

The purple-suit-wearing brother smiled, but he had no idea what Ant was thinking. Ant was five minutes ahead of his game, and on a whole different page.

"And good luck out there, man," he advised, like a snake to a rabbit. "Some of these girls got some long-ass nails."

Even the brother stinking up the restroom from behind the stall laughed.

"And don't let them feed you that shit no more, man!" Ant advised him, raising his voice above the black stall door. "'Cause whoever cooked you that meal, you need to leave *her* ass alone! That shit smell like *poison!*"

Back out from the restroom to join the party, Ant's testosterone level was at its highest. If he didn't know any better, he'd up and snatch the arm of the finest woman in the place, and tell her she'd be his company for the rest of the night, and for as long as he wanted her next to him.

Then there was Tone, right in the middle of the dance floor, already getting sweaty with some average-looking girl. Typical. Tone would take anything that was willing to be taken. But Ant? He searched the room like the sharpest young recruit of the Federal Bureau of Investigations. His mission: spot the five finest women in the club, and narrow down his mark.

"Hey, Anthony. Who are you searching the crowds for? Does she look like me?"

Dana Nicole Simpson was five foot three, slim, and caramel brown, with short-cut black hair and two dark daggers for eyes. She was so striking that looking into her eyes could paralyze a man as if he had been turned into stone, like the Greek legend of Medusa. Yet, Ant had seen, stared at, and sweated through every last inch of her, filling her up to full, like he did his '79 Chevy. Seeing her and *knowing* her like he did so well could just about make his already inflated head go POP! In fact, it was altogether dangerous. *Too* dangerous! So dangerous that Ant received the fatal message to his brain, *somehow,* and quickly, *wisely,* decided to take it down a thousand before he went bungee jumping with no damn cord.

"You wanna dance?" he asked her. Dana was wearing a shiny silver dress with no sleeves, accompanied by a silver purse and silver shoes. What a complementary match they made, without even trying. If push came to shove, Ant figured he could take her home again for their usual late-night romping. Tone sure wouldn't object to it. He absolutely *worshiped* her! "I would fuckin' marry that girl in a heartbeat, man! What the hell is wrong with you?!" he questioned his partner whenever Ant decided to play her. "You can't *get* no finer girl than her!"

Again, he didn't quite understand the game. Tone never played high enough. Despite the minor adjustments of Dana's less than round ass and her less than sizable breasts, her damn ego was as large as Ant's, and that was a *major* problem! So they played a game of who can out-think, out-charm, out-dress, out-sex, and out-control the other, deciding in the long run to just fuck and enjoy it. No mortal man like Tone could understand that. Ant and Dana were both on an unsettling level of wanting better, more, and all, and then having to settle for each other, but only sometimes, and never forever, because neither one of their egos would allow it.

Ant thought of it all, fantasizing, and could already taste her slippery, small tongue on his. But then she brought him back to reality.

"What if I'm here with somebody?"

"That never stopped you from dancing with me before."

Dana laughed, fantasizing as well on their great sex-making. How sweet it *always* was, as they would try so desperately to out-climax each other.

"But not tonight," she told him tenderly.

Ant read that as more danger, which only made him want her more.

"You got a jealous one this time?"

She smiled, touching his lower back, just enough, and not enough. A lesser man would have already wet his pants in expectations, brought on by daydreams that moved way too fast.

"Why can't I just be in love?" Dana asked him innocently enough.

He grinned, like playing the devil on an oversized screen with digital surround sound.

"Shit, you ain't in love. You ain't in love no more than *I'm* in love."

"You're in love with your car. So why can't *I* be in love with a man?" she hinted, bringing up memories of back-seat car romping. In a word, Dana's mental foreplay was *hot! Piping!* And only the strong could survive under such intense heat. Then she had that stare and those dark eyes of hers. She was the ultimate temptation, begging you to fall for her and be swallowed alive.

"You ain't in no damn love," Ant repeated, trying to snap himself from her trance. She *couldn't* be in love. Because if she was, then that meant their game was over, and she had won. Hell, he felt lonely already. Titanic. He was crashing into a glacier, breaking in half, and falling into the cold, deserted sea with no rescue.

She gave him one last pat on the back and said, "I gotta go now . . . before I get in trouble." And why did she have to smile so beautifully when she drifted away?

Dana had struck again, and Ant had been paralyzed, turned into stone, and was feeling cold, so damn cold. Some of those sisters had long-ass nails indeed. Raking.

"Damn!" he huffed out loud. Then he composed himself and said under his breath, "That girl's trying to ruin my damn night. Fuck her! I don't need her."

Oftentimes, when we lie to ourselves, we end up telling the truth with the intensity, or the lack thereof, in our emotions. So Ant went back to his searching, with a dagger in his heart, finding something interesting.

What the hell is she *wearing?!* He spotted a young woman who indeed could have passed for Dana's younger cousin: same size, same look, same hair, but with much less fire, flair, and experience. Maybe that was why she was wearing a black net dress that showed straight through to her black bra and panties. It may not have been as shocking on Toni Braxton at an American Music Awards show, but in St. Louis, most of the brothers seemed too stunned by her boldness to even approach her. Or at least not until the drinks got heavy.

Ant never needed any drinks to do *his* thing. That was only for men who needed to *lose* control in order to *gain* control, and would only end up being *out* of control, even when they *did* succeed. Then again, with the intoxication that he had just received from Dana, Ant was out of control his damn self, moving toward the sister with all body and no mind.

"What's your name, miss?" he pushed through her two girlfriends and asked.

Surprisingly, despite her girlfriends' obvious displeasure, his mark seemed attracted to his reckless authority.

"Shawntè," she answered him. She was pleased that someone was finally willing to talk to her after she'd gone to such drastic measures to make sure she'd be noticed that night.

Before she could step out of range, Ant clenched her net outfit with his fingers and joked, "Shawntè, I guess I caught you in my net tonight, hunh?"

It was corny, but what the hell? Although someone else may have thought of it, since no one else had said it to her, she laughed at it anyway.

"I'm not even gonna respond to that," she told him.

"Well, my name is Anthony Poole, I'm twenty-seven, I got my own place, and yes, I'm single."

Her girlfriends figured, *So what? Let's go.* But Shawntè could feel his persistence. She could sense his confidence. It surrounded him and floated up into the air like an exotic cologne. And he was choosing her and not accepting no for an answer.

"You a mind reader?" she asked him. He was in luck. She happened to be independent, and immune to the peer pressure that was sending her several messages to move on.

"I'm reading *your* mind," he responded to her. "That's why I told you what you wanted to know. Now can I buy you a drink, and ask *you* a few questions?"

It was an easy thought. *Why not?*

"Okay." As far as her girlfriends were concerned: "Um, I'll catch up to y'all later."

Ant smiled, knowing that he had picked the one. The ringleader. But hopefully she wasn't driving. When the ringleaders drove, more often than not, they ended up becoming baby-sitters after the party, breaking their necks to fulfill everyone's needs, as well as driving them all back home. However, a ringleader without a car would take a taxi in a heartbeat. That's just how much Ant knew about women.

So he asked her, "Are you driving tonight?"

"Unt-unh, my girlfriend drove," she answered as she slid onto a bar stool. Ant preferred to stand, so that he could remain sharp and up on his mental toes. Sitting down may have made him too comfortable to work things the way he wanted. Besides, he was still pumped with energy. Dana Nicole Simpson had made sure of that.

"What time is your curfew then?" he asked Shawntè with a straight face. He wanted to see what her thoughts would be to staying out late. All night if possible.

She was tickled by the question, as well as a bit offended. She realized that she was younger than most of the other women in the club, but she could hang, and she was nowhere *near* being a baby.

"You *can't* be serious," she said to him. "I haven't had a curfew for six years."

She was telling him too much information, letting him know that she was an amateur.

"You about twenty-two, twenty-three?"

She smiled, realizing she had told on herself. "Does it matter? I'm legal. That's all you need to know." Then she looked to the bartender. "I'll have a sloe gin fizz."

"And you?" the bartender asked Ant.

"I want whatever she got," he answered. "Unless it's harmful to me. Is that sloe gin fizz safe or what?"

He was asking Shawntè more than the bartender. The muscle-bound brother just smiled and went on about his business of making the twin drinks.

Shawntè grinned and responded, "It's safe. It's *always* safe. But it's not always available. Especially when it's in a new place."

Ant wasn't expecting that. Maybe she was a little more experienced than he thought. So he laughed it off.

"Oh, I see. It's like that?"

She nodded, "Yeah, it's like that," and took a sip of her drink as soon as it hit the napkin in front of her.

He read the speedy sip of her drink as nervousness. He watched her every move, listened to her every word, and collected her vibes, like an interrogation expert.

"So what's the most important quality that you look for in a man?" he asked her, taking a sip of his own drink.

She damn near choked on hers to respond to him. "What happened to just a regular conversation? God, I feel like I'm being interviewed," she complained.

He didn't even flinch when he told her, "You are."

She smiled. "For what position?"

"That depends on how well you interview."

The nerve of this guy! Who in the hell does he think *he is?* she thought to herself. Yet, she was intrigued like hell by him. Exactly how far was he planning to go with it all? By then, she was totally into him. No other man in that place would mean a *thing* to her. Ant had her undivided attention. But she didn't have his. Not really. He was still thinking about Dana. That's what made his game so uncharacteristically bold with Shawntè. He didn't exactly care if he failed or succeeded, because his mind was preoccupied with something else. *Who in the hell could* Dana *be in love with in here?*

Then he began to wonder, searching the room again with his drink in hand. He noticed the many eyes that were slashing back and forth at him and Shawntè. Even his partner Tone had spotted them. But were they all peeking because she was fine, and they were envious? Or was it more because she looked like a freak in her black net outfit, and they couldn't help themselves. Oh, men *will* stare at a freak, but few of them would respect her. Even fewer would want to be seen out in public with one, especially while in the presence of so many other fine women. It tended to make a guy look desperate.

All of a sudden, Ant grew self-conscious about it, and no longer wanted Shawntè's company. *Shit! What if Dana saw me with this damn girl? What the hell was I thinking?* he questioned. He could easily lose all of his cool points with Dana by lowering his standards and entertaining a freak. He didn't know Shawntè's reputation. He didn't know her from a dead-end street.

Before he realized it, Ant was drifting away from the bar area, fully conscious of every peeping eye, hoping and praying that two of them were not Dana's daggers.

Then he spotted her, all wrapped up and cheesing under the arms of a slim brother who looked at least six foot three. Maybe he was a baller for St. Louis University. But he couldn't be, because Dana was twenty-six and not at all into the youth movement. Most young guys couldn't handle her anyway. And judging from the guy's expensive style of dress, he obviously had some money. Yet, Dana was not into street hustlers either. She hated the insecurity of it all. It was a racket for reckless gamblers. Fast money led to fast failure. That had always been Ant's strong point with Dana; he was stable. Not rich, but stable. Not that glamorous, but definitely glamorous enough. And once she gave him an hour of opportunity to show what his one hundred seventy-five pounds of solid brown flesh was made of, he gave her all that she could handle and had her *always* pleased to slip and slide back to him for more. However, while she was wrapped up under supposedly loved arms at the club that night, it was as if Ant had never existed.

DAMN!

A shattered ego was a terrible thing to have.

"Hey, I'll be right back," Shawntè told him in his ear. "I have to use the restroom."

He barely acknowledged her, which only made her *more* intrigued by him. She was hooked, and he didn't even care anymore. What a shame. Now he had to figure out what he wanted to do with her. Would he just walk away and start all over? . . . He didn't have a clue. Until he took another look at her net outfit as she slipped through the crowd. Without any control, he could feel a hard-on coming. When all else fails, a new woman was *always* the answer. So even if he had to pay for it, *somebody* was getting penetrated that night. Why not Shawntè? She had Dana to thank for it. And as far as all the stares were concerned, *they can all go home and jerk off!*

"So how long do we have to stay here?" Ant boldly asked Shawntè when she returned to her seat.

She couldn't believe her ears. He was getting bolder by the minute. Too bold! *I barely know you,* she wanted to tell him. If she could.

Instead, she asked, "Where are you trying to go?"

He hunched his shoulders. "You wanna go to the casinos?" He was saying anything that came to mind.

"I don't gamble," she answered. And she didn't.

"I don't either. But right now, I'm just . . ." He lost all of his composure and said, "Bored. Bored to death."

Wrong comment. That changed everything. It gave Shawntè an easy way out.

"Is that what this is? Boredom?"

He tried to cover up his tracks with philosophy. "Look, in this world, you either go out there and try something new and different, or you end up just watching it spin by you. So what do you want to do?"

He was too hasty.

"I'm chillin'," she told him.

End of game. And he knew it. Or at least for that night. It made him so frustrated that he had to get away from her for fresh air.

He sighed and told her, "I'll be back," as he headed for the front door.

However, Shawntè knew the deal. She knew it when he first asked for her name. He wasn't coming back. He couldn't take no for an answer. She knew that already. But that didn't stop her feelings from being hurt.

Damn! No phone number. No good-bye. No nothing. . . . Guys are a damn trip. For real!

Ant had ruined Shawntè's night, and Dana had ruined his. The dominoes of love were falling over.

Ant walked outside onto Martin Luther King, and looked up into the dark sky, wondering why he was being punished. Was it payback for all of the girls and women that he had screwed over in the last ten to fifteen years of his dating life? Or did he bring it on himself over time, by never committing to love any of them? Either way, the emptiness was finally creeping up on him. It was finally running him down and taking him prisoner.

"Ant! What's up, dawg? What's up?" Tone asked, joining his partner outside.

Ant looked back and said, "I'm ready to get the hell out of here. It's just the same old shit."

Tone wasn't budging. "Yeah, well, that's *your* opinion, 'cause *I'm* stayin'." In fact, he didn't have any more words for the matter. He simply stepped back inside the club to continue enjoying himself. He wasn't a damn kid! He could take a taxi home. As for Ant, he was stuck somewhere between his desire to leave and his curiosity to stay. That's why he even bothered to go in the first place. Curiosity. What *could* happen? But his curiosity died a fast death each time that nothing did. Yet, he could at least use a new phone number. If only to keep his life interesting with fresh conversation from a woman. So he walked back in with that singular purpose in mind. A phone number. He just had no idea how easy it was going to be.

"Call me," Shawntè said, pushing her number into his palm as soon as she spotted him. *She* wasn't taking no for an answer either. She had chosen him. Whether he *wanted* to be chosen by her or not.

Ant felt sorry for her. It wasn't *her* fault that he was displeased with his life. It wasn't her fault at all. He even thought of apologizing to her. However, she seemed fed up with him for one night, and was only reaching out to him so they could start over again. All he had to do was call and act interested. So he left it at that. And he left the club. He left his parking space, behind the wheel of his car. And he left his friend Tone, to be alone again with his thoughts and wishes of fulfillment. He was still searching for a meaning of life in the American city of St. Louis, and in the world. And he realized that he would never find it amidst the dizzying lights and the human posturing that goes on inside an average nightclub.

Sometimes it's funny how one person's world can be so parallel to another's. Not parallel in another universe, or all the way around the other side of the world, but parallel in the exact same city. Someone else was looking for fulfillment and for a meaning of life as well, in St. Louis, while on a double date at the movies.

And the thing with double dates is, you always feel like an ice-skating couple, trying your best to impress the judges while hoping not to fall flat on your ass and have to cover it up with fake smiles to hide the embarrassment. Simply put, it's more like walking on eggshells than a fun date. Because if your man has any flaws, they suddenly become amplified: too short, too boring, too ugly, too immature, or too *something*. Or then, he's never enough of this, and never enough of that. Yet, you go through with it anyway, knowing damn well that you should have gone solo instead. Unless, of course, you were really with the man of your dreams. But on most of these double dates, you're absolutely *not* with Mr. Dreamboat! He ends up being more like Mr. Twoleftfeet, and can't quite catch the rhythm of your dance like you would like him to.

Sharron made her move, excusing herself in the middle of the featured film to fake a trip to the restroom. "I'll be right back."

"Where are you going?" Celena asked her.

"Do you *have* to know?" Sharron asked. *Show some darn manners and tact, girl!* she shot with her eyes.

"Oh," her girlfriend responded, catching on. "Well, hold on, I have to go, too."

That set off an alarm from Celena's bolder-than-average date.

"Wait a minute. Both of y'all have to use the bathroom at the same time? What is that?"

Celena moved to silence him with her own boldness. "Don't act like y'all didn't do the same thing, hangin' out on street corners, drinking beers, and pissing on trees."

"Yeah, but we don't do that shit now," he refuted.

His friend, who was with Sharron, let out a forced laugh, the kind that he could have done without. It only showed how incompetent he was as compared to his partner. It also made him seem more like a pom-pom-carrying cheerleader than a jersey-wearing player.

Embarrassed by it, Sharron made her way to the aisle and hustled out of the theater much faster than she originally planned. Both dressed casually in fitted blue jeans, Celena was hot on her tail as soon as she entered the restroom.

"Sharron, you don't like him, do you?" she correctly assumed.

"I mean, what's to like about the boy? 'My cousins did this. I got that. I can't wait till I do this,'" she ran off, mocking her date for the evening. "He sounds like a teenager. Are you sure he's twenty-five?"

Celena laughed. "Maybe he's not. You think he was lying about his age? He *does* look kind of young. Let's go to a club after this and see if he gets carded," she joked.

"I don't think so," Sharron snapped. "I'm ready to call it a night right now. This is not even an interesting movie, and he keeps trying to lean closer and closer to me."

Celena found it all humorous. *She* would. She was the one who had set everything up. In fact, far too many matchmakers suffer from a God complex, and they don't have the faintest idea why their matches don't exactly fit. They just think that they *know* what they're talking about, and with *your life!*

Sharron checked her hair in the mirror and said, "This is the last time for this. And I *mean it!*"

Her friend smiled, knowing better. "Until two months from now, when you're all lonely and watching late-night movies on cable again."

Sharron didn't even flinch. "We'll see," she declared, and walked out of the bathroom. Celena followed her out.

"You really wanna go home already? It's only nine o'clock, Sharron. What are you going to do with yourself?"

She smiled. "Well, with some things, I can just turn them on and off, and I don't have to worry about going through all of the other bullshit involved."

Celena frowned at her. "Girl, a real-ass man is *always* better than a vibrator."

"Are you sure about that?" Sharron responded. Realistically, she didn't own a vibrator. Nor did she ever use one, or even fondle herself. Sharron was more of a fantasizer, picturing herself with the perfect man, and imagining the perfect love, if such a thing existed. Her fantasies had often gotten her into trouble with reality, like with Mr. Married Man.

"Well, then again . . . I guess not in *all* cases, no," Celena answered with a chuckle. "But, I mean, don't you want someone to hold on to while you're feeling it?" she asked.

Sharron thought about it as they continued to linger out in the hallway. *Of course* she wanted to hold on to someone. She wanted to kiss someone's neck and massage someone's shoulders and lower back, and play an intimate game of Twister with someone's strong, warm, masculine body. But not just with *anyone. Who* wanted *anyone?!*

Overhearing their conversation, a teenage usher smiled sheepishly. Older women speaking so openly about sex could give a young guy a fast hard-on. Not all males were afraid of assertive women. Younger guys—because of having to deal with the immature giddiness of virgins and the insecure doubts of once-around-the-track girls—were *easily* attracted to older, more assertive women. Young girls were not as experienced in sex to talk about it in detail like older women could anyway. So the young usher began to have fantasies of his own, right there on the spot.

Celena was definitely his type, too: shapely and medium brown, with plenty of sexiness and gusto to match. She even appeared young, with her smallish head and facial features, accompanied by her youthful energy. Sharron, though, seemed too reserved for *his* taste, or at least from what he had heard from her. Reserved girls like her were a pain in the balls. At age nineteen, he knew enough about high-school virgins and hopelessly romantic college students to know that fact full well. So his fantasies were all about Celena, just like the average man's would be. As for Sharron, with her extra cock-blocking cognitive, she would surely get a fast boot. Because whenever a woman thinks too much, she jumps into asking questions that most guys don't want to answer, no matter *what* age they are!

Why do you do this? Why did you do that? What does this mean? What does that mean?

Truth be told, most males would rather their relationships with women just . . . flow, like a well-written novel instead of like a textbook, where they may be forced to answer twenty questions at the back of each chapter. Then they'd be quizzed on all of their answers, with a cognitive woman's high expectations of a grade A.

To hell with all of that! the young usher thought to himself. *Just give me a woman who can understand me and accept me for* who *and* what *I am, a hard-shelled guy with sweet, hidden chocolate in the middle. Like an Easter Sunday treat.*

Sharron and Celena, catching the usher's smile and snicker, decided to ease their way back inside to the featured film.

"That was a long-ass piss," Celena's date commented.

"That's because I had to take a *shit,*" she responded, strictly for shock.

Sharron shook her head, thinking, *How long do I have to live through this kind of stuff?!* Then her young date eased his right hand across her left knee and found himself rejected.

"Would you like to keep your hand, or do you want me to donate it to science?" Sharron snapped, handing his slippery brown invasion back to him.

"Oh, shit," his friend responded with a laugh. His boy was shattered, for caving in to peer pressure. He knew good and well that Sharron was not at all cordial to his advances, and trying to force himself on her would only bring to the surface the issue of their incompatibility.

For Sharron's part, the dramatic approach was against her nature. Instead of public confrontations, she would much rather slip away and disappear, like a ghost. But insecure men rarely allowed women to *be* ghosts. Especially when they hoped for more than just a movie and a car ride back home after dark.

At that moment, Celena knew that their night on the town was officially over.

"We might as well go," she stood up and announced.

"Why, just because *they* don't get along? They can both catch a bus back home."

And why were so many men hooked on the idea of boldness? Was it because so many women expected it from them? It was as if boldness were a requirement for maleness, and for serious dating. Women were used to it. Many of their fathers were bold, and their mothers' boyfriends, and their uncles, and their male cousins. Not to mention hundreds of heroes that they saw in films, or on network television, or performing in male-dominated sports.

Passivity was not acceptable. So the passive men, or *sissies*, became expendable. Of course, until it was time for appreciative cards, candies, and flowers. Women then seemed to want a sudden change—from well-worn T-shirts and Wrangler blue jeans—to a man who wears a nice tie and a soft cotton sweater across his shoulders. They want rough and tough with the crow of the rooster in their mornings, yet sweet and gentle as the sun goes down in their nights. Nevertheless, many men had obvious problems making such a dramatic character transition. Especially the men of the nineties era.

"You know what? I'm about tired of all the *shit* that's been coming out of your mouth tonight," Celena spat to her date.

"And what about *your* damn mouth?"

"What about it?"

"You were the one talking about you had to take a *shit,* so everybody in the fucking show could hear it! What about that?"

Women, believe it or not, were *hardly* immune to the ego, they simply had less of an awareness of their use of it. As if an out-of-control woman was a *good* thing. But it was mainly used to counteract a male society's expectations of meekness. Men who could not handle that fact created a defensive term to describe these women, calling them bitches. Which Celena had been referred to on *more* than a few occasions.

Fortunately, there weren't that many people in the theater. But for those who were there, public arguments between men and women nailed the point home that relationships were definitely something to be worked out, and could *not* just be *flowed* into, as most guys seemed to want. Nor was everything supposed to go perfectly on a first date, like many women expected.

Sharron stood and said, "Let's just go."

"Go 'head then," her shot-down date responded.

Sharron looked at him with a face of anger, but spoke with a voice of pity. "You need to really grow up. *Both* of you." If she had no tact of her own, she would have included her friend Celena in that advice. She had said it all before. A hundred times. Or was that a million?

"Are you just gonna ignore me all night long? God, it's just one date," Celena complained as she and Sharron climbed out of their taxi.

"He was just one guy, and it was just one boring show. I mean, what's the big deal?" she continued as they approached their second-floor apartment.

There wasn't much else for Sharron to say. One date, plus one guy, plus one boring movie eventually added up to a lot of unnecessary letdowns, all with the same results. Nothing! So why even mention names and descriptions, unless they really meant something? They all just became *the one.* Like in: *the one* who got drunk and acted like a damn fool; *the one* whose breath smelled like a trash can; *the one* who got arrested for doing "nothing" and called from jail to bail him out; or *the one* who lied about his age, his job, *and* his fiancée. After ten or twenty of *the ones,* what difference did it all make? Sharron had run out of words to continue explaining it. She was tired of it. Tired of caring, fussing, rationalizing, and tired of putting herself out in the meat market only to rot away in the window with no plastic wrapping for protection.

"What are you gonna do, go back to reading that damn book?"

Celena asked as Sharron headed straight for her room. "That book don't have no answers. I read it already. It's all the same stuff. Guys are just guys, so get used to it."

Celena would not let the situation die. She expected Sharron to respond to her. She expected her to respond like she always did, and then they would fall into another long discussion about how love *should be* but was not. And how love never quite reached a steady plateau. Or at least for a billion women. Guys, on the other hand, never seemed to want love. They seemed to want only the flesh, and the control of the heart. They wanted you to give yourself, while they would rarely give themselves.

So Sharron was speechless, knowing it all, and having control over absolutely none of it. While Celena just went with the flow, exactly how most guys liked it. And by going with the flow, she seemed to condone the nonsense, as if broken hearts and years of inner tears were meant to be normal.

It was not that way at all for some women. Some women were loved, happily married, and unbelievably satisfied. *So what is it with me?* The question is asked at one time or another. *Why do* I *have to suffer so much? What did* I *do? What could* I *have possibly done to deserve so much despair?*

Whenever Sharron became depressed, she thought about her mother and her two siblings in heaven. Then she thought about herself, and about her father, who had taken up seeing a new woman less than a year after his only wife's death. Sharron often asked herself as a younger woman, *How could he? Unless he never loved my mother as much as I* thought *he did. Or as much as he led me to believe.* But now, when she thought about her own gutter balls in the bowling lane of love, she finally understood what her father must have felt, and how he had to move on and love again with youth no longer on his side.

That sudden reevaluation of her father made her feel warm inside. It made her feel more mature. At the tender age of twenty-three, and approaching twenty-four, she realized that she had all the time in the world. She just hoped that it wouldn't equate to more time sitting in the meat market window without a sale.

Energized with purpose, she bolted from her room to retrieve the phone and pull it inside her room with her for privacy.

"Who are you calling?" Celena asked, stretched across the living-room sofa watching a video and eating hot popcorn.

"My father."

Good answer. Fathers were men whom Celena still respected, mainly because her own father had always been on the job. Maybe that was why she was never pressed or set on complaining about a man. Because when push came to shove, she understood that she could always get one. She simply wasn't ready to settle down and give up her adventurous freedom like her mother and younger sister had as teenagers.

"Hey, Daddy. How's everything been going?" Sharron asked in her room.

"Sharron! Hey, girl. How have you been making out up there? You need anything?"

"Yes and no," she answered with a smile.

"Yes and no?" he repeated. "What are you trying to tell me? Either you need something or you don't." No matter how old you get, fathers will always make you feel like a young son or daughter.

He was ready to lead her away from the subject, so she redirected things.

"Actually, I was calling you to apologize and to tell you that I finally understand. You know, how you felt after Mom died."

Total silence.

"Ahh . . . thank you, sweetie. Thank you." He didn't know what else to say. It was obviously an awkward moment for him. His daughter continued:

"I mean, it was real selfish of me not to see that you still had a life to live."

"Yeah, I just wish you could tell your aunts and first cousins that," he said with a chuckle. It had been eating him up inside for years.

Sharron took a deep breath and asked, "Is Lucille around?"

Silence again.

"Ahh . . . yeah."

Sharron had never been disrespectful to Lucille, but she had never been too cordial to her either. "Well, tell her I said hi, and thanks for sharing herself with my father." She could have told Lucille on her own, yet she figured it would carry more weight by saying it to her father, because Daddy was the one with whom she felt the most guilt.

It worked, too. She could feel her father's warmth smothering her straight through the phone, as if his shackles had finally been cut off, and he had been freed again to run in the sunshine.

"I sure *will* tell her, baby. I sure will."

Sharron laughed, imagining what her father must have looked and sounded like when he first met and fell in love with her mother years ago.

"Well, I don't want to hold you up from your movie. I just called to say that I was sorry, and that I'm happy for you."

"How did you know we were watching a movie?" he asked his daughter. He seemed surprised by it.

Sharron shook her head and smiled again. They always watched movies together. Movies or sports. Because they didn't like most of the new shows that came on regular TV, aside from *The X-Files,* which they both loved. Americans born in the forties and fifties would probably always have a thing for extraterrestrials and conspiracy theories. Just like those born in the eighties and nineties would have a particularly strong affection for music videos and computer graphics.

"I just know, Dad," she told him. "I just know."

And when she hung up, she envied them. She envied how grown-up men and women could just spend time watching movies and holding hands. They would go grocery shopping together and for long walks, totally satisfied with each other's company. When she was younger, Sharron couldn't wait to be older, like most humans. But now that she was older, she couldn't wait until she was a complete *elder,* to experience patient and giving love, from both sides. But first she had to find someone worthy enough to grow old with. *That* was the problem. Worthiness. How in the world do we measure it? And how long does it last?

Speaking of worthiness, how does a man in a free society determine which women are worthy enough to chase? Is it a body? Is it a face? Is it good hair and a keen nose? A good home-cooked meal and plenty of submissiveness? Or is it some kind of special mating ritual that we have somehow forgotten? One thing is for sure: men have the hardest time in the world trying to narrow the numbers down to just one. Many of them don't. And wouldn't. Not in an entire lifetime, whether their women accepted that reality or not. Because every new face, new scent, new outfit, and new curve made a man feel ten, twenty, thirty years younger. Like a brand-new baby boy in love with his momma and her nurturing milk all over again.

"How much would it cost me to get this thing fixed?" a confident woman's voice was asking Ant's boss, Paul Mancini, at his Fix It Shop. Paul had come up with his shop name just for people like her, who didn't know the first thing about cars and just wanted the thing *fixed.*

Paul was an Italian man in his midforties with strong presence and a six-foot frame. He looked over at the woman's dark green

BMW. It had been smashed on the left front end, not enough to stop it from running, but definitely enough to need fixing.

"I'll tell you what," he started with a grin, "I'd be able to tell you something a lot nicer if it wasn't a BMW." He shook his head, dark-haired with streaks of gray, and pitied the woman. "That there is gonna cost you a couple of quarters no matter where you take it. You start crashing BMWs, and you're not talking pennies anymore. What did your insurance people say?"

"I'm not using my insurance for this. And *I* didn't crash the car."

The confident woman was getting testy. Ant, who was working on new brakes for a Toyota, became curious to see what she looked like. Because she *sounded* like a brown sister. He could hear it in her voice tone.

Paul tossed up his massive hands and said, "I'm not disputing what happened, I'm just telling you that you're not looking at a nickel-and-dime job here. We're talking quarters. And if anyone tells you differently, they're lyin' to ya."

Paul had to put his business bid in, but he worked from integrity as well, and there was no way he could ease down the price of repairing an up-to-date BMW, a well-crafted German import.

"What year is it?" he asked her.

"A ninety-eight."

He couldn't help but smile, still pitying the woman. He nodded and said, "That's what I thought."

Ant slid out from under the white Toyota and acted as if he had to stretch in their direction, just to get a good look at her. He knew that she had money before he could even focus on her.

Shit! I'd fix that *for free!* he told himself, taking her sights all in. She had everything! The face. The hair. The body. The tailor-made dress code, and all the attitude of a regal black woman.

"Give her a quote, Paul. I'd work on it," Ant interjected.

Paul knew exactly what *Anthony* wanted to work on. He may have been Italian and married, but he still knew a good-looking woman when he saw one.

"Just calm down, tiger," he responded to Ant with a chuckle, inspecting the damaged BMW further.

Ant didn't like that so much. *Why the boss gotta show me up in front of this knockout? Maybe he wants her his damn self! Italians* do *go for black women. I've seen him in here spying a lot of sisters, and giving them extra discounts and shit.*

"I didn't say that I was definitely going to get it fixed here, I just wanted to get a price range. That's all," the regal sister announced.

Paul asked, "How long ago did this accident happen?"

"Just last night."

"And you didn't crash it, right?" Ant asked, overstepping his boundaries. He couldn't help himself. He just *had* to say something to her. Or he wouldn't have been able to live with himself.

"What difference does it make?" she sized him up and answered. She knew damn well where his mind was, and frankly, she didn't have time for the games. She was thirty-five years old with two small children. But she looked twenty-six and childless, until she opened her mouth with so much authority.

Ant was too taken by her presence to be bashful with her. So he kept on going, putting himself and his boss deeper in the hole.

"Well, excuse me for trying to be Mr. Fix It. *I'm* just trying to help *you* out."

"And what does that have to do with who crashed my car?"

"Well, if your husband did it, then let *him* pay for it. But if it was your boyfriend or something, then I understand why you'd be mad, and trying to cut corners."

Damn the boy was good! That just made her want to cut his f-ing head off! As it turned out, she had just recently divorced, and her new man was not *half* as responsible as her ex-husband was. She had run her responsible husband away with her proud dominance. Did she care? Not really. As she argued to her social-status group of friends, "If he's not *man enough* to handle me, then why should I settle?"

"Well, how much would it cost me?" she looked back at Paul and asked him. She decided to ignore the young, worthless, *asshole* of a black *boy* who had the audacity to question her about her business! Boy was she pissed at him! *And* at her new boyfriend! She often asked herself the question, *What the hell is wrong with* all *black men? Either they can't handle a strong black woman, or they end up having* other *damn issues!*

Paul was actually amused by it all. Ant never failed to impress or to entertain him. But he always took care of business *first.* That was what Paul liked about his young employee the most. Anthony Poole knew his job and was *always* reliable. The price of the damage on that BMW was going to run the sister more than three thousand dollars.

"I'll tell you what. Are you paying for this with your credit card, or with a personal check?" Paul was assuming that she was loaded with a house, and with plenty of credit. And he was right.

"It depends on what the price is," she answered.

He nodded. "You're looking at three thousand dollars and some change."

"How *much* change?"

"Two, three hundred dollars."

She frowned. "That's a whole lot of damn change."

"If you want me to go piece for piece, I will. But chances are, it's gonna end up running you a lot more than what I'm quoting ya."

"Well, that's what I would like to see. The details."

Paul paused and took another look at it. "Okay. I'll be right back out." He headed to his office for the paperwork.

Ant saw that as another opportunity to instigate.

"That wasn't a good idea," he walked closer and told her.

"Hey, Anthony, why don't you get back to work and get your wide nose from out of the air! You're sucking up all of the oxygen!" an Italian employee yelled from the garage. Ant was only one of two African Americans who worked for Paul. Paul employed up to eight men full-time, and six part-time. It was an all-man's zone. They worked the telephones and all.

Ant ignored his fellow mechanic and kept on talking. "When he comes back over here and does the real paperwork on it, it might come out to be more like *four* thousand and some change."

"Well, he needs to tell me that up front, and stop messing around with my time."

Ant paused. "Damn. Is your time that precious? We all need time to take care of things that need to be taken care of. I mean, how fast do you expect us to fix it?"

An alert lightbulb went off in her head. "How fast *can* you fix it?"

She didn't want her car out of commission for too long. Too long of a time in the repair shop would give her husband something else to complain about. After all, their divorce settlement was what gave her the opportunity to afford what she wanted without having to sweat him for everything. She would hate for him to start coming back around with plenty of "I told you so's" and "I knew you couldn't handle it's."

"You're looking at at least two weeks, depending on how long it takes for the parts to come in," Ant answered her.

"Two weeks? Shit!" she snapped. She had no idea whatsoever about cars. She was thinking more on a timetable of two days.

Ant could read her dilemma. She definitely had something to hide. Hell, he even felt like he was in some kind of a soap opera. "You could rent another green BMW if you had to. Replace the tag with your own, and nobody would know the difference," he told her.

She looked him in the eye and started to picture him more as a con man with every word he said. Maybe he was good for something after all. He still wasn't *her* type, but she had to respect him for being cunning. He was indeed smooth, and he was standing his ground with her. Of course, *he knew* that already. Ant prided himself on standing his ground with *any* woman.

"Okay, Anthony, could you help me out by finishing that brake job on the Toyota, please," Paul announced, with fresh paperwork to fill out on the Beamer.

"No problem, boss man. I'll get right to it." However, he still had his ears open. And when the final paperwork was done, the total cost came to four thousand, four hundred, thirty-two dollars.

A "Thank you very much" was all that the regal black woman had to say. Then she drove off as abruptly as she had driven up.

"What she say?" Ant asked his boss inside the office later.

Paul didn't even want to talk about it. He knew her type before he even opened his mouth. She was fast talk and slow action.

"I gotta tell ya," he said with a frown, "women like that are more trouble than they're worth to sleep with."

Ant smiled. *I knew the boss had the fever for the jungle in him,* he thought to himself.

Paul continued: "You have a lot more women these days that are like that, too. They want what they want right here and right now no matter what. Then they have these attitudes that you're just supposed to bend over backwards for them."

Paul looked into his young mechanic's brown face and wanted to make sure that Ant understood that his words had nothing to do with race.

"And I don't say this as a black thing, Anthony, because it's across the board with women nowadays."

"Oh, you don't have to apologize to me, man. I know exactly what you're talking about. I wouldn't plan on being with a woman like her for too long either." *But I'd damn sure hop in the bed with her,* he kept to himself with a grin.

"Those are the kind of women who give the caring, decent women of the world a bad name," his boss continued. "I went to high school with her type. And just because a girl's daddy had X amount of donuts, and they lived in such and such castle, they thought that they were better than everybody. But those kind of women are very seldom happy. Because their entire world is based on a facade with no real feelings involved. They'll just talk to whatever guy has the money and the status. And let me tell ya, that's a sorry-ass way to live."

Paul was on a roll, so Ant just let him talk himself out, as some of the other guys began to hover around and listen in.

"I'm sure glad I met my wife when I did back in the good old seventies," he said with a smile. "Because I feel sorry for some of *you* guys. Divorce settlements and child custody cases are running wild nowadays. And I'm not saying that you guys have nothing to do with a lot of that, but Jesus Christ! You'd think that a good old-fashioned marriage was some kind of a disease for a lot of people nowadays."

They all laughed and added their personal pieces to the conversation, before getting back to work. All the while, Ant began to daydream about Dana Nicole Simpson. Could *she* ever be happy with a man. *Really?* He doubted it. He doubted *that* strongly! So he figured it was a blessing in disguise to finally lose contact with her. All that a woman like Dana could do was mislead a guy into bliss, and then drive him crazy when he realized that she was insatiable.

•

After work, Ant drove the short distance back home to Nebraska Avenue, and smiled his behind off while listening to Master P shoot the rap game at high volume from his car's sound system.

"She ain't 'bout it 'bout it," he told himself of Dana. He was in a state of euphoria. A new revelation had cleared his mind of the stress of playing "Top This" with high-cultured women. *Who needs that shit in the first place? Let 'em all complain their asses off,* he told himself. *And just give me an around-the-way girl like L.L. Cool J's wife.*

Like clockwork, as soon as Ant got a chance to make it inside his second-floor apartment and relax, he had that expected phone call from his boy Tone.

"What's up for the night, man?"

Ant frowned and shook his head with the phone in hand. "Look, man, ain't nothin' up for tonight. I'm just relaxing. Can't I just come the hell home and relax for a minute. Damn! I mean, I *do* work every day. Maybe *you* should get a steady-ass job and try it out. So you can see how it feel to come back home and rest."

"Oh, okay, you in one of them solo moods again. Like a damn girl."

Ant got pissed off and said, "Look, man, what the hell are you saying? Only women can chill by themselves and get some peace of mind? Is that what you're saying?"

"Basically. Boys don't go out on each other like that."

"Aw, man, save that shit, Tone. Look, I'm chillin' tonight. So you go ahead and call me a girl if you want to. But if you ask *me,* you da one that seem more like a girl, by calling me *up* every damn day. What are you, lonely? You need somebody to talk to? I mean, damn! Let a nigga rest!"

"Yeah, whatever, man. So next time you got girl problems, don't call me up talkin' that shit you talk either," Tone countered.

"Man, that was just a few stray occasions, 'cause you *know* I got mines in check."

Tone said, "That ain't what I heard. Last time *I* heard, you was a lovesick crybaby."

"Yeah, aw'ight. I'm not lovesick tonight. So call me up when your ass got something to talk about. Like a job or something."

Tone started to get upset. "Hey, dawg, why you gotta keep talking that job shit to me?"

Ant gave a long sigh. "Can I get off the phone with you or what? Shit, man, I wanna call some girls up tonight. You tying up my line."

"I thought you said you was chillin'."

"I *am* chillin'. What that got to do with callin' a girl?"

Tone fell silent for a second. "She got a friend?"

They both burst out laughing.

"Come on, man, I gots to go. I'll get with you later," Ant told him.

"Aw'ight, man. Go 'head and front on me like that, dawg. Go 'head and front."

Ant shook his head again. Tone was unbelievable. And to think that he was only two years away from thirty.

"*Later* man! Seriously! I'll see you when I see you!"

He hung up the phone on his friend and felt hungry. He made himself a turkey and cheese sandwich and poured a tall glass of Pepsi from a cold two liter in the fridge. Then he stepped outside in the cool night air in a T-shirt, jeans, and flip-flops, with his sandwich, drink, and telephone in hand with new phone numbers jammed in his pocket.

"Damn, this a nice night out here," he expressed to himself with a bite of his sandwich. Kids were still out running the streets. It made Ant remember how good things used to be before he got older and started to have so many expectations for himself.

"I guess you just have to learn to take the bitter with the sweet," he mumbled in between bites of his sandwich. Some of the kids would look to see who in the world he was talking to, but Ant didn't care. Most people talked to themselves and were too ashamed to admit it anyway.

"Now who's gonna be the first lucky woman to get this phone call?" he asked himself once he had finished his sandwich and washed it down with his drink.

The first number out of his pocket was Shawntè's.

"On a night like this, she probably ain't home," he said as he dialed the number.

"Hello."

"Can I speak to Shawntè?"

"This is Shawntè."

"This is Anthony Poole. You remember me, from the club on MLK?"

Her voice became energized, and then it fell flat as she tried to catch herself. "Yeah, I remember you. Mr. Attitude."

"Hey, I was in a foul mood that night. I'm sorry about that. I'm not always that way."

"Okay, tell me anything. I've just about heard it all."

Ant began to chuckle. He liked her conversation already. She was going to try and make him work for it. A challenge. Just what the doctor ordered. He smiled and began to sink his teeth in for the slow kill.

"Oh yeah? Well let me tell you a few things about me . . ."

Damn the chase of a new woman felt good! The only way to compare it to what women felt was maybe by thinking about diamonds on their birthday. Nevertheless, some women had no use or desire for diamonds. But most men *definitely* had use for a new woman. A new woman was simply the *bomb!* An explosion of new energy. And I guess it would have to go down in the books of history as a man's *thing*. Women just couldn't understand.

Sharron Francis couldn't understand why she even desired to have a man sometimes. But she did. No matter how hard she tried to keep them off of her mind, she still wanted one. And the airport was flooded with men who had places to go. Progressive men. Men who had seen things and had been places. So less than a week after rearranging her priorities *away* from thinking about the opposite sex, Sharron found herself back at work, fantasizing about every interesting-looking guy who came into her direct line of vision: black, white, Latino, *and* Asian.

Do they think about us as much as we think about them? Or is it just me? she asked herself, watching and thinking as each new man walked by and stuck his head and body into the gift shop. Her thoughts were more intense about men when she worked as a cashier. But once she'd moved up to an assistant manager position, she no longer had so much direct eye contact with men who actually bought things. Things like postcards, breath mints, *Penthouse* magazines, and different sizes, shapes, and brands of condoms. So maybe they *did* think about women. The things that they purchased at the gift shops proved it. Embarrassingly. It made Sharron's new duties of counting inventory and stacking and rearranging shelves, moving from one shop to another, a needed relief from the embarrassing eye contact with so many men. And they all made her wonder, if not about them, then about the women whom they loved or lusted for.

"Ah, Sharron, can you take over at the register for me? I have to run to the bathroom."

Shucks! she thought to herself. *This is just what I* didn't *need!* The line was at least five men long, with three more hovering near the magazine stands. Perfect timing for a bathroom trip, right? But business was business.

Sharron nodded and headed behind the counter without a word. Filling in at the register was how she first met Mr. Married Man, only to bump into him again at the Grab-n-Go Cafe. It was as if it was fate. Or a *test* of fate. Like that famous apple in the Garden of Eden. And Sharron had fallen for it. The mystique. The charm. The lore of forbidden fruit. But not this time. She effectively turned herself into a machine.

TAP, TAP, TAP.

"Four seventy-two. Thank you."

CHINNNGGG! WHAP!

TAP, TAP.

"Two forty-one. . . . Thank you."

CHINNNGGG! WHAP!

TAP, TAP, TAP, TAP, TAP.

"Six eighty-five. . . . Thank you."

CHINNNGGG! WHAP!

"Looks like it's gonna rain today."

"It sure does. And we *do* have umbrellas for sale."

TAP, TAP, TAP.

"Three twenty-seven."

"How much are they?"

"The umbrellas are all seven ninety-nine. They're over to your left. Your total is three dollars and twenty-seven cents, please. . . . Thank you."

CHINNNGGG! WHAP!

"Boy, you have quite a line here."

"I sure do."

TAP, TAP, TAP, TAP.

"Four thirty-six. . . . Thank you."

CHINNNGGG! WHAP!

"How do you like your uniforms?"

"They're dark, gray, and ugly."

TAP.

"Sixty cents."

"Well, at least you're honest."

"Thank you."

CHINNNGGG! WHAP!

Thank God! she told herself when the cashier returned.

"I'm sorry," the young, vivacious woman told her.

"We all have to use the bathroom," Sharron responded, happily stepping away from the register. *And unfortunately, we all have a jones for men,* she thought. Because *some* cashiers *loved* to flirt. It wasn't just the young ones either. With all of those progressive and tempting men who flowed through the airport, flying around the country and around the world, Sharron had a new understanding of why so many knowledgeable parents had a real distaste for allowing their daughters to become flight attendants, including Celena's parents and her own. But *somebody* had to do it. Business was business. Besides, the majority of the flight attendants whom Sharron and Celena met were astute, respectable, and totally professional women.

When Sharron jumped back to her duties, stacking and rearranging the shelves, she found herself in full vision of a very familiar man.

"Sharron? Sharron Francis!" he called to her. Then he melted into her arms before she could prepare herself for a response, as if he had been waiting for years to see her again.

She was shocked by his outward affection and immediately pulled away. But she was gentle enough with her disengagement to keep his male ego, that soft pillow of a thing that men would *die* to protect, intact.

"Hi, Sean. How have things been?"

He looked twice as good as he did when they were boyfriend and girlfriend back in high school in Memphis. He was twice as confident. Twice as smart. And he was all grown up. However, he shook his head and gave her a face filled with pain when she asked about his life. She only meant it as a "Hello."

"I have to get your number," he said, pulling out a business card from a gold-plated holder with his name on it. "There are so many things I have to tell you. I don't know where to begin."

Sharron looked down at his card and was impressed. With everything! Sean Love was only twenty-four, and had already moved up to a management rep position for a hotel chain. She was just as smart as he was back in high school. But now she worked at the airport while he carried his own business cards inside gold card holders, while dressed in tailored suits with fancy ties. Not to disrespect herself or the other thousands of employees who worked at international airports, but often Sharron questioned if maybe going back to school and finishing her degree in nursing would be more fulfilling to her.

Of all people in the world to bump into, why oh why did it have to be Sean. Sean L-o-v-e of all things. Oh, sure, his last name was fun to talk about when they were teenagers in high school. But not anymore. And instead of losing her virginity to a young man named Love on prom night, after they had dated for three years with only kisses and no pressure, Sharron made the age-old mistake of moving on, only to lose herself to a college jock from California in her freshman year at University of Missouri at St. Louis. He transferred from St. Louis University to UCLA that next semester with not even a letter or a phone call.

"You know I have a beautiful daughter now," Sean said, snapping Sharron out of her daydream. He was pulling out his wallet-sized pictures before she could compose herself. It was all too fast and unreal, as if she were watching her own movie on fast-forward search.

"She has your eyes," she commented. His daughter looked as bright and as caring as he did.

Sean added, "I'm trying to gain custody of her. Her mother's a nutcase. We were supposed to get married, and I caught her cheating on me a week before the wedding. Can you imagine that? *A week* before the wedding!"

Actually, Sharron *could* imagine it. But only from men.

"Yeah, that *is* crazy," she responded.

Sean just stared at her, blankly, as if he couldn't believe his own story.

"What's your number?" he asked her again, pulling out a platinum-and-gold pen and a monogrammed notepad. "I just have too much to tell you."

With all of his fancy knickknacks, Sharron began to think of him as an Inspector Gadget or James Bond character. She smiled at her thoughts and gave him her number.

"I'm up in Chicago now," he said.

She nodded. "I see that on your card," she told him, holding it up to her face.

"So how long have you been in St. Louis?" he asked. "I wish I would have known. I could have taken you out to lunch or something. I've been here for three days at a conference."

"I stayed here in St. Louis after going to school here," she answered. Evidently he didn't remember. And why should he? She'd broken his heart when they separated. He had probably forced himself to forget. He'd ended up attending Purdue in Indiana, on an academic scholarship. Another recipient had decided not to attend at the eleventh hour, and Sean happened to be next on their list but was still undecided. Mainly because of Sharron.

All of those painful memories came back to her. She wondered if Sean remembered any of them. She was hoping that he did not. Because it all reminded her that she was definitely *not* a saint, and that she had not made all of the right decisions regarding love. Even with Mr. Sean Love. A smart, patient, caring, affectionate, and damned good man! The kind of man that women often bragged about. Or bragged about *wanting*. Because once some women received a man with the desired characteristics of such a "catch," they lost their interest in him. He found himself well on his way to being considered the most dreaded word in the male vocabulary: *Weak*.

"Anyway, I know you have to get back to work here, Sharron. But I can't wait to talk to you. Okay? So when's the best time to call you tonight? Do you work early tomorrow? What are you doing this weekend? I could even fly back down and spend time with you face to face. You're not married are you? I don't want to intrude on anything."

WOW! Sharron thought. Sean used to be a little stuffy with his words. But as a man, they were pouring out much faster than her mental cup could handle. His words were spilling all over the floor on her. *Slow down, horsey! Slow down!*

"Ahhh, let's decide all of that once we talk. It's just good seeing you again," she told him, trying to create some space for herself. Funny how desires can catch you off guard and then have you on your heels when they arrive a little too quickly for you.

"We'll do that," he told her. Then he forced her into another big hug before he hustled on his way, leaving her bedazzled eyes with too strong of a smile for comfort. A smile that she would be forced to deal with for the rest of her shift, and while awaiting his phone call that night.

Celena said, "Shit! I need some popcorn for all of this. So what time is he supposed to call you tonight?"

Sharron aired out her laundry while she and her girl took a shared break from work. She didn't know what else to do. She felt guilty. For whatever crazy reason, she didn't look forward to talking to Sean. Nor did she look forward to being with him again. It all seemed too forced. Love wasn't supposed to be about forced situations. Love was just supposed to happen. Like an accident. But most accidents seemed to hurt. Forced situations, however, seemed unnatural. And if it was unnatural, your body tended to reject it. But could we actually plan to wait for an accident of love to occur? It *all* seemed ridiculous as Sharron ran through a thousand different thoughts in her mind.

"Damn it! What is wrong with me?" she asked her friend rhetorically.

Celena just laughed at her. "I told you, girl. You might as well just let shit happen. As long as you don't get pregnant or catch no AIDS."

Half of the time, Sharron disregarded whatever Celena told her. She just needed someone to talk to, like most people.

"Well, I guess I'll just talk to him. I mean, it's not like I have to promise him a date or anything," she said, trying to convince herself.

Celena grinned at her, her mouth filled with tuna fish and chips, twisting in her elevated stool. "He's gon' want to do *way* more than *talk* if he makes a trip back down here to see you."

Sharron cringed. "Please. Can you finish eating your food first. You don't even know Sean. He's not like that."

Her girl frowned. "Are you sure?"

"Yes, I'm sure."

"So how come you don't want to see him then? That *is* what you told me, right? You don't wanna see him."

Sharron let out a long sigh. "It's not that I don't want to see him, it's just that . . . Well, this really caught me off guard, and I need more time to think it through, that's all."

"So you can find out a way to dump his ass," Celena said with a chuckle. "You dumped his behind before, and now you're trying to dump him again."

"And you would *think* that I had matured," Sharron stated.

"Matured to what?" her girl asked her. "I mean, a boring guy is a boring guy. It doesn't make a difference if he's twenty-five or *forty-five* for that matter."

"But we don't know that yet."

"*You* don't know that," Celena responded. "Because if *you're* having problems trying to decide if you want to go out with this guy, then I *know* he couldn't stand up to me."

Sharron smirked. "I don't know how *any* guys can stand up to *you*. That's why you keep getting those knuckleheads. You *force* them to be that way."

"Only the strong can survive, baby," Celena bragged. "I don't want no weak man. A weak man can't do nothin' for me but compliment my outfits and stare at my ass, wishing that he could have some. And that's *exactly* how I plan to keep 'em, watching and wishing."

Sharron chuckled and asked, "But don't you want a man who you can just chill with instead of fighting with all of the time? Because that arguing and stuff gets played out. Fast!"

"Yeah, I want a guy I could just chill with. But not right now. I still have to figure out what I want to do with my life."

"You don't know that by now?"

"If I did, I wouldn't be talking about it. I'd be *doing* it," Celena snapped. "Have you thought about going back to nursing school?"

"All of the time," Sharron answered.

"Me too. I've been thinking about going back to get my business degree. I just have to make up my mind to do it."

"You better make up your mind *soon.* Because if you keep throwing your money down the drain on outfits, pocketbooks, and fancy nails, you'll be too much in debt to go back to school."

"I'm not worried about that. My father would pay for school."

"Oh, well, what are you waiting for then?" Sharron asked her.

"What are *you* waiting for?"

In fact, Sharron had been saving up to make her move soon. Real soon. She just didn't want to announce it until she had figured out all of the details.

"Anyway, that's another thing that makes me hesitant with Sean," she said. "I mean, he's always known what he wants out of life, and he just goes for it. He may think that I'm confused. I hate when guys start talking to you as if you're a child who needs to get her life in order. I'm scared to find out if he's like that now." She even worried about what Sean Love may have thought about her working at an airport, without being a computer systems manager or pilot or something.

Celena said, "Didn't you just tell me that he had a daughter, and that the mother had cheated on him right before the wedding? Well, I think he *knows* that the world ain't perfect, so I wouldn't even worry about that. You're not *less* than him."

"I know I'm not *less* than him. But you do start thinking about how you measure up as a couple."

"So what? That's a part of life."

"Well, some people judge you on that."

"And you think he's gonna judge you because you work at an airport and he's some hotel rep? Because *I* would *never* let a guy think he's better than *me.*"

Their discussion began to lead into an argument of egos. Sharron decided to back out of it.

She jumped down from her elevated stool and said, "I have to get back to work now," and grabbed her lemonade from the small counter.

"All right then," Celena told her, not budging. She just knew that *no man* would play some upmanship game with *her.* And if her roommate felt that way about herself, then that was *her* damn problem.

Sharron thought about the question of parity for the rest of her shift, and then while riding home on the train, nervously awaiting Sean's phone call that evening.

Did she really feel less than him? The truth was that she did. She couldn't fight it. She just didn't want to be swallowed alive by him. That's all. She wanted to have her own space and dignity, and not have to cater to *his* thoughts, *his* aspirations, or *his* career. When she continued to think about it, she remembered that Sean was an Aries, and that he was always running forward with his head, banging into things. Not that she was particularly into zodiac signs, but Sean Love had always talked about those things, as if he knew it all. He had an answer for everything, and it all came back to her right before his phone call.

She took a deep breath and answered, "Hello."

"Did I catch you at a bad time?" he asked her.

Yes, at a bad time in my life right now, Sharron thought.

"No, you're right on time," she told him. Funny how we think one thing and say another. Fortunately, Sharron wasn't much of a phone talker. She would rather speak with people face to face, so that she could read them and feel them out.

"So how has life been treating you?" Sean asked. "Now that we have time to really talk to each other."

Miserably, Sharron thought. *Can't you tell?*

"I can't complain too much. I can't jump up and down about anything either," she answered.

"Well, life hasn't given *me* much to jump up and down about."

"What about your job?"

"What about it?"

"Don't you like it?"

"Sure."

"What's the problem then?"

Sean said, "You think that a good job is all that you need to be happy in life?"

Good question.

"Well, I guess not. Income isn't all that you need to survive."

"It's *definitely* not all. I mean, I expected to have a family by now, and all I have is a beautiful daughter who I have to fight for to even see."

"*All* you have?" Sharron questioned.

"I didn't mean to put it like that. I just expected a lot more. I expected to be a married man," he said, correcting himself. "But at least she has my name."

"Is that important to you?"

"Yeah, that's important to me. It's *very* important. Do you know how many kids are walking around today without their father's name? And do you realize that cuts them off from their history?"

"What about the mother's name?"

"Oh, we're seldom cut off from our maternal line, especially in the black community. I was around my mother's family all of the time. But if you're not married, and the child doesn't have the paternal name, then *your* side of the family may not even be thought of."

Sharron thought about her own family, and how many maternal cousins she was connected to as opposed to her paternal cousins. In her case, Sean was right. If her parents hadn't married, and she had not been given her father's name, her paternal line would have definitely been on the back burner, because her mother had a large and overbearing family.

"I see your point," she told him. "So marriage is about keeping your history in order."

"Not only that, but creating a legacy for yourself and for your children."

But what about love? she wanted to ask him.

Sean hadn't changed a bit. Sure, he was older, a college graduate, gainfully employed, and even a father, but he still talked more about things, concepts, and ideas than he did about real people, feelings, and ordinary life. His daughter was more than just a legacy and a name. She was flesh, bone, and blood, with a new heart that needed to know what love was.

No wonder Sharron didn't want to talk to Sean. He didn't have what she wanted. He didn't have what she needed. And speaking of names, she figured that he needed to change his from Love to something else, because he surely didn't project what his name alluded to.

"Have you ever been in love, Sean?" she finally asked him. He sure didn't sound like he had been. He sounded uptight, like a man who needed to release himself. His enthusiasm at the airport was just a front. The real Sean Love was revealing himself as damaged goods. She felt sorry for him. She felt sorry that he couldn't seem to have his way with life, a life without love.

He took a deep breath and said, "I've tried to. Lord knows I have. I even got saved and started going to church in Chicago to find myself. To find what I really needed out of life. That's where I met my daughter's mother, in church. Do you believe that? Even when I thought that I had someone to love, it turned out all wrong again."

Sharron couldn't believe her ears. Granted, she knew that all church girls were not what they portrayed through their tightly held Bibles. Nevertheless, the stories about them were shocking.

"Now she feels ashamed of herself, and she says that she can't take being around me after what she did," Sean continued. "She said that it was like the devil's last test, and she failed. So now I have to chase her around to even be with my daughter."

Sharron began to smile and couldn't help herself. At the same time, she felt so wrong. Sean was reaching out to her, like she wanted to reach out to others, and yet she was pitying him and rejecting him at the same time. The strength that one needs to love the brokenhearted is unbelievable. She was realizing that she didn't have it.

"What about you? Have you ever been in love?" Sean asked her back.

Yeah, she thought. *Of course I have.* But she did not want to be so direct with him. Maybe telling him pieces of the story would be better, and easier for him to swallow. After all, they *did* have a past together.

"I *thought* I was in love with a football player at St. Louis University," she answered him. "Actually, he played football, basketball, *and* ran track. But he obviously was not in love with me because he transferred to UCLA and never called me again."

"When was this?"

That's exactly *what I was afraid of,* she told herself. There was no way of getting around Sean's feelings. She simply hadn't chosen him to love, and what difference would it make to them now? She even regretted opening up the discussion.

Sean read her hesitancy and eased her turmoil. "I understand that you had to do what you had to do, Sharron. I can't hold that against you. But if we're going to be open with each other and start over again, then we have to be honest with each other."

He said, "I need your honesty right now. More than anything, I *need* honesty."

"My freshman year at UMSL," she answered.

"Was it that hard to be honest with me?" he asked. "Why? I mean, women talk about honesty so much, but then when they have a good and honest man like myself, they can't seem to be honest anymore. Or maybe I'm just meeting all of the wrong women."

Or maybe you hold yourself in such high regard that you make everyone else feel that they don't deserve you, or that they don't want to live up to the pressure of being perfect all of the time. Or of hurting your damn feelings every day, which is exactly how I feel with you right now! she mused with an edge. He was beginning to get under Sharron's skin, with an itchy kind of irritation that made her want to scratch him off, feverishly.

Sean had no idea how laboring he could be to a woman, even a good woman, with so much talk of his decency and of his suffering. Sharron asked herself, *Am* I *that bad with the men that* I *meet? Suffering like that? And showing it? Because if I am, then no wonder I'm getting nothing but suffering in return.*

The next thing she knew, she was giving her high-school boyfriend advice:

"Sean, you have to think more positive in order to have positive results," she told him. "I have to do that myself sometimes. Because I'm learning, day by day, that nobody gives a damn about your suffering. Not yours, not mine, not anybody's. Because we all have those days, and we all know how those days make us feel. So we choose to keep pushing forward and looking on the bright side."

"But that's not reality," he countered. "My fiancée was a bright and cheerful woman until all kinds of darkness climbed out of her closet. But if she had been honest with me in the beginning instead of projecting this Snow White and the Seven Dwarfs imagery of herself, we could have both dealt with her demons outright instead of being embarrassed by them later."

Sharron shook her head and grinned, stopping herself just short of laughing out loud. She could just imagine how corny her girl Celena would have thought Sean was if she heard his terminology. She would have laughed out loud and embarrassed him. He was definitely no match for Celena, nor could he hold up to Sharron's standards.

I'm sorry, Sean, but you will never *be more than a friend to me,* she leveled with herself. *Because life is much too short for this kind of drama.*

"Well, when did she get pregnant?" she asked, for more information on the story.

"About a month after we started dating."

A month?! Damn! Well, you both *had* demons *to begin with,* she thought.

Sean interrupted before she could speak. "Now I know what you're thinking, but I knew her for about three months before we started dating. So I knew, or at least I *thought* that she was a good woman when she became pregnant. And since the Lord our Savior doesn't make accidents, we realized then that we were meant to be a family."

Sharron was speechless. Who could argue with the Lord our Savior? So she left it alone. But one thing was for sure: Sean Love had a lot more drama going on in *his* life than she *ever* had in hers!

"I don't know what else to say to you, Sean," she told him. The words just tumbled out of her mouth without any thought behind them. She just wanted to end their conversation. It was depressing. She didn't need to be depressed, she needed to be uplifted.

"Yeah, I guess I shouldn't be talking about my problems to you like this, but sometimes you just need someone who doesn't know, or who hasn't been around you, to just hear you out."

Sharron nodded and didn't say a word.

"Well, maybe you can call me back and start over again when you've cleared your mind about things," she told him. And it was a good line. A line that she hoped and prayed would work. Unfortunately, it didn't.

"I have a better idea," he told her, filled with new energy. "How about I fly to St. Louis and take you out on your birthday next month? It's June twenty-seventh, right? You're a sensitive Cancer. I remember."

I'm not that *sensitive,* she thought. "Well, we'll have to see about that, okay? I mean, I don't know what I'm doing for my birthday yet."

"Well, now you do," he told her.

"No, no I don't," she countered. "So just call me in a week or so, and we'll talk again. Okay?"

She was trying her best to end their phone call without being short or rude to him. Nevertheless, he was really pushing her to the edge of her calm sanity.

He paused and finally agreed to let her go.

"Okay. That's fair. I'll call you in a week then."

Sharron hung up the phone and said, "Jesus Christ!" Then she caught herself. "I mean, God, I didn't mean that. I mean . . . What am I saying?!" she finally stopped and asked herself.

She was *that* confused and frustrated. She actually felt ashamed of herself for rejecting Sean again, because love was what she wanted. But the suffering part of love, she wanted to push away. She desired only its sweetness, the bright yellow sunshine of love and never the suffering dark grays. Because the suffering part of love was too painful. Life was far too short to have to face such . . . pain. Knowingly. So Sharron vowed to avoid it, like she would avoid Sean.

Pain and suffering was what Ant had to endure every time his partner Tone wanted to tag along with him. However, Ant could take the pain because he loved his partner. Dearly! For as nagging as Tone could be, Ant felt committed to him, responsible for him, and driven by him. And Ant no doubt suffered an everyday gray, while forcing his boy to understand that life was meant to be lived and experienced, and not just talked about or bullshitted through.

"Man, *you're* the one who keeps talking this stuff about being bored. I'm *always* out to do stuff," Tone refuted, decked out again in his red Cardinals baseball jersey. Ant had been compelled to take his own St. Louis Cardinals jersey off, for fear of showing up like twins. He redressed in a plain blue Wilson Athletics T-shirt with his jeans.

Ant had control of his wheels, *and* control of their destination to the skating rink on Lindbergh Boulevard, northwest of St. Louis, and not far from the airport. On Thursday nights, the grown-ups got their groove on. Tone was simply concerned about how *grown* they would be.

"It's gon' be a bunch of old folks in here, man. Watch," he continued to complain.

"Aw, man, you probably scared 'cause you can't skate," Ant joked.

"I can skate. I just don't want to run over no old folks."

Ant stared into Tone's face in disbelief. "How old do you think people are going to be in here? *Seventy?* I mean, we're almost thirty our damn selves. Grow the hell up, man!"

Tone looked away and out of the passenger-side window. "Yeah, I hope they're our age. You just remember that this was *your* idea," he turned and said to his friend.

As soon as they pulled up into the slowly filling parking lot of the skating rink, Tone noticed more couples than singles walking from their parked cars and moving through the short line.

"Are you sure that this is old heads night, or is it *couples* night?"

"When you get our age and older, most people start connecting like that. We ain't teenagers no more," Ant responded. "I'm not out here to meet nobody anyway. I'm just out here to skate. You know, to do something different."

Tone shook his head and grinned, deciding to leave his partner alone as they reached the front entrance. He knew that *he* wanted to meet someone regardless of what *Ant* was there for.

Tone whispered, "Damn, she look *good!*" referring to the cashier, an attractive sister who was full of body. "Look at that backyard in there," he added.

Ant smiled and looked the woman over himself. "Are you gonna be collecting money all night, or do you go out there and skate?" he asked her.

She smiled, real reserved, and nodded. "Yeah, I skate."

"We'll be out there on the dance floor lookin' for you then," Tone interjected.

"My husband will be looking for me too," she responded as cool as water.

"We don't wanna see him," Tone countered as they moved along to the skate rental booth.

Ant stopped him and asked, "Why you always gotta jump in on *my* shit?"

"Aw, dawg, I saw her first. You wasn't even payin' attention."

Ant shook his head and said, "Anyway, I told you, sisters start hookin' up once they get a certain age. I bet her husband is having *big* fun with that! No doubt!"

"No doubt indeed!" Tone agreed with a smile. "That's exactly why we don't need to be in here. It's gon' be a bunch of old, worn-out, divorced, and kid-having women up in here. We need to hook up with some college girls, or girls who just got out of college. You know, still wet behind the ears and shit.

"Look, it ain't even that many people up in here yet," Tone continued whining.

Ant said, "You know, it's CPT time. Black people always come late."

"Oh yeah? Well, we black, so how come *we* up in here so damn early?"

Ant had finally heard enough. He sat down to jam his rented skates on. "Damn, man, can you stop complainin' so much and just enjoy yourself? I mean, you act like a kid brother sometimes. Are you sure you're older than me? My name need to be Tone and *your* name should be Ant," he added with a chuckle.

Tone said, "You can talk that kid brother shit if you want, but I'll whip your ass. Now how many kid brothers can do that?"

Ant smiled, tied up his skates, and headed for the disco lights that flashed on the skating rink, while the DJ played the hit song from Usher "You Make Me Wanna . . ." But when your body hasn't performed a certain task or used specific muscles for some time, it's amazing how out of shape you can feel. Both Ant and Tone felt like amateurs. They skated right out into the rink, trying their best to be cool, black, macho men. And it wasn't working.

"Shit, man! These things hurt my feet!" Tone went back to complaining. "We need some better skates, dawg. They gave us the damn welfare department skates. Mine don't even turn."

"They're not supposed to turn. Your *legs* are supposed to turn the skates," Ant said with a laugh. He wasn't making the curves too comfortably himself. The rentals felt more like stiff ice skates than roller skates. The real skaters had their own wheels, and were grooving along to the bass-driven song as if they were born for it.

By the fifth lap, Tone was already looking to retire. It was a pity, however, that he failed to guide himself to the edge of the rink instead of stopping in the middle of traffic:

BLOOMP!

BLOOMP! BLOOMP! BLOOMP!

SQUUEEEEETT!

SQUUEEEEETT!

CLACKK!

CLACKK! CLACKK!

Tone created a three-skater wipeout, with two breakers and three jumpers.

Ant nervously headed for the walls, regaining his balance before he wiped out himself from laughter.

Tone climbed to his feet and gingerly made his way from the rink to recover. *I knew this shit was a bad idea,* he thought to himself. He felt like his right arm was broken.

Ant made it to his partner, filled with laughter. "You aw'ight?" he asked, still chuckling.

"Shut up, man. I hit my damn funny bone. My arm feel like it's broke," Tone responded, cradling his right arm.

"Aw, man, stop whinin'. Who the girl now?"

They stopped right in front of twin basketball machines and read each other's mind.

"You too hurt to get it on?" Ant challenged.

Tone smiled, worked out his arm, and faced the machines. "We can get it on."

"I don't wanna hear no excuses about your arm, Tone. I'm not tryin' to hear that shit."

"Just get your money up," Tone huffed.

"How much we playin' for?"

"Twenty dollars a game."

"Twenty dollars a game?" Ant questioned. "What, are you trying to make an income off of me, man? If we playin' for twenty dollars, we gon' make it two out of three games," Ant said as they headed for the nearby change machine.

Another skater headed for the basketball machines before they made their change.

Tone said, "Dawg, we 'bout to play for money over here. You wanna get in on it?"

The brother smiled and shook his head. "Naw. Just let me play a quick game before you get started then."

Tone sucked his teeth. "Scared money don't make none."

The brother ignored him and finished up his game before returning to the skating rink.

Tone looked at his meager score of thirty-two points and said, "Shit, he had *reason* to be scared. I would have taken *all* of his money."

Ant shook his head. He said, "I don't believe you in here trying to hustle people."

"Yeah, yeah, just shut up and put your quarters in."

They played two furious, trash-talking games, with Ant winning them both with the same approach: nailing long, three-point baskets to seal his last-second victories, 56–53 and 64–60.

"Give them twenty dollars up, boy!"

Tone was hesitant. "Wait a minute, man. You know I couldn't shoot them three-pointers with my elbow being messed up."

"Naw, naw, man. I told you, I don't wanna hear that shit."

"I'm sayin', dawg, you won off of three-pointers. So let's play two out of three games where we just shoot short shots, you know, because I'm a handicap right now."

Ant started to skate away. "Let me go back out here and skate then while your little arm heals." He didn't want to take his partner's money anyway. Tone needed it.

"Yeah, whatever, man. Anybody wanna play me for money!" Tone went back to challenging.

While they played basketball, the skating rink had filled up a bit. It wasn't wall-to-wall skaters or anything, but it was enough. There were a lot more singles who had shown up with the later crowd as well. Tone didn't know what he was missing. And although Ant said he wasn't there to meet anyone, he just couldn't help himself. The brother had a real weakness for available women. One of the skaters even looked familiar to him. She was in blue jeans and a thin green blouse that trailed in the wind as she skated. Ant put a little extra in his stride to catch up to her, hoping that he wouldn't wipe her out in a clumsy crash, or look too damned anxious and blow his cool.

"Hey, miss, don't I know you from somewhere?"

She looked straight into his face, recognized him, and grinned. It was the "piece of me for a piece of you" man. She couldn't help *herself* either, smiling at him again. A smile like hers tended to send the wrong message to a man. A message of easiness. Easiness was the last image in the world a woman wanted to present to a full-grown player like Anthony Poole. Knowing as much, Sharron Francis continued to skate away from him. Her reasoning: *If he wants me, then he's gonna have to come and get me, whether I've been thinking about meeting him or not.* And she *had* been thinking about meeting him again. Constantly! But she realized the game of seduction and counterseduction had to be played regardless. She couldn't just stop and talk to him. Especially after smiling like she did. Or could she? Could she just stop all of the bullshit and ask him what he wanted from her without scaring him away like a dog with his tail caught between his hind legs?

Guys just *had* to play their games. Otherwise, they didn't seem to know how to function. Besides, the game was good in the beginning. All of the mental foreplay was hard to outright ignore. Yet, how long did men and women have to continue playing games? She loves me. She loves me not. Or maybe she just loves my pocket knot. He wants me. He wants me not. Or maybe he just wants my pleasure spot.

As Sharron skated around the rink to the DJ's driving rhythms, Ant remembered her. She was the only woman whom he had used his precious line on. How could he forget? He had wasted it on her. Or maybe not. Because she was smiling again. And he still wanted to find out what that meant. That smile. And *this* time, she was *not* getting away from him.

"Who was that?" Celena skated in and asked, much swifter on her own skates than Ant could ever hope to be on rentals.

"I don't know yet," Sharron answered. "But why don't you skate ahead so I can find out."

Her girl looked and grinned. "Oh, it's like that now."

"Yes, it is. Now go on somewhere," she advised, with no apologies.

"Is he *that* important, Sharron?"

Ain't it a trip how your friends can know *exactly* when they're getting in the middle of a good thing? It almost makes you want to throw them a stiff elbow. Instead, Sharron put on the brakes and let Celena skate right by and out of her damn face, causing Ant to do exactly what he was trying so hard to avoid, clumsily wiping out and taking his chase down with him.

BLOOMP! BLOOMP!

"Damn! Now you done made me embarrass myself," he complained. "Why did you just stop like that?"

Sharron smiled again and remained sitting while the crowd skated around them.

"Why were you right behind me like that?" she asked him.

Weird. How is it that we can feel an automatic connection to someone we've never been around before? A complete stranger.

"Come on now, you knew I was trying to catch up to you. This is the *second time* you walked away from me," he answered her. "The first time was on Kingshighway Boulevard." He wasn't trying to pick himself up either. They had the floor all to themselves.

"I bet you don't even remember that," he added. He knew damn well she remembered. He just wanted to hear her say it.

"Are you going to help me up, or are we just gonna sit here? You *did* knock me down, you know," she commented instead. She had a feeling he didn't exactly *need* ego boosting, so she wasn't planning on giving him any.

Ant climbed to his feet and proceeded to help Sharron to hers. And they were on shaky ground, just like they would be on a first date.

Then came Celena again. "Are you okay?" she asked, peeking at Ant.

"Yes, I am," Sharron stated. She hated to be so frank, but it was time for Celena to experience some of her own blunt medicine.

"Well, excuse me for asking. I'll just leave you two crash-test dummies alone," she responded, amusing herself as she skated away.

"You're the nice one, aren't you?" Ant asked Sharron with a knowing smile. She didn't even have to answer. He knew it already.

"Let's go sit down and talk," she told him, grabbing his hand to lead him away from the rink.

Ant smiled, realizing who was in charge, and with better skates and form. Or at least until he got the hell off of that rink and out of those cheap rentals.

Sharron lead him straight to the red refreshment booths.

"Are you hungry? I'll buy you a slice of pizza and a coke," she told him.

Wait a minute, Ant asked himself. *What the hell is she trying to do?*

"Naw, I can buy my own food, sweetheart. I don't need you to do that. Do I look like I'm broke or something? I'm not even hungry."

Amazingly, Sharron was in a comfort zone. She was just feeling it. Since she *knew* that he was a player, she planned to have a good time with him. She figured she could use some enjoyment in her life anyway. But while he may have had plans of playing her, she was thinking deeply about playing him right back, and letting him feel the complete impact of his game.

Sharron looked him straight in his eyes and said, "When you asked me if I wanted to make a trade, a piece of *you* for a piece of *me,* what exactly did you mean by that?"

In other words, she was effectively saying, *Show me what you got. Explain yourself.*

Ant smiled as tellingly as she had. She *did* remember. He was flattered. His precious line *wasn't* wasted. Sharron had no idea how much that meant to him.

"So you understood what I was trying to say to you?" he asked.

"Not really. I'm still trying to understand it now. So tell me what you meant."

Ant frowned at her, not annoyed, just perplexed. "It's not like it's some . . . thousand-year-old riddle or something. I'm just saying a piece of me for a piece of you, like we sharing each other, that's all. Sharing."

So far, so good.

Sharron smiled, wanting more.

"Sharing what parts of each other? I mean, is that just physical or what?"

Of course some parts were physical. But it was more than that too. Nevertheless, how exactly could he explain it as a man to a woman, when many women couldn't understand?

Ant smiled, intrigued by the challenge. He felt like a con man in a million-dollar card game. He was *pumped!* But like all real players, he showed her nothing but calmness.

"Well, it's physical, mental, spiritual, and a whole lot of other things," he answered.

Somehow, Sharron didn't expect him to use the word "spiritual." Not a player.

"Spiritual?" she was forced to ask, confused. "Explain that to me."

"Well, I believe in God. I got to. How else can we explain half of the things in this world? And sometimes, when I'm working on people's cars, they look at *me* like *I'm* a god. Ever since I was a teenager. But I just know what I'm doing. So the concept of God is real. It gotta be. And when a man and woman really get into each other and they start moaning and groaning toward that thing, you know, that climax, that's *more* than physical. That's *godly!* Spiritual."

Sharron broke up in laughter. "I can't believe that you're actually equating sex to God."

Ant looked confused. It made perfect sense to him. Why didn't it make sense to her?

"How can we *not* equate it to God? How do we reproduce? By sharing each other, right? I'm telling you, sex is godly."

"I see. So you like having sex *that* much, hunh?"

Sharron was in a *zone,* and willing to let it all hang loose. Why not, when she had been so uptight for the past couple of weeks? Ant had caught her at the wrong time. Or in this particular case, it could have been the *perfect* time. He had been wanting to let himself hang loose as well.

"You don't like sex?" he asked her. "I mean, when it's good. 'Cause I'm not talking about that wham, bam, thank-you, ma'am, shit. I'm talking about real, sweaty, deep-breathing stuff. You know what I mean? Howlin' at the full moon and shit."

Sharron laughed out loud. "Is that what your women do, howl at the moon?"

"I do it too, when it's good. It makes it complete. I wouldn't be giving you a full piece of myself if I didn't."

A full piece of himself? Interesting, she thought.

"And what does a 'full piece' mean? And how come you don't say *all* of me for *all* of you?"

Ant stopped her in her tracks.

"You know what? Think about that question for a minute. I mean, really. Can you actually give me *all* of you, and expect to get *all* of me? That's unheard of. To do that, you would have to live my entire life with me. I can't even remember all of that shit. Nor can you. Nobody gets all. The closest thing to *all* would be identical twins. And everybody who's ever been around twins can tell you how weird that shit is, that they can be so much alike. But they're also different, because it's usually a nice twin and a mean twin. Alter egos and shit.

"So, naw, we don't give *all* of ourselves," he continued. "What we do is give important pieces that build up to a whole, little by little. That way, you're always looking for that next piece. Because when you give somebody too much too fast, they don't respect you for that anyway. They get bored with you. So you show 'em something new every day. In *full* pieces, and none of that half-steppin' shit. That's why a lot of guys can't keep their women now. They don't know how to go deep enough to reach a woman. Reach her to where she really knows you, trusts you, and respects you. And I'm not talking about for the meantime. I'm talking about for *life!*"

Enough said. *Wow!* Sharron wasn't expecting all of that. Not from a player. It was just supposed to be a line. He wasn't actually supposed to understand it. And he damn sure wasn't supposed to be able to explain it. Before she realized it, she was staring across the table in awe. She was speechless. As was he.

Ant had no idea that he could open up to a woman like that. He wanted to. Someday. But he doubted if women could really handle it. The full, unleashed mind of a man. But Sharron had asked him the right questions at the right time, and got the right answers. And wow! With such buildup, what else could they possibly say to each other?

"Hello, my name is Celena Myers." Sharron's friend appeared from nowhere and addressed Ant with her hand extended. "And your name is?" she asked him.

"Anthony Poole," he answered, taking her hand in his.

Sharron hadn't even asked. Nor had Ant asked for *her* name. And did it matter? Was a name more important than searching a person's soul? What could be more important than a person's views on God, sex, and human life. Given names said more about a person's parents and culture than they did about the individual being anyway. Nevertheless, it was embarrassing not to know them.

"Sharron Francis," she announced, with her right hand extended across the table. "And that's spelled Shar—S-H-A-R—ron—R-O-N."

Celena frowned, horrified. "Well, what the hell were you two talking about all this time? Y'all didn't even know each other's names?"

"What's up?" Ant's friend Tone interrupted, crashing in on the party.

"This is my boy, Anthony Wallace," Ant filled in.

Celena jumped all over that.

"Wait a minute. You both have the same first names?"

"Yeah, but I'm older," Tone said proudly.

Only in age, Sharron thought to herself. She could tell who was whom between the guys, just like Ant could tell between her and Celena. The party crashing had brought them down from their high and back to earth, because for a minute there, they were both floating with no place to land.

Ant said, "We were just having a deep conversation here." He was rather annoyed that their friends had broken it up.

"It must have been *deep* if y'all didn't even know each other's *names,*" Celena noted.

"I mean, is a name *that* important?" Tone asked rhetorically. "Your name could be Jane, Judy, Jackie, Jill, or whatever, and the conversation would still be more important than that. Unless your name was Janet Jackson. Now *that* would be something else."

Ant chuckled. His boy Tone never failed to amaze him.

Celena presented the same bundle of surprises for Sharron.

"Well, in *some* cultures, *names* actually *mean* something," Celena countered.

Sharron let out a long sigh, reading where things were starting to go.

"Can we go back to skating?" she asked her new companion, holding his hand again.

Ant had other ideas in mind, but he went along with it just to regain their privacy. He broke away once they hit the skating rink.

"Look, ah, I don't mean to hurt your feelings or anything, Sharron, but I don't really feel like skating anymore. I just wanted to talk to you alone again."

She slipped into another smile. Now *that* was a man. She guided him over to another empty spot where they could be alone again.

"Actually, *I* didn't want to skate anymore either," she leveled with him.

"Good. Because my damn feet are killing me! I'm about ready to return these skates. Do your skates feel comfortable?"

They sure *looked* comfortable. They were all black with black wheels and red tassels.

"Of course they feel comfortable. Rented skates are just to get you rollin'. They're not supposed to feel good. That's why *real* skaters buy their own."

"So I guess you can tell that I'm not a *real* skater, hunh?"

"Definitely. So why did you come here tonight?" she asked curiously. "Was it just to meet more women?"

He began to untie his skates as he looked up to answer her. "Naw, it just could have been fate. It was meant for us to meet again. Because evidently you must have been thinking about me."

She grinned, captured by the truth. "I guess you had too many women on your mind to think about me; you know, with your godly sex and all, howling at the full moon," she mocked him.

He laughed it off. "Now you gon' rewind it and play it to death on me. How many people have you told about my line already?"

"Actually, I haven't told anyone," she answered. "It was my own private secret. Why? How many women have you used it on?"

"About a thousand," he lied, just for a reaction.

"That many?"

"You wouldn't believe me if I told you, so why bother?"

"Try me anyway. That's what life is about, isn't it?"

"All right then. You really wanna know how many women I said it to?"

"I'm asking."

He said, "One. Some girl named Sharron Francis. And she walked away from me, smiling. Then my boy laughed at me, talking about it wasn't gon' work. And I thought I wasted my damn line, and that this girl was gonna go and tell everybody. So I didn't even want to use it again."

Sharron couldn't believe her ears. She was really tickled by it.

"You mean, you went through all of that stress over a line?" she asked him, laughing.

"Well, you obviously remembered it."

She nodded. "It was different."

He smiled. "Well . . . *I'm* different."

"Everybody's different in the beginning," she said.

"Have you ever had a beginning this strong? I mean, not just physically, but mentally?" Then he grinned, adding, "And spiritually?"

She grinned right back at him. "Honestly, no. But then again, there's a first time for everything."

He nodded and pulled off his skates. "You know what your problem is? You think too damn much. You're trying to have a comeback line for everything I say. Learn to just go with the flow. Just make sure that you don't lose yourself."

"But isn't that what you want me to do, lose myself? Honestly?"

He started to chuckle. A player being called for a hidden deck of cards.

"You know what? I wanna lose *myself*, too. That's what women can't understand. Guys want to fall in love. But then we wake up with nightmares, thinking about that pretty girl way back in high school or junior high who gave us the okeydoke. Then we freeze up and say, 'Naw, man, I ain't goin' through that shit again.' And that's the truth. Whether guys want to admit it or not."

"But you *have* to admit it. That's life," she told him.

"You know what? That *is* life. You're right," he agreed. "So we have to get back on that wild horse and ride it, hunh? Ride it good."

She smiled at him, mischievously. That deep, penetrating natural smile of hers. "*Or,* you could let the horse ride *you* for a change. *If* you could handle it?"

Hmmm! What a proposition! he thought. And he was *definitely* interested!

"Dawg, when we first met this girl, you said she wasn't all that. Now you meet her again at the skating rink, and you spend the whole damn night with her. What's up with that?" Tone wanted to know. It was after midnight. They were on their way back home.

Ant was too satisfied to even respond. He was driving as if he were floating in a spaceship on cruise control, thirty-thousand miles away from earth. He was already thinking of his future with Sharron. How long would the honeymoon last? They always seemed to die somehow. Crashing and burning into oblivion.

"Hey, man, are you daydreaming or what? YO-O-OH!"

Ant snapped out of his deep thought and said, "What's wrong with you, man?"

"I'm sittin' here trying to talk to you, and you over there spacin' off and shit," Tone explained.

Ant said, "Look, man, I had me a good night. Aw'ight? So let me just enjoy it in peace."

Tone said, "Her girlfriend was snotty as hell. That's all *I* know," he complained. He actually tried to talk to her, but Celena wasn't having it. Nor was Ant paying any real attention to him. He was off in his own world, blocking everything out, even when he arrived up the street from Tone's mother's house, off of Grand Boulevard.

"Don't crash on the way home while you spacin' out over this girl, man," his boy advised him as he climbed out of the car. "'Cause it look like she got your ass whipped just through holdin' hands and shit."

Ant was in such a love high that he could only laugh.

"I'm whipped without even gettin' no ass yet, hunh?" he reiterated. "That's the way it *should* be. Because once I hit the G-spot, the excitement all fades away," he told his partner.

Tone stopped and thought about that for a minute with the passenger door still open. "Yeah, I don't know about this one, man. This girl seem like she got you on some old spooky-type shit. Fuckin' voodoo."

Ant laughed even louder. "Naw, man, you trippin' now. She ain't got me that bad. And I got *her*, too. Don't forget that. She back home thinkin' 'bout me now."

"Yeah, whatever. Go on home and have wet dreams about her. But just remember, *I* hooked you up with her."

"What?" Ant questioned with a frown.

"Aw, don't act like you don't remember now. You wasn't even into this girl. I saw her first and *made* you talk to her on Kingshighway. You was talkin' some trash that she was too tall."

Ant nodded. "Aw'ight, I'll give you that. You spotted her."

"I *know* I did," Tone said. "You just don't forget that shit," he added, closing the passenger door. Then he walked off toward his mother's house.

Ant drove off and remembered that Tone had spotted Dana Nicole Simpson for him as well. He thought about it all, and began to pity his partner as he headed farther south to Nebraska Avenue.

How did Anthony Wallace really feel about being second fiddle for so many years? Ant had thought about that before, but never seriously. He figured that it *had* to hurt. How damaged had Tone's ego been over those years?

No wonder he seemed to lack drive, direction, and consistency. He was forever being left out and shot down. And while Ant had a great damn time with *his* life, Tone had only learned how to live through Ant, and *his* women, and *his* adventures.

Ant jumped on the phone line as soon as he arrived at home and called up his boy to let him know that he cared. And he *did* care, because Tone was his lifelong partner.

"I just wanna let you know that I love you, dawg. No doubt."

"What? Man, that girl done drove you crazy already," Tone responded drowsily. He was long due for a rest. When you stay up halfway through the night for the majority of the week, the need for sleep will surely catch up to you.

"I'm not thinkin' 'bout her, man. I'm just talking about me and you now," Ant told him. "We been through a lot together, man. And I just want you to know that I appreciate you, that's all. I love you, man."

Tone paused and let it all sink in, tired or not. "Yeah, man, I guess I love you, too. But I love pussy a lot more, so don't *ever* think about gettin' funny on me, man, calling me up to tell me that you love me after midnight and shit."

Ant broke out laughing. "Gettin' funny," as Tone called it, was absolutely out of the question! Nobody loved the sweet silk of a woman more than Ant did. No doubt!

"You don't have to worry about that from *me,* man," he commented. "So go on back to sleep. I gotta get up early for work tomorrow."

When they hung up, Ant undressed, laid down, and thought all the way back to their childhood in Jennings. Then he laughed to himself, reminiscing long past midnight on the love he had for his boy, and all of the crazy times they shared together while running the streets that emptied into Florissant Avenue.

Celena Myers was crazy, *period,* sometimes. Like when she demanded to know every detail of Sharron's personal life as though she were her mother reincarnated, *and* some. Who gave her that kind of power? Who ordained her? Better yet, how *dare* she have that much audacity? Handle your *own* business and get out of that of others!

"Look, Celena, I don't have to tell you everything about everybody I know, or how long I've known them, or where I met them. I mean, if I *do* tell you that kind of stuff, then fine. But don't make it out as some special *privilege* that I *owe* you, because I *don't,*" Sharron huffed. It was after midnight. "You damn sure don't tell me everything that *you* do, nor do I *ask* you about it."

"Look, I'm just trying to protect you, Sharron. I mean, you just go from lows to highs and back down to lows again. And that shit ain't healthy."

"Well, what do *you* know about being *healthy* with guys, Celena? I mean, really? When have *you* had a steady man in *your* life besides your father?!"

"I don't want one!" Celena hollered back.

"Well, *I* do! So don't get in my damn way!" Sharron snapped. She was so pissed that she slammed her bedroom door as Celena continued to run at the mouth.

"Now see, when you find yourself brokenhearted again, don't come runnin' back to me, because *I* won't have no more *advice* for your ass!

"Didn't even know the guy's damn name," she added.

"SO WHAT?!" Sharron yelled through her closed door.

That caused Celena to stop herself and laugh. They were acting as silly as two kitty cats wrestling over a big ball of yarn. They knew it, too. But Celena had started it, like she always did, with her extreme assertiveness. Sharron wasn't some big, crybaby pushover. Sometimes she had to remind Celena of that, very decisively. However, her girl Celena was protecting a loved one. And after Sharron's mother had died of cancer, with her father taking on a new woman, and her aunts and cousins bugging her to return home to Memphis, Celena had somehow, through her strong support, amassed more power over Sharron than what was presently needed.

Sharron thought about that herself, while sulking in her room. A room filled with large, stuffed animals, most won at Missouri's Six Flags amusement park. Sharron had been fairly lucky at Six Flags. She only wished that luck could spill over to her relations with men.

I appreciate what you've done for me over the years, but I can take care of myself *just as much as* you *can,* she reasoned. She was gathering the right words to let Celena know that the protective shell she had developed for her over the years had to go.

Where would you *be with your* debt *situation if it wasn't for* me *making you take some of those* addictions *that you buy* back *to them damn stores where you got them from?* You're *the one that needs help!* she thought.

Then she smiled. "No, I can't say that," she told herself out loud. "That would be mean, and then we'd go back to arguing again."

"Are you in there talking to yourself, again?!" Celena yelled, close by the door. "See, that's exactly what I'm talking about. You goin' crazy."

"Aw, girl, don't act like you don't talk to *yourself!*"

"Not like *you* do!"

"What's the difference?!"

Celena smiled. "*I* make sense when I do it."

Sharron had had enough. She jumped back up out of her bed and headed for the door. She swung it open like a madwoman and challenged, "You want some of me?! Is that it?! You want some of this?!" she asked with her hands up in a boxing stance.

Her girl laughed and backed away. Sharron brought the static right up to her face.

"Come on, then. Show me what you're made of, St. Louis. You got all of the mouth. Let me see the action."

"You better get up out of my face," Celena warned jokingly.

"Or what? Hunh? What?"

Celena lost her cool and rushed at her. Sharron, filled with playful energy, immediately countered the move and grabbed her shorter friend in a headlock.

"Now what, St. Louis?"

"OOUUWW, GIRL! MY DAMN EARRING!" Celena yelled at the top of her lungs.

Sharron let her go only to find *herself* being grabbed in a headlock.

"Now what, Tennessee?! Hunh?! What's up now?!" Celena asked, mocking her friend.

"You wanna play a game of horseshoes now? Hunh?" she continued.

Sharron just laughed, helplessly, until her girl let her go.

"Dummy," Celena sneered.

Sharron gathered herself and said, "You can't beat me, Celena. Remember, I *let* you go."

"Whatever."

"Because if we were in a real fight, I wouldn't have cared about your damn earrings."

"If we were in a *real* fight, you wouldn't have grabbed me like that," Celena argued.

"Celena, you cannot beat me. I've fought girls bigger than you way back in high school."

"So. That was in Tennessee. I mean, what were y'all fightin' over? Corn dogs?"

Sharron stopped herself and sighed. "Oh my God. You *have* to come to Memphis with me this summer, that's all there is to it."

"I guess I have to practice my horseshoe toss?" Celena joked, winding her arm back.

Sharron was impelled to challenge her again, but Celena, more poised than last time, sidestepped her with her hands held high in a boxing stance of her own.

"Come on wit' it then," she challenged.

Sharron held her hands even higher, and jabbed out her left arm with an open palm, connecting with her target, right smack across Celena's small face.

"Shit!" She ducked the next one and slipped under a right-handed hook with an open-hand smack to the back of Sharron's head. Both of them, not wanting to be hit up close, grabbed each other and began jockeying for openings to attack as if in a real fight.

"POW, POW, POW!" Celena gestured with a superior inside opening to the taller Sharron.

Sharron backed up and gestured with a right-handed fist that may have ended it all.

"BANG!"

Celena sucked her teeth as they disengaged. "Girl, I wouldn't have let you hit me with that."

"Whatever."

"I would have tied your arms up and just beat your face in."

"What, with them little hits? I would have knocked you out with my one punch."

"I didn't have to let you go to *get* that one punch, Sharron. I would have just dug my nails into your face while I had you."

"You wouldn't have gotten that close. *I* landed the first hit in case you forgot."

"Because you're taller than me."

"That's why you can't beat me."

"Sharron, I've fought plenty of tall girls before, and I whipped every one of their asses, *including* my sisters'. Just because you got the first hit, *doesn't* mean that you'll get the last."

Sharron finally smiled it off. "You a tomboy anyway," she said, jumping in for the last word.

"So what?"

By that time, it was close to one o'clock in the morning. They both had to be up early for work. Nevertheless, Sharron couldn't get any sleep. She had a man on her mind. She was too pumped with energy to even close her eyes. So she sat up in the dark, under the covers, thinking every little thought that managed to pop into her head.

I wonder how crazy it would be if I called him up and told him to drive over here and give me some, she mused with a grin. *Celena would* really *think I was crazy after that. But damn, I have all of this energy and I don't know what to do with it now. I'm freakin' restless!*

She shifted her body from side to side under the covers, and had another outlandish thought. *I wonder how crazy it would be if I like, showed up at his apartment or something in a taxi. I wonder if he would even be up. Or how about if he's out somewhere sexin' another woman anyway? Since he likes* sex *so much. I wonder if he's any good, howling at the moon. Because I had other guys who bragged on their Johnsons and couldn't even get the job done.*

Guys talk so much shit sometimes. Seriously! I wonder how I *would be if* I *was a guy. Shit, Celena's already a guy! I don't even have to* imagine *how* she *would be. She would probably be the kind of guy to tell a woman to give her a piece, then turn around and not call her anymore. It's not like she, or he, would be interested for the long run. She's not interested in the long run as a woman now.*

I wonder if Anthony is like that. I mean, he says that he wants that deep love stuff, but that could just be part of his game. Then again, at least he can explain himself. Most guys can't explain. A lot of them are too damn scared or immature to even try. And I'm talking about old guys, too. Age don't mean a thing. So at least Anthony is courageous enough to speak his mind. I admire that in him. Because most guys are straight-out cowards. Don't bullshit with me, tell me what the hell you want. And be man *enough to accept whether I give it to you or not. But that's their number one problem; they want to have their cake and eat it too. Always half-steppin'. I just want to see if he's gonna half-step with me, or if he's gonna give me* his *full piece.*

•

When Anthony called Sharron that first weekend, she planned on sticking it to him just like she had started off, in a zone and holding nothing back. She wanted to give him *her* full piece. That way they would have no excuses to claim later on.

"What do you like to do on a night like tonight?" he asked her from his front steps. He had another sandwich and drink in hand. Outside phone calls and snacks were Anthony's ritual of winding down after an honest day's work at Paul's. It was Saturday night, just after eight o'clock, with the sun making its way west, as the mellow darkness settled in.

"What are you doing right now?" Sharron asked him back.

"I'm about to eat a turkey and cheese sandwich and chill on my front steps."

"And then what?"

"The night is still young, and I don't have to work tomor'. Who knows where the wind may take me?"

"Well, why don't the wind bring you over here to pick me up?"

She was making it too easy for him. He wanted to push her away to create respectable distance between them.

Anthony chuckled. "Sounds like you bored. And you know what they say boredom does."

However, Sharron was on a mission not to play hard to get but, rather, hard to *forget*.

"Do you want to pick me up, or do you have something else to do?" she asked, pressing him.

"Damn, don't get spicy on me," he complained, munching on his sandwich.

With that, Sharron figured to go a little softer on him and use what she knew about men. Their egos could always get the best of them.

"I don't mean to sound demanding and all, I just want to see you. It's not that I'm all that bored, because I could go out with anybody. I would just rather be with you."

If he could see her smile, he would have realized how big of a trap she was setting for him. Nevertheless, Anthony was no pushover.

"What if I wasn't able to see you tonight? Like, if I already had plans?" he asked.

"But you don't. You already told me that."

Damn! he thought. *She's ridin' me. And I don't like how this shit feels.*

He was already being elusive, running away with his tail between his hind legs. Sharron was fully prepared to call him on it.

"Look, I'm just trying to give you a full piece of me. Now, you asked me if I wanted to make a trade, but now it seems like you don't want to come up with your end of the deal," she told him.

Shit! I told this girl too much! Now I gotta *see her,* he thought to himself. He couldn't let her down *that* fast. They had just met and he was still curious about her. He just didn't realize how curious *she* was about *him.*

"What time will you be ready?" he asked her. He felt like he was on a leash and being yanked in by his new owner. Players would much rather be in charge of the situation and have the *woman* on the leash. But Sharron had flipped the script on him, using his information against him. That's why most men kept their fat mouths shut. Women had some expert memories of conversation. They could draw on just about anything. Right on down to how often a guy trimmed his mustache. That kind of recall was dangerous. Especially for men who showed no consistency in what they said versus what they actually did.

"I'm ready now," Sharron answered. "How long will it take you to get to here?"

"University City? Ahh, give me about an hour. I gotta freshen up first." They'd already had most of their small talk on where they lived, what they did, and so on, before they left the skating rink on Thursday night.

"Okay," Sharron said. She agreed to his time, gave him her exact address and apartment number and directions. When she hung up, there was her girl Celena again, breathing down her neck.

"Sharron, you sound as desperate as a teenager in love. And you just *met* this guy," she piped. "He could be a damned rapist or anything."

Sharron smiled at that. "You don't know how many times I thought the same thing about the guys *you* go out with," she commented.

"Yeah, but *I* know the difference. *You* don't. Because you usually don't date guys like this."

"Guys like what?" Sharron wanted to know.

"Well, don't get me wrong here, but this guy Anthony seems a little faster than the usual guys that you date. That's all *I'm* saying."

Sharron smiled. "So what are you *really* saying, that I can't handle myself with him? I was doing quite well Thursday night, before *you* stuck *your* nose in it."

"Yeah, right. You didn't even know his damn name."

"Here we go with that again."

"I'm just reminding you of that."

"Oh, yeah, because I forgot the first *eight* times that you told me. You know, since I'm turning seventy next month, I don't recall things as well as I used to," Sharron joked.

Celena smirked at her. "You can get smart if you want to, but just be careful. That's all I'm telling you, to be careful."

"Okay, Grandma. Holding hands only, and *no* eye contact, because that can get you in *deep* trouble," Sharron said.

They paused, taking a moment to stare at each other before rumbling in laughter.

"All right, girl. Do what you want. I just don't want to be the one telling you 'I told you so.'"

"Good. Then don't."

By the time Anthony made it over to pick Sharron up, Celena, not to be outdone, had set up a date of her own. Her man arrived at the same time as Anthony, driving a black Toyota Supra. They approached the stairway to their dates' second-floor apartment simultaneously.

"What's up, dawg?" Celena's energetic date addressed Anthony. The light brown, tall, and slim young man was bubbling with enthusiasm. He spoke to Anthony out of pure friendliness. He was not the usual kind of hard-knocks man that Celena dated either. But he still had the ego intact. What would a man be without that?

Anthony nodded to him. "What's up?"

"You here for Sharron?" Mr. Bubbly asked him, going on information from Celena.

"You here for Celena?" Anthony asked him back, assuming as much. Celena seemed like the big-mouth type anyway.

"Yeah."

"Same answer," Anthony told him.

Not to be rude, but Anthony didn't feel up to chitchatting with the guy. He didn't even want to be there. In fact, he stopped himself short on the first step.

"Do me a favor and tell Sharron I'm out here."

"What's your name?"

"Ant."

"All right then, Ant. My name is Ronald."

They shook hands and separated. Ronald continued up to the apartment door. Anthony returned to his car and turned on his CD player.

Sharron walked out a minute later, flowing down the steps with her small, brown leather pocketbook, wearing blue denim shorts, a red Cardinals T-shirt, and no socks with her brown sandals.

As soon as she slid inside his Chevy, Anthony smiled and said, "You gotta go change your outfit." Outside of the sandals and pocketbook, he was wearing the exact same thing, a red Cardinals T-shirt and blue denim shorts.

Sharron looked him over and laughed. "Oh my God! This is embarrassing."

"Who you tellin'?" he responded, still grinning at the coincidence. "Now go back in the house and change."

"I'm only changing my shirt."

He nodded. "Aw'ight. That's a deal."

Celena's man was on his way back out as Sharron made her way in. You know how some women are; they're never ready. And few men are patient enough to wait. So Ronald decided to sit and wait in his car and listen to music as well.

On the way to his sports car, he walked over to speak to Anthony through his open window.

"I like what you did with your ride, man," he commented, looking over the '79 Chevy's chrome wheels, shiny paint job, and spotless interior.

"Thanks," Anthony told him with a nod.

"This car has hydraulics?"

"Naw."

Anthony was still moody and uncommunicative. He answered

Ronald's questions out of respect for Sharron. He didn't want to give the wrong impression of himself. But he still wasn't too happy about being there. It was Sharron's idea, and *he* wanted to be the one calling the shots. Particularly when there was no sex involved.

"No hydraulics? What about the sound system. Is it booming?" Ronald asked him next.

Anthony said, "Everybody got a sound system, man. I don't have none of that block-shaking shit, but it's loud enough for me and my passengers to hear."

"Yeah, I know what you mean," Ronald responded with a nod. "Sometimes them systems give you headaches anyway."

When Sharron made it back out, wearing a plain white T-shirt, she noticed Ronald at Anthony's open window. She smiled, thinking, *I wonder how well he gets along with people,* and climbed back in on the passenger side. Anthony had the car hot for her arrival.

"Aw'ight, man," he told Ronald. He backed out of the parking spot and pulled off.

Celena walked out and locked the apartment door a second later, wearing a floral dress that showed off her toned arms, shoulders, and legs, and smelling of sweet perfume and hair oil.

"Damn you look good!" Ronald told her. "And smell good, too."

"Thank you, thank you," she said as he opened the car door for her. That was a courtesy *Anthony* hadn't bothered to offer either time for Sharron.

"So what do you think about Sharron's friend?" Celena asked curiously. She figured that Ronald had met him. And she was right. Ronald was friendly that way.

"Well, he wasn't too talkative. But other than that, he seems all right to me," he answered.

"Yeah, but *you're* talkative," she responded with a grin. "You talk enough for *both* of y'all. So take me to get some ice cream first. That way, I can listen to all of your chatter and just lick my ice-cream cone."

Ronald looked at her and smiled. "So what am *I* supposed to lick?"

Celena looked at him with half a grin and half a frown as she nestled into the tightly modeled sports car. "You know what?" she began. "No, I'm not even gonna respond to that. Let's just drive."

Back in Anthony's Chevy, Sharron was just buckling her seat belt; the cranberry interior was as soft as a pillow.

Man, this feels good! she thought to herself. *And look at that wooden dashboard, and the cool steering wheel. He put more money into this car than I first thought.*

Out of the blue, Anthony asked her, "Is that the kind of guy your girl talks to?"

Sharron smiled. "No, not really. She's just bored tonight."

I know the feelin', Anthony thought with a grin. But he didn't dare say it. He'd told Sharron enough about him already. He expected her to ask him for more, and he planned not to tell her much. Surprisingly, she didn't seem pressed at the moment to ask him anything. She was just enjoying the ride. After a while, with no clear destination in mind, he got curious.

"So, where are you trying to go?" he asked her.

She thought about it and decided to be creative.

"I don't know. What's it like up on the moon?"

He looked over to see if she was serious. Once he noticed her staring up at the full moon, right smack in the middle of his windshield, he decided to play along with her lead.

"As a matter of fact, I was just up there last week. And we couldn't go up there dressed like this. We would need snowsuits," he joked.

She looked at him and smiled, deciding to keep it going. "What's there to do up there, you know, besides looking around?"

He said, "Well, we could go moon skiing, or play basketball on twenty-foot hoops."

"Could you dunk the ball up there?"

"Like Jordan."

"Me too?"

"It depends on how strong your legs are."

She looked at him and flirted. "My legs are *very* strong."

He looked back and returned her flirt. "So is my lower back." Then he grinned.

"What kind of workouts do you do?" she asked, grinning back.

"Mainly push-ups, lifts, and curls," he answered.

How silly can we get? they both wondered. It felt good to unwind with silliness. Everyone has it. And it sure does break the ice.

"So where would you take me if I let you take me anywhere? And don't *lie* either," Sharron challenged.

Here she goes with that shit again, Anthony thought.

"You ever read encyclopedias before?" he decided to ask her instead.

"As a matter of fact, I did."

"I can tell. Because you wanna know *every* damn thing!"

"And *you* don't?"

He thought about it. "Sometimes I do, and sometimes I don't. Because sometimes . . . you just don't wanna know," he told her. "That's what gets women in so much trouble, wantin' to know everything. So dead cats are laying up in the alleyways from here to California.

"And you know why?" he asked her.

"Why?"

"Because y'all only got nine lives, but y'all be asking twenty fatal questions. Then y'all find out answers that y'all can't handle and start jumping out of twelve-story windows."

She smiled, amused by his analogy, but not convinced of it.

"Not *all* of us."

"Yeah, just *most* of you," he said with a chuckle.

"Don't think I forgot about my question, either," she told him.

He shook his head and grinned. Then he came up with an idea. "Aw'ight then, I'll tell you what. I've been wanting to do something for a while now, I just haven't found anybody to do it with. So, since you have a million and one questions, you gon' find out exactly what's on my mind right now." And he continued to grin, knowing that a woman's natural curiosity would drive her insane with wonder. Then she would be pleasantly surprised. Or maybe not. Maybe she would think his idea was corny. Nevertheless, she was intriguing, playful, curious, and free enough to find out. Free, because she did not seem imprisoned by boredom and pressed about being entertained.

Some women needed entertainment *constantly.* And they were the worst women in the world to go out with. Especially on an unplanned date. Because they never knew how to enjoy the moment, transforming every decision or nondecision onto the man, whether he was up to it or not. Sometimes men were just not up for taking charge of every single situation. And God help the man who ends up with a woman who depends on his every move or thought for life. But this was Sharron Francis, a down-to-earth girl from Memphis, Tennessee, who knew how to live in empty space, filling it up with thoughts, ideas, and actions of her own.

So she responded, "Okay," and waited to see what he had in store for her.

Anthony turned onto Lindbergh Boulevard and headed north toward the airport. Then he second-guessed his idea, thinking that Sharron had seen enough airplanes as it was. She worked at the airport. But he had already started on his mission, so he drove to the parking site where mainly white American couples watched airplanes take off and land.

"Now that I think about it, maybe this wasn't a good idea for you. You work over there, right?" he said, referring to the St. Louis airport.

"So," she told him. "*You* don't." She jumped out of the car before he did to enjoy the clear sight of the airplanes.

"Don't you get tired of seeing these things though?" he asked.

"Not really. I'm never outside. Celena would get tired of seeing airplanes before I would."

"Hmmph," he grunted. "She's the kind of woman who gets tired of everything." And *he* would know. He knew all of the types. But that didn't mean he could never fall for a woman. As long as he was willing to be loved and to love back, with courage and a woman that he could trust. But first he had to learn to trust himself.

Anthony thought about the idea of trust and love as they watched planes together in the cool night air, while leaning against his car. Then Sharron grabbed his hand.

"Does this make you feel uncomfortable?" she asked, expecting to let him go.

"Why do you ask?"

"Because a lot of guys don't like holding hands."

He smiled, knowing that the truth was simple.

"When were we ever into holding hands in the first place? I never did that shit. I didn't even hold my mother's hand. Then I had two older brothers, uncles and boy cousins. And none of us held hands."

Sharron snapped her hand away from his, playfully.

"So, what are you saying, that holding hands is only for girls and mommy's boys?"

"Basically, yeah," he admitted with a laugh.

Then she slammed her backside into him and tossed his hands around her hips.

"And this makes you feel uncomfortable, too, right? Because it makes you want me."

He broke out laughing and never answered her.

"So what's a woman to do, you know, when she just wants closeness? Not penetration, but closeness?" she asked him seriously. "I mean, don't you ever want to be just . . . close to a woman? To smell how clean she is, and to touch how smooth her skin feels, and to stroke her hair and stuff."

He chuckled, thinking silly thoughts, and said, "What if she don't smell too good?"

"First of all, you need to find one who does," she answered. Then she stepped away and turned to face him. "Are you trying to tell me something?"

He broke out laughing, watching the horror on her face.

"Naw, you smell good. I'm just saying. Come back here," he told her, reaching for her hand of all things.

"Why? You're not a mommy's boy, right?"

"You know I'm not. But I'm not a murderer either. I'm human. And I like closeness like you do," he said, pulling her back to his cozy spot.

"I'm not even supposed to be leading you on like this. This *is* our first date," she told him, holding her ground and moving away.

"So what?" he commented, teased by her.

"So . . . I don't want to give you too much too early. I want to give you a piece at a time, like you told me."

Aw, man, he pouted to himself. She could read the disappointment written all over his face as he let her hand fall away.

"See that? Now you know why we don't tell y'all nothing," he complained out loud.

She knew she had the upper hand on him then. He wanted her. But she wasn't giving in to him until *she* was ready. The power of the booty. It was legendary.

"So, if I was willing to give you some tonight, would you take it?"

He smiled.

"Dumb question, right?" she asked him.

He took the Fifth and kept his mouth shut. Nevertheless, his grin told her everything. He was a M-A-N. He was *made* to penetrate.

Sharron shook her head and didn't find the idea as humorous.

"That's the kind of thing that makes me wonder why we even go through it all. And it doesn't matter *what* woman it is. If *she's* down with it, then *you're* down."

Anthony denied it. He had taste.

"Naw, it ain't that simple," he told her. "Not for me."

"Well, it seems simple enough to *me,*" she responded.

"Then why do y'all do it then? Why do y'all keep chasing after guys?" he asked.

"Because it's natural to want somebody," she snapped. It was obvious. She moved closer to him and whispered, "You know how pussy feels, right? So why do you keep fuckin'?"

Anthony was so surprised that he nearly covered his ears with his hands. He didn't expect for a woman like Sharron to use such words. It didn't fit her personality. That made him even *more* curious about her.

"You didn't expect for me to say that to you, right?"

He was still speechless, staring at her.

"Naw, you right. I didn't," he answered with a chuckle.

"I usually don't. But I know girls that do."

"Yeah, like your roommate."

Sharron paused for a moment and thought about Celena, her rambunctious friend with the yuck mouth, who generally received twice as much respect from guys as she did, even though Celena slept around and treated them more like thrill rides than companions.

"Would you rather be with her than with me? Tell the truth," Sharron asked Anthony. She had no clue that she would ask him that. The question simply slipped out of her mouth. She was in a zone. A love zone. And she didn't even realize it.

But *he* did. Sharron was reaching Anthony, deep down inside, with her honesty.

"Does she ever keep any of her boyfriends long?" he asked of Celena.

Sharron shook her head and smiled. "You know, you're very good at avoiding questions. And to think that *I* thought you might have been different."

"I *am* different."

"And so is everyone else."

She stood there and leaned up against him on his car again.

He answered, "I would choose you. Because it would last longer."

She thought on his answer for a second. *It would last longer? What* would last longer? The sex? The relationship? The love? The intrigue? Or all of the above?

"Everything would last longer," he answered without her asking him.

She smiled and squeezed his arms tightly around her. Was this still a first date? It seemed like a hell of a lot more. To *both* of them! And Anthony was used to calling the shots. Maybe a little uncertainty was good for him. It sure had his full attention.

"Sometimes, I envy how close white couples are on *their* dates. It just seems like black love doesn't get that close. Or at least not in public," Sharron said out of the blue.

Anthony frowned and asked, "Where did you come from with that?"

"I mean, just look at them. Puppy love. At all ages."

And it was true. They were surrounded by it. Old couples and young. Apple-pie Americans.

"That's because they don't have as much shit to worry about as we do. And they do more," Anthony responded. "I was even unsure about bringing you out here. Not so much because you worked at the airport, but because you might have looked at me funny for doing it. My boy Tone would *never* bring a girl up here."

"Nor would my *roommate* want to be here," Sharron countered. "But that's them, and this is us. That's what stops couples from being themselves, judging what everybody else is doing."

"You're doing that right now by talking about white couples," he reminded her. "You don't know how black people are in other countries. I hear that black guys in the Caribbean are supposed to be real affectionate."

Sharron sucked her teeth and said, "They don't seem affectionate to me. They seem just as rough as American men, and just as egotistical, if not *more.*"

"So, you're saying that black men are not affectionate *at all?* Is that what you're saying? Because I heard that white couples in Europe barely touch each other. What about them?"

Sharron shook her head and turned to face him.

"You know what, we're both talking about a bunch of stereotypes. The bottom line is this: Are *you, Anthony Poole,* willing to be affectionate with *me?* That's what *I* want to know."

He pulled her gently into him and kissed her square on the lips before breaking away. A confident move.

She smiled, covering her lips, embarrassed and pleased by it at the same time.

"Does that answer your question?" he asked her.

"That wasn't really affection though. That was more like . . . passion."

He grinned. *This girl is a trip,* he thought to himself. But he was enjoying it. It was a new challenge for him, not being able to predict anything, while being forced to work a little harder. And as for Sharron, she knew that Anthony could take it. An intelligent edge in a woman was *always* attractive to a player. Intelligent women gave them a chance to test how strong their game was. Or how weak, so that they could return to the lab and work on it.

"What's the difference?" he asked her.

"It's simple, really. Affection is showing closeness, and expressing that you care in small ways, like holding hands, giving hugs, asking if everything is okay, and stuff like that. But passion is more assertive. Passion is like . . . taking over, and immersing yourself into the moment. Like, jumping into the bottom of the well. And there's a big difference in the two.

"Because a lot of women end up in passionate, sexual relationships, when all they *really* want is affection," she added. "And most *guys* would rather be passionate, because passion may lead straight to sex, where affection may not."

Anthony chuckled at it. Sharron was telling the truth. Passion was for guys like him, who usually got the panties. Affection was for the softies. The mommy's boys, walking around holding hands and forever being told, "No. Let's wait."

Fuck that waitin' and debatin' shit. I'll take passion over affection any *day!* he told himself. Then he chuckled and blew his cool.

"See, that's what I mean," Sharron responded, reading his smile. "You know it's true. *And* you know the difference," she told him.

"Don't you want to be passionate?" he asked. He couldn't imagine her *not* wanting passion. She thought too much not to. Sharron thought too much to do without *many* feelings.

"Of course I want it. But I want it in a balance," she answered. "A little bit of affection. A little bit of passion. And then both at the same time. But I would rather that a man be more passionate about loving me as a complete being than about just screwing me. You know what I mean?"

He nodded and understood her point. Men wanted to be loved for more than their wallets and the drama in their lives. Sometimes, they just wanted to chill, like *they* were doing. And before they knew it, it was close to one o'clock in the morning. They were one of the last couples standing.

"Damn! Where did all of the time go?" Anthony asked rhetorically.

"That's the way it's supposed to be," Sharron responded to him. "Off the clock. Because we have all night long to be with each other."

"We do?"

"Well, not tonight. No," she answered quickly, heading back to her side of the car.

Anthony ran around and beat her to it, opening the passenger-side door to help her in.

"Is this affection?" he asked her, cheesing all the way.

"No. Opening car doors is more like chivalry and respect."

Anthony looked at her and was stunned.

"Damn! We got manners, respect, chivalry, affection, passion, and what else?"

Sharron added, "Commitment, loyalty, trust . . . And when I think of more, I'll be sure to let you know."

He laughed and said, "Yeah, I'm sure you will."

When Sharron crept back into her room that night, it was well after two in the morning. Celena had been waiting up for her.

"So where did you go, and what did y'all do?" she appeared in the dark and asked.

"SHIT, GIRL! WHAT THE HELL IS WRONG WITH YOU?"

Sharron had undressed and was in bed already. A surprising voice in the dark is not exactly the best homecoming after a late-night date.

"I thought your behind was asleep," Sharron snapped, composing herself.

"Yeah, you *wanted* me to be asleep. So what happened?" Celena asked again.

Sharron sighed. "Did I walk into your room and ask you what happened on *your* date?"

"Well, if you *must* know . . ."

"I *don't* want to know," Sharron snapped, cutting her off.

Celena went ahead and told her anyway. "Ronald kept dropping hints about what he had an *urge* for, so I tested him to see if he was serious. And he was. *Very* serious!" she revealed with a spreading gesture of her thighs.

Sharron shook her head. "Well, we had none of that going on on my date. We just had deep conversation and watched the airplanes go by."

Celena frowned. "You watched the *airplanes* go by?"

"Yeah. We parked in a lot across from the airport where couples and families watch airplanes."

"Was that *your* idea or his?"

"His."

"It fig— What?" Celena stopped herself in midsentence and asked, "It was *his* idea, to go out and watch *airplanes*?"

Sharron laughed, tickled that Celena was unable to mark her new friend.

"We talked more than we watched planes. But it *was* peaceful. And different. *Very* different."

Celena grunted, "Mmm-hmm. I think I better watch out for this guy. He might have some unusual *scheme* in mind for you. So Mr. Nameless is an airplane lover?"

"I don't think he loves airplanes all that much, he just wants to do different things, and he was willing to share that with me."

"Mmm-hmm. Because he wants *you* to share something with *him* later on," Celena assumed. "Don't get it confused, girl. He can take you to the airport if he wants to, but he's still a damn player to me. *I* know it. I can feel the vibes on his ass."

"Yeah, whatever. It sounds to me like you're jealous. I think you're just mad that he didn't bump into *you* at the skating rink," Sharron countered with a grin.

"Ha, ha," Celena mocked, leaving the room.

Could *she be jealous?* Sharron thought to herself. *Why? Because Anthony is more* her *type, and* I *have him? I better watch out for that,* she told herself. *Close girlfriends or not, Celena has to respect my space.* And *respect my men. But she's right about* one *thing. He* is *a player. A player with a heart. I just wonder if I can really get to him, and make him fall in love with me somehow. Hmmmm.*

And she fell asleep with a smile on her face.

Ant found it hard to fall asleep on *that* night. He was *falling* all right, but not so much in love; he was falling more into confusion. Usually, he had to be *mad* about a girl for her to get to him. Mad about her physically more than anything else. And it wasn't that Sharron was not an attractive woman, because she was. She simply was not jumping off of the scales the way he liked it. Dana Nicole Simpson scales. However, those hyperscalcs were exactly what he was trying to get away from. The insecurity of trying your best to handle a fast-paced woman was torturous to a man no matter *who* he was *or* what he had. Even the iciest pimps feared them. Because women who tipped the scales could break a man's entire stable. They were just too damned dangerous to keep. Likewise, Ant was dangerous to Sharron. Yet, he was just what she needed. He kept her excited about life. And she was just what *he* needed, an intelligent, around-the-way girl to take his mind off of the everyday stress of human competition; competition that wore men into the ground.

"Shit!" Ant yelled at his phone after hanging up the line. His boy Tone was nowhere to be found, and he needed someone to talk to.

Desperately! About girl problems. Oh yeah! Guys talked about girl problems. Even the players. Women were just rarely allowed to participate in those conversations. But that did *not* mean they didn't exist.

So Ant called his cousin Michael "Rico" Poole, who still lived in an apartment complex in Jennings. Rico, with Puerto Rican blood from his mother, was seductively reddish brown, with thick, black, wavy hair, and had enough loose marbles in his head to send women absolutely crazy for him. Even scale-tipping women found him hard to resist, including three who bore him children: two boys and one girl.

Ant would not let *any* of his women near Rico with a twenty-foot pole. He despised even talking to his older cousin *about* women, because Rico had absolutely *no* loyalties. Women to him were like chips in a petty card game. They were completely disposable. So calling his cousin up for advice was another torturous task. Nevertheless, Rico was sure to have some answers. A master player.

"You know what fuckin' time it is?" he answered the phone. His youngest son's mother was stretched across his chest, which was nicked up from too many street battles, the scars of passion run wild and other close calls of fatality.

"Yeah, I know what time it is. Why, did I disturb something?" Ant asked him.

"Naw, that would have been a couple of hours ago." Then his cousin smiled and added, "And a couple hours after this."

"You got time to throw down with me for a minute then?" Ant asked him.

Rico tensed up. "Somebody got squabbles with you?"

"Naw, man, I'm talkin' 'bout game and women."

Rico eased up and laughed. "Some girl got you whipped?"

"Naw, man, I ain't even hit it yet."

"Oohhh. She mind fuckin' you then."

Ant *hated* to admit that. "I can't really say—"

"Yes you can," his cousin cut him off. "If you callin' me up at"—he gave a look over to his illuminated clock—"two thirty-six in the morning, then this girl is *definitely* mind-fuckin' you." Then he laughed at the idea.

Damn! I shouldn't have called his ass! Ant told himself. It was too late for that.

"What you do, right, is go out and get yourself a piece to get your mind off of it," Rico explained to him. "You know that shit already, man. You ain't no damn rookie. Why you even callin' me up with this?"

Yeah, why am *I calling him?*

"You right, man. I'll catch you later then," Ant responded, rushing to end his call.

"Anthony?" Rico piped before he hung up. "Are you ready to be a daddy yet, man?"

What?! Ant was shocked that his cousin was even asking him such a thing.

"Oh, naw. Not me," he answered.

"Well, when you *do* knock this girl off, you make sure you keep your head covered. *Both* of 'em. Because once you have a kid with a woman—" he stopped and looked down at his youngest son's sexy mother, amazed that she could sleep so damn hard, "shit can get *real* complicated."

Ant smiled and knew exactly what Rico was referring to. His children's mothers were driving him as crazy as he had driven them. Some of those scars on his reddish brown chest were there to prove it. I guess Rico was no master player after all.

Nevertheless, Ant hung up the phone with the full intention of taking up his big cousin's advice. He needed to entertain himself with other flesh and bone, and as soon as possible to clear his mind from thoughts of Sharron.

"What did you do last night? I called you twice," Shawntè asked, relaxing against the same comfortable interior of Ant's car that Sharron had leaned against the night before.

"You didn't leave me no messages," he told her.

"Because I don't like answering machines. It makes you seem pressed."

Ant looked at her and frowned. "Shit, if that's the case, then why even call? All you had to do was give me a number where you were.

I could have called you back and hooked up with you," he told her, using her information to his advantage. It's a pity. Some women have no idea when the cards are already stacked against them.

"Yeah, I guess so," she responded with a smile. She fixed her makeup in the vanity mirror, far too into herself for her own good.

"How many times you gon' look at yourself in the mirror?" Ant joked with her. "That makeup ain't changed since you sat in the car."

"I'm just trying to make sure that I look right, that's all."

She *did* look right. In fact, she was just a touch from glamorous in a blue, form-fitting tank dress with spaghetti straps to hold it up. Yet, she was too damned eager to be there, which made her pressed anyway. And a bit insecure. She was a vain rabbit up against a hungry rattlesnake. Too bad she couldn't hear the rattle of his tail while sweating herself.

Ant, dressed in olive green, with a black belt and black shoes, was taking her over the bridge to East St. Louis of all places, just to show her off, get her drunk, gas her head up, and take her back to his place for the late-night deserts.

"Which club are we going to over here?" she asked him.

"Do you have a preference for one?"

She shook her head of short-cut hair. "Not really. I was just asking."

He smiled, reeling her in. "I'm thinking 'bout going to whichever spot has the least amount of people in it. That way we can do our thing without bumping elbows and shit."

She chuckled. "Yeah, because last time I didn't even get to dance with you. You was acting like you lost your best friend or something. I felt sorry for you."

That surprised him. He looked her in the face to make sure he heard her right. "You felt *sorry* for me?"

"Yeah. I mean, you were acting really miserable that night, like you had just come from a funeral that day."

"Naw," he told her with a frown. "Is that why you gave me your number, to make me feel better?"

She stopped herself in full knowledge of his ego. He had already revealed his nasty bite to her the night they met. She surely didn't want to go that route again. So she thought before she answered. Intimidated.

"I gave you my number because I liked you," she said with a smile.

Good answer. But it was also the naked truth with no clothing left to strip free before intimacy. Like Ant had told Sharron on their night at the skating rink, you don't want to give too much too fast, because it's liable to be taken for granted.

So he smiled at Shawntè, already predicting her fate for the end of the night. Then he went with his killer instincts, grabbing on to her knee and squeezing it just right to let her know what it would feel like to be caressed by him. Caressed all over. Then penetrated and brought to a powerful climax. *All* through one squeeze.

The right touch could say a thousand words. And Anthony Poole had spoken. Loudly! So by the time he had chosen a low-key club, lightly speckled with a thirty- and forty-something crowd instead of their own twenties crowd, Shawntè walked in with him hand in hand and was all his before the first drink, the first dance, and the first kiss.

"I guess we'll grab a quick drink first so we can get loose on the dance floor and show these old heads how to move," he told her.

Shawntè looked around at the boogeying dance floor of grown-ups in dresses and slacks, sweating the night away, and begged to differ.

"I don't think we can show them *anything*. They already got it all down in here," she responded with a chuckle.

Ant looked around and agreed, but only halfway.

"That's just because they like this old song they're playing," he countered.

"Who is this?" she asked. "Didn't Biz Markie do a song off of this beat a few years ago?"

"Yeah. It's McFadden and Whitehead. 'Ain't No Stopping Us Now' My uncles used to *love* this song!"

"Are they gonna play oldies in here all night?" Shawntè was concerned. She wanted to get her dance on and not with a bunch of old songs that she wasn't particularly familiar with.

"Why, you don't like the seventies jams?" Ant asked, snapping his fingers and swinging as if he was forty himself.

She looked at him and broke up laughing. "Stop it. Okay? Otherwise, I'ma have to talk about you," she warned him. "What made you choose this place anyway?"

"I told you, I'm not trying to be bumping into people tonight. Old heads know how to give each other space."

Shawntè still disliked the idea, and was ready to pout. "Are we staying here, for real?"

Ant read her displeasure and decided to use his age and experience on her.

He said, "I thought that when a woman really likes a man, she can go anywhere with him and just enjoy herself because she got what she wants. Then again, if you don't like me like that, then maybe I need to hook you up with one of these old players in here, and tell 'em that you like his feathered hat and polyester jacket."

Shawntè broke up laughing again and confirmed her interest in him. "Don't even go there," she said. "You know I like you. I wouldn't even have walked into this place if I didn't."

"But you think I'm corny now. I can tell. You don't really wanna be with me. You wanna be with some younger guy." He said, "You want to run around with some guy talking about shooting people and getting high every night.

"But me? I told you, I like to have elbowroom and fresh air," he continued, pouring it on thicker than southern gravy. "I just like to chill and go one-on-one with whoever I'm with and school 'em like Michael Jordan."

Ego revealed, Shawntè sighed with a grin and decided to excuse herself from the bullshit.

"I have to go to the bathroom now," she told him.

Yeah, I got her, Ant told himself as he watched her slip away to the ladies' room. It felt damned good to be a young man on top of his game. *Damned* good!

"Hey, young blood? How's it goin'?" an older man asked him. "Look like you stole my outfit for the night," he added with a chuckle. He stood over six feet and was dressed in the same olive green as Ant.

"Good thing I'm leaving. We don't want to look like no twins in here," he commented, smelling of too many drinks.

"Yeah," Ant admitted to him. Something like that could screw up his night. It would have given Shawntè something to laugh and talk loud about with her friends. He would rather she went home and *whispered* about the strong loving he planned to lay on her after midnight. *"Girrrl, let me tell you this . . ."*

Luckily, the old-timer made his way out the exit door with his lady friend before Shawntè returned from the restroom and spotted him wearing a similar, olive-colored outfit.

And since the proof had left the premises, Ant decided to share it with her anyway. It wasn't as if she would believe it without the proof. Innocent until *proven* guilty, right?

"You'd never guess what just happened," he told her, wide-eyed.

"Some old man had your same outfit on," she responded effortlessly.

"How'd you know that?"

"I saw him when we first walked in."

"You did?"

She nodded. "He was sittin' right at the bar. But since you were so busy getting your groove on, you didn't even look in his direction."

"Damn! You sharp," he told her.

"You thought I wasn't?"

Uh-oh. This girl may be harder than I thought, he mused.

"You wanna get a drink now, or you wanna tell the DJ to play one of those old, slow songs?" he asked her.

"It doesn't matter to me."

"Oh yeah? Well, let's get them drinks then. Sloe gin fizz?"

She smiled. "Unt-unh. Sex on the beach."

He chuckled, caught off guard by it. "The drink, or the act?"

Her smiled disappeared. "You tell me," she countered and walked away.

It was apparent at that point the male game plan was all bullshit indeed. Because if Shawntè had her own plans and they included sex on the beach or *wherever,* then *Ant* could have just as well have been playing right into *her* game. He was curious to find out if that was the case.

"What time do you need to be home tonight? You go to work in the morning?" he asked her.

It was a Sunday. Ant had to be to work early himself. Fortunately, knocking over new women provided a strange energy boost, mainly with women whom he couldn't refuse. New women like Shawntè and Sharron. And goddesses like Dana Nicole Simpson of course. But he would rarely lose sleep over old women. He'd send them right home and tell them they'd hook up again when more time allowed.

"I'm not working right now," Shawntè answered him.

Curiosity made him ask, "Why not?" Ant didn't particularly like broke women. They were the quickest way in the west to a headache. They were too damned needy and greedy for comfort.

"I'm just in between jobs right now."

"For how long?"

She shrugged her shoulders. "Three months."

"Three *months?" Where the hell do you get your money from then?* he thought of asking. He figured his tone of voice was quizzical enough to spark an explanation without asking her.

"It takes time for some people to figure out what they really want to do," she answered. "And I don't want to work just to be working. I want to *enjoy* what I do."

He nodded. There was no sense in getting into her economic life. He just wanted her *physically.*

"Like having good sex," he hinted to her. "You don't want to just do it, you want to *enjoy* doing it."

She choked on her drink. "Where did *that* come from?"

"From my mouth," he told her.

"Preconceived notions, hunh?" she asked with a twinkle in her eyes.

"You don't have any?"

She smiled even wider with soft pink lips on her straw and nodded. "I do."

"On what?"

She chuckled, teasingly, but wouldn't answer. That all but made Ant want to pack it up for the night and head west, back over the bridge for St. Louis and Nebraska Avenue to his cozy, second-floor apartment.

To break the tension, as soon as Shawntè set down her drink again, Ant asked her if she wanted to dance.

"Come on," she told him.

He hadn't even ordered anything. He was too busy guessing and second-guessing her availability for the night. And how much *she* may have had planned for *him.* Like his curiosity for the panty line that he failed to notice through her dress. And when they danced, she wasn't at all concerned about the rhythm of the beat, just the closeness that they shared, making him feel awkward in front of so many grown faces.

They were so close that he got a good, long sniff of her hair, which smelled of sweet oils.

"What did you put in your hair? It smells good."

"Ginseng oil."

"*Ginseng?* You used *ginseng* in your *hair?*"

"Yeah, it's called Ginseng Miracle."

He grinned. "I guess you can use that for a lot of things then."

She grinned back at him. "I guess so. What do *you* use it for?"

"I don't need to use it. But I know other guys who do."

"What do *they* use it for?"

"Ahh, to stay ahh . . . awake. Yeah, that's it. Awake," he answered with a laugh.

"You stay awake naturally?"

"Yeah," he answered her with pride. "Naturally."

"How long are we planning on staying here?" she questioned, bored again.

"Where else you want to go?"

"Actually, I'm kind of tired. I just need to lay my head down and relax somewhere."

Shit! Is this girl fuckin' with me or what?! he asked himself. Ant took her answer to mean she wanted much more than grinding on the dance floor. She was turning on the heat, and they weren't halfway finished with their evening together. It was only eleven o'clock.

"And what am *I* supposed to do while you lay down and relax?" he asked, just for kicks.

She smiled. "I guess you do what you want."

He smiled back at her. "Let me get a drink before we get out of here."

Sometimes, when you got it good, things just seem to float along like a dream. But the night was real. And on the way back to St. Louis, while crossing the bridge, Shawntè reached over with her left hand and began to tenderly stroke the nap of Ant's head, sending chills and thrills to all the right places.

"Girl, you gon' make me crash doing that," he warned her.

She didn't heed his warning. Instead, she undid her seat belt and slid in closer to him to nibble on his ear, something she wouldn't have been able to do in bucket seats. Ant's comfortable old Chevy came in handy that way.

Damn, she's in heat! *I may not be able to* make *it to the crib!* he thought. *We might end up having to pull over on the side of the road somewhere.*

"I thought you told me you wanted to lay your head down and relax," he said, leaning away from her. Hell, he still had *driving* to do!

"I *do* want to lie down," she said, still chasing his ear with her tongue.

There was no doubt in his mind at that point, Shawntè wanted to strip down and dance on bedsheets. *His* bedsheets. Or maybe not. Maybe the back of the car would do her just fine. Or even the *front* of the car. Nevertheless, Ant wanted to get her back home so that he could possess her full body, and teach her a lesson. You never outplay a player. Unless you're the ultimate shit! And Shawntè was not. So he could not allow her to get away with her insane advances to him while on the bridge of all places.

Shawntè wouldn't stop. When she went for his olive pants and gripped his hard-on, it became embarrassing. Ant then switched the wheel to his left hand and pushed up her slippery blue dress with his right to grab a handful of her pudding, poking his way to her entrance. And he got an immediate response, as if she were an iceberg waiting to be thawed.

"Girl, you gon' make me explode on you right in this car," he warned her again.

All she did was giggle, continuing to lead him on. "Do what you gotta do?"

SHIT! This girl's a freak*! And I didn't even bring any rubbers with me. Fuck was I thinking?!*

He surely wasn't thinking that she would turn into a real-life viper on him. He was unprepared for it. But players had rules. Screwing without condoms was one of them. Especially new freak bodies. You *don't* do it! Yet, rules were all meant to be broken. It's only human nature that they were, because there was no such thing as *objective* perfection, only *subjective* perfection. In other words, there was no absolute, only situational. All human rules became malleable depending on the urgency of the situation. Some situations made it easier than others to follow the rules. But then you had those cases that did not.

Shawntè had become urgent. *Very* urgent. The situation was unbearable. Even for a practiced player. Fortunately, the law won out. Literally. As they entered downtown St. Louis they came upon a swarm of flashing police cruisers, gathered for some downtown disturbance.

"Put your seat belt back on," Ant snapped to Shawntè with a shove. He didn't want to be pulled over with a full-blown hard-on. Fear of male humiliation was more urgent than sex.

"God, you don't have to *throw* me out the window," Shawntè huffed.

"I didn't push you that hard. Stop whining."

"You did *so* push me hard."

He read her face to see if she was serious, and decided to lighten things up.

"You gonna get *pushed* all right. And I'ma give you something worth whinin' about," he told her.

That turned Shawntè's fake frown into a real smile. She behaved herself and sat quietly until he got her to his place, all cleaned up and ready for her arrival.

"Aren't *you* neat," she said, taking in the tidiness of his living quarters. Ant had everything he needed in his living room: a nice sofa, a La-Z-Boy chair, a coffee table, and a massive television set. In his miniature kitchen he had a small dinette set. He had Tupperware on his shelves, silverware in his kitchen drawers, and food inside his refrigerator and cabinets. He even had clean facecloths and hand towels, soap, and toilet tissue in his bathroom. And in his large bedroom, he had quality dressers, a huge vanity mirror, and a perfectly made bed that included matching shams.

OH MY GOD! Shawntè thought to herself in a panic. *What kind of man do I have here?* She didn't expect him to have all of that. And it wasn't as if anything was extra expensive. It was just all there. As if he paid strict attention to the details. Guys who chased after the cute smiles and sexy skirts were not supposed to have completed apartments. They were supposed to have just a place to sleep and do their business. A crib. But Ant had much more than that. He had a home. That scared Shawntè half to death. Because she realized that she would like him more now. He was a man with a complete place of his own, and not in his momma's home or some makeshift apartment with too much traffic running through it. Ant was self-contained and stable. The same thing that Dana Nicole Simpson had found out and fell for.

Shawntè found herself floating toward the bed, helplessly, as Ant carried her in to her fate. She squeezed him, desperately, knowing that it would hurt. Not so much physically, but in the heart, because she realized there was no way to stop herself from extending it to him. Especially if he was able to take care of business downstairs. Because the *upstairs* was already accounted for.

And when her clothing was tugged off and thrown to the floor, she felt nothing, and yet *everything*. *Nothing,* because every other thought on her mind had disappeared. And *everything,* because his cool, wet tongue on her bare nipples stimulated excitement in a trillion nerve cells running from the hair follicles in her scalp, down to the skin beneath her toenails.

All that she could do was shake her head with her eyes closed, with no strength for words, only illegible moans of pleasure. But Ant could read them. It was the language of physical bliss. He had become an A student of that a *long* time ago. He teased her with his tongue, all the way down to her inner thighs, causing her to cling to the sheets for help.

Help me, somebody! Oh God, help me! Pleeease!

When she felt it, she melted, becoming a full body of soup as he stirred her with his ready spoon. She kissed his lips, devouring his tongue like a serpent while he prepared her serving like the chef she prayed he *wouldn't* be. Why? Because it hurts so bad to love so good and not know if you could keep that loving forever.

Forever!
Forever!
Ooohhh, my God, *forever!*

"You okay?" Ant asked Shawntè, exhausted in his sweat-drenched bed.

She was barely awake. After all, it was only six o'clock in the morning, and he had pushed her far beyond her limits until half past two.

"What time is it?" she mumbled, praying that she could stay there and recuperate for another three and a half hours. At least!

"It's time for me to get ready for work. I have to drive you back home first."

Can I just stay here for a while? Shawntè thought of asking. But she knew better than that. Pressing the issue would only buy her a faster ticket home for the next time she wanted to stay. That's why it hurts so bad. She would be forced to deny herself what she would desire so torturously: Ant's time, trust, affection, and dedication.

"Well, I'm 'bout to take a shower. In the meantime, I need you to do me a favor and get yourself ready for yours. Okay?" He waited for her answer to make sure she understood him.

"All right," she whined. "I'll be up when you get out."

While the warm water smacked Ant's face and body, washing the midnight's lust away, he thanked his lucky stars for being born a boy. Then he proceeded to wash his tool like it was the most treasured item in the world. And it was. The magic wand of *all* creation.

Girls held the *keys* to creation. The soil. And they were usually well-rounded. More so than boys. They knew more. Felt more. Read more. Expressed more. Not just about things and statistics, but about life in general. How to hold on. Keeping it all together; maintaining the earth, and all that was in it. In fact, if it were not for girls growing into nurturing women, mother earth would have starved and died a million years ago.

Men, on the other hand, were more concerned with trying to blast off into outer space and land on the friggin' moon. Many of them only succeeded in crashing into the deep blue ocean and drowning, pulled down by the reality of gravity. But that was what men were born to do. Explore new heights. So women had to push them to do that. Push them to be "the man." Push them to conquer, while praying that their fickle minds would not forget who was there through thick and thin to help them reach their lofty goals of manhood. So Sharron understood how tough it was for Sean Love to feel complete and manly without attaining his life's goals, even as she tried her best to avoid him.

"I just need someone to share my dreams with sometimes," he was telling her, long distance from Chicago.

"We all need that, Sean," she responded.

"But do we *all* get it?"

Of course we don't, she thought. But she would never say it to him. Sharron was too courteous and respectful of his feelings.

"Life isn't fair for any of us. We *all* have our bad days," she reminded him instead.

"I'm not just talking about *bad days* here, Sharron. I'm talking about a worthless *life!"* he snapped, becoming agitated. Sharron was not feeling his urgency. He wanted *answers! Right now!*

"Your life isn't worthless," she told him. "Think about your daughter, if nothing else. She *needs* you. She's a part of you. So think about her."

"But I'm talking about my *own* life here, Sharron. I can't live through my daughter. What kind of a life is that?"

What else could she say? Sean had made his bed, and he had to lie in it. Just like everyone else. Nevertheless, men had this thing about them that made them feel as if they were the only organisms alive who could not have things their way. And yet, *they* never had to worry about cycles of bleeding every month, with regular visits to the gynecologists to make sure everything was all right, or breast cancer checks, weight struggles, bad-hair days, the pill, the waiting game of double-standard dating, less pay for the same jobs, slower promotions to management, constant resistance to their authority, and the worldwide pressure to forgive their man for *his* faults while eliminating *all* faults of their own.

NO! Men could just rock and roll and get their things wet as much as they wanted. All they had to do was slip on a condom, yet they refused to do *that* half of the time because they "can't really feel it that way." However, to *tell* them these things would only send them into fits and immature rages. So Sharron decided only to listen. Listen and learn what she already knew. Men thought only about themselves and could not seem to get past the extensions of their petty erections. Because as powerful as they may be, they were *hardly* the only *things* popping up in the world.

"Sharron, can I ask you a question?" Sean asked.

"Sure."

"Have you ever thought about suicide?"

"No. Not at all," she answered.

There was an extended silence between them.

"Why?" she asked him back. He couldn't *possibly* be thinking of killing himself. No way in the world would she believe that. Then again, Sean had always been a tad bit emotional. Could emotion push him over the deep end? Could it? Realistically?

"I thought about it," he said. "Not like I would do it or anything, but just as a thought, you know, as if you could start your entire life over again."

"But you *can't* start all over again," Sharron told him. *It's a cop-out to even* think *that way,* she thought.

"I know. It's crazy, right? But I *do* think about it. I can't lie about that," he admitted.

Why are you telling me this?! she wanted to ask. But she knew already. He was reaching out to her. He had no one else to understand his pain. Not like she could. They had a history together. They had a history of the minds that had never included the body, and the change of perception that clouded the mind because of it. His connection to Sharron was still pure, and still needful. And Sean still wanted Sharron to realize that she loved him in some way. Even if he had to shove her in through the back door with a desperate cry for help to deter his own fatality. Men could be that damned petty. They could *be* that damned *childish!*

"So, what do you want me to say to you, Sean? I mean, I still don't understand," she finally addressed him.

"I don't really know. I guess I'm just . . ." He ran out of words to explain himself. Men usually did. Oh, sure, they could break down every part of politics, economics, war, and sports, but could never seem to explain their own emotions.

"I think you *do* know what you're trying to say, or what you're *trying* to do," Sharron snapped. She was beginning to lose her poise. The *nerve* of him, to use their closeness like that!

"All I'm asking for is your support."

"My support for what? I'm *giving* you my support, Sean! I *always* have! But it seems more like you're trying to twist my arm or something. Why are you even telling me all of this?"

She was hurt. Not to say that she didn't care, or that she did not feel for him. He just hadn't bothered to adjust his emotional state since the last time they had spoken. And it wasn't fair to her, to stress her out that way. Long distance. But Sean failed to see it. That pissed her off the most. His lack of courtesy. A *friend* uplifts and *looks* for upliftment. Friends do *not* wallow in the mud and ask you to jump in with them.

What the hell is his problem?! Sharron thought venomously. *No wonder his baby's mother ran away from him.*

"You just don't care about me at all, Sharron. Is that it? I'm just an *old* friend to you. You have your *new* life in St. Louis. It's always been that way. Hasn't it?"

Sharron sighed, trying her best to regroup. She was not one to lose her patience. But *boy* was Mr. Love pushing her buttons!

"Sean, you can't keep blaming *me* or anybody else for wanting to live their life. You just *can't* do that," she pleaded to him.

"Yeah, I understand. Everybody wants to get up and walk away from the fire when it gets too hot, and just forget about all of the ashes that are left behind," he countered.

"Well, those ashes are for *you* to clean up, and not anyone else, Sean. It's *your* life. And you can't impose yourself on people like you're trying to do to me. It's just not fair. You can't see that?"

"I see it all right," he responded tartly. "I see that you don't want to be bothered with me anymore. So I'll just leave you the hell alone now. And have a nice life, sister."

When he slammed the phone down, it rang in Sharron's eardrum, damaging her faith in goodness. Why be so supportive in the first place if you could never be supportive enough? Why care if you could never care enough? Why even respond, when your every response pushes you closer to making decisions you wanted no part of to begin with. But that was how many men had *forced* it to be, pushing a woman's back up against the wall until it broke. Then as soon as it broke, they didn't want you anymore. They would move on to hunt for new, improved women with stronger—or even weaker—spines, so that they could break *their* backs as well. Yet, they would complain to an empty wine bottle when you, the woman, jumped off of that wall and kicked their asses with your *own* power. Kicked their asses with your *own* mind. And kicked their asses with your *own* destiny. Oh, how they would cry like babies whenever a woman represented for herself. As if you were never supposed to do so. *Ever!* Or at least not without their permission and full acceptance, which of course had to be noncompetitive with their own softer-than-an-infant's-ass egos.

So Sharron was forced to reject Sean, again. *And to hell with him!* she told herself. *Because as long as* I'm *alive, I want to see my heaven, misguided or not. Because* heaven *is not* promised *to* any *of us. But* hell? *Hell is just a dime in the bucket. And my life is worth* a lot *damn more than a dime!*

Dimes were all that *some* people allowed themselves to have in life. People like Anthony "Tone" Wallace. And while they dreamed of Benjamins—the face of American hundred-dollar bills—fortune, and fame, some people failed to understand that you had to *work* for it. *Hard!* Because real success was not based on a lottery system, *or* the luck of the draw. Nor was real love available without passion. In order to have it, you had to *want* it. *Badly!* And not just sometimes, but at *all* times. However, wanting it was not enough. It was only the beginning. You had to chase it, and be pressed about it, to the point of near perfection. Perfection, like that which Anthony "Ant" Poole chased in everything he attempted.

"So how was she, man? Did you tighten her up?" Tone asked his partner across Ant's small kitchen table. He was referring to Shawntè's first weekend.

Ant smiled, chomping down a hot plate of homemade chili and rice. "I'll put it to you this way: in the morning, she didn't want to leave here."

Tone laughed. "You had to drag her out of your bed?"

"Basically," Ant mumbled through his mouthful. "I told her,

'Look, I'm 'bout to take a shower. Make sure you ready for yours when I get out.' And she was like, 'Okay. I'll be ready.'"

"She sounded like she wanted to cry, hunh?"

Ant nearly choked on his food with laughter. "You know how I get 'em."

"Not Dana, though," Tone alluded.

Ant frowned and said, "Man, I'm not thinkin' 'bout that girl no more. And why you gotta keep bringing her up?"

"Because she's *fine*."

"So what? It's other fine girls out here." Every guy had a Dana Nicole Simpson in his life, just like every woman who wanted a man enough would eventually end up with reference to a heart-breaker like Anthony Poole. Their yearnings set them up for it.

"Whatever, man," Tone piped. "So, what's up with the other girl? What's her name? Sharron?"

"Hold on," Ant told him as the phone began to ring. "Hello," he answered.

"It's Sharron Francis from the skating rink, Kingshighway Boulevard, and the airport."

Ant smiled. "I know who you are. My boy just asked me about you, as a matter of fact," he told her.

"Tell him that I'm doing fine, and I thank him for asking."

Ant smiled some more, and ignored her request.

"What are you up to?" he asked her instead.

"You're not gonna tell your friend what I said?" she pressed him.

"Naw. Why, you want to tell him yourself?"

Tone looked up in alarm. *What she wanna tell* me? he asked himself. The next thing *he* knew, Ant was handing him the phone.

"She got something to tell you, man."

"Hello," Tone answered.

Sharron said, "I like your friend a lot, because he makes me happy. And as long as he makes me happy, I'm gonna keep calling him and hanging out with him. I just wanted you to know that."

She was still in a zone, doing whatever she felt. She knew Ant was a player, right? So why act naive and confused about it?

"What if he stops making you happy?" Tone asked her. Many young women had wanted Ant's long-lasting attention, but few of them had succeeded in getting it.

"Do you think that's possible? Does he stop making *you* happy?" Sharron countered. "You've been his friend for how many years now?"

Tone was shocked. He looked up into Ant's face and knew that he had a rough one on the phone. No doubt about it! Sharron was a thinker. She would be hard to shake, and hard to break.

"What she say?" Ant asked him, reading the alarm on Tone's face. Ant didn't want his boy screwing up his chances with a new woman. He was eager to reclaim the phone before his partner said the wrong things to her.

Tone, excited by her mind state, leaned away with the phone.

"You know how boys are. Our bond is forever," he told her.

She said, "And your friend can't have that same bond with a woman? Would you step in the way of that? I don't want to take him away from you, I just want to share him."

Tone smiled bigger than a circus clown. He couldn't believe his ears. Her logic was crystal clear.

He said, "You make it sound like I'm his girlfriend or something."

"No, you're his boy. And I understand that. Y'all go way back together."

By then, Ant was dying to get the phone back.

"Hey, man, give me my damn phone."

Tone went as far as to stand up and step away from him.

"Hold on, man. I'm talking to her."

"Look, man, she called here for *me*. Aw'ight?"

Tone ignored him.

Sharron said, "Is he that possessive about everything?"

Tone laughed and said, "Yeah. You'll find out."

"She'll find out what?" Ant wanted to know.

"You think he could be that possessive about me?" Sharron asked Tone.

Tone thought about it and decided to lead her on. "Yeah. Why not?"

"Because he wouldn't care enough," she responded.

"How do you know?" It wasn't as if she was wrong. Tone just wanted to hear her logic.

"Because he's not supposed to, right? That would get him in trouble, wouldn't it? If he really started to like me? Being whipped by a woman is not a good thing," she answered.

Tone was tickled by her. She was right on point and not afraid to say what she knew.

"So, why even go through it then?" he asked her. He *had* to. She knew too much. Maybe she could teach *him* a thing or two about the logic of women. Why did they fall for the game in the first place? Or at least for *Ant's* game. Because not many women fell for Tone's.

"That's the way it was meant to be, I guess," she answered him. "If it wasn't, then why would a woman even take off her clothes for a man?"

Good answer, Tone thought.

Ant was fed up!

"Tone, give me my damn phone before I have to kick your ass out of here! This is kid shit!"

"You the one acting like a damn kid!" Tone snapped back at him. He was irritated himself that Ant was bothering him. "You told me that she had something to tell me and handed me the phone. Now you wanna act like a damn kid about it!

"Here then, man. Take your damn phone!" he said, jamming the black cordless back into his partner's eager palms.

Ant was embarrassed by Tone's outrage. Tone was showing off. Just like *he* was. They were both showing off for a woman. Maybe they were already whipped. *Both* of them. And too egotistical to even see it.

"Why are y'all arguing over a phone?" Sharron asked Ant. She was instigating, just for the hell of it.

"Oh, don't act like you and your girl don't have petty arguments about things," Ant said, trying to cover it all up.

"Are you saying that you and your friend are just like us?"

"Naw. I'm not saying that. I'm just saying that *humans* have disputes and arguments."

"Oh, so now I'm not a human?" she asked him.

"I didn't say that either. You puttin' words in my mouth."

"So what *are* you saying?"

"I'm saying that you need to stop asking me so many damn questions," Ant finally snapped at her, frustrated by the entire phone incident.

Sharron was shocked! They *both* were. Or all *three* of them were, because Tone had not left yet. He was packing himself a serving of Ant's chili in a Tupperware bowl before making his way to the door. But then he looked back to see how Ant's tantrum would be handled. Sharron had effectively pushed him past his cool zone. And Tone had come to like the girl. He felt for her. She was all right. The kind of girl that a guy could really chill with. Because she told the truth, and she could deal with the real answers.

She said, "I guess I can't ask you what you were doing before I called you now. Is it time to hang up? Do I need to call you at another time with no questions at all? Actually, that's another question, so I shouldn't be asking you *that* either.

"I'm sorry. I guess I can't help myself," she added. "I guess I want too many pieces too fast."

Ant couldn't help but smile. She was riding him to death with his *own* line. She was making him feel ridiculous about his outburst. He was just short of apologizing. He couldn't apologize anyway with Tone in his face, because he would never be able to live that moment down. So he poised himself and responded to her.

"I was eating chili."

Silence. More questions? Or not?

Ant was broken like a horse.

"Look, you can ask me questions if you want. I didn't mean to go off like that. You just ask a whole lot of 'em, that's all."

"Are you sure you won't shoot me?" she joked with him.

"I can't promise you that," he told her with a grin. With *his* gun, he liked to *shoot* a lot. So much that he began to chuckle about it and gave himself away.

"Guys just *have* to think with their *other* head," she told him, catching on.

"What do women think with?" he asked her.

"We think with our minds, and with our hearts."

"You mean your *hearts* and *then* your minds," he responded, correcting her.

"No, that's only for *some* of us," she countered.

Tone had heard enough to make his own conclusions. Sharron could hold her own. He only worried if *Ant* could hold his. So he packed up his bowl of chili and headed for the door.

"Where you going, man?" Ant asked him.

"I'm going home."

"No, I'm talkin 'bout with my food."

Tone smiled. "Like I said, I'm going home. I'll bring your bowl back tomor'."

"Man, you can't just come up in here and eat my food. You got food in your own crib. You leave *my* shit here," Ant said, reaching for the bowl.

Tone avoided his reach.

"You got all the food that you need right there on that phone."

Ant ignored it.

"Tell him I said bye," Sharron said. "Or do you want *me* to tell him?"

"Naw, I'll tell him. She said bye, man," Ant responded, passing on the message.

"AW'IGHT NOW! KEEP THAT *WHIP* OUT ON HIM!" Tone yelled toward the phone.

Ant frowned at him and showed him out.

"Aw'ight, I'll see you later, man."

"Hey, Ant, she aw'ight, dawg," Tone added before he left. "She gets *my* vote." Then he grinned his way out of the door with chili to go.

Sometimes people and situations inspire others to do more. Tone was inspired by Sharron and what she attempted to have with his partner Ant. Even if Ant was only a lover out to score, Sharron had her heart and soul already set for the mission. Tone admired that. Could Sharron actually make Ant fall in love with her, giving up his freedom to hunt new women? Could she?

Everything in life is dependent upon an opportunity. That was all Sharron was asking for. An opportunity to try when plenty of others had failed. And Tone was inspired by her courage. He felt that it may be *his* time to try as well. His time to love something. To love someone for real, and not just for play. Because many people bullshit themselves in life and extend it to others. Especially guys. They go on to hurt women who are much more serious about love and life than they are.

Tone had already hurt women who cared. The first being his

mother. She cared so much about her only son that she ended up accepting *anything* from him, instead of pushing him to do more. He had become passive. Way too passive for comfort. Way too passive for real manhood, where one explored progressive things and didn't just talk about them, dream about them, and think about them but *acted* upon them.

So Tone ate his friend's chili in the silence of his messy, disorganized room and thought about how he could make amends with the women who had attempted to love him. He'd start by seeking out his mother in her room.

She seemed dazed by the television set illuminating the darkness, as if the entertainment world of Hollywood was the only light left to live for.

"Hey, Mom." He spoke to her from the door, and was ignored. He waited a few seconds for her response before calling her again. "Hey, Mom."

She laughed out loud and kept her eyes glued to the tube.

"MOM!" he snapped impatiently.

She turned and faced him, tired and annoyed. "What do you want from me now, Anthony? What? Can't you see that I'm watching something?"

He was stunned, standing there in her doorway.

What do you want from me now, Anthony? What do you want from me now?

Her words hung on his mind and turned him away with guilt. He had worn his mother's love into the ground. He realized that now. But he did not know what to do about it.

"I was ah . . . just seeing how you were doing?"

"Well, I'm fine, Anthony. How are you?" she piped at him. Then she went right back to watching television, while her son hovered there for a few minutes in her doorway before fading back to his chaotic room, a representation of his chaotic life.

"Damn. She don't even have no words for me," he mumbled to himself. "Talk to me like I'm a damn kid." Then he looked around and realized that he was still living in her house, twenty-eight years old, with no household of his own.

Guys get depressed too. *All* of them. They just don't talk about it as much as women do. So we figure that they're all right, when they're actually not. Just posing cool, and not actually living what they project. Inside, many of them are *three times* as insecure as women express to be. But in expression comes peace, like the evaluation of being sick and the arrival of proper medicine to heal the wounds.

Men don't get healed. That same peace that women receive, many men never allow themselves to have. Always lying to themselves. And if you cannot tell *yourself* the truth, then when will you ever be able to stand on solid ground with the rest of the world?

Too many men die young and miserable without ever attaining solidified goals in life. Not just dying physically, but mentally, spiritually, emotionally, every day. Nevertheless, men don't *want* love. Don't *need* love. Right? . . . Wrong? Simply put, *humans* cannot *live* without love!

Tone wanted to live again, love again, and revive himself from the dead by reaching out to someone, *anyone* who would listen. But when you turn off so many ears with silence in the past, who will be willing to listen to your present and future? Yet, Sharron had inspired him, and it was his time to *try* an opportunity for love. So he jumped on the phone with hope. Hope and energy, calling up an old girlfriend whom he had led astray, and had pushed away.

"What's up, girl? It's been a long time. It's Tone."

Silence.

"Mmmph. It has," she answered him with a grumble.

"So what's been up?"

"You tell me."

"You know, I'm just living it. Nothing special," he answered.

"WHAAAHH!"

What was that?! he asked himself.

"You got a baby now?"

"Mmm-hmm."

Silence.

"When did that happen?"

"Three months ago?"

"With who?"

"You don't know him."

Silence.

Shit! What do I say now?

"Are you still with him?"

"Am I still with *you?*"

Funny. That's what Tone was calling for, to get back in the picture. But what about now? Things had gotten complicated. She had a brand-new baby from another man.

"Is it a boy or a girl?"

"A boy."

"He look like his father?"

Pause. "What is this, eighty questions? I mean, you haven't spoken to me for what, two years? Now you call me up out of the blue and want to know everything about my child."

"Actually, I was just calling to see how you were doing."

"Well, I'm doing just fine. As fine as I'm *ever* doing."

"WHAAAHH!"

"Okay, boy! God! Greedy little thing!"

"What are you, breast-feeding him?"

"Yeah. And he's as greedy as big boys. Don't want to let it go."

Until it gets pregnant on you, Tone thought with a chuckle. Then he stopped himself, and thought about his own father, who had been missing in action, twenty-eight years and counting.

"That's fucked up," he expressed out loud.

"What?" she asked him.

"That you got a baby . . . and no father."

"You wanna be my baby's father?" she snapped at him.

"It's not my child."

"Well, don't concern yourself with it then. In fact, I have to go. You called me at the wrong time." Then she added, "You should have called me *two years* ago," and gave him plenty of time to respond to her.

"I should have done a lot of things," he admitted.

"Mmm-hmm," she mumbled. "OWW, BOY!" she complained to her son attached to her breast. And how much would she love her son? More importantly, how much would her *son* love her back?

It's a damn cycle, Tone told himself. How could he deny it? The evidence was right there in front of him. Right on the other end of the line.

"Well, I have to go now," she told him.

He didn't quite know what to say, or how to end it.

"Ah, yeah, aw'ight. I'll get with you later," he told her.

"Don't make *me* no promises," she said. "Because *I* don't need 'em no more. And that's the *truth!*"

Tone hung up and was stunned for the second time, feeling even lower than he did with his mother. But he was driven to keep trying. He made a second call to a stray love with more hope.

"What's up, girl? It's been a long time."

"Who is this?"

"Tone."

"*Anthony?* What are you doing calling *me?*"

"Just seeing what you up to."

"Why?"

"Why not?"

Silence.

"Hmmph. I don't go out like that no more," she told him.

"Go out like what?"

"Where you can just call me up and try and get what you want."

He laughed. "I'm not calling you for that. I'm just calling you to talk."

"Talk about what?"

"You know, life."

"Hmmph. You never wanted to call me up and just *talk* before," she reminded him.

"That was then and this is now."

"Oh, is that it? So you're lonely now?"

"Why I gotta be lonely?"

"Why else are you gonna call me up out the blue and talk about life for?"

"Because I haven't talked to you in a while."

"Correction. You didn't talk to me at all. You just wanted to fuck me."

He was taken aback by his own truth. The harshness of it.

"Why you gotta talk about it like that?"

"That's what it was, right? Fuckin'. It wasn't nothin' else," she snapped.

This just ain't my damn night, Tone told himself.

"So, I guess *you* don't have words for me now either then," he commented.

She laughed at him, knowing that she was on the mark. Tone was lonely and *feeling* the full weight of it.

"How many other girls did you call?" she asked curiously.

"Fifteen of 'em," he lied.

"*Fifteen?* I didn't know you *had* that many."

"Me neither until I sat down and thought about it," he responded with a chuckle.

"And none of them wanted to talk to you?"

"Nope."

"So now you're callin' *me?*"

A trap. He backed up from it.

"Actually, I didn't call that many girls."

"Don't lie to me now," she told him. "So, what am I, number seven?"

He paused. "Seven is a lucky number."

She started to laugh again. "Not this way it ain't. I'm sorry, but you gon' have to try number eight. Because I have to get my life in order."

"I have to get *my* life in order, too."

"Do what you gotta do then," she advised him.

"That's why I'm calling you," he said, losing himself and saying anything.

"That's why you're calling *me? I* don't have anything to do with your life. Not hardly! We spent maybe three hours at a time together, *if* that. What the hell are you talking about?"

Damn, women could be rough! Tone was finding out.

"Well, we could start all over again." He didn't believe that himself. He was still talking out of his neck and not processing his conversation in his mind.

"Is this some kind of a joke?" she asked him. "Do you work for a radio station now or something? Because you got me, you really do." She continued laughing out loud.

Talk about humiliation. Tone was *hardly* thinking about making any more phone calls *that* night. Not on his life! But he still felt miserable. He felt like crying to his mommy. And not even his mommy was listening. She had heard it all. The bullshit. About getting his life together. About doing the right thing. About finding a steady job. About staying clear-minded without the Mary Jane sticks, while respecting the house, black women, *and* himself. They were *all* tired of hearing that SHIT! *Say* what you mean, and *mean* what you say. And accept the consequences of your actions instead of running away like a scared boy who changes his mind every three hours, dashing away from the hardships that he creates like some damn Gingerbread Man! Catch me if you can. Why don't you catch your *damn self, BOY?!* . . .

That's exactly how Tone felt, like a confused, running-for-his-life boy, who was just beginning to understand that the world was no longer chasing his ass. The world no longer cared, and was continuing to go round without him. Tone had to learn to care about himself, and get back in the ball game of life with new dedication. He needed to try a new system that worked, with a new coach to teach him the ways if he needed it. Because before you can find someone to love, to listen, *and* to care, you had to have something inside of yourself *to* love, something to express, and feelings of your own to share right back with them, to show them that *you* care.

If Tone could cry, he would have. If he had any tears. If *men* had any tears, they *would* cry. Every day. Like women. And then they would resurrect themselves. Every day. Like women. Women lived longer and to the fullest anyway. Unless, of course, they were waiting around for the love of a Gingerbread Man. Because a Gingerbread Man like Anthony Wallace would only keep his woman waiting . . . to exhale . . . in vain.

Waiting was something Sharron Francis was no longer interested in. She wanted a piece of her pie, like *right now!* And Anthony Poole happened to be the one guy at that urgent moment whom she wanted it from. Whether he was fully aware of it or not was *his* problem. Whether he could handle it or not was *his* problem. Whether he was up for it or not was *his* problem. Sharron *knew* what she wanted, and it was *him*. One hundred percent! She even had his phone number on the job.

"Who is this?" he answered, as oily as an auto mechanic would be on a busy day.

"Sharron."

"Unh-hunh," he mumbled, in a what-do-you-want fashion. She was stripping away all of the small talk and getting to his real nerves, something many woman dared *not* do. Yet, a man was a man, and if he was rough around the edges, it would all come out in time. Sharron was simply speeding up the process.

Why should I let him just play his game with me without having some fun of my own?

She was taking that page right out of Celena Myers's book. Beat them to the chase. Beat them to the attitude. Beat the man to the sex. Beat the man to the mind. And the man will beat *you* to the altar. Celena had been asked five times already. Sharron only once, by Sean Love, when making the transition from high school to the university. Celena's approach seemed surefire, it was just that few women had the courage, or the tits, if you will, to carry it out. Then again, Sharron was in a zone with her chase. And in her zone, she was attempting any and every thing.

"I was wondering if you would mind picking me up from work tonight," she asked him.

"All the way from the airport?" St. Louis International was on the far northwest, the other side of the city from where Anthony worked at Paul's Fix It Shop on the southeast. To drive to the airport just to take Sharron home from work sounded absurd.

"We can get a bite to eat," she offered. "My treat. I just want to see you."

"What if I can't make it all the way out there tonight? I'm tired as I don't know what. I've been working on a transmission all morning. Them things ain't nothin' to play wit'. Trust me!"

"If you can't make it, you can't make. I'll survive. I just thought I'd ask, since I was thinking about it."

"So, you just gon' ask me anything that you think about?"

"Yeah. Why not?"

He smiled. Many women *wouldn't* ask. They insinuated. They assumed. They guessed. Or they only wondered. And he was impressed by Sharron again. She definitely kept his pot of mental stew warm on the stove.

"Well, let me think about it," he responded to her. "I'm not making no promises either. So don't get your feelings hurt if I don't come."

When he hung up, he smirked and tossed up his hands. The boss, Paul Mancini, took in his puzzlement and chuckled at it.

"You got one chasing you down, tiger?"

"Definitely. And you wouldn't think that *this one* would be that type. She's one of those always-thinking women."

Paul nodded. "I know the type. Before I got married to my wife, eighteen years ago, she wanted ice water in hell. And I was fool enough to try and get it for her. But she hung right in there with me and kept pushing."

He stopped himself and sighed with a smile.

"Yeah, those *thinking* women are a lot of work," he added. "They make *you* think. And the more you think, the more work you do. That's why I'm successful now. I'm always thinking of a better way to do something, and I owe that all to my wife."

Then he walked away, allowing Anthony a chance to think on his own, and to make up his mind on whether he'd drive all the way across St. Louis before eight o'clock to pick up Sharron for a bite to eat after work.

"Shit!" he cursed himself, deciding that he would go ahead and do it. But he wouldn't let *Sharron* know. He would just show up at her job and surprise her.

"Was that your boyfriend?" asked the young cashier at the gift shop, minding Sharron's phone call. She was wide-eyed and ready for girl talk.

Sharron realized the younger woman would never last long on the job. She had been around her type before. The young, flashy women who tried their best to accessorize everything they wore, even down to the dull gray airport uniforms, could never swing it. She would burn out and drift away to another job, like many other unsatisfied young women had done.

Sharron tested the young cashier to see if she was right about her lack of perseverance.

"Yeah, that's him. He won't even pick me up from work," she answered, misleading the younger woman.

"My man would *have* to pick *me* up from work. I don't play that!" the cashier bragged. She had an innocent enough face, but her can't-miss body would get her into trouble every time with black men who treasured well-roundedness.

"You got him wrapped around your little finger, hunh?" Sharron teased.

The young woman backed down. "I'm not saying all that. But he *does* know what time it is."

"How long have you been with him?" Sharron asked her.

"Two years."

"How old is he?"

"Twenty-nine."

"Twenty-nine?" she responded with a frown. "And you are how old again?"

"I'm turning twenty-two later on this month."

"You're twenty-one then."

"Right now, yeah."

Sharron was only turning twenty-four herself. But she *felt* as if she was *twice* as old.

"And when does your boyfriend turn thirty?" she asked.

"Well, he's not exactly my boyfriend. But he turns thirty in October."

He's not exactly your boyfriend, hunh? Sharron thought to herself. She knew plenty about older men. They were five times worse than younger guys. Older men seemed to do *everything* a woman wanted, except be true. Because some of them had hundreds of skeletons in the closet, layer after layer just waiting to give a young girl a heart attack! At least the younger guys were true to their immaturity. Many of them had not found out exactly who they were or how to be what they wanted to be. But older men? They *knew* who they were. They had plenty of time to find that out. And they became the most fatal poison in the world to young-minded women who didn't know any better. So Sharron felt sorry for her. The young sister had a lot to learn, just like *all* women.

"So, he's been with you since you were what, nineteen?"

"Okay, I know what you're thinking, that he's too old for me, right? But it's not even like that. We started off as friends. And he was helping me out with my problems, you know, understanding my boyfriend and all, who was just way too immature for me. Then we just clicked like that and we've been close ever since."

That's because older guys have more patience, you fool! Sharron found herself thinking.

"How did he approach you in the first place?" she asked. And to think that they had started off talking about *her* so-called boyfriend.

"I went to the movies by myself and was crying and everything after having a fight with my boyfriend. And then I met Marcus on my way out."

She had to hold her comments as male customers crowded the register. Her young spirit, body, and energy teased the eager eyes of every one of the men in that line. What power young, unassuming women had over men. And what power fully assuming men had over young women.

Sharron was afraid to continue the conversation, predicting where it could go. But it happened anyway.

"The first time we did it," the young sister whispered when the line was gone again, "I had never had an orgasm before. Boy did he change that!"

That's enough! Sharron told herself. *I don't want to hear any more about it! Please!*

However, her co-worker went on, sharing *all* of her business.

"He went downtown on me and everything."

Okay, I have to get over to the other store now, Sharron thought.

"Are you gonna be okay at the register over here?" she asked, changing the subject. "I have to make rounds to the other stores."

"Yeah, I'll be all right. Are you coming back?" She was actually eager to tell more.

"Ahh, I'll have to wait and see," Sharron told her, with no promises.

"Okay. Well, please do if you can. I have some more to tell you," she announced with a wink.

Sharron couldn't wait to have her usual workday snack and chat with Celena.

"Would you ever tell somebody *all* of your business? Somebody you barely knew?" she asked her rhetorically. Of course Celena wouldn't. She had too much to tell. And unless you knew much of her relationship history to begin with, she would only confuse you.

"Why? You talking about that young girl Nadine who works at the register? She tells *everybody* her business," Celena commented with a mouthful of pepperoni pizza. "She was talking about some older man, right? Twenty-nine? Jason or something?"

"Marcus," Sharron corrected her.

"Yeah, whatever his name is. And he ain't no damn *twenty-nine,* either. I saw him pick her up last week in an ugly-ass car with tinted windows, probably to hide her young behind. He *looks* more like *forty.* He probably got eight damn kids somewhere. But he *totally* blew her damn mind. That girl don't know if she's coming or going."

Sharron shook her head with a grin. If there was news to be gotten, Celena Myers would be on it like a seven-digit-income reporter. She was like a witch doctor with her work, seeming to know everyone and everything.

"Well, anyway, how has your day been going?" Sharron asked her.

"You know, it's just the usual. The guys make dick jokes, and then I talk about pussy."

Sharron cringed over her slice of mushroom pizza. "God, can I eat in peace? What is wrong with you?" she complained.

Celena chomped down her slice and shook her head.

"That's how *guys* talk. So I don't know why *we* want to water everything down. *They* don't water shit down," she commented. "But see, that's why I like my girls Lil' Kim and Foxy Brown. They just tell it like it is."

"They tell it like it *sells* is more like it," Sharron countered concerning the popular New York rappers. "They sound like real-life sluts. *Both* of them. They need to take a lesson from Lauryn Hill."

Celena looked at her and said, "Yeah, you seem like a Lauryn Hill fan. Oh, love me, love me, love me. Learn to love your *damn self,* girl."

"You don't think that Lauryn Hill loves herself? I would think that she loves *herself* a lot more than Lil' Slut and Foxy Slut."

"Oh, now why you gotta call them out their names?"

"Call them out their names? I don't even *know* their names. At least Lauryn Hill is brave enough to *use* hers. That's because she's the truth."

"Aw, so what, girl. She's more like a singer. All singers use their names. Mary J. Blige. Janet Jackson. Brandy Norwood. You name 'em. In fact, Mary J. Blige is the same as Lauryn Hill. Always singin' 'bout some love me, love me, love me.

"Those two *needed* to sing a damn song together, they want to be *loved* so much."

"Foxy Brown and Lil' Kim need to make one, too: fuck me, fuck me, fuck me, they want to be *fucked* so much," Sharron countered.

Celena laughed so hard her ribs felt ready to cave in. She had to spit out her food and leave the table from embarrassment. She returned with tears in her eyes.

"For real," Sharron added, chuckling herself. "Everybody needs love. That's the truth."

"Yeah, yeah," Celena told her, wiping her eyes.

"What time are you getting off tonight?" Sharron asked her, just in case Anthony was unwilling to pick her up.

"Eight."

"You are?" she asked. She expected her to work until midnight.

"Yeah. Why?"

"We might be able to ride home together then. Usually, we work different schedules."

"Well, you better be ready to go then, because I got somewhere to be later on. So be ready at eight on the nose, or I'm gone."

Celena had her father's old car, a black Maxima. However, Sharron still hoped Anthony would take her up on her offer to meet her after work. She could not count on it though. Not yet. She didn't know him well enough to count on him. Only time would reveal if she ever could. Time would reveal all things. She was forced to wait after all.

When seven fifty-five rolled around with no phone call from Anthony to confirm his pick-up, Sharron got ready to leave with Celena.

"What's wrong with you?" Celena asked of her roommate's silence as they drove home.

Sharron shook her head in denial. "Nothing." That usually meant everything.

Celena shook her head. "I told you to stop chasing this guy like a maniac. You're riding him *way* too hard."

Sharron said, "What do you have, relationship ESP or something?"

"Sharron, I can *always* tell when you're thinking about guys.

That's when you don't want to talk anymore. Then I have to force it out of you. It never fails. It's the same way with you *every time.*"

She smiled. "Yeah, I guess you're right."

"I'm *always* right," Celena piped at her.

"I don't know about all of that."

"Well, like I told you, this guy is a player. That means that you can't count of him for *nothing.* They want to be with you on *their* time, and on *their* time alone. That's why, if I can't have my way up front, then I don't even bother with it. And I'll call the next one up in a heartbeat."

After they arrived at their apartment, Celena showered and got dressed to go out, while Sharron sulked and wound down for bed, before nine o'clock. She was pissed off, too! *Don't* shit *seem to work for me! No matter* what *I do!* she told herself, with another book in hand. This time it was *Li'l Mama's Rules* by Sheneska Jackson.

"Don't cry all night, Sharron. Or should I call you Mary?" Celena teased, peaking her head into her roommate's room before she left.

Like the R & B singer Mary J. Blige, Sharron just wanted to be happy. She was *tired* of crying about it, physically, verbally, spiritually, *and* otherwise.

"Dang, girl!" she snapped, responding to Celena's ringing of the front doorbell just minutes after she had left. "I *should* just let you stay out there! Stop forgetting your damn keys!" she yelled through the door before opening it. What a surprise she found on the other side. Anthony "Player" Poole, dressed in an all blue denim outfit, and smelling as good as he looked.

"What kind of fool you take me for, girl?" he snapped at her. There was not even a hint of a smile on his face. He was *twice* as pissed off as she was!

"Now you gon' have me drive all the way to the other side of the world to pick you up from work and then you gon' leave before I even get there."

Sharron smiled. She was delighted by the idea. He had actually showed up. On time!

"I didn't know you were coming," she responded. "You didn't call me back and tell me."

"So what? You asked me to pick you up, didn't you? You should at least wait to see if I'm gon' show up. I was there at eight o'clock on the nose," he said, taking a peek at his gold-plated watch, five minutes ahead. "And they told me you had just left."

Sharron was flattered by it. Anthony was *not!*

"So I just came over here to tell you the hell off, because I don't appreciate that shit, and my time is very valuable to me," he hissed at her from the doorway.

Sharron was so pleased that she didn't even feed into his tantrum. She had other ideas in mind.

"My roommate's not here," she told him, still grinning.

Anthony calmed down to evaluate her information for a second.

"So? And?" he asked her, still pissed. He was curious, too. Naturally.

"You don't wanna come in?"

"Of course I wanna come in," he responded with his first smile. "I've been driving around for two hours." How quickly male minds can change.

Sharron chuckled and thought, *What would he do if I told him he can't?*

"What took you so long to get here?" she asked him instead. The airport was only twenty minutes by car from where she lived, unless he got lost.

"At first, I wasn't even gon' come over here. I was just gonna say, 'Good riddance,' and not talk to your ass again. But I was so pissed off that I said, 'Naw! I gotta see this girl face to face and tell her.' That's how mad I was. I even got off work early for this."

Talk about being happy, Sharron was growing cheerier by the second. She had really gotten under his skin. Believe it or not, that was a *good* thing. A heated man expressed a lot more than a cool man on any day of the week. And evidently, Anthony could be counted on. He was punctual. He cared very much about extending his time to someone. And he was *not* going to be walked over by anyone! Sharron respected that. *All* of it!

"You wanna come in or what?" she teased him again.

The first rule in Sheneska Jackson's book was that you never invite a man into your house. You think Sharron was listening to that advice? Heck no! She was *definitely* letting him in!

Anthony looked over her long, baby blue nightshirt and immediately wondered what she had on under it, exactly like her book had warned. But hell, that was all a part of the territory with men.

"I thought we were gonna get a bite to eat on you?" he asked her. But he wouldn't mind if plans had changed.

"We can still do that. Let me go get dressed," Sharron told him, leading him in and over to the tweed sofa in front of the 19-inch television.

"Well, we don't have to go if you just want to chill. I'm tired myself."

She stopped and looked back at him from her bedroom door. She smiled, thinking, *Would you be too tired to fuck me if I let you? I don't* think *so.*

"Well, what do you *feel* like doing?" she hinted.

He smiled, way too wide, giving away the full intentions of his manhood.

Sharron sucked her teeth and said, "Is that all that men *ever* think about?"

He laughed it off and said, "Look, if you wanna go out, we can still go. You see I'm dressed for it." After all, he didn't want to seem too pressed about getting into her stuff on his first invitation to her place. He could wait for that. Or at least for a little while.

Sharron had a better idea.

"What if I just wanted to sit next to you and talk, like this?" she asked, displaying her outfit, with no bra, pert breasts, and blue panties underneath. She was really working it, trying anything that came to mind. She wanted to see up close and personal how much discipline he could have.

Anthony smiled and said, "I don't think that's a good idea."

"Why not?" she asked him. She was already walking over to join him on the sofa.

He shook his head as she approached him.

"I'm sayin', it's just ah . . . It's just not a good idea."

"But what if I want to?" she asked him, sitting right next to him and touching, arm to arm and leg to leg.

Anthony looked into her face and said, "What are you trying to do, test me or something?"

"Am I?"

All of a sudden, she looked twice as good to him, with perfect symmetry in her brown face. The elements that photographers looked for in models. But Sharron wore little to no makeup and had a natural look. She was an everyday woman. And boy did he want to touch her. All over. So he did, starting with her knee, which felt as soft and as plush as new carpet.

Sharron grinned and said, "If I was testing you, I guess you would have failed already. You just couldn't keep your hands off of me," she told him, planting his hand back on his own knee.

Anthony laughed again, busted, and wondered what her next move would be.

"Look, you ready to go out and get something to eat or what?" he asked her again. He couldn't see himself passing her test. She felt too good to even imagine trying to. He was already wondering what the rest of her felt like. He had reloaded his wallet with condoms. He had more out in the car to make sure he wouldn't have a replay of the incident with Shawntè, where he was unprepared.

"I don't want to go out anymore," Sharron told him. "Why, are you hungry? We could order Chinese food if you want."

She stood up and walked to the phone on the kitchen wall. Anthony watched her behind jiggling. It was the perfect size and roundness. Not too big, not too small, and definitely grippable.

Damn! he thought to himself. *She gon' drive me crazy up in here!* He had to compose himself before he went out like a mark and ended up in a trap. Sometimes women could throw a guy off by appearing to be down for whatever and then pulling away, producing awkward relationships that become irreparable.

What did Rico say again? Anthony asked himself about his cousin's advice. He had talked more about cars and sports than women with his older brothers.

He said to get the panties on your *time and not on theirs. And this would be* hers, *because this whole night was* her *idea. Now she's teasing me with no clothes on,* he told himself. *Yeah, this shit is all a setup. So I can't touch her until it's* my *idea.*

On Sharron's end, she was thinking, *God, I can't believe how things are happening! This is unreal! But he's* not *getting any tonight no matter* how *I feel. We're not doing anything until* I *want to! And I don't want to yet. Not yet. No way!*

These are the games that humans play. So they ordered fried rice, ate it, and talked while sitting nervously for the rest of the evening. Then they didn't know how to say good-bye.

"Well, I gotta get up early for work tomorrow," Anthony finally announced, standing up from the sofa and stretching.

"Okay," Sharron told him, ready to lead him to the door. She didn't seem too pressed to have him leave. He noticed her hesitancy.

"What do you want, a hug or something? That would be affectionate, right?" he asked her with a grin. Women rarely would turn down a good hug, especially from a good-looking, good-smelling man whom they were fully attracted to.

"You trying to read my mind?" she asked him back, moving in to receive her hug.

He held her soft body and he didn't want to let it go.

"You want a fried-rice kiss with that hug?" he asked her with a laugh. But he was serious.

She chuckled herself and leaned in to kiss him. And with her eyes closed, Sharron dreamed of making it last forever. That same ice-cream dream was common to *most* women: to keep a man's sweetness forever, whether the flavor was chocolate, vanilla, coffee, or lemon sherbet.

But how do you pull away from the dream and deal with the reality of time revelation. It's not supposed to be perfect the first time. You have to wake up, and *stay awake,* to make it last that long. Because dreaming is unconscious, but decisions made were usually not.

So before the kiss got too good to her, Sharron forced herself to push him away until next time. Or next time. Or next time. As long as there would still be time. And from what she was able to learn so far about him, Anthony wanted to finish what he started, like with his automobiles. So she was confident that she would have the time that she needed.

Anthony broke off their kiss, looked her in the face, and knew it. *I gots to have this girl! And I'm gon' get her! No doubt!*

"Well, I'll call you whenever," he told her.

"Why can't you call me tonight?" she asked.

"You wanna know the truth?" he asked her back.

She nodded. "Yeah."

"Because I had enough of you for one night. And I can't take no more."

Sharron broke up and said, "At least tell me that you got home safely."

He wasn't promising her that either.

"We'll see."

Realizing she couldn't push him into it, Sharron decided to let it slide, to look forward to their next time together. Because she knew that they were nowhere near being finished yet.

Anthony wasn't even finished with his night. Once the door closed on Sharron's brown face, separating them, he knew that, once again, he would not be able to sleep. Not without some kind of a climax. Sharron had built up too much unused energy in him. And men, when set off, were like time bombs that were impelled to explode.

Anthony drove fast to the first pay phone he could find and pulled out his book of numbers he was fortunate to have carried along with him in the car that night. He started dialing at close to midnight on that Tuesday.

"Hey, Shawntè. It's Anthony."

"I know who you are," she answered too excitedly.

"Oh, yeah. Well, that's a good thing," he told her. "But what are you doing right now? Are you in for the night, or what?"

First she paused. Then she asked the automatic question: "Why?"

Booty calls are fairly obvious. If the opposite sex calls you up on a Tuesday night, closer to Wednesday, chances are, most restaurants are closed, along with the theaters, amusement parks, and shopping centers. And unless you happen to be the greatest cook in the world, and your opposite-gender partner has the eating tendencies of a nocturnal werewolf, chances are, they are *not* hungry for food. However, they may indeed be hungry; hungry for something else. Maybe that's how the werewolf legends began in the first place: late-night hungers for OPP—other people's property.

The automatic question to Ant's late-night investigation lingered. . . . "Why?"

"You feel like seeing me tonight?" he asked Shawntè instead of answering it.

Of course she wanted to see him. She wanted to see him *daily* if she could. Not just for sex either. But what could she do about it? Realistically? Some women are just dealt a better hand of cards than others. That was her dilemma. She did not miss the underlying message of being second fiddle. The other woman.

Sharron Francis controlled the deck. Or at least for *that* particular night. Especially when it came to this man, who couldn't stay away from the playing table. Who would deal the deck in the next game? However, second fiddle or not, Shawntè still wanted to *be* fiddled. So she was not in a position to say no, no matter how much she wanted to. No matter how much she needed to, if only to gain some semblance of respect for herself.

"Where are we going?" she asked hopelessly.

"Wherever you wanna go. My car is warm," he told her. *And I got rubbers on me this time,* he told himself.

Shawntè sighed, wishing there was another way to see him, and during the daytime, where there were other things to do outside of pointless humping.

"Where are you coming from? Give me twenty minutes," she told him. She was already dressed for bed. But did *he* care? Are you kidding me? If he cared, he would have never called and put her in such a precarious situation. He just wanted to blast off into outer space, burning away all of the emotions as part of the fuel.

"Aw'ight then," he told her.

Lickity-split. He walked back to his car as happy as a kid on Santa Claus's knee. He was on his way to pick up his Christmas present, like it or not.

When he arrived, Shawntè was waiting outside on her front steps, dressed in a dark blue shorts outfit. She walked over to the car as soon as Ant pulled up to the curb and climbed in, closing the door behind her. She sniffed the aroma of his cologne and surveyed his clothes as physical proof that she was second fiddle for the night. She was the dessert, not the full-course meal. The quick cherry pie, not the well-done sirloin steak that cost more. Nevertheless, she was still there. Game bait.

Ant looked her over and asked, "Are you sure you weren't sleeping? I didn't mean to wake you up."

What difference does it make? All you wanna do is fuck me, she thought to herself.

She could no longer hold her thoughts on the matter.

"Where did you go tonight? You sure *look* good and *smell* good," she hinted.

Here we go, he mused. He had prepared himself for just that question while on the way to pick her up.

"I was over the bridge in East Boogie with my cousin, and I really ain't feel like hangin' out tonight, so I had to wait for him to hook up with another ride home, and then I left and called you."

Excellent answer! It was loaded with enough information to lead her completely away from the hunt.

"How come you didn't call me *before* you went?" she asked, still filled with attitude. But at least, based upon his exquisite lie, it wasn't another *woman* in the way.

Ant faked an attitude deserving of an Oscar award. "Come on now, it was a guy's-night-out thing."

"But you said you didn't feel like going."

"Haven't you done things that *you* didn't want to do, and then changed *your* mind. Everybody does that," he snapped.

Shawntè calmed herself, and was *too* calm, because the snake was *well* in the grass.

"I mean, aren't you happy that I called you? At least I was thinking about you," he added.

Shawntè looked away and out of the passenger-side window to stop herself from smiling. At a red light, Ant leaned from the wheel and took the opportunity to plant a soft kiss upon her neck, sealing the fate of his prey.

Women had more to lose in a world ruled by instincts alone. And Shawntè wanted to stop herself before things ventured out of hand.

She pushed him away and said, "No, we can't do this."

"Do what?" he whined, playing the innocent.

"You know what."

"Are you sure? I mean, you really don't want to?"

Ant was admitting it. He was admitting his instincts. The hypocrisy of humanity was a bitch! Because *she* wanted to be instinctive as well. *Badly!* But couldn't. Or wouldn't. Or could. And would.

Yes, I want to, she thought painfully. *I mean, no, I don't. I mean, I don't know. I mean, I can't. It's not right. I shouldn't.* We *shouldn't. We can't! No, don't touch me like that! Don't touch me there. Don't kiss me there. Pleease! STOP!*

And then she verbalized it.

"No, we can't, Anthony. I don't feel right about this."

But he was rock hard already. And she was wet. Yet, Ant understood her plea. Women were not supposed to be easy. They were supposed to be talked into in. Tricked into it. Slicked into it. Otherwise, humans would rarely do it. Or definitely not as much as the *males* wanted to.

So he thought of a way of convincing her. It was what men were supposed to do. Otherwise, humans would rarely reproduce. Or not as much as they did. That's why players were players in the first place; they understood the power of human sexuality, the reproductive selection system. Good-looking, charming, well-dressed, fast-thinking players were at the top of the charts, along with men who commanded surplus currency.

"You wanna go back to my house then? Would that make you feel better?"

Compromise. And make everything all right.

"Don't you have to go to work tomorrow?" she asked, stalling and avoiding the question.

Damn it felt good in his bed last time! she thought.

"Yeah, but *you* don't," he countered.

Ant was already heading east, toward Nebraska Avenue. Home.

Shawntè sighed, with no control over their destination.

"I don't like getting up early like that," she pouted.

Compromise again.

"You wanna go to your place? You got your own room, right? But what would your mom say?"

"Oh, that's out of the question," she responded, firmly shaking her head with a grin.

"Where do you wanna go then? Because I have to get up for work tomorrow regardless," he told her.

She was tempted, but she *knew* better. Nevertheless, if he was that pressed about it, then he would have to compromise a third time.

"Just let me stay there until I'm ready to leave then. I'll lock your door and take a taxi home."

Oh, that's out of the question, he thought to himself with a grin.

Another rule: Let no woman chill at your place unattended unless she was unquestionably number one. Shawntè was *hardly* in that position.

Ant said, "I don't really feel comfortable with that. I mean, if we lived together or something, and you had a key—"

"If we lived together and I had a key, this wouldn't even be an issue," she snapped, cutting him off.

He denied her with his silence, still heading home at the wheel.

"I just wanted to be with you tonight, that's all. And I apologize if I caught you at a bad time," he told her.

"Well, it took you long enough to decide that you wanted to be with me. It's after midnight now," she pouted.

"What does that mean, that I'm supposed to wait until tomorrow?"

"You *could* have. I mean, at least we would have had more time together."

But I want some now, he thought with another short grin.

"I'll make it up to you then," he promised her with a squeeze of her inner thigh. "Okay?"

She was sold without another word from him. She decided to just let it happen. *Stop fighting the process, and let the chips fall as they may,* she told herself. What was the use of fighting? She wanted him as much as he wanted her. Or as much as he wanted *it.* The sweetness of a woman.

On Ant's end, his mind reflected back to Sharron. He had to make certain that he turned his phone ringer off and came up with a clever excuse for her in case she called him that night and received no answer.

The rest? Well, who needs regurgitated details. A man takes a woman. A woman accepts a man. They tire themselves. Then they fall asleep. But many times, the women are not *half* as tired, particularly when men are more greedy than they need to be, taking all and giving none. Which was the case that night. Shawntè felt cheated, not so much physically, but mentally and emotionally. So she went sleepless in St. Louis. But did he care? Are you kidding me? He just wanted to blast off into outer space.

That next day at work, Ant was terrified. It's funny how women can seep into a man and become a part of his daily consciousness. Women may not believe as much, but it's true. Even for fast-thinking guys like Ant. *Especially* for fast-thinking guys like Ant! After all, he had to stay ahead of his own game, and the deeper it got, the more he was forced to think about it.

Sharron Francis was seeping into him. As he worked, he wondered about the numerous phone calls she had made the night before, only to hang up on his machine.

Damn! She even has my number at work! he thought. *How did she do that? And what the hell was* I *thinking when I gave it to her? That girl asks too many damn questions, that's her problem. And now it's* my *problem for even trying to answer 'em.*

So he waited for the phone to ring, all day long, thinking that every ring was for him. Sharron would call with an earful of questions that he would attempt to duck and dodge. Why? Because he wasn't finished with her yet. She hadn't given him a piece of herself. She was still testing his waters with her toes, thinking before she jumped all the way in. He was forced to respect her for that. But a booty call? Shawntè? What about her? If she was easy to him, she could be easy to someone else. The hypocrisy of humanity was a bitch indeed!

"Hey, Anthony, your friend is out at the front," a co-worker told him close to lunch hour. He had a big smile on his face that made Ant suspicious.

"My *friend?*" he asked quizzically. "Is it a guy or a girl?"

His heart skipped four beats as he slid out from a Chevy Nova that needed to be trashed rather than repaired. The rusty, dark green car had a million different problems with it, but the owner refused to let it die. And why should he, when Paul gave him such good deals for being a committed customer for over twelve years?

"That guy who always comes to get ya. Tony, right?" his co-worker asked him.

"Oh, Tone," Ant responded, relaxing. For a minute he thought Sharron had gone bananas like a wife showing up unannounced at her husband's job to beef about another woman. Since that was far from being the case, he walked out to greet his partner with a huge smile of relief.

"You goin' to lunch soon?" Tone asked him.

"Yeah, give me twenty minutes."

A good talk with his partner Tone during lunch hour was just what he needed to free his mind from Sharron. But on the way back to the garage, his boss stopped him.

"Hey, Anthony, what's with this friend of yours? Does this guy have a job or what? What is he gonna do, wait around and go to lunch with ya again? How many times is he gonna do this? Get a *life* for crying out loud."

Ant was surprised by it, but not *that* surprised. He knew his partner's shortcomings. And he knew that Paul could have a lack of patience for underachievers. So he blew it off and went back to work until lunch.

"Is your boyfriend still waitin' for ya, tiger?" his fellow mechanic asked him, teasing him when he returned to the garage.

"So that's why you were smiling," Ant responded with a nod. "Paul was cracking on my boy, making jokes and shit on him."

"I mean, is the guy lonely or what, man?"

"That's my boy. He'll get his life together. He ain't dead yet."

"Yeah, and that's about the *only* thing he's not."

"Yeah, whatever, man." *And if you keep talking that shit, you gon' have a fight on your hands,* he thought, in defense of his longtime friend. But the issue was dropped as quickly as it started as both mechanics got back to work.

Nevertheless, Ant felt self-conscious about Tone's lack of direction. He pulled out a cheap white sheet to lay across his Chevy's interior for cruising again at lunchtime.

"Where was you at last night, man? You had another girl with you?" Tone asked him as soon as he hopped in on the passenger side, wearing his St. Louis Cardinals jersey again.

Ant thought about that as well.

"Damn, man, you ever thought about buying another shirt that you like?" he asked him.

Tone said, "Why, I wear this one too much?"

"Yeah, man. Like every day."

"Aw, dawg, I don't wear it that much. So where were you at last night, man? I called you about five times," Tone lied. It was more like *eight* times.

Ant looked at him and was pleasantly surprised. "So *you* were the one with all them hang ups on my machine. I thought it was Sharron."

"I told you to pick up the first two times, then after that, I just didn't leave no messages," Tone explained. Then he smiled. "You thought it was Sharron, hunh?"

"Yeah, man. I left her crib last night and hooked up with Shawntè again, so I turned my phone off. Then I checked my answering machine this morning and got all of them hang ups."

"You was nervous about that?" Tone wanted to know.

Ant hated to admit it. And he didn't. Not directly.

"I'm sayin', man, I still ain't got with this girl yet. I just didn't want to mess it up."

Tone broke out laughing.

"Yeah, dawg, she got you. You sniffin' yourself all over, making sure you smell good."

"I'm just sayin', man, I don't want to fuck it up. At least not until I get with her first. You know how that goes, because after that, who *knows* what'll happen. It'll be back to business as usual, just like with this big-butt girl over here. God!" he exclaimed, watching a well-curved woman in form-fitting black pants who waited at the bus stop.

Tone looked and smiled.

"You're saying that you don't really like this girl?" he asked, pressing for an answer. Just a month earlier, Ant seemed to be running out of gas for women. But all of a sudden he seemed rejuvenated and back in the hunt for more. Or was it a last hurrah?

Ant thought about that for a minute and hunched his shoulders.

"I don't really know, man. Who knows? I might like this girl more than I *think* I do."

Tone nodded, and smiled again. "*I* do," he said.

Ant grinned back at him. "I know you do."

Tone said, "Yeah, this girl make you think, man. In a good way."

"But she be overdoing it though," Ant told him.

Tone thought about that. *Overdoing it?*

"Well, maybe that's what you need. Because a lot of girls don't make you think enough. They're either too easy or they don't want to talk to you at all," he commented with a laugh. "Or at *least* not to me. Then you got girls who want to talk all the time but never give you no ass. I don't like them much either."

Ant broke out laughing. "What if this girl Sharron is like that? And she don't like to fuck?" he questioned rhetorically. "I was over her crib last night, and she was dressed for bed in a long nightshirt, and she stayed like that while we ate fried rice and talked, teasing the hell out of me."

Tone looked at Ant incredulously.

"And you *let her* do that to you?" he asked.

"Man—"

"Aw, yeah, dawg. She's the one," Tone cut him off and commented with a laugh. "She's playin' with your Johnson and everything. She even had *me* going home callin' up old girlfriends and whatnot," he confessed.

"Speaking of calling up old girlfriends," Ant said, "have you tried making calls anywhere about a job?" He was dying to get at it, he just hadn't found the opportunity to bring it up without forcing the issue. Tone needed direction and some kind of purpose in life.

"As a matter of fact, I have," he responded. "I thought about calling up this carpet cleaning service out Richmond Heights."

"Richmond Heights? My boss lives out that way in Ladue," Ant said, surprised. "My boss got like a mini mansion out there. He let me ride out there with him a couple of times. I even ran ball with his two sons."

Tone looked into Ant's face and asked, "He got it like that? A mini mansion?"

"Yeah, he invests his money in stocks and bonds and shit. Paul's a smart guy, man."

Tone smiled. "Are you sure he ain't a part of the Mafia? That repair and body shop might just be a front."

Ant shook it off. "Just because he's Italian with some money don't mean that he's into Mafia shit. That's like saying we both hustlers because we black."

"I *have* hustled," Tone said with a smile. "I was just never good at it."

Ant thought about that.

"What *are* you good at?" he found himself asking his partner as they cruised up to a Taco Bell drive-thru.

"I was just thinking about that myself. It don't seem like it's shit that I *can* do."

Ant started laughing, but it wasn't funny. It wasn't funny at all.

"I mean, I'm twenty-eight years old, man, and I got no skills," Tone said. "I mean, you, you got that car shit that you into, but I was never really into that. And then you got into gamin' women and whatnot, and I just had to take what I could get."

Ant stopped laughing and ordered his food.

"Yeah, gimme three soft chicken tacos with plenty of hot stuff."

Tone wasn't even hungry, he just wanted to talk.

"That's why I was calling you last night, man," he said. "Now I know what you were talking about when you said you get bored a lot. It feels like I haven't done shit with my life."

Ant was sorry he even started the conversation. Tone was trying his best to depress him.

"Yeah, well, you ain't dead yet," Ant told him. "So just call up this carpet cleaning place and see what's up."

"I'm gon' do it," Tone said.

"You sure you ain't hungry, man?"

He shook his head. "Naw, I ain't hungry. But thanks for asking. You a good friend, man," he added. "One of the only *true* friends that I got. I just wish that some of your enthusiasm about shit could rub off on me somehow."

"You need some inspiration, hunh?" Ant asked, stuffing his mouth with his first bite.

"Exactly. I need some inspiration," Tone admitted with a smile.

"Well, like they say, man, where there's a will, there's a way," Ant mumbled through his taco. "You just have to stay at it and keep yourself busy. And once you do that, only time will tell."

Time will tell indeed. And time can never be rushed with friendship. You can try your best to speed up the process to make fast friends, but in the end, time will eventually kick your behind, and untested friendships will eventually betray you. A commitment to anything has to be walked through. And as corny as it may seem, the computer age held nothing on the old-school principle of getting to know each other as friends before lovers through time. Yet, the year was 1999, and now the end of June; the beginning of summertime. And as young Americans arrived at the last summer before the year 2000, they seemed *more* than ready to do away with time's lessons of faith and patience, while fast-forwarding to get to the good parts—the good life, the good money, the good sex, and the good love—as if time was running out on them. Unfortunately, in their rushes of immaturity, too many of them made hasty decisions with their new opportunities, new friends, and new lovers, ending up with a fast hour of pleasure, followed by a full decade of misery.

Like it or not, Sharron had the right idea, to slow things down and discover one another inside and out before indulging each other. *Let's just enjoy the good things in life like my twenty-fourth birthday, before we ruin things,* she thought. So she had Anthony take a drive through slow-moving traffic on Natural Bridge Avenue on her birthday, Sunday, June 27, 1999, in the midst of St. Louis teenagers celebrating their youth and another summer of the mating game.

Sharron smiled, relaxing in the passenger seat, dressed in a new skirt outfit of cream-colored cotton with brown leather sandals. "I haven't done this in *ages,*" she said, referring to cruising the avenue amongst the giddy teens blowing horns, walking the streets, and showing themselves off to one another.

Anthony chuckled, dressed again in all blue denim. He didn't believe he was even driving there on Natural Bridge during the weekend. Nevertheless, it was something to do, and something to see, on a long birthday date for Sharron. He enjoyed her company that much, whether he admitted it to himself and to his partner Tone or not. She had given Anthony peace. And he had given her peace. But how long would that peace last? Again, only time would tell. Yet, with faith in one another, they had all the time in the world.

"So, this is what you want to do on your birthday?" Anthony asked Sharron. He was embarrassed. What if someone saw him there? Embarrassment stopped guys from doing many simple things in the first place; simple things like holding a woman's hand for a walk in the park. Macho men laughed about those things, or at least while they were still young and didn't know any better.

"Why?" Sharron asked. "You don't feel comfortable here? We can drive somewhere else. It doesn't matter to me. We got all day, right? You promised."

Boy did she know how to hold a man to his word. All Anthony could do was smile. He *did* promise it to her. They would spend the entire day together.

"I'm just saying, Sharron. There's a million other things for us to do outside of driving around with . . . these people."

"Aw, don't act like you never came up here before, and to O'Fallon Park, to check out the tight jeans and high skirts. Don't even try it," Sharron snapped at him with a grin.

He laughed and didn't deny it.

"Yeah, but it's different now. I'm older."

"There's guys older than you out here," she countered. And there were.

"And those are the kind of guys that I don't want to be with either," he told her.

Sharron thought of his friend and could not hold her tongue.

"What about Tone? I don't think *he* would mind being out here."

"Me and Tone are two different people just like you are Celena are different."

"Whatever happened to the saying 'Birds of a feather flock together,'" she said with a laugh.

"That's bullshit," Anthony responded. "You mainly hang out with people you know, and who you like, whether they act like you or not. We ain't all twins out here. I told you about that before."

"Yeah, when you talked about sharing pieces," she remembered glowingly.

Anthony looked over and grinned, shaking his head at her.

"Are you ever gonna forget that line?"

She looked him straight in his eyes and answered, "Of course not."

He nodded. "That's just what I thought."

"Why? Would you want me to?"

Hell yeah! he thought to himself. It was as if his one line had given her permanent keys to the workings of his mind. She could lock him up whenever she wanted to.

"Sometimes I do," Anthony admitted, grinning.

"Yeah, well, you can forget about that," she told him defiantly. "Because I *won't* forget. Unless you knock me in the head and I catch amnesia."

He laughed a little too hard for comfort. Maybe those thoughts *had* come to his mind a few times to release himself from her vice grip on him. His laugh made her curious.

Sharron looked at him real hard and asked, "Have you ever hit a girl before? You know, for getting on your nerves or something? And you just hauled off and punched her in the mouth?"

Anthony nearly crashed into the car in front of them. He couldn't *believe* Sharron! He turned and looked at her with horror.

"Girl, you just say anything that comes to your mind. I mean, most women have a conscience that tells them 'No, I'm not gonna ask him something like that.' But you just don't care."

Sharron found his statement ironic. Usually, she allowed her conscience to control too much. Questions that needed to be answered went unasked. But not anymore. And not with him. Because she was tired of assuming and complaining to girlfriends. She wanted a man to speak up for himself, and *be* a man.

"You still haven't answered the question," she pressed him.

Anthony snapped, "No! I ain't never been into that shit!"

"Never?"

"Naw!"

He hadn't. He was too busy sexing them up.

Sharron, tickled by his outrage, egged him on some more.

"Am I getting on your nerves right now?" she asked him with a knowing grin.

He ignored her.

"If I am, just remember that it's my birthday. So I can do that. When your birthday comes around in February, I'll let *you* get on *my* nerves. Okay?"

He tried his hardest not to laugh. *Don't go out like no fool, man,* he told himself. *She's trying to play you out.* But he couldn't help it. So he chuckled at it anyway. She was projecting that they would still be together when next February rolled around in year 2000.

They relaxed in the middle of the heavy, slow-moving traffic on Natural Bridge Avenue, pleased with each other's company. Anthony forgot about his embarrassment while they made their way through the weekly teenage crowd.

"Where are you taking me to now?" Sharron asked him, curious about their next destination.

"To the *Admiral,*" he answered, referring to the boat casino that sat on the St. Louis side of the Mississippi River. Then he took a last-minute detour and headed north on Jennings Station Road, toward his old stomping grounds. Home.

"Ah, isn't the river the other way, or are you trying to take Route 70?" Sharron asked him.

He smiled. "I just wanted to show you where I grew up first," he told her.

"Oh," she responded. "That's nice." She was actually surprised by it. "Does your family still live here?" she asked, setting him up for her next big question.

"Yeah, they still live here."

Then she smiled. "So, are you gonna introduce me to your mother?"

He smiled back at her. What the hell? Sharron was a good girl. His mother would probably like her. Like her a lot.

"I gotta go in the house first to make sure that she's dressed for visitors," he responded.

Sharron was surprised again. He had no hesitation about it. That made her a bit nervous. What kind of a mother did he have anyway? Was she protective? Was she tough? Anthony had already told her that his mother had raised three boys, and contributed to raising a few of his cousins. In fact, the Poole family seemed loaded with men, and was very different from her own extended family of women down in Memphis.

Sharron sat quietly and was still nervous as they pulled up to a nice, working-class, three-bedroom brick home with a healthy green lawn and a private garage.

"I'll be right out," Anthony told her and ran inside.

Oh my God! Sharron thought to herself in a panic. *I wasn't prepared for this. What if his mother doesn't like me?*

It was too late for worries. Anthony was already on his way back to the car, and was smiling.

"What she say?" she asked him as soon as he opened the door to help her out.

"She said, 'Bring her on in!'"

He made his mother sound tough already. What kind of a woman used such language? *Bring her on in!* Or was that Anthony's paraphrase?

Sharron hit that front door and nearly tripped into the house, she was so nervous. She had never dreamed of meeting the mother of a player. Many a woman would wonder if loose men even had mothers. But they did.

"So this is the birthday girl?" Mrs. Poole asked, embarrassing Sharron at first sight. "Well, go on. Sit down."

Sharron didn't know what to do with herself. She was only bluffing Anthony. He went ahead and marched her in out of the blue to meet his mother, a medium-sized, dark brown, intense woman with a short natural do. And, when Mrs. Poole looked at you, she *really* looked at you! That didn't do Sharron's nerves a bit of good. She took a seat on the sofa across from Mrs. Poole's black leather La-Z-Boy chair and crossed her legs like a lady.

"So, where are you from, Sharron?" his mother asked her.

"Memphis," she answered. *I wonder what he told her about me,* she pondered. If *he told her* anything, *being a player and all. He probably said that I ask him a bunch of crazy questions. Oh my God!*

To make matters worse, Anthony left her alone in the living room with his mother in search of snacks and juice in the kitchen. He didn't hurry back either. Was it payback for all of the questions she had tortured him with? What a cruel joke to play on a woman on her birthday.

"Memphis? What are you doing all the way up here?" his mother asked.

"I went to school at the University of Missouri at St. Louis."

"UMSL? Did you finish?"

"Not yet," she responded self-consciously. She did *plan* to finish someday.

"Mmm-hmm," Mrs. Poole mumbled, pulling out a cigarette. "Do you mind if I smoke?"

Sharron *did* mind, but do you think she planned to say so?

"No, I don't mind," she answered quickly enough.

Mrs. Poole lit up so fast she might as well have never asked the question.

"Being around so many men all your life can work your nerves," she commented through her first drag. Sharron took in the neatness of the room and imagined how hard it would be to keep a place so nice with no other women around.

Mrs. Poole added, "I got three boys, a separated husband, two brothers, three brothers-in-law, and plenty of hardheaded nephews.

"If you were around all them damn boys every day, you would have started smoking too," she added. "But Anthony is a good man. He ain't never been in no kind of trouble. Or at least not the kind that you can go to jail for."

Sharron relaxed, trying her best not to cough, and took it all in like a lecture before a final exam.

Mrs. Poole took another drag and said, "Anthony's hard on women. I might as well let you know that." She took a peek at the kitchen to make sure he didn't overhear.

"All of my boys are. They got it from their daddy," she said. "The man just couldn't keep his hands *off* of women. Seemed like every other *week* I had to chase a new girl down with my knife. After a while, I just couldn't *do* that shit no more. You know what I mean?" she asked. "If your ass wanna be a damn alley cat, then you *stay* your ass out in the alley!"

Sharron had to stop herself from laughing, because it wasn't funny. She didn't know how Mrs. Poole would take it anyway. Anthony reappeared with cookies and juice in his hands, and an extra glass for Sharron.

"Mom, you out here talking about Dad again. Y'all know y'all still love each other."

His mother planted that intense stare of hers on him as Anthony sat down next to Sharron on the sofa.

"Love ain't crazy no more, boy. No more!"

Then she looked at them both as they sat together comfortably.

"So, how long you two known each other?" she asked them.

Anthony started to chuckle, but Sharron was horrified.

Shit! she thought. *Why did she have to ask us that?* She wished they had never come to visit. Or at least not without her preparing for it. What a cruel, cruel joke Anthony was playing on her.

After neither one of them answered quickly enough, his mother said, "What, a week or two? How long?"

Anthony was still chuckling.

Sharron spoke up and said, "Longer than that."

That only made him laugh harder at her vagueness.

"I see," Mrs. Poole mumbled. "It sounds to me like you two have a lot of getting-to-know-each-other to do."

"We sure do," Sharron agreed. "I know that already."

That stopped Anthony's silliness *quick*! He realized what she meant. He would have a much longer wait for the flesh.

Fuck! he thought to himself. *Time to get the hell out of here! Damn! I'll never get with this girl the way things are going.*

"Well, you know what you have to do, girl. If you're as smart as I *think* you are," his mother responded to her. "You know what *they* want, so you have to know what *you* want."

SHIT, MOM!

"Don't look at me like that, boy," she snapped at her son.

Anthony shook his head, pissed at himself for deciding to bring Sharron to meet his mother. The doctor didn't order *that* apple. No way!

"I didn't appreciate that at all," Sharron told him on their way downtown to the Mississippi River. By that time, it was nightfall. "That was *not* funny. And you set me up for that."

Anthony didn't consider it a piece of apple pie and ice cream either, but he had to laugh at it because it *was* funny. Sharron knew it too. That's what life was made of. The unpredictable.

"It's not funny, Anthony," she insisted.

"Well, stop talkin' 'bout it then, and let's just finish your birthday."

Sharron sulked for another few minutes in silence. Then she went back to her usual questions.

"So, your daddy was a player, too," she said, almost as if she were talking to herself.

Anthony smiled. *I guess it's in my genes,* he thought. He knew he could not express *that* thought to her. At least not until he got her, then he could finally get bold with his words.

"How was *your* daddy?" he asked her instead.

"My daddy was a good man who wanted good love. And he still is."

"Did he get good love?"

"Yes, he did. And he still does."

Anthony said, "What kind of woman is your mother?"

Sharron paused. She hadn't talked about her mother with a man in a while. It was too painful. They didn't care half of the time anyway. She wondered if Anthony would care.

"She died of cancer," she told him flatly. Too flat. And she got the effect that she wanted. Shock.

Anthony looked over at her and said, "Damn. My bad. I didn't know."

She looked into his face to read it. "How could you? Unless I told you."

"You did tell me. And . . . I'm sorry about that."

Few men were inhumane enough to blow off someone's mother dying of cancer. The most precious woman in the world to a man was his mother. So it should have been obvious that Anthony would care, just like he would care about his *own* mother dying of cancer.

"Did she smoke?"

Sharron nodded. "Mmm-hmm."

Anthony didn't know what else to say.

"Turn the radio on," she told him.

He obliged.

She said, "I don't really feel like going to the *Admiral.* I just want to get something to eat. Okay? Some seafood or something."

"It's your birthday, right? We'll do whatever you want," he told her.

She looked into his face and read it again. He *looked* serious enough.

"Whatever I want?" she asked him to make sure.

"Don't go overboard with that," he responded, grinning.

"I won't. Just remember that you said that," she told him.

They went ahead and had a nice dinner at The Sailor restaurant on the Mississippi, and talked and laughed until it was close to eleven o'clock at night. The waitress was hovering near their table, anxious to collect the check and her tip for their meals.

"I think this waitress is trying to send us a message," Anthony told his birthday date.

Sharron laughed and said, "I know." Then she gathered herself to leave, after a trip to the bathroom. When she returned, she knew exactly how she wanted their night to end.

"What do you want to do now?" Anthony asked her on their way out. Sharron was yawning. A bad sign for a player. She was too tired for dessert.

"Let's go back to my place," she said to his surprise. She made it sound as if she wanted him to stay for a while. And she did.

Finally! Anthony told himself. *It took a little while. But I figured she'd want some on her birthday. That's why I didn't mind spending the whole day with her. It ain't all that bad to treat a woman to everything she wants every once in a while. It ain't that bad at all.*

He drove back to Sharron's apartment in University City in silence, while listening peacefully to soft music on the radio. Sharron had requested it, and Anthony was willing to grant her anything that would keep her in the mood.

As they pulled into the parking lot of her complex, she asked, "You ever listened to the rap group The Pharcyde?"

Anthony looked her over, wondering where the question was coming from. "Yeah, why?" he asked, confused.

The Pharcyde? What the hell is she talking about? I thought she wanted to listen to smooth *music.*

"What about their second album, *Labcabincalifornia*?"

"What? 'Can't keep runnin' awaaaay'? That one?"

She laughed at his attempt to sing. "Yeah, that one."

"I mean, I don't have the CD, but I liked that song."

She nodded. They parked and climbed out of the car.

"It's another song on there that I want you to listen to," she told him.

"I didn't know you listened to rap music like that," he said to her, still confused about it.

"Actually, it's Celena's CD," she responded with a smile.

"Oh. Well, that makes more sense. She *seems* like she listens to more rap."

"She does," Sharron confirmed.

She led him up to her apartment and greeted her roommate, who was stretched out in the living room and watching a *Hellraiser* video with a pillow to her face.

"Girl, you got nothing else to do but watch a horror movie in here, scared to death by yourself? You need to at least turn that thing down some," Sharron snapped at her.

Celena viewed Anthony walking in with her before she responded.

"You ditched me on your birthday, so what else *could* I do?" she commented.

Sharron gave her the evil eye and led Anthony to her room of stuffed animals.

"Damn. Look like a circus in here. You need a hug that bad?" he joked to her.

She didn't deny it. "Yes, I do. And I'll be right back, so make yourself comfortable," she told him.

Anthony ventured right over to the bed to lay down on it amongst the teddy bears and other stuffed animals, pushing them aside to make room for himself.

"What are you doing?" Celena asked her roommate apprehensively. She just *knew* that Sharron was not planning on jumping bones for her birthday with Mr. Noname, whom she'd met only a month ago. That wasn't even Sharron's style. And the whole Married Man thing was just an experiment.

"I'm minding my own business," Sharron told her. "Now can I borrow one of your CDs?"

"Sean Love called you today to wish you a happy birthday," Celena said, ignoring Sharron's plea.

"That's nice."

"Aren't you gonna call him back?"

"What do *you* care, Celena? It's too late for that anyway."

"Yeah, I guess you can't, 'cause you got company now," she said.

"Look, I'm just gonna go get the CD then."

"What CD?" Celena asked.

"The Pharcyde."

"*The Pharcyde?* Girl, that ain't no music to get busy to. What are you thinkin'?"

"Who said I was getting busy?"

"What are you doing then?"

"Like I said, *minding* my own business."

Sharron marched into Celena's room, found the CD, and attempted to march back out before Celena jumped up and stopped her at the door.

"Sharron, you're not gonna regret this in the morning are you?" she asked, still concerned about her roommate's intentions for the night.

"Regret what?"

"You know."

Sharron pushed her aside. "No, I *don't* know. Now please, turn this TV down so I can hear myself *think* in here."

"It's not that loud."

"Yes it is."

Celena grabbed on to Sharron's arm before she reentered her room with her company.

"If you need me, girl, just holler."

Sharron looked her in the face and shook her head with a smirk. "Girl, please." She walked back into her room, shut and locked the door, and told Anthony to take his shoes off while on the bed.

"Don't you have any bed manners?" she teased him.

He smiled. "I got plenty of bed manners."

"I'm sure you do." She slipped The Pharcyde CD into her Aiwa stereo system on the tall dresser. "Okay, you told me that I can have anything I want for my birthday, right?"

He was hesitant. "Yeah, I said that."

But not anything *anything,* he thought. *What is she getting at?*

"Well, I want you to listen to this Pharcyde song. Okay?"

Anthony smiled, as confused as ever. What the heck did The Pharcyde have on that second album of theirs?

Sharron clicked on her night lamp, put on her song, and scampered back to the bed to get cozy with her company. Anthony listened to see exactly what the hell was on her mind. He found that out as the four-member, West Coast rap group crooned over a smooth rhythm while each expressing a girlfriend's desire to be accompanied for a night without the greediness of sex. "She Said," in a word, was a song that catered to a woman's need for affection. Even late-night affection from a man, without the cloudiness of sex. And Anthony understood Sharron's message, loud and clear. The song sounded good anyway. *Real* good. And he granted her wish, because it made sense. So they held each other and talked through the night, listening to the entire CD before falling asleep in each other's arms with their clothes on.

"You did *what?!* And you didn't even *try* to take her clothes off? Because of a *song*? Aw, man, dawg. You was my hero! But like they say, heroes ain't nothing but a sandwich!" Tone joked over the phone as he was given the word on Sharron's birthday date. Ant didn't feel embarrassed by it at all. He felt enlightened. Relieved. Relieved of the pressure of having to score. Women just didn't know how stressful it was for a man. Ant didn't know himself until it was no longer an issue for him.

"It felt good though, man, that I could actually do it without getting the hell up out of there, Tone," he explained.

Tone sucked his teeth. "Aw, man, I had to do that shit *plenty* of times," he admitted. "It didn't feel that great to *me*. I was waking up with blue balls. Every single time."

Ant laughed. "Well, that wasn't something that *I* was used to."

"Now it is. 'Cause you may not *ever* get this girl."

"But think about it though, man. We've only known each other for a month."

"And? What that mean? That ain't stop you before."

Tone had a point.

"I guess you was right then, this girl got me. At least for right now," Ant responded.

Tone said, "There you go talking that 'right now' shit again. You been saying that for weeks."

"That's because everything changes once you get it. You know how that is, man."

"Yeah, we'll see. Anyway, I got that new job out Richmond Heights, cleaning carpets. I'll be in training this week."

"See that? All you gotta do is *try,* man. Now you gotta *keep it.* Because you had *jobs* before," Ant said with a laugh. Nevertheless, he was happy for him.

"I know," Tone responded, chuckling himself. "I think we make like seven dollars a hour."

"You *think?* You better *know,*" Ant told him.

"I'll find out."

"Anyway, man, what else has been up?" Ant didn't want to dwell on Tone's new job. He wanted to wait and see if his partner could actually keep one long enough to celebrate. It was similar to Ant's own ability to hold on to a woman. He couldn't do it.

"I need to be asking *you* that," Tone responded. "So now that you don't have Shawntè no more, what are you gonna do when your rocks get hard? Are you goin' back to old ass, or are ya gonna start chokin' ya' chicken," he added with a laugh.

"Naw, dawg, you won't have me grabbin' low at *my* shit," Ant said. Realizing that things would never go her way, Shawntè had already stepped away from him.

"You tellin' me that you never jerked off a day in your life? Get the hell out of here!" Tone doubted. He considered it unbelievable, based on all of the times when he had to take pleasure into *his* own hands.

"Look, man, everybody ain't hard-pressed like you," Ant countered with a laugh. He had a strong hunch that Tone had been around the block a few times with the five-finger method, but he had never asked. It wasn't his kind of conversation.

"You think girls don't do it? Ask Sharron," his friend challenged.

"Man, I wouldn't even talk about nothing like that with her."

"Have you asked her when was the last time she had one?"

"Naw."

"Well, you better ask her *something,*" Tone advised.

Ant laughed it off. "All of that stuff will come out in time."

Tone said, "How many guys you think she's been with? She just turned twenty-four, right?"

Ant began to shake his head with his black cordless phone in hand.

"Come on, man, you trippin'."

"Aw'ight then. What about if she asks you how many girls *you* had? Are you gonna tell her?"

Ant had stopped counting. It was a plenty large number, too. Large, like in *three* figures. But at least he had begun to slow down over the last few years.

"You think I would tell her something like that?" he asked honestly.

"I'm saying, though. What if she asks you?"

"I'd lie, and tell her that I had somewhere around forty."

"*Forty? I* had more than that! You think she would believe that?"

"Man, trust me. Most women don't have a clue, because they're always lying to themselves. Like Chris Rock said in *Bring the Pain,* they don't even count their one-night stands. But *we* do."

"Damn right we do," Tone agreed with a laugh. "Shit, if it wasn't for one-night stands, I couldn't count *twenty* girls right now."

Ant said, "Yeah, so when we count everything, women actually think we had relationships with all of these girls. And that shit is crazy! I mean, do they actually think that when Wilt Chamberlain said he slept with twenty thousand women, that he had relationships with all of 'em? That don't even make no sense. He would have to be a thousand years old."

Tone said, "Man, I don't even think you can fuck twenty thousand women in one lifetime. Wilt Chamberlain lying his ass off. His dick would be purple by now."

Ant laughed and said, "It probably is. All bent up from too much stroking."

"Hey, man, you ever thought about how big Shaquille O'Neal's Johnson is?"

Ant stopped laughing and asked, "What?" He didn't believe that Tone was asking him something as far out as that. Tone kept right on with his query unabashedly.

"I mean, he wear a size twenty-one shoe or something like that, right? And the boy is *huge,* man! Seven foot one, three hundred twenty pounds! I mean, I wonder what women are thinking when he asks to go out with them. I would be afraid that he would break me in half or something."

Ant started to laugh again. "You crazy as hell, dawg," he told his friend. "I'm not even thinking about no shit like that. You got *way* too much free time on your hands."

"I'm serious though, Ant. If *I* was a girl, and a big ma-fucker like Shaq asked me out, I'd be like, 'Oohh, no! No damn way!'"

Ant had tears in his eyes and had to hold the phone away while he laughed.

"Hey, man, you had some chronic earlier or what?" he assumed.

"Yeah, I had a little somethin' somethin'," Tone admitted.

"I can tell."

"Anyway, man, when you think you gon' finally get wit' her?" Tone was going back to the discussion concerning Sharron.

"Why are you so worried about it? I mean, it's not like I didn't have to wait to get a girl before."

"Yeah, but you always had five, ten other girls on the side. Now you can't even keep one. That Shawntè girl was all right. She dressed kind of freaky, but she was aw'ight."

"You want her or something? I'll give you her phone number to call her if you wanna keep talking about her."

Tone paused and thought for a minute.

"I want Sharron," he admitted with a laugh.

Ant said, "You high right now, man. Stop fuckin' around like that. Seriously."

"But I'm sayin' though, dawg. If you're gonna get rid of her anyway, then why should it matter to you that I want her."

"Because I ain't fuckin' finished with her yet!" Ant snapped. He didn't realize how upset he was over the idea. With any other woman, he would have more than likely laughed it off. But the reference to passing on Sharron Francis triggered something extra inside of him. He was becoming close to her. She was beginning to mean something to him and he was willing to protect her.

"Hey, man, don't say shit else about Sharron. And that's on the real," he warned Tone.

All the fun and laughter stopped right there. At least from Ant's point of view. Because Tone was still planning to have a good time with it.

"Why don't you just give her my number when you through with her?" he added with a chuckle. "She already talked to me before. She might even like me, on the down low side of things."

Tone wasn't the least bit afraid of Ant. Fighting was something that he *could* beat his partner in. Not that Ant was a wimp or anything; Tone simply had a harder life and had learned how to make things hard for others in physical disputes.

Ant said, "It sounds like it's time for me to hang up."

"Why, you don't love me no more? Over a *bitch!*"

An overload of energy shot into Ant's brain and ricocheted into his right arm, bringing the cordless phone down against his kitchen table.

CLAAACCKKK!

The phone snapped into three pieces: a mouthpiece, a battery, and the battery clamp.

"THAT MOTHERFUCKER!" Ant yelled at the walls. "He always gotta start some crazy shit! If he can't handle that weed, then he needs to leave that shit alone! DAMN!"

He put his phone back together and sat down to calm himself. As soon as the phone was back in order it rang again.

Ant answered it and said, "Hey, man, don't call here no more when you high, all right? That's all I have to say to you right now," and was ready to hang up.

"Anthony, this is Paul Mancini. What are you talking about?" his boss asked with a chuckle.

Ant was embarrassed by it. "Oh, my bad, Paul. I thought you were someone else."

Paul paused, thinking. "It's not that guy who comes by the job for you all of the time is it? Because if it is, you need to really think about finding a better friend. And I'm not saying that to bad-mouth your friends, I'm just telling you as someone who knows, *and* as your boss. Because if this guy is getting high, and then coming around *you* during work hours, then that doesn't look good for *me, or* for you. You understand me?"

Shit! Ant thought. The boss already disliked Tone. Now he had a more concrete reason to not want him on the premises.

"Naw, it wasn't him," he lied. "And I'm not saying he's perfect or anything, but—"

Paul cut off the bullshit and said, "Look, Anthony, I was calling up all of the guys tonight to see if you all wanted a half a day tomorrow, because I have to make a trip out to Kansas City tonight, and I won't be back until tomorrow afternoon.

"Now, I don't want to get in the middle of you and your friend, but business is business, and I don't think I want him on my premises anymore," he added. "Now, if he shows up and he *does* happen to be under the influence of something, then *you* no longer have employment with me, and I *will* have your friend arrested on the spot!

"Do we understand each other? Anthony?"

"Yeah, we do."

"Do you want tomorrow morning off?"

"Yeah, I'll take it off."

Ant hung up the phone and was crushed. He had no words for himself. Not even thoughts. He was simply numb.

He sighed and finally mumbled, "You try your best to be there for a ma-fucker, and look what happens. Now the boss gon' be lookin' at me all sideways and shit, thinking that *I'm* doing something. DAMN!"

He stood up and paced his apartment, brooding for a few minutes before deciding to call Sharron. Who else could he talk to? Women were sensitive, sensitive to everything that mattered. Calling another guy would likely get an *insensitive* response of "Fuck it, man! Just do what you gotta do."

Ant wanted more than that. He wanted someone to understand what he was going through. *All* humans wanted someone to understand what was weighing down their minds. So he went ahead and called her up.

"What are you doing right now?" he asked, as soon as he heard her voice.

She seemed excited. "I was just about to call you."

"I know," he told her. "I felt it."

"Like The Force, hunh?"

He chuckled. "Yeah. Obi-Wan Kenobi."

She laughed at it. Hearing her laugh turned him on. He wanted to lay down with her right then and there for the real deal to connect with her, body and soul.

"What if I wanted you to visit me tonight? Would you say no?"

She paused. "Are you asking me?"

"What if I am?"

"What if?" she countered.

Shit! I don't have time for this cerebral bullshit tonight! I just want to do what comes natural to us, he thought to himself, tiring of the mental foreplay. He got desperate.

"I'm coming right now to get you. Aw'ight?"

Sharron laughed at it. "Just like that, hunh?" she asked. She realized that it sounded out of character for him. But so what? Being out of character was a good thing for a man to show a woman. It meant that she had broken him down, and had lowered his shield of cool.

"Yeah, just like that," he told her.

"And where are we going?"

"I'll tell you when I get there."

She paused again. "Okay. Come and get me."

Sometimes women say the damnedest things and don't even know it. Men take those things, run with them, say them a dozen times or so, and paint whatever fantasies they want with them.

Okay. Come and get me . . . Come and get me . . . Come and get me.

I'll come and get you *all right,* Ant thought with a grin and a fast hard-on.

"How long will it take you to get here?" she asked him.

It was close to nine-thirty that post-birthday Monday night.

"Twenty-five minutes."

"All right then. I'll be ready."

Ready for what? he mused. Maybe she thought they'd go cruising and talking again. Ant was *hardly* in the mood for that. He had already run out of patience for the waiting game before sex. He just wondered if *she* had, and if driving over there to pick her up would be a big mistake. Maybe he should have just called up an old acquaintance for the night. He had too much to lose with Sharron to react in haste. Every possible scenario ran through his mind while driving west to University City. Nevertheless, he kept driving there, as if he were on a mission: Superman flying around the globe at light speed to save the life of Lois Lane.

When he reached Sharron's apartment parking lot, he hesitated.

"Aw, man, what if she still thinking about chillin' with no contact?" he mumbled to himself. The Pharcyde song "She Said" was still ringing in his head. But before he could back away, there she was, walking down the steps of her second-floor apartment and toward the car.

Why am I so worried about this? Just go for what you know, he told himself. Sharron opened the car door and hopped in.

Ant smiled and said, "You really meant it when you said you'd be ready. I was gonna come up and get you."

"I didn't want my roommate ridin' me again," she said.

"Does she always act like that with your friends?"

Sharron smiled, looking as tempting as a woman *should* look when a man is on the prowl for her. "No. Really, it's just with you," she responded.

"Why is she so worried about me?"

He had a guilty conscience. He knew damn well why Celena was concerned about him. He was a player. And Celena knew *more* than a few, where Sharron rarely attracted them. They said a word or two to Sharron, and her responses always let them know that it would be a long, scoreless ball game.

"I guess she figures that you're bad for me," Sharron answered, face to face.

That made Ant feel worse about his predicament. He turned away. All of the time spent. The hours of talk. The desire for closeness. It all came down to a pressed night for the flesh anyway. But hell, he wasn't going anywhere. They could still do the same things they did before. The sex was only physical. Why would that stop their *mental* connection?

"And what about you? Do *you* think I'm bad for you?" he asked Sharron. He wasn't supposed to ask her that question. He was supposed to convince her that he *was* good, and worth every second of her time. But frankly, the bullshit was tiring! And Ant was getting older, realizing his emptiness. Empty like most men, looking to be filled up with something. Just like women were. Loveless or lovesick, and *all* in need of healing.

Sharron said, "I don't know. *Should I* be afraid of you? I'm not."

"I don't want you to be," he told her. "And you shouldn't *have* to be. But . . ."

How exactly would he put the truth in words?

"It's kind of hard to stop, Sharron. I mean, once you figure out you got this power to do what you want with women, it's just hard to give that shit up. I mean, I'm always feeling it," he told her.

"Feeling what? What is it that you feel?" she asked him. "And is it just you? Or is it in *all* guys?"

He shook his head and frowned. "You can never say that it's a part of *all* guys. That would be like saying that drug addiction, or alcoholism, or crime, is in *all* guys. And that's not the case."

"So, what *is* the case? I mean, *you* tell *me*."

He shook his head again, trying to come up with the perfect word to explain it. "It's a drive, Sharron. A drive for life. And once you find out how good that shit is, it's addictive, and you never want to let go of that wheel. So somebody has to pull it out of your hands. Either that, or you end up crashed the hell up on the side of the road somewhere. And what do you do after that?"

"You get another car and you drive more carefully," Sharron answered on cue.

Ant shook his head. "That's not as easy as it sounds."

"How *do* you cure yourself then?"

Ant thought about it. "You take *turns* with somebody you can trust," he told her. "Your turn, my turn, your turn, my turn. Like that."

And *damn* it sounded good! Because it made sense. Sex was a very powerful thing. Not many men *or* women were willing to give it up. Not completely. However, its trusted and shared power was much more meaningful than selfishness and reckless freelancing.

Sharron, feeling the moment of truth, reached out for Ant's hand as they sat in silence for a moment. "Do you trust me?" she asked him.

"I want to. And I want *you* to trust *me*," he told her. "But you know what's funny about trust. You can never really trust someone until you give them a chance to be trusted with something in the first place. And how long does *that* shit take?" he asked with a chuckle.

"Until you feel comfortable with your decision," Sharron answered him. "And too many times we don't feel comfortable, and that only leads to disaster. Every time. Especially for women."

"You don't think that *guys* have things to distrust *women* about?"

"I didn't say that. I *know* better. I have a roommate," she commented with a smile.

"Yeah, well, those decisions are just as hard for us to make. How much do you tell a woman? 'Cause she gon' use everything you tell her against you. So you end up with a bunch of lies instead. Then you gotta keep track of all of 'em."

Sharron smiled. "It sounds like you know a lot about it."

"Oh, I do. That's what I'm trying to tell you."

"What have you lied to *me* about?"

"Nothing. That's what I'm trying to tell you," he repeated with a chuckle. "Do you know how many women I've introduced to my mother in the past five years?"

Sharron had actually thought about that during her birthday date. But she was too stunned by her surprise meeting with his mother to even ask him about it. She had thought about many things that night. But sometimes our minds can go blank, and we fail to process it all.

"How many?" she asked.

"None. I haven't done that since I first got out of high school. But you? I just took you right over there to her. So what am I telling you with that? In a sense, I already trust you, with a lot of things that I told you already. And with a lot of things that I've already done with you.

"I never took another woman up to watch airplanes and shit," he said. "Who would do that? Especially your first time out. But I thought that I could do that with you. So I did it. And it was nice."

She squeezed his hand. "Yes, it was."

"Don't do that," he told her, pulling his hand away.

"Why not?"

"Because I want to be more than just held and kissed tonight. And talked to."

Sharron stopped and stared out of the window, pissed off for some reason.

A typical fucking guy! But what did I expect? What did I really *expect?!* she thought to herself.

Then she nodded, defiantly. "Okay then. If that's how you want it, then let's do it then. Let's just get it over with."

Ant stared at her. He was speechless.

You try and tell a woman the truth, and what do they do, they fuckin' get attitudes with you! Man, I knew this shit was dumb! I should have just stopped off and picked up a hooker somewhere. I got money on me.

"What are you waitin' for? Let's go to your house. You want me, right?" Sharron pressed him.

"And what's so wrong with that?" he asked honestly. "You want me too. I mean, I *assume* that you do. Why else would you spend so much time with me?"

"Because evidently I *like* your ass!" she yelled at him. "Didn't you listen to the song last night? Or were you just *faking* it. And *lying* to me?"

"Yeah, I listened to the song. And I liked it. But this is real life here. And if we ever expect to go further than where we are, we gon' have to trust each other. In *everything!*"

"Like sex, right?"

"That's a part of everything."

"Yeah, it *sounds* more like the *only* thing to me," she told him.

Ant got pissed off himself and said, "Look, the fact that I'm even sittin' here tellin' you this shit shows that I like you. I don't even talk about sex with women. I just do the shit!"

"You talked about *sex* with me, *howling* at the moon. You remember that, Mr. Lie Alot?" she asked him sarcastically. It seemed comical to her. All of that wasted effort on her part to end up with the same result. A panty chase.

"I did a lot of things that I don't usually do with you," Ant told her.

"And I'm actually supposed to believe that now? After you told me that you outright lie? So what are you gonna tell me next? That I'm special to you? That nobody makes you feel like I do? And you want to take it to the next level?"

Sharron was having a good time with it. Why the hell not? There wasn't anything else she could do to change things. Men were men. And they were *mostly*—since she couldn't use the word "all"—terrible, in one way or another.

Ant grinned at her sarcasm.

"That ain't even my style. That stuff sounds like a corny Babyface song."

"Well, *I* happen to *like* Babyface. And maybe *we* just don't have enough in common."

"And we took all this time to find that out, hunh, that we don't have anything in common?"

"All what time? I've only known you since May. It's not even July yet."

"And we already shared your birthday together, from sunup to sundown," he countered.

"That doesn't mean we know each other all that well."

"Yeah, not like you know Celena."

"And not like *you* know Tone."

Ant shook his head and smiled again. He said, "I hear that's why a lot of black men get with white women, because sisters always gotta argue their point with everything."

"Oh, so we're just supposed to say, 'Sure, honey, do whatever the hell you want, and I'll still love you anyway.' Well, to hell with that!" Sharron snapped at him.

"Look, I'm just makin' a point. I don't go that way."

"Well, good for you, Anthony. Very, very good. Anthony Poole doesn't date white women, he only dogs out the black ones. Well, *hurray* for us!"

Obviously, Ant had gotten underneath Sharron's skin as well. So what were they to do with each other?

"It's gettin' late," Ant said, watching his car clock reach quarter to eleven.

"I don't have a curfew," Sharron told him. "And you can walk inside and tell *Celena* that I said that," she added.

"Are you saying that you're coming with me then?" Ant wanted to make sure he knew what the plan was.

"You still want me, right? Or at least for tonight," she responded.

He denied her assumption. "That's not the case at all. You make it what you make it."

"So *I* have a say so? Really?" she asked him.

"I mean, it's not like I'm gon' drop off the planet. That's why I'm telling you that you have to trust me," he told her.

"Don't you have to go to work tomorrow morning?" she asked.

"Not until one. What about you?"

"Twelve. So I have to leave home by eleven. Which means I have to be back here by no later than ten. Which means you have to be up to drive me back by nine. Which means I have to get to sleep by one o'clock tonight, so I can get my eight hours of rest. Which means that you have between now and one o'clock to get me to your house and do what you have to do. But first, I have to go back inside and get a few things to take with me."

Ant just broke out laughing. *This girl is stone-cold crazy! And I like her for it,* he thought.

"You make it sound like we robots or something," he commented.

"Why should I put any emotions into it? You just want some, right? What does that have to do with my mind? You just want the body."

At that point, Ant decided the play the game *her* way by pulling out his wallet.

"All right then, if it's like that, then how much is this gonna cost me?"

"Five hundred dollars."

"For a whole week?"

"Hell no! Until one o'clock, like I said."

Ant did the math. "By the time I get you back to my place, we're looking at less than two hours. That means I want your clothes off as soon as we hit the door."

"How 'bout I just ride over there naked?"

How 'bout we just screw in the car? Ant thought with a chuckle.

"Oh, and I don't *do* cars, so don't even think it," Sharron added, reading his devious grin.

"I'll be right back," she told him, leaving the car to go back inside for her things.

Ant sat there with half a smile on his face and wondered, *Is she bullshitting me or what? She might have me sitting out here looking like a damn fool, and then get her girlfriend to come out and tell me that she can't go. Or maybe they'll call the damn cops and say that a man is outside stalking her. I mean, how is she gonna go from being pissed off about me wanting to do her, and then agree to it? Because if* that's *the case, I probably could have pressed her real hard before and got it.*

After a few long minutes of waiting out in his car, his car clock reached eleven, and Ant nodded his head, telling himself, *Yeah, she got me good. She's not coming back out here. I just played myself. That's just what I get!*

He started up his engine to pull away. He was disappointed. Not only with the fact that he would have to start from scratch to find someone to sleep with, but also at the loss of Sharron's very interesting company. However, right as he put his car in reverse and began to back out of his parking space, Sharron headed down her steps and over to the passenger side of his car with a big brown bag of things.

"Sorry about that," she told him as she hopped in. "I couldn't find everything I was looking for."

Ant nodded and smiled at her. Not only because he wouldn't have to start all over and call someone to be with for the night, but because he would be spending more time with Sharron Francis from Memphis, Tennessee, who had quickly dug her way to his heart and didn't even realize it.

Confidence. How many people really have it when it comes to relationships? Are we all insecure about ourselves and how others perceive us as men and as women? How weak we are, or how strong. How attractive, or unattractive. How intelligent, or unintelligent. Or how hip we are to the ways of the world, as opposed to how others *perceive* us to be. How much do we *care* about all of those perceptions? How much do they affect our relationships? And how much do those perceptions sway the confidence that we *think* we have in ourselves, or that we *think* we have in our mates?

I'm gonna hate myself in the morning. I know it! Sharron thought to herself as she rode in the passenger seat of Anthony's car. *And Celena's going to be right. She was right from day one. I should have never stopped and let Anthony knock me down at the skating rink that night.*

We all second-guess ourselves based on our own *lack* of confidence, and the perception from others that we could do better. And in those periods of confusion concerning who *we* are and what *we* really want out of life, we somehow lose our sense of direction and forget which way is up.

"Why are you so quiet over there?" Anthony finally asked her. "Is it somewhere else you'd rather be?"

Sharron thought about it and answered his question honestly. "No."

"So why do you seem so quiet now? You don't want to do this?"

Anthony was second-guessing *himself* as well. How badly did Sharron want to be with him? Was her attraction to him real, or just for play? Because sometimes women fell more in love with the *dream* of how a man *could be* instead of accepting who he was at that moment.

"I do and I don't," she answered.

"Would it be better if we waited another month, or another three months, or another *ten months* for that matter? Would it make you feel more . . . respected?" he asked.

"Not necessarily respected, but more comfortable, like I said earlier," she told him.

"Why are you doing this then, if you don't feel 'comfortable' about it?"

She looked Anthony in his face and took in his relaxed mood. He was sure asking a lot of questions for someone so pressed about sex. One would get the impression that he was trying to talk her out of it.

"Do *you* want to do this?" she asked him for the third time. "Because it sure doesn't sound like you're up to convincing me."

He hunched his shoulders. "You're going to do what you want to do regardless."

She was appalled at his insinuation!

"Oh no, don't put this all on me. *You* wanted to have me over to your house. And *you* called me up with this on *your* mind, and not the other way around," she snapped.

"Yeah, but *you* have the power to make this happen or not," he countered. And he was right. "Women always have the power," he added.

"I wouldn't say *always,*" she commented. "Just like you told me never to say *all.*"

"When *don't* they?"

"When they're raped."

Anthony looked at her and frowned. "I'm not talking about rape incidents. I'm talking about consensual stuff."

"Some men rape a woman's mind to make her *think* that it's consensual when it's really not."

"So are you saying that women are that helpless, that they can't make their own decisions, and that men are always mind-controlling them? You think that's what I'm doing with you?"

Where are all of these questions coming from tonight? Sharron asked herself.

"Why all the questions tonight?" she decided to ask him. "I thought *I* was supposed to be the one with all of the questions."

"To tell you the truth, I needed someone to talk to about things tonight. And at the same time, after I talked to you on the phone, I was feeling . . . a little bit horny," he admitted with a smile.

"Okay, so it's *my* fault again, right? It's always the *woman's* fault."

"You was the one talking that 'come and get me' stuff," he reminded her.

"And you were the one who wanted to have me over in the first place," she countered.

"Anyway, I wanted to talk to you, and then I started feeling horny in the process," he reiterated.

Sharron stopped and thought about that. Was her mind and conversation turning him on to sex?

"So, in other words, I guess that I should be flattered. Is that what you're trying to tell me? Because I don't *feel* flattered. Plenty of men are turned on by women *sexually* for all kinds of reasons. And I want to be *more* than just a *turn-on* inside of your *pants*."

He laughed and said, "You are. You just can't see it yet."

"When *will* I see it?"

"I guess when we celebrate *my* birthday," he told her.

Good answer. It projected longevity. Just like *she* had projected on him. Anthony's projection, however, was a lot more unstable. February 8, 2000, was more than eight months away. Anthony had never been in a steady relationship with a woman past five months. They just never lasted that long. Fortunately, she never asked him about it. Sharron, on the other hand, had dated Sean Love for three full years before even graduating from high school. Her stamina was proven.

"You sure you wouldn't be bored with me by then?" she asked Anthony with a smile.

He didn't answer that immediately. How could he?

"I mean, you have to wait and see for something like that. *You* might get bored with *me*," he looked her in the eyes and answered.

"I doubt that," she responded.

"A lot of people doubt things," he countered. "Then they happen."

She nodded. He had a good point.

"Okay, you're right. Maybe I *will* get bored with you. Have you had that happen before?"

"Yeah, plenty of times," he admitted. *They get bored with not being around me as much as they want,* he thought to himself. *Shawntè got bored in three weeks.*

Men could rarely express their every thought to a woman. And despite how much women *claimed* to express to their men, they rarely addressed every thought on their minds either. What kind of impolite world would we have if everyone did? Who knows the scattered, insecure, selfish, disrespectful, hasty thoughts that run through our minds? And who would really want to hear them all? Better yet, what would someone do with that kind of knowledge of us? Men knew, far more than women, it seemed, that knowledge of the conscious mind was indeed power. And they were not willing to give that much power away.

"How did that make you feel when they got bored with you? Were you heartbroken?" Sharron asked. She was thinking again about Sean Love. *He* sure seemed heartbroken. She felt sorry for him. But she still did not want to be with him.

Anthony hunched his shoulders. "Not really. You just move on."

But sometimes you don't want *to move on,* Sharron thought. She was tired of moving on.

"But don't you get tired of that? Just going from one person to the next?" she asked him.

Anthony nodded. He *did* feel tired. But not three years ago when he was in his prime.

"I guess you do get a little worn out from it, yeah. It seems like, the older you get, and the more you mature, the more it starts to get to you. But then, when you try to stop, that shit seems almost impossible." Anthony had been trying to stop his own bed hopping for months, and the months had added up to nearly a year.

"It's just a . . . dick thing, hunh?" Sharron asked him with a smirk.

He smiled back to her. "Yeah. It really is."

And what is his dick going to do to his mind after he gets me, she thought. That's when the lack of confidence sets in. The insecurity. The fear of loving a black man and the effects of his idolized penis.

"Is there such a thing as a *woman's* thing?" she asked him, just for the hell of it.

He answered, "Yeah. Love, and a menstrual cycle."

She smiled even wider. "*Love* is a woman's thing? So you're telling me that men are not capable of love. Do you love your boy Tone? Do you love your mother?" she quickly asked him.

He grinned and said, "Of course I do. But I don't dwell on it. It's a given."

"Women dwell on love?" She knew better than that. Of course they did! A lot more than men. Men dwelled more on success. Not that women didn't care about where they stood in life, they just didn't dwell on it. Success, for many women, was a given. They would simply work hard until they met their goals. Whereas many men seemed to have too many goals and not a smidgen of the work habit that they needed to get there.

Anthony answered, "Yeah. Just listen to the songs that women sing."

"Is something wrong with that? Don't *you* want love?" Sharron asked him.

What a question *that* was. Of course he wanted love! As badly as *she* wanted it. He was just very picky about where that love came from, and where he wanted to give it back. That was a man's dilemma. *If I can only love* one, *then who in the world will that* one *be? His* insecurity was in picking one woman to love out of a hundred. That made a male decision a hell of a lot more crucial than that of a woman, picking one man out of maybe two or three. Because women, on the average, were a lot more selective about who they went out with.

Her question slipped his mind as they pulled up to the parking spot outside his apartment.

"Well, this is where I live," he told her. It was eleven-thirty.

Sharron looked out at the clean, brick-front two-story building and was pleased with it. Even the block that he lived on was peaceful, yet lively enough to never feel alone.

She grabbed her brown bag and climbed out of his car to follow him up to his place on the second floor. She was impressed with the inside as well, a fully furnished and clean apartment.

"So where is your maid?" she joked. She just *knew* that Anthony couldn't be so clean himself. Or maybe he had organized everything specifically for her visit there that night. Then again, his car was always clean. But that was his pride and joy. Could his apartment be an extension of that?

"How long have you had my visit on your mind?" she asked.

He smiled again. "Are you asking me that just because my apartment is clean? What, I'm supposed to be a pig, and can't cook or do dishes or laundry just because I'm a guy?"

"Yeah," she answered.

"I'll ask you this then," he said. "Does my mom seem like the kind of woman who would do all of those things for three boys and a husband? Because she *didn't*. She used to tell us all the time, 'If your narrow ass don't learn how to do it, then it *won't* get done, and it *will* get done! You understand me?! Because every narrow-ass nigga in this house is gonna do it!'"

Sharron could imagine it. She could even see it. She broke out laughing.

"My mom didn't play that shit," Anthony told her. "And I guess that if she had a daughter or two, I could have gotten away with not knowing how to do much. But since she didn't have any daughters, she was like, 'To hell if *I'm* gonna clean up the house behind them every day after I come home from work. I'll kill 'em first!'"

"Your mom used to say that?" Sharron asked incredulously.

"Yeah," Anthony answered. "She meant that shit, too."

Sharron thought about it. "Is your mom really that violent?"

"Yeah."

She laughed again at his candidness.

"So both of your brothers know how to clean and cook?"

"My brothers, *and* my cousins. Or at least the ones who came over our house a lot. They knew the rules."

"But she still couldn't stop your father from cheating," Sharron commented.

"I mean, it's not like he did it in her face," he responded. "She just kept hearing about things floating around in the streets."

"Did she ever try to kill him?"

He smiled. "Plenty of times. That's why he had to leave. You want something to drink?" he asked her, breaking from the subject.

Sharron shook her head. "Not right now, but maybe later."

Anthony walked into the kitchen to serve himself while Sharron looked around in his living room and at the collection of mostly rap CDs. They sat in a CD rack that stood beside his massive stereo system. She was still thinking about his mother and the relationship she had with his father. Her own father was a very loyal man, loyal to his wife to the grave. Then he picked right up with a new woman soon after and became loyal to her. But what kind of man would Anthony be with such a bad example from *his* father. Could *he* be loyal? Ever?

She picked up an empty CD case from the stereo system and looked it over as Anthony walked back into the room with juice in a tall green glass.

"This *Makaveli* CD is old. You still listen to this? You like Tupac Shakur like that?"

Anthony nodded. "I was just listening to it the other day. Tupac was raw, man. He was the truth. And everybody knew it."

"From what I heard, he made up a lot of things," she said as she looked over the artwork of the slain artist/actor/poet/hip-hop activist on an illustrated crucifix.

"Even when he made shit up, it was the truth. Because he wasn't really glorifying nothing. He was just tellin' it like it was."

He wasn't glorifying *anything? Shit, he could have fooled* me *then, with all of that West Coast Gangsta stuff!* she thought with a frown. But she didn't express it. However, she *was* interested in what particular messages Anthony listened to and how they reflected on his life.

"Which one of these songs is your favorite?" she asked him.

"I like the whole album," he answered, taking a seat on his sofa. "But I wouldn't listen to that for me and you."

"Why not?" she asked, curious.

"You don't listen to that with no woman. You listen to Faith, Brandy, or Levert or something."

Sharron smiled. "But this is what *you* listen to."

"I can listen to other things. I have other kinds of music."

"Like what?" she walked over and searched through his CD rack, finding nothing but rap.

"R & B. Movie soundtracks. Slow jams. Oldies. A lot of different things," he answered.

"What's your favorite slow song?" she asked him.

"Ahhh . . . Damn, that's a good one," he commented with a chuckle. "I like a lot of that old Jodeci stuff, when they were still together."

Sharron sucked her teeth. "All of that freaky whinin' and stuff."

Anthony shook his head and smiled. "See, now that's a trip that you even said that. Because women talk all the time about men not expressing themselves. Then when they do, like Jodeci and R. Kelly and them, then we hear women complainin' about them whinin'."

"Because they *are* whinin'," she said with another laugh. "You can sing without doing that. Look at Boyz II Men. They *sing,* they don't *whine.*"

With that, Anthony sucked *his* teeth. "Aw, girl, they can't even write their own music. That's Babyface's stuff."

"They *did* write their own music on their last album."

"Yeah, the one that didn't sell nothin'."

"Whatever."

"Name one of their songs from that last album," he asked her.

Her mind went blank because she hadn't listened to it in a while.

"That's what I thought," Anthony said before she had a chance to come up with a song.

"So is that what you want to listen to while we make love?" he asked, shocking her. She smiled and took it in stride.

"'I'll Make Love to You.' That was one of their latest songs," she said, referring to Boyz II Men.

"I don't have them. Pick something else."

"I wasn't talking about us. I was just naming a song."

Anthony looked at his watch. "It's getting late. I only have until one o'clock, right? That's what you told me."

Sharron's heart started to beat. *Here goes nothing,* she told herself. She spotted the bathroom. "I'll be back," she said, heading inside with her brown bag of things in hand.

Inside the bathroom, she pulled out a green satin chemise and proceeded to undress. "I don't even know why I'm putting this thing on," she mumbled. "Men don't care about any damn outfits. They just want to get to what's under them. I should just walk out of here wearing nothing."

Then again, wearing nothing wasn't exactly her style. Not that she was ashamed of her body, because she wasn't. She was tall, lean, and well curved in all the right places. She just didn't want to seem too blunt about things. Wearing a green satin chemise with no panties and bra was blunt enough.

She sprayed a small can of vanilla-flavored mist around her most sensitive parts: neck, shoulders, breasts, and inner thighs. Then she added the final touch with cherry-flavored lip gloss to kiss him with.

She took a deep breath, grabbed the door handle, and mumbled again, "Here goes nothing," as she walked out. But instead of returning to the living room, she walked straight into Anthony's dark bedroom.

He followed her in and said, "I like the color. It looks good on you."

"Thank you," she said awkwardly. Anthony was still fully dressed, right on down to his shoes. "Should I climb under the covers and wait for you to join me?" she asked.

He chuckled at the idea. "Yeah," he told her. "You do that." Then he began to undress.

As Sharron pulled back his covers and climbed inside, she couldn't help but imagine how many other women had been there. It soured her mood immediately. She felt so disturbed by it that she thought of climbing right back out and returning to his living room. She would rather go to the floor than use a bed that may have held up to thirty other women.

"How many other women have been in this same spot?" she couldn't stop herself from asking.

Anthony couldn't believe it. She would ask questions right down to the last second. She would probably even ask him questions during the act. By then, he planned on flat-out ignoring her.

"If you don't want to do this, I understand," he said, tired of it all. She was wearing him the hell out! But he still wanted her, especially since he was finally so close to the sweetness.

"I'm asking you too many questions again?"

"Yeah," he told her, dropping the last piece of his clothing and standing butt naked before her. Sharron liked what she saw. A lot! Every raw, brown, muscular inch of him.

"I just want to ask one more question," she said, pleased with the sight of him.

"Aw'ight, go ahead and get it over with," he snapped, still standing naked before her like a silhouette in the darkness. It was almost as if he were showing off, striking a black naked Superman pose that made her laugh.

"What's so damn funny?" He failed to find anything humorous. He was too ready for the naked dance of life.

"Nothing," she said, holding her thoughts to herself.

"Well, what is your last question? And remember, you told me this was the last one."

"I know that," she responded. "I just wanted to ask you if you had any protection."

Anthony calmed himself and smiled. "Reach under that pillow behind you," he told her.

Sharron looked at him quizzically and searched behind the pillow, pulling out two attached Sheik condoms. Anthony began to chuckle at her reaction.

"I don't find that funny," she told him. "Now did you put them there tonight, or do you always have them there?"

"Actually," he said through his laughter, "I put them there while you were in the bathroom."

"Is that the truth or another lie?"

"It's the truth. I don't lie about small things like that."

"Oh, you just lie about big bad things," Sharron countered his hasty words.

He shook his head and frowned. "Didn't you just say you only had one more question?"

"One question can lead to many. Especially in *your* case," she told him.

He said, "Do you want me to climb in there and warm you up real quick or what? Let me know."

"Real quick?" she questioned. "How long do you expect this thing to last?"

He looked at his clock on the nightstand. "You told me I have until one o'clock, right?"

"Why do you keep saying that?"

"Because that's what you said. Then I have to get up and take you back home for work in the morning after you get your eight hours of sleep."

"Are you telling me that you actually listen to everything I say? What if I told you that we can't do this until I have a ring for marriage."

Anthony just stared at her. "What?"

"That's what I thought," she told him. "Come on, get in. I definitely don't want you to just stand there with no clothes on."

"Why, is it turning you on?"

She smiled and was speechless.

"Yeah, that's what I thought," he said, mocking her as he approached the bed.

When he slid inside the covers, she huffed, "Damn, you're warm. Do you have a fever or something?" as his body met with hers.

"I have a fever all right. A fever for the . . ." He never finished his statement, deciding better of it.

"A fever for the what?" she asked.

"That's about four questions past your limit now."

"What limit?"

"The limit that you set for yourself," he told her as he felt his way around under the sheets. "No panties or bra on. Interesting," he commented with a smile.

"What did you think?" she asked him. "And what if I walked out of the bathroom butt naked?"

"That wouldn't have surprised me. Or maybe with *you* it would have. Because you don't seem that bold."

"You're right. Because I'm not," she answered.

Anthony quickly slid under the covers without another word and began to moisten her nipples with his teasing tongue. Sharron contemplated whether to caress him, deciding that she would not, just to see what his response would be. Did guys really want a woman's involvement, or could she simply lay there like a Barbie doll that needed to be moved and positioned every step of the way.

"What's wrong?" he asked, sensing her limpness.

"Nothing. It feels good."

"Well, shit, I can't tell," he pouted.

"Do you need me to tell you?"

"Yeah, and in some way. Body, mind, voice, or *something!* Damn! Don't just sit there."

"Would it disturb you if I wasn't really into that, you know, responding to it?" she asked him.

"If that were the case, you wouldn't be human," he snapped, climbing back up to face her.

"Some people *do* have that problem. They just don't feel anything," she said. However, she was *not* one of them. Sharron felt *everything!* Nevertheless, it was more mental than physical for her, as it was with many women. But the physical still had to be workable.

Anthony rolled over on his back and said, "Yeah, I know what you mean. With some people, you just want to get it over with as soon as possible. Then with others, you don't want that shit to stop."

"You would do a woman and want it to end. Why? Because you just wanted to get a nut?" she asked him candidly.

"Basically. Yeah."

"So, what is it with me?"

He sighed. *I just can't fuckin' win with this girl! Why am I even goin' through all of this?* he asked himself.

"I don't know what it is with you. Sometimes I just wish that you would shut the hell up and enjoy my damn company for a change," he told her.

"I do enjoy your company," she responded, smiling. "Because trust me, if I *didn't,* I wouldn't ask you *half* as many questions, and I *damn* sure wouldn't want to spend entire days with you."

He thought about that for a minute.

"You want to spend entire days with me?" he asked. It wasn't as if other women didn't.

"We already have. And I wasn't bored for one minute. Were you?" she asked him.

Surprisingly he wasn't. He wasn't bored with her either, even with her irritating quiz games.

"Naw," he told her. "And that's the truth," he said before she asked. "I don't lie *that* much. In fact, I should have never said that to you, because it don't even really apply to you. You ask too many questions to lie," he added with a laugh. "For a guy to lie to you, he would have to lie on about five different levels."

Sharron relaxed and touched him, the rough ripples of his abdomen, the bulging curves of his chest, and the smooth swivel and dip inside his hips.

"You're turning me on again," he told her with a grin. "I just wanted to let you know that in advance."

"That's what I'm here to do, right?" she leaned over and asked him with a greedy kiss.

"Mmm-hmm," he mumbled through her lips. "Exactly."

"As long as I turn you on in the mind, too," she leaned back and reiterated to him.

"You do."

"Do I?" she asked, caressing him with her soft hands.

"Yes. I told you that."

She searched again for the condoms under the pillow and took one out for him to slip on, while asking him something else.

"Am I gonna regret this?" Simultaneously, she lowered herself upon him and connected her puzzle to his.

Anthony stared up at the empty ceiling and breathed, "Naw."

Sharron proceeded to give him the moment, but definitely not her all until she was sure that she could keep him, piece by piece. However, her confidence in him and in herself was still on shaky ground. So while Anthony fully enjoyed *himself* on their first night of bliss, Sharron faked it, filled with too many thoughts on her mind to let herself go. Thoughts about longevity and the vulnerability of making so many decisions where you seemed to have so little control over the final results.

Fear, like confidence, is a very mental thing based on *personal* perceptions. Some people seem to fear nothing, but that is only a perception as well. *All* humans fear *something*. It's a built-in condition. A fear of the dark. A fear of monsters. A fear of death, loneliness, tragedy, poverty, and the ultimate fear of losing control over the elements of your life to a woman. Men feared that *dearly!* They wanted to lose themselves to a woman, but fear like the devil the prospect of unleashing their emotions to a woman who may be untrue. That became Ant's dilemma. The closer he got to Sharron, the more he began to fear her.

"You know I was high that night on the phone, dawg. I ain't mean to dis your girl like that," Tone said, apologizing to his partner at a north St. Louis park.

It was a perfect night as they sat out on top of a wooden bench. Ant was daydreaming about his new treasure, Sharron Francis, who was more pleasurable than he ever thought she would be.

"You hear me, Ant," Tone said, pressing for forgiveness.

It was no big deal to Ant. They had crossed each other and regained their friendship plenty of times. That's what friends are for. How else can you make friendship last for twenty years?

"I'm not worried about that, man," Ant finally responded to him. "But you can't come to my job no more for lunchtime and shit now."

Tone looked puzzled. "What the hell that got to do with anything?"

"My boss called like two minutes after I hung up on you. I thought it was you and said the wrong things. So that led to conclusions, and he said that if you came near the job anymore, and you happened to be high, he'd fire my ass on the spot and have you arrested."

Ant said this all as a matter of fact.

Tone snapped, "Man, fuck him!" Since he knew that Ant was loyal to his job, he planned on leaving it alone. But he couldn't.

"What do you think about that?" he asked Ant.

"It won't make no difference with your new job. You won't be down there to see me anyway."

"I bet he don't say that shit about them white boys that come up there to the shop."

Ant shook his head. "Don't make it no black and white thing, man. Just go on about your life."

"Yeah, I would have told that motherfucker something if *I* was you."

"If you was me, you would have done the same damn thing I'm doing now; tell your boy to stay away from the job. That's all. 'Cause I gotta get paid."

Tone grimaced. "Aw, man, it ain't like he got the only repair shop in the damn city."

"Yeah, but I don't want to mess up a good thing over some stupid shit."

"Whatever, man. It sounds like he playin' you like a damn fool. Racist ma-fucka'."

"If he was so racist, he would have never hired me in the first place."

"Naw, if you didn't know what you were *doing* he wouldn't have hired you," Tone responded. "He knew what he was doin' when he hired you. You one of the best mechanics in St. Louis. Fuck that! You could even run your own shop, and I could set up your appointments for you."

Ant laughed and said, "Yeah, man, just stick to that carpet cleaning business."

Tone chuckled to himself and decided to change the subject.

"What's up with Sharron? Or you don't want me to ask about her no more?" he questioned.

"Why do you ask about her so much anyway?" Ant asked him back.

"Because I'm jealous," Tone admitted.

Ant laughed at his blunt honesty.

Tone said, "Seriously, man. I can't even lie about that shit. I wish it was *me* that had her. Your ass don't even care about the girl. Or maybe you *do* care about her after you hung up on me like that," he added with a laugh. "You sounded pissed than a ma-fucka'."

"I *was* pissed. And I *do* like her. That's my girl, man," Ant said with a grin.

"Oh, she your girl now? You must have fucked her then," Tone responded. "What it feel like? What she taste like?"

Ant stopped and shook his head. "Here you go with that crazy shit again. I don't even think I wanna talk about her with you anymore. She's off-limits."

"Off-limits? You sound like you try'na make her your wife. You looked at any rings yet?" Tone joked.

"Come on, man. Change the subject."

One of the neighborhood park hangers walked over to the bench to speak with an extended hand. "Hey, Ant. Haven't seen you around here lately. What's up, dawg?"

"Yeah, well, some people gotta work every day," Ant responded with a handshake.

The park hanger with sagging blue jeans, a white tank top, and a marijuana joint rolled behind his right ear, didn't appear to enjoy his statement.

"So what you sayin'?" he asked.

"I'm sayin' exactly what I said."

Tone stared the beef down, and the park hanger decided to blow off his steam elsewhere.

"You need to check your boy, Tone," he said, walking off to a more crowded section of the park.

Tone was speechless. He addressed Ant after the scene was clear again.

"You could make yourself a little more friendly when you come around here, man. They already don't like you around here. Seem like you had too many girls in this area," he added with a chuckle.

"What am I supposed to do, man? Come around here and smoke a few joints and shoot the breeze. I don't have time for that shit. It's almost the year 2000. I'm starting to think about buying houses and raisin' kids."

Tone looked at him surprised. "Oh yeah? You been thinkin' 'bout that?"

Ant had discussed it all with Tone before. Tone just hadn't paid him any attention at the time.

"I'm *dead* serious, man. We 'bout to turn thirty in a couple of years. *You* before me. Don't *you* think about that shit?"

Tone smiled and started laughing. "I was thinkin' 'bout that the night you hung the hell up on me. I was tellin' myself, 'The next fine girl I get with, I'm gon' fuck her raw and drop a bomb on her.'"

Ant frowned at the idea. "Aw, man, you crazy. You ain't goin' out like that. We ain't been using rubbers all this long to just start shootin' missiles in the ocean. I already got two loose nieces and a nephew from my brothers goin' out like that. And Rico got *three* loose kids."

"Like you said, dawg, I'm gettin' old, and I ain't got nothin' with my name on it yet," Tone responded.

"What, you thinkin' 'bout marrying somebody, too?"

"Why the hell not?" Tone answered. "That way *my* kids won't be loose. And I'd get me a girl that got a nice job and her own money, and just turn her ass out in bed. It's plenty of working girls out here looking for some good meat to keep."

Ant just laughed. Tone made no sense at all. Even when he was sober.

"You ain't thought about busting one in Sharron yet?" he asked his friend.

Tough question. Ant actually *did* think about it. He wondered what the consequences would be: how she would respond to it, how he would respond to her, and where they would go from there.

"I told you, man, she's off-limits," he repeated.

Tone looked through the night lights of the park and saw too many of the wrong people gathering.

"Hey, man, let's take a ride in your car," he said. Not that he was intimidated by anyone. He just didn't want any unnecessary disputes to break out in the park with Ant. He loved his partner too much to mix him with crowds that Ant had consciously stayed away from.

"You wanna ride back up to the old 'hood in Jennings?" Ant asked, reminiscing.

Tone smiled and said, "Yeah, let's do that." They stood up and walked to the car.

Once they were headed farther north to Jennings, Ant said, "I was out this way for Sharron's birthday last week, and I messed around and took her to the crib to introduce her to my mom. That shit was funny."

"I thought you told me she's off-limits," Tone cracked.

"Man, fuck that, I feel like talkin' 'bout her," Ant snapped defiantly.

Tone grinned. "I knew you would talk about her before the night was over. You can't hold no shit like that to yourself. So let it all out."

"Yeah, well, anyway, my mom was in there tellin' Sharron that my pop was a player. And she asked *me* about that."

"And what you say to her?"

"You know me, man, I dodged the question. All men got a little player in them. Even loyal guys. They just too scared to admit it."

They laughed loud like two young and free men would.

"She asked you to go steady with her yet?" Tone joked.

"*Go steady?* What, you been watching *90210* or something? Naw, she ain't asked me no shit like that."

"What she been kickin' to you? I know she got some kind of plans for you. *All* women do."

Ant nodded and thought about it. Plans. "You know, she ain't really pressed the issue on that yet. But I know it's coming."

"Did you fuck her yet?" Tone asked him again.

"Come on, man. Stop that shit."

"Well, tell me then and get it over with."

"That ain't gon' get it over with. 'Cause then you gon' ask me how it felt."

Tone laughed, admitting it. "So you *did* fuck her then," he responded, putting two and two together.

Ant ignored him with a telling smile.

"Was it good?" Tone asked for the hell of it.

They broke out laughing again, until tears came to their eyes.

"You know you always tell me, man. So go ahead and do it," Tone pressed him. "Come on, dawg, get it over with."

"What, you just want to hear me say it? It sounds like you know it already," Ant commented.

Realizing it was the truth, that his partner had scored once more, Tone went silent, feeling jealous and lonely again.

He said, "Damn, man. Sometimes at night, I just wake up with a hard dick, and it be nobody there to do anything about it."

Ant smiled and said, "That happens to everybody. Especially after a few drinks on the weekends. I've been there before. Plenty of times."

"Yeah, and then you call somebody up and take care of it. I call bitches up, and they be like, 'Tone who?'"

Ant laughed but had to stop himself.

He said, "That's why it's always good to keep a home base, man. Somebody you can always call. That's why I ended up gettin' Sharron when I did. I didn't have Shawntè anymore, and I didn't feel like calling up no old girls. That would have been boring as hell."

"Yeah, I know what you mean. But boring is better than nothin'," Tone commented.

"Is it though? I mean, think about it. If guys wasn't bored, we wouldn't need so many girls in the first place. 'Cause I get bored *fast*."

"Are you bored with Sharron yet?" Tone asked him.

Ant smiled. "Naw. Not yet."

"But you think that you will be?"

Ant paused. "I can't really say, you know. She asked me that same question, and I told her the same thing. We just gotta wait and see."

"What if she fuck around and get bored with you first?" Tone joked.

Ant smiled again. "That's what I asked her. And she said that it was impossible."

"*Impossible?* She said that? Damn! She really into you then."

"What girls are not? Even Dana was lovin' me when I had her," Ant bragged.

"And you fucked it all up," Tone responded.

"No I didn't, man. You just don't understand. You can't keep no girls like her. She don't know what the hell she want. All she'll do is drive a ma-fucka' crazy. I feel sorry for the guy who ends up with her."

"I just wish he was me," Tone responded with a grin.

By that time, they were cruising the familiar Florissant Avenue, where Ant recognized a house on a corner that held too short of a sweet memory for him.

"Remember that girl Leanna Brady used to live there?" he asked Tone, pointing to the house.

"Yeah, I remember her. She was pretty as hell!"

"She said that she would be my girl right before her pop moved her ass to Denver. You remember that?" Ant asked.

Tone said, "Aw, man, we was like eleven and twelve years old. So what? That wasn't nothin' but puppy love."

"No it wasn't either," Ant snapped. "She said she was gon' write me and she never did. I was asking my mom for mail for weeks."

Tone broke out laughing.

Ant said, "That shit wasn't funny, man. I used to go to sleep *dreaming* about that girl. And every time the Denver Broncos came on TV, I used to change the damn channel. My brothers was like, 'What the hell is wrong with you?! That's John Elway!' And I was like, 'Forget John Elway! I *hate* Denver!'"

The hard laugh brought more tears to Tone's eyes.

"She probably lost your damn address, man," he said through his laughter.

Ant made a U-turn and drove back to take another look at the house.

Tone said, "What are you doin', man? She's gone, dawg. You can't bring her back."

Ant reflected on those lonely nights he spent as a young boy anyway, where he prayed to the stars at night to send him a letter in the mail from Leanna. It was a letter that never came. And he was crushed. So crushed that he never wanted that disappointment to happen to him again. *Ever!* And although women believe that men forget everything, they *do* remember *some* things.

"Yeah, I thought about getting Sharron pregnant," Ant admitted, making another U-turn on Florissant. "I thought about it with a lot of girls. I just wasn't stupid enough to do it."

Tone nodded and said, "Yeah, I know what you mean. I had to pay for two abortions."

Ant was surprised as ever. He faced his friend and said, "You never told me that."

"I know. I was too embarrassed to tell you. And I ain't want no kids if you didn't have none," Tone responded. "I was real young back then, man. But now that I think about it, that shit didn't make no sense. And both of them girls are married now with children. Ain't that a bitch?"

"How do you know that? You stayed in touch with them?"

"Naw, man, this was years ago. One girl was two years older than me. Last I heard, she moved with her husband to Texas somewhere. The other one hooked up with this dude right after she broke up with me and got pregnant by him. I guess she *wanted* a baby."

"Damn!" Ant exclaimed. "And you never told me that." He shook his head, still finding it hard to believe. Not that Tone had gotten two girls pregnant, but that he had never told him about it. Boys told each other *everything*. Especially boys like Tone. Or at least Ant *thought* that they did.

He shook it off and said, "But that's what I mean, man. Time is movin' on. I think about that more and more now. I've been tellin' you that for months."

"I know," Tone conceded. "It's just now startin' to sink in on me. Every girl I call now got something else going on. You kind of think that their world stops as soon as you stop calling them, but it don't."

Ant nodded, agreeing with it. "Dana claim that *she* in love now, too. And I *still* can't believe that shit," he commented.

They rode around until late at night, reminiscing on the girls they'd had and the ones who'd slipped away. Then they discussed what kind of a woman they both hoped to have for themselves in the future. But when it was time for Ant to head back in, the only woman *he* could think of was Sharron, and her two hundred questions. That scared the hell out of him. Because sometimes, we actually get what we really want. We get what we really need. Then many of us choke up and drop the ball, scared straight, and not really knowing how to handle the pressure.

Pressure can make us think and do the most ridiculous things. Things that make you stop and say, "What the hell was I thinking?" Of course, that statement is usually uttered well after the fact, and when the pressure is long gone. But in the process of the act, when the heat is still on, we make our moves, and therefore, we must learn to live with them. Yet, learning to live with our mistakes is a hard thing to do. And when embarrassing or hasty decisions are made under pressure, many of us try and run from them. We form attitudes to distance ourselves from these mistakes, while making up excuses, or simply trying to move on without facing the music that we previously chose to dance to.

Sharron felt embarrassed and insecure about even continuing a relationship with Anthony. Or whatever it was that they had, because they had never bothered to officially define it. And why was she so insecure? Because she *didn't* have *"plans"* for where they were supposed to go *or* how they were supposed to get there. She had planned things in her relations with black men before, and they had never worked out. Now she had gone ahead and slept with a new one, and she didn't quite know what to do about him yet. What women did? Love was supposed to be a great big accident waiting to happen. Or was it?

Do we just continue like we've been doing? Will he back away now that we did something? Or will he only call me now to get some more? she asked herself, second-guessing all of the way.

Unbelievable! The position that men were able to put women in after the first time. So without wanting to, Sharron found herself becoming standoffish with Anthony, like other women had become with *their* insecurities. And they had all lost that way, under pressure of a broken heart, in the mix of confusion with a free man. No wonder Anthony only talked about pieces. He wanted to remain free from the get go. Free forever.

"It's Anthony," Celena said, pulling the phone into Sharron's room.

Sharron sighed and reached out for it.

Celena noticed her displeasure and placed her hand over the receiver.

"What, you don't want to talk to him? I'll tell him to call you back. All you have to do is say the word."

Sharron hadn't told her roommate anything. Celena was just a pro at getting rid of hassles, particularly *male* hassles.

"No, I'll talk to him," Sharron told her.

"Okay, well, we'll talk about this later then," Celena commented.

"Great," Sharron huffed, sarcastically. *That's just what I need right now, an I-told-you-so talk with you,* she thought.

She held the phone to her ear and faked contentedness.

"How are you?" she asked.

"I'm fine. How 'bout you?"

"I'm okay."

Silence. What a dry conversation. It was that way after the first time for a *whole* lot of women.

Anthony began to laugh, breaking some of their unusual ice.

"What's so funny?" Sharron asked.

"I know what you're thinkin', and it ain't even like that," he told her.

"What are you talking about?" she asked.

Anthony said, "You're feeling like what we had was the beginning to the end. And it's not."

"Why would I even think that way?" Sharron countered. "It sounds like you're telling on yourself. Is that how *you* were thinking, that it was the beginning to the end?"

Anthony paused far too long for it to be a positive. He was usually fast on the draw. But it's funny how your gun gets stuck in the most important battles, the ones you want the most.

"Can you handle the truth?" he finally asked her.

"I've *been* handling it, haven't I?"

"Yeah, so far."

"Well, how much more *truth* do you have? Or in other words, how many more *lies* do I have to see through?"

"About a hundred or two," he joked. "Naw, seriously. Everything is all right between us."

"Everything meaning what?"

"You know, how we feel about each other."

"And how *do* we feel?" she asked, breaking his back.

"We still both like each other, right?"

"Why wouldn't we, unless we didn't expect to?"

Anthony broke out laughing again.

"*You* sure haven't changed with all of your damn questions, that's for sure," he commented.

Sharron finally cracked a smile and loosened up. She realized how petty she was becoming. Why give him that much power over her because of a one-night sleepover? It was silly. He didn't own her just because of one night. Nor did she own him. Take it like it was, and go back to being yourself, the girl who sparked his curiosity in the first place. Exhale. Men don't like uptight women. Women don't like uptight men.

"So did you tell your friend yet?" she asked him, still smiling.

"Did you tell Celena?"

"No."

"Okay, well, you got me on that then. But I didn't just come out and say it. It was like he already knew."

"She knows too. She just hasn't said anything to me yet. But she will after I hang up."

He asked, "Have you ever thought about having your own apartment somewhere?"

"Of course. But I had no reason to do it."

"What about for your private space?"

"What, so we can take showers together, and then lay around the apartment butt naked all day?" she teased.

He chuckled. "That's my girl. Use that imagination."

That's my girl? she thought to herself. *Hmm!*

"What do you call me when you talk to your friend?"

Anthony was full of giggles that night. That was a good sign, because coldness could have meant distance and resistance. Every woman in the world wanted nothing but closeness after the first time with her new man. Closeness after *every* time.

"Believe it or not, I just started calling you 'my girl,'" he answered her.

"Oh, and you had to wait until you got some before you could do that, hunh?"

"Yup," he piped. "That's the way it goes."

"So, when can I start calling you 'my man'? And why can't you call me your *lady* or something? Why do we always have to be 'girls'?"

Anthony thought about that and agreed to it. "Aw'ight, I see what you're saying. Okay, *my lady*. Does that make you feel better?"

"Yes, it does. Now what do you want *me* to call *you?*"

He hesitated. "You can call me your man."

Sharron chuckled and shook her head against the phone. She could hear the uncertainty in his voice.

"Are you sure? I don't want to make you feel uncomfortable about it. I know how leery guys can get when talking about relationships."

He laughed it off. "We talk about relationships. We just don't do it around *y'all*."

"I know," Sharron countered with a grin. "Because all I ever hear are guys talking about sex, sports, and rap music, all day long. And, oh yeah, makin' money."

"Well, that money gotta be made. So don't act like it ain't important. Because as long as we livin' in America, *it is*."

"As long as it's not the most important thing," Sharron stated.

"What are the most important things to you?" he asked her.

Good question.

She said, "Hmm, let me think about that. Well, I have to be attracted to you number one."

"That's more superficial than money. What if I was a beautiful guy *inside* with an ugly-ass face?" Anthony asked.

"You'd be shit out of luck. And I'm just being honest."

"Damn. Is that what they teach y'all down in Tennessee? I thought you'd go for any man who was good to you."

"Not hardly. We *all* have our images of who we'd like to be with. I know *you* do. And I do too."

"What's after the attraction part?" he asked her.

"Respect. Because you can't allow yourself to be with someone who doesn't respect you."

"True, true, I can agree with that.

"Then what, honesty and loyalty and all that?" Anthony asked as if he had heard it all before. He had. Most guys had heard it before when they were willing to listen.

Sharron caught on to his sarcasm. "And what's so wrong with those things, since you're being so smart about it?" she asked.

"Nothing. I mean, I guess they all apply."

"What's important to you then, outside of good sex?" Sharron assumed that "good sex" would be *high* on any guy's list. And it was. It just wasn't as high as many women *thought*.

"Ahh, I'd say that dedication was pretty high with me. Because I need a woman who can stick it out with me, no matter what. Like on that Tupac album you asked me about, *Makaveli*. He got this one song called 'Just Like Daddy,' where he says, 'When I'm dirt broke and fucked up, you *still* love me!'"

Sharron sucked her teeth and said, "Yeah, that's typical of a guy. But y'all won't do the same for us. If I wrote a song talkin' about 'When I'm fat as a cow and can't see my feet, you're still sweet,' most guys wouldn't want to hear that."

Anthony had to hold the phone away from his mouth he laughed so hard.

"You trippin'," he told her.

"But that's the truth though. Tell me it's not."

"You *will* get fat like that when you're pregnant."

"I'm talking about *after* the babies."

"Well, you gotta stay in shape. That ain't *my* fault."

"And it ain't *our* fault when guys lose their damn jobs. You gotta get back out there and get another one."

"I'm not ever gonna be without a job. I got too many skills for that," Anthony countered. "As long as we all drive cars, I'm *staying* employed. Trust me! I'm just saying that it's good to know that a woman has your back through whatever."

"But we always have. Guys just make it extremely hard for us to keep forgiving them." *Like your mother told me about your father,* Sharron thought to herself.

"So, you tellin' me that you never cut a guy loose, and said, 'Fuck 'im'?"

Sharron thought of Sean Love and declined to comment.

"Yeah, that's what I thought," Anthony said, confident in what he knew about women.

"So, how many kids would you want?" she asked with a grin, deciding to change the subject.

"Like twelve of 'em?" he answered for effect.

"*Twelve?* Well, how many wives you plan on having? Because *nobody's* thinking about having *that* many kids anymore. The baby boom era is *long* gone!"

"Naw, I'd probably be cool with three or four."

Sharron nodded, wondering if she should tell him about her mother's other children, who didn't make it. Then she decided that she would.

"I would have been the middle child of three myself," she said.

"So what happened? Don't tell me you had brothers and sisters who died at birth or something."

"One did. A stillbirth. The other one died in the crib."

Anthony was silent. He felt for her.

"Damn. It sounds like you had a rough life. How do you feel about all of that?"

"I mean, what can I do about it? I'm still here, so I gotta keep living."

"Yeah, you do," he told her. "Did your parents talk about it much?"

"No. Not really. But we did talk about my mom's cancer when she had it."

At that point, Anthony wanted to match her pain with something of his own to let her know that the world wasn't all peaches and cream for him and his family.

"When one of my older brothers went to jail a few years ago for car theft, my mom said, 'I'll see you when you get out.' We all thought that she was joking, but she wasn't. She didn't talk to him or answer his letters until he came out. They haven't really been close ever since. So I said to myself, 'I ain't never going to jail if my mom won't even write or come to see me.' But I think my pop had a lot to do with that, you know. My mom was just tired of extending herself. That's why I talk about dedication like I do. I need a woman who got your back through *anything*. That shit is important to me. Because you only live once. And it's a lonely-ass world out here."

What a happy day the morning brings to a woman who knows that her man is still with her. Sharron didn't even have to avoid the drill sergeant routine with Celena. By the time she got off the phone with Anthony, her roommate had been unconscious and in la-la-land for three hours already.

To top things off, Sharron received a surprise phone call from Anthony while she was at work that afternoon.

"You want another ride home tonight?" he asked her.

She smiled. "Are you gonna be on time again?"

"I'm always on time. You don't know that by now? You can count on me," he assured her.

And she believed him, because he *had* been accountable. Or at least so far. A lot of men were accountable in the beginning.

"Well, I get off at eight o'clock again. You can meet me at the pick-up entrance. But I might be a little late tonight, like eight-fifteen. Okay?"

"As long as eight-fifteen doesn't turn into eight-thirty."

"What if it does?" she asked, just out of curiosity.

"You don't want to know," he warned her.

"Okay, well, I'll see you then."

As soon as Sharron hung up the phone, the young cashier Nadine was all up in her face.

"You gettin' a ride home tonight?" she asked, grinning.

Sharron thought of telling her, "No! Mind your damn business and grow the hell up!" Instead, she said, "Yes," and went back to her work.

However, some people don't know how to take hints. Nadine walked out from behind the cashier's booth and right up into Sharron's face for more girl talk.

"Do you know what I found out about my man?" she asked.

No I don't and nor do I care, Sharron thought.

Nadine proceeded to tell her anyway.

"I found out that he has an ex-wife and three kids, and one of his kids is with some woman he was seeing in East St. Louis."

"*Was* seeing?" Sharron couldn't help but ask.

"He says he's not seeing her anymore. But he *does* see his son. Do you think he's lying? *I* think he's lying," Nadine said.

"And you're probably right," Sharron told her, pointing back to the register where customers were gathering.

"I'll talk to you about this later."

No you won't either, Sharron mused with a sigh. Nadine was really beginning to test her patience. *Maybe I need to find something else to do when she finishes with these customers, because I am just about ready to tell her ass off in here!*

"Everything's okay on this end?" Sharron's boss asked, appearing from the busy airport crowd. Brenda, in her late forties, was a kind, brown woman with three daughters like Celena's family.

Everything but this ridiculous cashier of yours, Sharron thought. She'd been there when Brenda gave Nadine the job. A surrogate-mother thing could be a blessing, because Nadine definitely needed some guidance, just *not* at the expense of Sharron's daily peace of mind.

"Yeah, things are pretty much in order," she answered. "I just have two more shelves to stock."

"Good. How is Nadine doing?" Brenda asked, taking a look at her new employee at the register doing her natural flirting thing.

"She's ah, taking care of business," Sharron answered, biting her tongue.

Brenda watched Nadine for a second from the distance and shook her head. "Boy, she has a way with men, doesn't she? Smiling all the way."

She does a lot more than that, Sharron thought. "Yeah, she does get her kicks in here," she responded.

"Well, let me know if you need anything." Just like that, Brenda vanished back into the traffic inside the airport terminal's hallways.

At quitting time at eight o'clock that evening, and after being dodged for the majority of the day, there was Nadine again, getting off work with Sharron.

"So, I guess I get to see what your man looks like tonight," she commented.

Out of competitive instincts, Sharron took a peek at the younger woman's fully rounded behind and was through with her.

"Why are you so interested in my man?" she asked with plenty of attitude. Some people can get right under your skin and make you say and do things that you don't want to.

"I'm just being nosy. I didn't mean anything by it," Nadine answered, visibly shaken.

Sharron shook her head, let out a sigh, and calmed herself down. "Okay, it's just been a long day, and we both need some space right about now," she said.

"No problem," Nadine responded with a hint of spice of her own.

Nevertheless, the young woman still found a way of arriving at the pick-up entrance when Anthony pulled around in his '79 Chevy.

Sharron hopped into his car with a bone to pick.

"That damn girl is getting on my *fuckin'* last nerve!"

Anthony took in her angry mood and smiled it off. "Who you talkin' about?"

"You know who I'm talking about. That damn girl waiting outside with the big, fat ass! And I *know* you looked at her, so don't even try to deny it."

Anthony could only laugh. He *did* see that whopping behind on her. How could he not? The girl seemed to be displaying it for all lookers, knowing full well the power that it held over black men.

"What's wrong with you?" Anthony asked, still chuckling as he pulled off.

Sharron ignored him. The pressure of female competition was astonishing.

"I don't know if this will make you feel any better, but big asses are only a *sexual* turn-on," Anthony commented. "You already told me that you want to be *more* than that, right? Well, when girls have asses like hers, it makes it hard to concentrate on anything else. So they end up using more of their bodies and less of their minds. It's the same thing with them six-foot-four, two-hundred-twenty-pound guys. They ain't all that bright a lot of times," he added with a smile.

It made Sharron feel better immediately, and she agreed with his assessment.

"I remember I went out with this guy when I first started working at the airport, and all he talked about was his chest size and biceps and how he liked to work out. I was thinking, 'So what? I can see that you're built already. God! Talk about something else.'"

"You know what I noticed about you?" Anthony noted.

"What?"

"You seem to hold back a lot of stuff on your mind from other people, but then you say anything that you want *to me.* I noticed that shit."

Sharron broke out laughing. He was on point. She *did* say a lot more to him. She was in an Anthony Poole zone, and she had forced herself to be as up-front with him as she could.

"That's true," she admitted.

"Why is that? You started off that way with me ever since that night at the skating rink."

She thought about it. Then she told him, "You just caught me at a time when I was fed up with the games that guys play. So I said hell, since I know it's all a game, then I might as well play it too."

"In other words, you really didn't expect much out of me. You was just playing along."

"Well, not exactly. I mean, I *did* want to ask you what you meant in the car that day. You got me with that one."

Anthony smiled and said, "Yeah, and now you won't let me forget."

"That's one that I'll probably tell our kids about," Sharron added.

WHAT?! . . .

Anthony didn't express it with words, but the shock was written all over his face. Then he just smiled, feeling a slight tingle in his pants.

Sharron smiled it off herself. "I don't even know why I said that," she commented.

Anthony nodded. "That's just what I'm talking about," he said. "Anything comes out of your mouth to me."

"Well, it's *your* fault," she said with a grin.

"*My* fault? How is it *my* fault?"

Because you got me open like that, she thought to herself as they drove down Lindbergh Boulevard and headed south from the airport exit.

"So, where are we going?" she asked him. "Or are you just trying to get me home again?"

"Naw. I'm thinking about ice cream," he answered.

She smiled and said, "Oh, so you're gonna try and bribe me with an ice-cream cone first. Am I that cheap to you?"

Anthony shook his head. "There you go again."

"Well, if it bothers you so much, then why do you put up with it?"

Good question.

Anthony thought about that. Long! *I guess you got me open like that,* he thought. But instead of telling her his real thoughts, he answered, "I don't know."

Sharron smiled again, realizing the truth. He liked her. She was feeling more confident about Anthony by the second, like a cat carrying her kittens back to safety. He was almost hers.

They stopped off on Page Boulevard, halfway to her apartment in University City, and had ice-cream cones, as giddy as two teenagers on prom night.

"What do you want to do after this?" Anthony asked her. "You want to go to a show or something? I still haven't seen that new *Star Wars* movie yet."

"I can't go to a movie dressed like this," she said, referring to her dull airport uniform.

"What difference does it make? It's dark in the theater anyway."

"Leave it to a guy to say something like that. You don't know *who* I might see in there."

"What, it's somebody there who's more important than me?" he asked her. He was actually concerned about it. Was it jealousy, or was it just his male ego talking? Either way, Sharron was flattered and speechless.

She sighed and said, "Let's go see a show then."

They even held hands down the aisle, sharing Twizzlers and popcorn for the science fiction film from George Lucas. It took them back to the time when they were kids themselves, loving the dark ambiance and technical excitement of the theater and its monster sound systems. They even kissed, during and after the movie, an *un*playeristic thing for a guy to do. Other moviegoers may have gotten the impression that they were in love. Or close to it. Maybe they were. And by the time Sharron made it home that night, Celena was back in the mother zone, worried sick about her friend.

"Where the hell have you been?! I've been calling all over the place for you. I even called the police and found out what I needed to do for a missing person report."

Sharron said, "I was *hardly* gone that long. I got off of work at eight o'clock."

"And it's now close to one o'clock in the morning. Were you over at Mr. Noname's house again?" Celena huffed.

Sharron stopped and frowned at her. "You know his name, Celena. Okay? So *learn* to *use* it," she piped as she headed to her room.

"Well, you better start telling *Anthony* to have you home at an earlier time on weeknights. You could have at least *called* me and told me where you were. I do that for you."

"Why, were you scared that I would walk in on you, *doing* something?" Sharron cracked with a smile. She had walked in on Celena before, all over the sofa with company, half naked and heated.

"Girl, shut up," her roommate countered, still embarrassed by it.

"Leave me alone then. And go get yourself some sleep before you end up with bags under your eyes in the morning."

"And it'll be *your* fault if I do."

"Yeah, whatever," Sharron said, reaching her room. She felt at peace, undressing from her work clothes with the radio on, listening to soft, late-night, quiet storm music. Before she knew it, Anthony was calling from home to inform her that he had made it back safely. What a way to finish off a perfect evening.

"Well, I really enjoyed myself tonight," she told him.

"Yeah, it was all right," he responded, sounding much more reserved about it.

Sharron was a little spicy in response to him. "Oh, so I guess it's not *the bomb* for you unless we end up in bed," she commented.

"Of course," he answered with a chuckle. "I'm a guy."

She shook her head and grinned. "At least you're honest about it." And when they hung up late, for a second night in a row, Sharron felt fully satisfied with her new man, and comfortable that she could call him that, even though they had still not made it official. She was satisfied with what they had so far.

Satisfied? A young man? *Never!* They *always* want more. More of everything. More chicken and gravy. More horsepower in their cars. More success. More property. Money. Women. And definitely more sex. So by the time the first week of July rolled around, Ant was on a serious mission.

"Come on, Sharron. Why not?" he was pleading. They were stretched out across his sofa on a calm Sunday afternoon. "Why we gotta go back to this waiting game stuff? We broke the ice already."

Maybe you *have, but* I *haven't,* Sharron was thinking to herself, hesitant to indulge. Not that she didn't want to. But did they *need* to? That was a more important question.

"This is a very easy way of making our relationship more physical than it needs to be," she pouted.

"Well, what do we need, to never touch each other? All affection and no passion?"

She smiled, all twisted up in his arms and legs in their summertime clothes.

"I didn't say that," she told him.

"What *are* you saying then? We gotta have a special event every time we do it? Or do you just want me to beg all the time? Because that's not my style."

"Well, what is your *style,* since you like to bring that up so much?"

"We just feel it, go with it, and get into it," he answered.

Sharron laughed. "That sounds like *every* guy's style," she countered.

Ant backed off his statement. "Naw, sometimes I like it to seem special, like when you don't expect to get none. But you don't want it to be that way *all* the time. Sometimes you just want to get busy. I mean, what do you think our parents did? You think they had to sit down and think about why they wanted to get busy?"

"Oh my God! I don't believe you're bringing *parents* into this," Sharron responded. "How *low* can you go?"

"I'm serious, though. I don't want to have a reason to do it all of the time," he argued, holding on to Sharron's hips for dear life.

She got to thinking about it. *Well, I* did *hold myself back last time. But when guys get as pressed as* he is *right now, it usually doesn't last long. They get too damn anxious! So I'll have to slow the whole process down again.*

"You wanna take a warm bath?" she asked him.

"A *bath*?" he asked back. He wanted to get right into the sex. But her idea of a bath meant that she would get naked with him. Nakedness meant that he could stimulate her. And stimulation would lead them right to where he wanted to go, penetration. So he quickly agreed to it.

"Aw'ight. Let's take a warm bath then. With our clothes off, right?" he joked with a smile.

"No. Fully clothed," she joked back.

"That ain't no fun. Then our clothes will end up all heavy. We'd have to take them off, wring 'em out, and throw 'em in a dryer."

Sharron said, "Are you kidding me? It's so hot outside that we could hang our clothes out the window and have them dry in ten minutes. That's why we're *inside* today."

"Aw'ight, so, you know, let's go take that bath."

Damn he's anxious! Sharron thought again. She grinned at him as he pulled her to her feet and led her to his bathroom.

"Do you have any candles laying around anywhere?" she asked him.

"Naw, ask Dracula," he joked with her.

Sharron just smiled at him. "Smart-ass."

"Yeah, I know. Now let's get naked."

There comes a time in relationships with women where guys drop their swords and shields and become fully human. They become emotional and caring, silly and serious, petty and thoughtful, happy and sad, eager and poised, patient and impatient, predictable, surprising, and totally vulnerable. However, the level of their revealed humanness depends on the woman. If she's too easy, she may receive nothing but the negatives. If she's too tough of a shell to crack, she may receive an overdose of the positives up front, and then be shattered by the negatives later on. But if she's just right, sort of like in the story of "Goldilocks and the Three Bears," then she'll get a perfect mix of everything, the way that it *should* be.

Sharron Francis was just right, and had come around at just the right time in Ant's maturing life to receive all of the perfect small pieces that would eventually add up to a perfect whole. *Perfect,* meaning to possess *most* of the elements that each woman and each man could find themselves comfortable with. Because no one on *earth* was perfect like in *flawless*. Looking for flawless attributes could only lead one astray.

So as they ran the warm bathwater in the lime green porcelain tub, and stripped naked inside the bathroom, watching and giggling at each other, they were no longer embarrassed by each other's thoughts, words, and actions.

"You weigh about one-thirty, hunh?" Ant asked Sharron.

"One twenty-seven, to be exact."

"Well, you wear it well," he told her, gleaming.

"Why, thank you. You wear your weight well, too. What are you again, one-eighty?" she asked, rounding up on purpose like he did.

"One seventy-four, to be exact," he answered, mocking her.

They climbed into the water with Ant leading the way.

"Whoa, this may be *too* warm," he pouted, tensing up as his body hit the water.

"No it's not. It's just right," Sharron said, joining him.

"Yeah, because *you* don't have any exterior parts," he whined.

"What about my breasts? And if the water was *really* hot, I would feel it, too."

Ant doubted her. "I don't know if your stuff is as sensitive as mine is," he said.

Sharron smiled and shook her head. "Shut up and pass me the soap," she huffed at him.

"Shut up?" he asked, frowning. "You better watch what you say to a guy when he got you butt naked. That could be dangerous."

She ignored him. "I like this bathtub," she commented of the green porcelain, taking the soap and lathering her hands with it.

"Yeah, I did too when I first moved in."

"You don't like it now?"

"You get used to it. Then other people talk about it."

Sharron smiled and asked, "So how many women have you had in here? You don't have to answer if you feel uncomfortable about it," she added.

"Why even ask me then?"

"Okay, I take it back."

Ant shook his head. "You can't take it back. You asked me already. But I never took a bath with someone before. I mean, what are we supposed to do in here? We can't even really get comfortable. It's not enough room for both of us."

Sharron sighed and said, "Just relax." She reached out and rubbed the lather of soap onto his muscular chest and shoulders. Ant lathered up *his* hands and did the same to her, realizing how soothing it felt.

"How many *guys* have you done this with?" he asked her. As soon as he did, he wanted to take his question back as well. *Now what the hell I ask her that for?* Unless she gave the right answer, it would do nothing but sour his mood. Men *hated* to think of other guys with their women in *any* circumstance. Yet, they asked those painful questions anyway, all out of competition to find out if they were the one and only or the best.

"One," Sharron answered, getting the stress out of the way. "But it was nothing like this."

"What do you mean, 'It was nothing like this'?" Ant asked her. He was all ears.

"I didn't really like him that much."

Ant frowned. "So why'd you do it with him?"

She shrugged her shoulders. "Because it was something different to do, I guess."

Ant shook his head, thinking, *I* knew *I shouldn't have asked her that shit.*

Sharron leaned forward through the water and kissed him on the lips, right as he began to worry about her past.

"I like you *four* times more," she assured him.

He smiled. "What's that supposed to do, make me feel better?"

"I'm just telling you," she answered, grinning. With the touches of soapy water on her face, hair, and body, her grin and smooth brown skin were enticing. Exciting! Delicious! Ant could feel his heart rushing blood to that exterior tool that he treasured so much.

Sharron smiled, and drove her soapy hand through the warm water, caressing him. When he felt the full rise, he reached out to titillate the nipples of her firm breasts with his own soapy hands. And as they enjoyed the silence, they forgot about all other men and all other women, immersed in only the heat of themselves.

This is beautiful! Ant told himself. *DAMN, THIS IS BEAUTIFUL!* He lost all of his hunger for the immediate sex, understanding that they had all day, all night, and all of a lifetime. As long as they continued to enjoy each other and block out the rest of the world, like they were able to do while in that small, crowded, lime green bathtub, they would be just fine. And then a minute turned into ten minutes. Ten minutes turned into twenty. And twenty minutes turned into a full hour, and they had become two brown prunes.

Sharron stared at the shriveled-up flesh on her fingertips. "Okay. Time to get out," she said.

"Yeah, the water's not warm anymore anyway. And I have to take a leak," Ant added with a chuckle.

Sharron shook her head and continued to smile. *Guys!* she thought to herself. She stood up out of the tub and wrapped herself in a towel. "I'll see you in the bedroom, mister," she said, teasing him as she walked out.

Ant was so tickled he nearly slipped and wiped out on his bathroom floor.

"Aw, I'm gon' love this," he mumbled to himself. He couldn't *wait* to join her. But he was no longer anxious about it. He was perfectly calm, and in full control of his senses. He even thought again of going natural with her, depending on how *she* felt about it. So when he slid into the bed beside her, he was without condoms.

"I notice that you don't have your protection behind the pillow again," she commented.

He laughed about it. "Naw. They're in my drawer." *But we don't have to use them if you don't want to,* he thought but did not vocalize.

Sharron slid her thighs onto his and whispered into his left ear, "Can you go get them please."

Ant laughed. Sharron had rules of her own, and she was still disciplined, no matter *how* sweet their bath together had been. He respected that, because rules of other women were too easily broken. So were the rules of many men, which, under the wrong circumstances, easily led to disaster.

Ant heeded her sound advice and pulled out *their* protection; Sharron decided to do the duties of putting it on.

"What, you don't trust me or something?" he asked her, half joking and half serious.

"It's not that I don't trust you; I just wanted to be the one to put it on. Is something wrong with that?"

There wasn't. In fact, it seemed rather sexy to him. It was assertive and confident of a woman to feel that comfortable about the intimacy she shared with her man. And as long as Ant was not embarrassed by the size of his tool, which he was not, he was all with it.

"Naw. I don't mind. As long as you put it on right."

"Why? You don't *trust* me?" she asked, mocking him.

"It's not that I don't trust you; I just want to make sure that you know what you're doing."

Sharron took care of business before Ant could count to five. That made him wonder again.

"How many times have you done that?" he asked her.

"Never," she told him. "Only with you." And it was the truth.

"So, how come you decided to do it with me?"

"Because I wanted to. And stop asking so many questions," she told him with a kiss as she straddled him.

He smiled at her ironic sarcasm, finding himself asking questions he had never bothered or felt a need to ask other women before her. And as he leaned up to kiss her back, and to stroke her breasts with his fingers, he wanted to solidify his hold on her.

"You know what?" he said in her right ear. "I wanna be on top this time."

Sharron chuckled and fell limp to the bed, and was ready to receive him, all the way. And she did, holding on and digging her fingernails into anything she could anchor herself to, while making sure that her nails never injured his skin, because guys hated that. She wanted him to love her. All the way. And he did, bringing things out of her that she had only fantasized about. Because Ant had something to prove, as though his life depended on it: opening her up and making her feel everything that a woman *should* feel from a man she wanted to love.

But it was mostly mental. They thought about it, giving their all, and then the physical part fell right into place, all night long and until the next morning arrived.

"Damn! It's six o'clock. I gotta get ready to go to work," Ant said, taking in the time.

Boy is he dedicated to his job, Sharron thought, with her eyes still closed. Dedication to employment was a good thing. Definitely! She respected that. But she wasn't looking forward to being taken home so early on a Monday morning, knowing that she did not have to be to work until noon.

He knew her work schedule, and she knew his. So Ant thought about that early morning drive to University City as he took a quick shower. And he decided to break his own house rule, and let her stay until she was ready. As long as she didn't answer his telephone. Fortunately, since he had cut back on the cat-and-dog game, he didn't have many women still calling. Nevertheless, players could never fully let their guards down, so he decided to turn his ringer off as a precaution.

"You go to work at twelve again?" he asked her to make sure.

Sharron was out of bed and ready to shower.

"Mmm-hmm," she answered him, still drained from the night before.

"Well, I'll tell you what. You go ahead and get some more z's, and when you get ready to leave, just make sure you lock the bottom lock on my front door. Okay?"

Sharron was surprised by it. She knew how protective Ant could be about his things. That was a good thing as well. That meant he would take good care of anything that meant something to him.

"Are you sure?" she asked him.

He nodded, convincing himself. "Yeah. You got money for a cab?"

She nodded back to him. "Yeah, I have money."

He pulled out a twenty-dollar bill from his wallet and handed it to her anyway.

"I said I had money," she told him, pushing it back.

"Just go ahead and keep it. Now if it was a *Benjamin,* I'd take it back. So take that cab ride home on me, because I brought you over here, and I should have driven you back."

She smiled and asked, "Do you feel that way about everyone?" Knowing that he was an adventurous man and sex-crazed with an ego to boot, she doubted it.

Ant smiled back at her and said, "Naw. But we talking about you now."

She gave him a kiss on the cheek, and said, "Thank you," before climbing back into his bed.

He gave her one more look before he walked out and headed for work. He was confident he had done the right thing. Imagine that. After not allowing any of his women to remain at his apartment, unattended, for close to three years, Ant let Sharron stay when he had known her for less than two months.

As he cranked the engine of his car he gave one more look up to his second-floor apartment. "Fuck it," he told himself. "All rules are meant to be broken in time anyway." *And she's a good woman,* he thought. *I can trust her.*

Trust had to be earned. It was rarely a given. Ironically, people who trusted themselves were more likely to trust others. Maybe that was why Celena Myers trusted no one. She didn't trust herself. Since she had thought and done too many ridiculous things in her life to count or want to remember, she assumed that others could be just as conniving, demanding, short-fused, and hopelessly insecure as she was. Not to mention having too many aggressive, masculine traits for her own good. Assertion was one thing, but aggression was entirely something else. Something few *rational* women hungered to attain.

"Well, don't call here no fucking more if you feel that way, Darryl!" Celena shouted through the phone.

"Oh, now why you gotta cuss me out? I'm just trying to talk to you about it."

"I'm not ready to have just one man in my life right now. Okay? And I *do* as I please."

"Aw'ight, then. You know what? Fuck you then, 'cause I don't have any more time for your sorry ass."

"Yeah! Fuck you too!" Celena spat, slamming the phone to the receiver.

Sharron stared at her reckless roommate as she paced the living room, obviously still teed off.

"What did he *say*?" Sharron asked. Celena was constantly having arguments with guys. In fact, she argued with anyone who didn't see things exactly as *she* saw them.

"He was talkin' some nonsense about *'spreading'* myself too thin with too many different guys."

Sharron thought about that and smiled. "Well, you do."

"And it's *my* prerogative to do so," Celena huffed.

"So are you saying that no one can even say anything to you about it?"

It was an honest question.

"For what?"

"Well, weren't you seeing Darryl?"

"Yeah, and?"

"*And* he obviously has some concerns about all of the guys who you go out with."

"Well, if he can't handle that, then he needs to step to the curb."

Sharron stared at her again. What else could she say?

"Mmm," she grunted. "Whatever happened to *your* faith?"

"Faith?" Celena asked, stunned by even the use of the word. "Faith in what?"

"Faith in being able to enjoy one person."

Celena sucked her teeth and sighed, not sure how she wanted to answer the question. "What happened to *their* faith in *us?* If Darryl really wants to be the one like that, then he would hang in there with me until I was ready for something real. But obviously he doesn't have any patience for that."

"Patience?" Sharron repeated. She laughed at the idea. "Who are *you* to be bringing up *patience?* When have *you* had patience with anything?"

Celena shook her head and started toward her room, worn out from the conversation already.

"I have no time for this," she commented, waving her right hand as she went.

Sharron followed her into her room. "Maybe you need to stop running away from your fears and just face them," she advised. "If you don't trust guys enough to be with just one, then you have to at least admit that to yourself."

"Okay. I admit it. Are you satisfied now?" Celena shot back. She stretched out across her bed, mentally exhausted. "Now can you just leave me alone for a minute?"

Sharron smiled and didn't budge.

"You don't leave *me* alone when you have something to tell me about *my* life."

"Yeah, you just close your damn door on me," Celena countered. "Maybe I need to get right up and do the same thing to you."

Sharron ignored it and looked around at how barren Celena's room was compared to the fullness of her own. "How come your room looks so . . . deserted?" she asked, taking it all in as though she had never noticed it before. Maybe she hadn't paid Celena's room that much attention because Celena was forever invading *her* room for some reason.

"That's because I put stuff away instead of leaving everything out for showpieces, like *you* do. It looks like a damn safari in your room, with all them stuffed animals and carrying on," she cracked.

Sharron shook her head, grinning, while thinking of a crack of her own.

"You don't want any of these guys to know too much about you, hunh?" she assumed. "When we were in school at Missouri, I knew guys like that. My first love, in fact. And he left me to go back home to California with not even a phone call."

"So what are you trying to say?" Celena piped.

"Well, when you run away from other people, you also run away from yourself, because you never face up to your situation. And those are your favorite words: 'I don't have time for that shit.' Well, what *do* you have time for?"

Bang! That's what friends are for. Honesty. Celena was speechless. Sharron walked out of her room, leaving her good friend with that, and giving her time to think to herself.

Once Sharron had left the room, Celena mumbled to herself defensively, "Mmm-hmm, now she got all that mouth just because she all into Mr. . . . *Anthony* now, hunh?" But after her short moment of denial, she realized her Memphis, Tennessee, roommate was actually right for a change. How many men had Celena left at the crossroads? She was afraid of taking a step further and being run over by a truckload of emotions that she was terrified of having to experience. So she would have fits, quit, turn back, and start all over with a new man, only to arrive at the exact same crossroad for a replay. Why? Because she hated the vulnerability of being a woman. Why did *she* have to be the one who ended up brokenhearted? Nevertheless, she was forced to suffer anyway. Like many *men* suffered, so full of themselves that they eventually became constipated, ending up tortured for life, by never allowing themselves to experience the greatest science of the world. Love.

But do they really care about me, or just themselves? Celena questioned as she stared up at the ceiling. *They only want me because I'm unavailable to them. And once they really know that they got me, it's game over, and they'll move on to their next* challenge. *Because that's all I am to them. A* damn *challenge! I know what I'm talking about. And I'm* not *gon' be some damn "yes" girl like my sisters are for some man. I don't have time for . . . that.*

She stopped and chuckled to herself. *That damn girl is right, ain't she?* she thought, referring to Sharron. *But what are you supposed to do? And how do you know which one is real, and which one is just playin' games. I mean, so many of us have made the wrong choice that I don't want to be just another damn dummy.*

This shit is so fuckin' confusing, man. I mean, why am I even thinking *about this?! I know what I'm doing. Or at least I* thought *I did. But now Sharron got me all confused.*

"Dammit," she huffed. She stood back up and headed for her roommate's open door. Sharron smiled at her from her own bed when Celena walked in.

"You think this shit is funny, don't you?" her roommate asked.

"It is," Sharron admitted. "I knew you'd be in here sooner or later," she added, with a new book in her hands.

"What book is that?"

"*A Do Right Man,* by Omar Tyree."

Celena smiled. "Does it tell you where to find one?"

First Sharron laughed at the idea. Then she thought about how to describe it correctly.

"Let's just say that it's good for us to know all of the things that guys go through, and all of the decisions they have to make in their lives, to understand them a little better. So next I'm buying *Men Cry In the Dark,* by Michael Baisden."

"Isn't he the one who wrote *Why Men Cheat? Never Satisfied,* or something?"

"Yup."

"Well, you feel like going for a car ride, or would I be disturbing your reading time?" Celena asked, itching to unwind out in the wind somewhere. It was slightly after ten o'clock at night.

Sharron closed her book and stood. "Let's go."

As soon as they jumped into the old black Maxima and cruised up Olive Boulevard, Celena got to asking more about Sharron's new man.

"So what do you think about him? Really?"

"What do I think about who?" Sharron quizzed.

"Anthony." Celena hadn't asked much about him before. She only assumed things of him.

"Oh." Sharron thought about it and smiled that easy smile of hers, expressing herself without a word.

"You think that much, hunh?" Celena asked, reading the immense joy in her friend's face.

"Have *you* ever felt that way? Where you don't even have to talk about it? You can just smile and know?" Sharron asked back.

Celena nodded. "Yeah, I've felt that way before. Everybody does. But it never lasts. That's the problem with it. That's the problem with *all* relationships. They don't *last* anymore. Somebody needs to write a book about how to make it last." Then she forced herself to say the word, "Forever."

That shocked Sharron. A lot!

"You *do* have feelings then," she commented.

"Of course I do. I'm *human* ain't I?" Celena piped. "What kind of statement is that? I'm not some kind of dating robot. I have feelings. I just don't like to . . . put 'em out there like that."

Sharron nodded. She knew the feeling. *Yeah, hold back so you don't get burned.*

"But eventually . . . you have to," she said. "There's no other way around it. It's like . . ." She thought of a new analogy, something that was fully relatable. ". . . admitting that your hair is nappy."

Celena looked at her and broke out laughing. "Are you trying to tell me something?" she asked, feeling the nape of her neck with her left hand.

"I'm not saying that *your* hair is nappy right now; I'm just saying that when it is, you verbalize it, and then you go and do something about it. Right?"

"Damn right, you right," Celena agreed.

"Well, relationships are the same way. Eventually, you have to verbalize what you feel, and then you have to do something about it."

Celena looked at her and frowned. "Now you know good and well that guys aren't into that kind of stuff. They be steady talkin' 'bout, 'Baby, you know how I feel about you. You my Boo, ain't you?' " she said, mocking a deep voice tone.

Sharron laughed out loud. "But eventually, if they really care, they're gonna have to say it, if just to admit it to themselves. That's just how it goes," she reiterated. "That's why a lot of guys are *afraid* to say it. Because after they do, they know they have to do something about it. They have to prove it with their actions, loyalty, dedication, affection, and everything else. So they don't say it because they don't want to do all of the work. They're lazy."

"Don't I know it," Celena agreed again. "But they *surely* don't have a problem telling you when they want to fuck. They're not lazy about that. Unless you want them to eat it. Then they get lazy again. 'Aw, girl, I don't feel like it right now.'"

Sharron smiled and shook her head. She had a hell of a lot more tact than her roommate. But Celena was Celena.

"Has Anthony told *you* anything?" she asked, getting back to her interrogation.

"In ways he has. But he hasn't verbalized it yet, no," Sharron answered her. "I mean, we've only known each other for what, two months now?"

"I can't tell with the way you've been all up under him lately. I hardly get to see you anymore," Celena responded. "*I* used to be the one on the go all the time and *you* were the one sitting home."

"You've been sitting at home lately?" Sharron asked her, doubting it.

"No, I'm just sayin'—"

"That's what I thought," she concluded, cutting Celena off.

"Girl, I can't stay home that long. I even read my books on the go. I can't see how you do it. Or how you *used* to do it. Because you damn sure don't do it no more, with Mr. Noname coming around."

"Celena, *I told you* about that," Sharron warned her.

"You know I know his name. I'm just teasing you. Anthony Poole. Okay? You satisfied now, Mrs. Sharron Francis Poole?"

Sharron smiled, liking how that sounded. "That actually sounds good," she admitted.

Celena looked at her and cautioned, "Don't get ahead of yourself with that. You'll be setting yourself up again."

"You're the one who brought it up," Sharron reminded her.

"So you're saying that you haven't even thought about that? Because I *know* you have, Sharron. I know how you think. You're *way* old-fashioned."

"What's so wrong with that? Old-fashioned people made it last. We need *more* old-fashioned people nowadays. But I never put Anthony's name on the end of mine like you did."

"It doesn't sound bad, though. Poole. It's just kind of . . . plain. But not in an unattractive way," Celena said, smoothing out her words to make sense.

"I know what you mean. It just works well," Sharron added.

"Francis works well, too, because my name sounds like I'm selling hot dogs or something. Myers. That's the one thing that I *do* envy about my sisters. They got to change our last name."

"You hate your name that much?" Sharron asked, laughing. "How would your father feel about that?"

Celena said, "I still have it, don't I? It's not like I changed it on my own or anything. But that's another thing I don't like. Why do *we* have to change *our* names? My mother's maiden name is Duval. Celena Duval. You hear how elegant that sounds? Like royalty or something."

"Aw, girl, go 'head with that."

"I'm serious, Sharron. That's why I kept your Francis in the mix. Don't go changing your name for no man. That ain't even right."

"So what *do* you like about being a woman then?"

She smiled. "Getting things my way, and getting my kitty cat *purred* just right."

Sharron couldn't believe her ears. She smiled and shook her head again as they continued to ride aimlessly, with the windows down, heading north on Route 270.

"You know, that sounds just like something a guy would say, having five women at a time and getting his dick sucked," she commented.

"So what?" Celena said. "What's good for the gander is good—"

"That right there is bullshit!" Sharron snapped, cutting her off with a raised palm. "That's exactly why you're so untrusting now. You don't do what they do just because *they* do it. That's like saying, 'Since everybody else got a gun, let me go out and get one.' And you only end up with more dead people.

"That don't make any sense at all," she added, noticeably ticked off. "So instead of women trying to be *more* like men, we *should* be trying to make *them* more like *us*. Or if not, then maybe we really *do* hate ourselves."

With that, they fell silent for a couple of miles before Celena mumbled, "I like myself." And they began to smile.

Nevertheless, Celena could not help but notice how strong Sharron's views and personality had become through her association with her new man. Sharron seemed so sure of herself. Confident. Poised. Men were supposed to drain the intelligence and confidence of a woman, *not* add to it. Or at least from Celena's perception. Could she be wrong about it?

As if it were a sign, the car began to act up with a slippage of the transmission, grinding noisy gears with no acceleration.

GGRRRNNNNNN!

"Here goes this damn car again," Celena stated.

Sharron smiled. "Ant could fix it."

Celena said, "Yeah, I forgot they called him that. A Mr. Fix It, hunh?"

"That's what he does, fixes cars. And there are plenty of them out here to fix, too."

"Tell me about it. I'm surprised this car hasn't just broken down on us yet."

"It will if you don't fix it soon."

"But I'm always fixing this damn thing. One hundred dollars

here, two hundred dollars there. I'm tired of that shit." Then she thought about Sharron and her mechanic boyfriend again. "I guess you won't have that problem when *you* decide to get a car, with Mr. Fix It around."

Sharron just smiled at her. "Guys need fixin' too, Celena," she commented. "It's a partnership. And if you have nothing to offer a guy except what's between your legs, then you won't even be with him long. Because eventually, he'll get rid of you."

"So what do you offer Anthony then?" Celena asked curiously. It wasn't as if Sharron had any money or anything. And she was hardly glamorous enough to be considered a challenge for most guys, especially for a player. What was so enticing about an ordinary sister from Memphis, Tennessee? What could *she* offer that no one else could?

Sharron said, "I just make his life interesting, basically. Some couples match up well together, and others don't. Some women like guys for who they are, and support what they do, and others don't.

"I mean, think about it, Celena. A man can have all of the money in the world, but if he doesn't have a woman to celebrate it with, a woman that he really *likes* and gets along with, then he might as well give it all away," she added. "Because he'll still feel empty inside. So, for whatever reason, I obviously have that connection with Anthony."

Celena was shocked! What kind of game was this Anthony guy using on Sharron to make her so knowledgeable about relationships? It was like an overnight flash-card session that she was absolutely *killing!*

Celena said, "I never really thought of it like that. I mean, I *thought* of it, you know, guys gettin' money to get women and all, but I never really understood it the way *you* just made it sound. You make it sound like a jigsaw puzzle or something. But see, some of these damn guys are so greedy that the more money they get, they start wanting *twenty* women."

Sharron said, "But you're still focusing too much on the money aspect. The thing is: What do you *add* to his life? He can *buy* a woman anywhere," she stated. "And as far as guys needing twenty women, you know what I figured out about that?"

Celena was all ears. "What?"

"If you need twenty women to make you happy, then you really have none. Because no man can really focus on that many women. *I'm sorry.* And if he *thinks* he can, he's just fooling himself."

Celena didn't want to hear anymore. No Memphis, Tennessee, girl was going to school *her* on what *she* knew about relationships no matter *how* close they were. No way! So she turned the radio on to drown out anymore talk. And it just wasn't her night. Because as soon as she turned up the volume on her stereo, the celebrated love crooner Lauryn Hill was crying out her heart on a penetrating rhythm about how bad it hurts when you choose to love hard-rock men.

Sharron smiled her face off for about the tenth time that night. "Where exactly are we driving to?" she finally asked of their destination. Celena had connected to Route 70 and was heading east toward downtown St. Louis.

"I'm just driving in a big circle, girl. Heading the long way back home." Meanwhile, she thought, *Now I have to figure out what I got going for my* own *love life, because whatever Sharron is getting is obviously* the bomb! *For* now, *anyway. Because if I know* anything *about guys in the 1990s, it's that they don't have any stamina for long-lasting relationships. So I'll just wait this thing with Sharron and this new guy out, and see how long it really lasts.*

Stamina, for many men, was *definitely* a problem. Or at least it seemed that way if you happened to know all the wrong kind of men and the women who mixed with them. They could all make it seem as if the sky was really falling, and that the old-world concept of man and woman forming a bond to make children and maintain a family was extinct. However, there *were* old relics of strong bonding still left out there. There were people who actually knew how to hold things together for thirty and forty years, on old-school principles of community purpose. But the youth, stressing too much individualism, had created chaos for themselves in the *absence* of community. And they found themselves constantly running out of breath.

Me, myself, and I, as a philosophy, led to nothing but harder work and longer periods of loneliness. And rarely could a stable home, family, and community be built on such individual methods. No wonder relationships were so hard to work out in the 1990s. *Me, myself, and I* was in order. But *life* was about *sharing* responsibility, and so was love. Only *then* could home, family, and community become meaningful. But some people failed to comprehend, while wondering out loud, why they lacked the stamina to attain what they wanted in life. People like Anthony "Tone" Wallace.

"Man, you should see some of these houses that we clean, dawg. I'm starting to think that seven dollars ain't good enough," Tone commented to Ant on their way to the barbershop. Ant liked to keep his hair cut to a smooth, low height, and Tone decided to tag along with him and get himself a needed haircut.

"I could say the same thing about some of the cars I work on," Ant responded from behind the wheel of his Chevy. They headed north on Grand Boulevard to their usual barber.

"Oh no you can't, either," Tone argued. "Because even if you worked on a car that costs eighty thousand dollars, that car got nothin' on these half a million dollar houses."

Ant smiled and nodded. "Yeah, I guess you're right."

Tone thought about it and said, "It makes you wonder how it is that some people have so much, when others don't have shit. Especially black people."

"That's America, man. Get used to it. A lot of white people don't have shit either."

Once they made it to the barbershop, Ant parked his car on a side street, and they walked around the corner and into the rusty shop for immediate entertainment from lively black male chatter, just like in every other barbershop in black neighborhoods all across America.

"That's Eriq La Salle, ain't it? The brother from *ER*?" someone asked, watching a public service announcement on the 13-inch color television set that sat on a tall stand. After work hours, there was always a wait for the better barbers. Only the older men and young kids who didn't know any better sat in the chairs of the less respected barbers. That's just the way it was. If you couldn't cut respectfully, you found yourself at the lower end of the pecking order. So Ant and Tone waited and listened to the black male talk, sometimes joining in if they had anything to add. Usually they only laughed, agreeing and disagreeing with the many opinions that were thrown around.

"Yeah, that Eriq La Salle is married to a white girl, ain't he? A model or something, right?" a thirty-something brother said from the barber's chair.

"Naw, he ain't married to her is he? She was just his main squeeze," a barber answered. That's usually how it started. The conversations would expand from one barber to another, and then to the customers in the shop.

"All I know is that she's a *fine* white girl," another barber added. "So at least he didn't sell himself short."

"Wesley Snipes got a white girl, too, don't he?" someone else started.

"Naw, he got himself an Asian girl."

"So does Russell Simmons from Def Jam," a younger customer put in. The conversation spread around the shop.

"We must not like the sisters no more, hunh?" one of the older barbers concluded.

"That ain't the case here. I've been in love with my wife now for twelve years and countin', with three kids," a reserved customer added. He felt he had to. He was joined by a few others who agreed with him.

"Yeah, I gotta have *me* a black woman. I wouldn't be able to bring anything else home to my momma," one of the younger barbers added for a more humorous approach.

Ant and Tone looked at each other and laughed.

The young barber continued: "Usually, the kind of brothers who marry white women got a whole different approach to themselves, like they *above* other blacks. Even Wilt Chamberlain said it. He said ah, 'White women knew more about the finer things in life,' and that he could relate to them more."

"Hmmph," another barber grunted. "I wonder what his ass *related to* when he was poor and black in Philadelphia. They call it the 'City of Brotherly Love' don't they?"

"Wait a minute now, just because he grew up black and in Philadelphia didn't necessarily mean that he was poor. Let's not jump to stereotypical conclusions," someone else spoke up.

"Look, most of them brothers who go for white women don't even associate with real black folks like they need to. That's all I'm sayin'. They got a different way about them."

"What's so different about them?" a customer in a blue Nike sweat suit asked.

"They just got different ways, different looks, and different hang-outs, man."

The young barber was really putting himself out there with assumptions.

The customer in the Nike sweat suit went on to drop a bomb on the entire barbershop. He said real casually, "I have a white wife, and we got two kids, a boy and a girl. Now would you know that if I didn't tell you?"

All eyes were on him. And most of the brothers in the shop would have never guessed. He looked like any other brother from the St. Louis 'hood.

"You bullshittin' me just to make a point, ain't you?" the young barber asked him.

"No I'm not either. My wife is straight from Germany. I met her while I was stationed over there in the reserves."

After that, the barber was able to relax a bit.

"Oh, well, that's different," he said. "You probably ain't have enough sisters over there to choose from."

"That wasn't why I married my wife. I dated plenty of sisters," the brother refuted. "But when you get with a woman, and she looks out for you and does things for you that other women wouldn't, then you gotta respect that, man. Then I messed around and fell in love with her. And when I got her pregnant, I did the right thing and married her," he said.

"But I like to throw that out there to people, man, because you don't break the respect for your family for *no* color. And this is *my* family now, whether my wife is white, black, green, orange, or whatever.

"Because you got a lot of brothers who walk around and talk more black shit than Malcolm X, and they got three and four kids by three and four different women, and ain't did the right thing with *one* of them," he added. "So I stand strong with my wife and family. If anybody got a problem with that, they fixin' to get hurt. And you can talk all the bullshit you want, as long as you don't fuck with me and mine," he ended with a smile. And every black man inside of that barbershop took him seriously.

Tone looked over to his partner Ant and smiled, thinking about Ant's father, his older brothers, his *own* father, Ant's cousin Rico, and too many other black men who left the sisters hanging with a bag of brown kids, not only in St. Louis, Missouri, but all over America.

"So now, are we saying that black men have lost their love for the sisters and for black family or what? Because we still have some brothers who *are* married to black women who *do* go out of their way for their man," the shop owner mused out loud. Danny was in his early fifties and had been around for a while. He was married to his wife of over thirty years, but he had surely witnessed the changes in how black men and women were mistreating each other over the past two decades.

Ant felt compelled to speak on it, as if confessing his sins to the world. And it was all because of his relationship with Sharron.

"A lot of it is really on us, man," he commented to Tone's surprise. Ant, after all, was a player who could rationalize just about *anything*.

He went on and said, "There's a whole lot of sisters out there who are willing to go to the edge of the world and back for us, man, and we just don't seem to care about them. We're too busy thinking about ourselves. I know *I* was."

"Man, that's bullshit. They too busy thinking about *themselves,* too," another young customer snapped. "They know good and well who they're dealing with. They go out and choose who they want to choose, and then they get up and cry about it."

Tone laughed and nodded his head. "Yeah, that's true," he agreed. Women had chosen him *knowing* he was only out to score. That went *quadruple* for his partner Ant.

"It still don't change the fact that we in control of that situation," Ant argued his point. "I mean, we can choose to be with any one of the women on our list any time we get ready."

"Yeah, and then as soon as you get ready to choose, that's when all of a sudden you can't find that same girl who was crying her eyes out when you had them three other women on the side," the other customer countered. "Then she'll start talking about she ain't ready for no real commitment on your ass."

The barbers all laughed at it.

"Sound like you talkin' from personal experience," one of them commented to him.

"Yeah, I'm talking from personal experience. I had that happen to me before. *Twice!* And as soon as I stopped being a player, they ain't love me no more. So after that, I told myself, 'Aw'ight then. If that's the way they want it, I'ma be a player for life.'"

Tone started laughing so hard he could hardly compose himself. Those same thoughts had run through his mind recently.

Danny jumped back in and said, "What it sounds like to me, is that we have a lot of hurt and confused men *and* women. And you're all scared to death of each other. So as soon as the rocky roads start up, you both jump out of the car and let the thing roll off of a cliff. But if you *both* learned to hang in there, you could steer the damn thing clear back to safety and keep on rolling. That's what *I* think the problem is."

"Yeah, and there's a whole lot more guys afraid than women," Ant agreed. "And I *know* because I was one of 'em. I just didn't want to give up my player's card." Then he laughed, joined by the other customers and barbers in the shop. They all knew the feeling. Women just couldn't understand. Then again, some of them could. Women who were players themselves, and just couldn't imagine living without the roller-coaster ride of a man of mystery who was there only for a few hours at a time and had no strings attached. Women like Celena Myers.

"This girl Sharron is really gettin' to you now," Tone said as he and his partner rode back down Grand Boulevard after their haircuts.

Ant smiled and said, "You called that shit before it happened, didn't you?"

Tone smiled back at him. "I could just feel it, the way she was reachin' for you."

"But all of 'em ride me like that when I get 'em good," Ant responded.

"Naw, man, you know when you gon' get the girl. You know how it's gon' be and everything. But with this one, you didn't know," Tone explained.

Ant thought about it and tried to put it into perspective.

"There were some girls that I didn't get. I mean, I don't get *every-*

body, man," he admitted. "I'm not the mack like *that,*" he added with a laugh.

"Yeah, but I don't hear you *talkin'* about them girls you didn't get. I think you would have talked about Sharron. In fact, I *know* it. Just by the shit that she was askin' when I was on the phone with her. And the way you went and hung up on me for her," Tone reminded him with a grin.

Ant fell silent, missing Sharron as Tone continued to talk about her.

"You thinkin' about her right now, ain't you?" Tone asked.

Ant broke out grinning.

"Yeah, she got ya' ass aw'ight. She-e-e gotcha," Tone teased.

Ant said, "Why are you jealous about it then?"

Tone paused for a second. Then he answered, "Because I wanna be got, too, man. I want some ho to turn me out so bad I don't know what to do."

Ant chuckled and asked, "But do you want her to be a ho?"

Tone said, "Naw. I want a virgin."

They broke out laughing again. Men wanted so badly to be the first and only to every virtuous woman who ever walked the planet, while never being quite as virtuous themselves. So when Ant got back in that night and called up Sharron, he actually asked her what she felt about that.

"Would you talk to me if I was a virgin?"

Sharron laughed herself. "What?"

"Would you talk to me if I was a virgin? You heard me."

"How would I know?" she asked.

"What if I just told you I was?"

"I wouldn't believe you."

"Why not?"

"I just wouldn't."

"Because it seems like I've been with women before?"

"Yes."

"And what if it didn't seem that way?"

Sharron thought about it and went blank. "I don't know."

"Would you still ask me so many questions?"

She smiled again. "Probably not."

"Because I wouldn't have shit to talk about, right?"

"No, I didn't say that."

"You don't *have* to say it. It's already in the things that you *do* say."

"Like what?"

"All the things you say to me just to see how I'll respond to them. If I had nothing to be curious about, you wouldn't even be saying all of that stuff."

"Why are you even asking me this, late at night?"

"Me and Tone were at the barbershop tonight, talking about relationships and whatnot, and this one guy said that women know exactly what they're getting into before they do it, and then they cry about it as soon as things don't go their way."

"And it's not the same for guys who chase after women like my roommate?" Sharron asked. "It's the same thing. Celena and I were just talkin' about that the other night."

"So when do we all stop the bullshit and just hook up with each other?" Ant commented.

"Hmmph," Sharron grunted. "I don't know. *You* tell me. I've *been* tired of it."

"Why you choose me then?"

Hypocritical. Sharron just laughed at it.

"Okay, I guess I'm *not* tired," she admitted. "But you just made me curious about you, so I went for it. So why did you stick with me? Or at least *so far?*" she questioned.

Because I'm in a slowdown period right now, he thought. But he held that thought to himself.

"Why not?" he asked instead.

"Because you can have five other girls, howling at the moon," she mocked him.

"Yeah, well, some of them don't howl the way I want them to."

Good answer.

She laughed again. "I don't *howl* at all," she commented.

"You don't have to. I feel you anyway."

Another good answer. Ant was on a roll. But when wasn't he?

"That's why I chose you," Sharron told him, seemingly out of the blue.

Ant failed to connect the dots. "Hunh?"

"That's why I chose you, because you're smooth like that. And women like smoothness," she answered.

"Not all of them," he countered, remembering those women who never trusted him.

Sharron said, "I'll take a smooth guy over one who doesn't know what he wants to say."

"But that guy who doesn't know what he wants to say may actually be better for you."

Sharron thought quickly of Sean Love and Omar Tyree's novel *A Do Right Man.*

"Well, in that case, they need to learn," she stated. "And sometimes it takes a while. But it's not my fault."

Ant chuckled and said, "Oh, it's like that."

"Yeah, it's like that," she told him.

"Well, at least you're *honest,*" he mocked her. "I guess that some parts of being a player ain't bad, hunh?"

Sharron answered, "As long as you know when to stop playing and start being serious."

"Oohhh," Ant moaned. He didn't know what else to say. It was the truth. He had been telling himself the same thing. Then they were stuck on the phone, not knowing what move to make, or what to say, and the awkwardness made them laugh.

"Is there something you want to say to me?" Sharron asked, beating Ant to the punch.

"Is there something *you* want to say to *me?"* he asked her back.

They laughed again, as silly as teenagers.

"I don't know," she answered.

"I don't know either," he countered.

"I thought *you* would know everything."

"Why would I still be curious about *you,* if I *knew* everything? I would move on with my life then, right?"

"Because you don't have all of the *pieces* of me yet," she countered.

Ant grinned. She always caught him off guard with that.

"Like I said, I'll never forget you said that to me," she told him.

"And you'll pass it down to our kids," he added.

"That's right."

It all sounded good to him. Good and natural. As if it was normal behavior for them to talk about their future so matter-of-factly.

"Have you ever talked to another guy about kids and stuff before?" Ant asked her.

"No. I just thought about it."

"Yeah, me too. Wondering what they would look like."

Sharron laughed and said, "Conan O'Brien does that on his late show. He takes celebrity couples and puts their features together for the looks of their kids. It's hilarious."

"I saw him do that before. They trip out on that show."

Then they were silent again. Sometimes, silence was not bad. It could tell you if you were comfortable with a person. Ant and Sharron obviously were, because neither of them were forcing the conversation. Sharron wasn't even a phone person. But Ant was. He used the phone to break the ice, so that when he came face to face with a woman, he could jump directly into more intimate things. But with Sharron, her multifaceted questions made it seem as if they were picking up from nowhere. It was what rappers called freestyling: an unplanned flow that tested your skills to the fullest. That was what made Sharron such a turn-on to Ant. He could never work his straight magic with her. She was indeed stretching out her pieces.

"Are we having a hard time hanging up or something? Because I have some early runs to make tomorrow before work," Sharron said with a chuckle.

"Your day is no earlier than mine," he told her.

"Yes, but I have to take public transportation. All you have to do is drive your car for about ten minutes," she answered.

"*Five* minutes," he teased. "Aw'ight, well, I'll let you go to sleep then. And I'll call you tomorrow. I just felt like calling you up before I crashed tonight."

"And I'm glad that you did. I always look forward to your calls."

Ant grinned and thought, *Yeah. I got her too,* before they hung up. And when he crashed soon after in his comfortable bed, he thought about how nice it would be to settle down with Sharron. All he had to do was continue to enjoy her company, and then make up his mind, once and for all, that he would stay put with her. Like he mentioned earlier in the barbershop, men *did* possess the power to stay.

But *thinking* about progressive decisions has *always* been easier than *executing* them. Sometimes things just seem to get in the way. Big tests, if you want to call them that. Hurdles to overcome. Relationships, like everything else in life, have plenty of them. Hurdles. So just when everything is going well, you can always predict a few unexpected twisters to swoop down and throw you for a loop.

"The telephone is for you," Nadine informed Sharron. She was behind the register at the airport gift shop.

Sharron, understandably, had grown hesitant to answer the phone around Nadine. They remained *less* than friendly to each other since their testy encounter, weeks ago. It wasn't as if they held any grudges, they were just in two different ballparks of maturity.

"Hello," Sharron answered, guarded. She wanted to make the phone call as short as possible to keep Nadine's nosiness at bay.

"How are you doing, Sharron? I haven't heard from you in a while."

It was Mr. Married Man! Sharron was so shocked she nearly dropped the phone. He had made himself disappear so easily that she had all but forgotten about him.

He said, "I told myself, or at least I *tried* to, that I would move on and do what I needed to do with my family, but I couldn't stop thinking about you."

Sharron was speechless. With her silence, she figured Nadine would soon work herself into a frenzy of wonder while she rang items at the register. So Sharron forced herself to at least mumble, "Unh-hunh, I see," in response. The last thing in the world she wanted her co-worker to know about was her short-lived relationship with a married man. That would make her seem just as naive, whether she'd *known* that he was married or not. In fact, since Sharron *had known* that he was married, that made her feel worse!

"Now just hear me out for a minute," he was telling her.

Sharron expected a lecture and swiftly cut him off. "This is a real busy day today, so I'll call you about it when I get home," she told him. She was ready to hang up the phone on him but her manners did not allow her to be so brutal, which gave him time to continue.

"Sharron, I would have never called you if my feelings for you were not as strong as they are. I guess I realized how attached I felt to you while we were apart."

If she could have thrown a pot of hot water on him right through the telephone, she would have filled up a *bucket* instead and scorched his ass from head to toe!

"What I'm telling you is that we are very busy right now," she repeated. And they *were,* because air travel picked up a great deal in the midst of the summertime, especially after grade schools had let out. St. Louis International was an absolute *mess* with traffic.

He said, "I understand that. Just hear me out for a second."

She was tempted again to hang up on him.

"I've already purchased a ticket to fly down this weekend, and I just wanted to let you know so that we can sit and talk to each other face to face."

"Why?" she asked him. *Why in the* world *would I want to do that? I don't even want to* remember *you. Just go the hell away!* she thought frantically.

"Because I have too much to say to you to do it all over the phone. And I just want you to know that they are all good things about *us. Us* as a couple."

She couldn't ask him, *What about your wife and kids?* She couldn't call him an *ASSHOLE!* And she surely couldn't scream, *Are you out of your FUCKING mind!* like she wanted to. Not with Nadine standing right there in front of her at the register. The gossip would spread throughout the airport quicker than a hurricane. So she just sat there and took it, like a boiling pot of spaghetti rumbling to explode.

"Okay, so call me tonight then," she said, hanging up the phone before he could spit out another word. She *had* to do it. But then she got nervous about it. *What if he calls back?*

BLUP, BLUUUUP!

An outside call. Sharron's hand met Nadine's at the receiver.

"Customers," Sharron hinted with seniority at the job. *In other words, get your ass back to work!* she thought.

Nadine got the message and let go. If it was for her, Sharron would hand it over anyway.

"Sharron Francis, please."

"Speaking," she answered.

"Why would you hang up on me? This is childish. All I'm asking you to do is hear me out. Do you realize how difficult of a situation this is for me? My wife and I are separating."

So what? Do I care? NO! That's your *damn problem!* Sharron snapped in her mind.

She asked, "Are you purposefully trying to get me fired? I mean, I know this isn't much of a job to *some* people, but it *is* a job to me. So I'll call you later on. Okay?" she pleaded.

"Are you promising me that call?" he asked, twisting her arm.

"Yes," she answered, *if only to light your ass on* FIRE *when I get home!* ASSHOLE! she snapped to herself.

"Okay," he told her. "I'll talk to you then."

Sharron hung up for the second time and wanted to call it a day. Five minutes on that phone with Mr. Married Man, who was attempting to make *her* life as difficult as he had made his own, seemed more like five *hours!* She was noticeably drained, and looking at the clock.

"Almost five o'clock," she mumbled to herself. "*Three* more hours to go!" *SHIT!*

Closer to seven, when she had finally gotten a chance to calm herself down, Nadine was calling her to the phone again.

Why do I always *seem to get phone calls whenever I'm in* this *damn gift shop?!* she asked herself, referring to the shop where Nadine worked, close by the airport's entrance. Sharron tried her best to spend less time in that shop by working quickly whenever she was there, but it didn't seem to matter. And she wouldn't dare to tell Nadine to take a message like she could do elsewhere.

Damn this girl is a pain!

"Hello," she answered the phone again. This time she was expecting trouble.

"Why are you avoiding all of my phone calls? I thought we were much closer than that. I can't believe this."

It was Sean Love. What else could go wrong? Sharron hadn't exactly been avoiding him, she was just too wrapped up in her time spent with Anthony to get back to him. Nor was she anxious to do so. She didn't feel like talking to him right then either, especially after she had calmed her nerves from the first sneak attack.

She said, "How about I just fly up there to Chicago for a weekend? Would you like if I did that?" she asked sarcastically. She no longer cared about Nadine overhearing. She dared her to run her mouth. She even gave the cashier a stern eye to send her a message.

"Would you be willing to do that?" Sean asked her.

"Call me at home," she told him.

"Why, so Celena can tell me that you're not home again?" He sounded as bitter as he was the last time Sharron had spoken to him.

"I'll be in tonight," she lied to him. Actually, she was developing other plans. She wanted to get away and think, to recuperate from the day's drama. In the meantime, she would let Celena handle the phone calls however she wanted.

"You're getting off at eight o'clock again?" Sean asked.

"Yes."

"So you'll be home by nine?"

"Yes."

"Well, I'll call you then. Okay? And you'll talk to me, right?"

Sharron said, "No, I'll just answer the phone and breathe."

"Hmmph. Very funny. So how has everything been going for you otherwise?" he asked her.

"Call me tonight, and I'll tell you all about it."

"All right then. I'll talk to you later on. Hopefully."

Sharron hung up the phone once more and thought, *Not* hardly *will I be home for that! I'm gonna make sure I stay out as long as possible tonight.*

Then she called Anthony to see what *he* would be up to for the evening, only to find out that he had left early from work. He usually worked late.

Hmmm. I wonder what he's *up to,* she mused. She called and left a message at his apartment to get in touch with her as soon as possible.

Sharron arrived home before nine and checked her phone messages to see if Anthony had called her back. Once she found that he hadn't, she wasted no time changing into a pair of blue jeans and a red knit tennis shirt. Then she called for a taxi. Her destination: the skating rink on Lindbergh Boulevard for time to herself. However, as she waited with her skates in hand for the taxi to arrive, she anticipated the phone ringing, hoping for Anthony's last-minute call, so that he could join her. She felt attached to him and was not looking forward to being alone.

Man! How did this *happen?* she asked herself. Sharron rarely had regrets about enjoying her own personal time. It was usually *Celena* who couldn't stand being alone. So Sharron talked herself into it, going skating by herself, like she *used* to do. She decided that it would be a good thing. However, as soon as she arrived at the skating rink and laced up her skates, she felt all alone again.

I will not *call him,* she told herself. *I will* not *do it!*

Twenty minutes later, she was on the phone again, hanging up on Anthony's machine.

"Where the hell *is* he?" she mumbled, pissed and insecure.

Then she caught herself. "I can't believe this. I can't even *skate* by myself anymore," she stated with a chuckle. *What the hell is wrong with me?* she thought. *This is exactly how women* lose *men, by clinging to them and losing their own personal space. I should* know *better than that by now!*

Nevertheless, she was tempted to leave Anthony another message on his machine to meet her at the skating rink.

No, that doesn't make any sense. I don't even know how long I'm gonna be here, she reasoned.

"Excuse me, you're not here by yourself, are you? A fine black woman like you. Tell me you're not here by yourself," a tall brown man asked. He even had the nerve to look good. Real good! And he could skate well at that.

Sharron looked into his pleasant face and said, "Okay, I'm *not* here by myself," and skated off, leaving him in the wind.

Why did I just do that? she questioned. *I'm not even like that. Now he'll think that I'm stuck on myself. Damn, I just can't win! Would Anthony do the same for me, if a good-looking sister stepped up to him? Where is he right now?*

She caught herself worrying again.

Oh my God! This is terrible! What is happening to meeee! DAAAAMN! she agonized. She forced herself to skate it off.

Yeah, this is typical of my life, she continued to muse, rounding the skating rink. *I'm just changing songs with flashing lights and different people, and all I'm really doing is skating around in circles, whether it's fast or slow, backwards or forwards. This love shit is a* trip! *It really is.*

As she skated, she decided she needed to hear a song that fit her mood, and made a request with the DJ in his elevated booth that overlooked the skating floor.

"Do you have Lauryn Hill?!" she shouted up at him.

"Lauryn Hill? Of course I got Lauryn Hill," he answered. "Which one you wanna hear? 'Doo Wop'?"

"No! Do you have 'Ex-Factor'?!"

He grinned and said, "Oh. So you got a love jones in here."

She smiled back at him and responded, "Yeah, don't we all!"

"In two songs, I'll put it on for you," he promised.

"Thank you!"

When she returned to the floor, she noticed that good-looking brother with the skating skills watching her every move.

What if I just made friends with him? she questioned. *What would be so wrong with that?*

Before she knew it, Lauryn Hill's ode to love hit the speakers and sunk into the minds and souls of every skater on the floor.

Where were *you-uuuu . . .*
when I neeeed-ed yuuuu?!
Where were *you-uuuu . . .*

"Did you make a request for that?"

That handsome-ass tall brown man was right back in her face again. His *breath* even smelled good. Like peppermints. Unless you didn't *like* the smell of peppermints. But it sure beat the smell of cigarettes or marijuana. Peppermint breath was a good first impression.

"Yeah, I requested it," Sharron told him.

"You wanna sit down and talk about it? My name is Damani. Damani Richardson," he said, extending his hand to her while they skated forward.

She politely declined his hand and skated alongside him, giving him her undivided attention.

"Where are you from?" she asked. He was *not* from St. Louis. She could tell. He was a player from another place, with a different *style* about him.

"Cincinnati," he answered, smiling. "Why? You can tell?"

She nodded. "Yeah." *And why not sit down and talk to him, if just to amuse myself while I'm here?* "I'm not from here either. I'm from Memphis," she told him.

"And your name is . . . ?"

"Sharron Francis."

"So, would you like to sit down and talk about it, with no strings attached, to a stranger. At least until we get to know each other," he added with a confident smile.

She smirked, knowing better, and was tempted to do it anyway, *with no strings attached, to a stranger.* So she agreed to it.

"Sure. Why not?"

He led the way to a table, while reaching out again for her hand. A hand that she still refused to give him. At least not until they got to know each other. Which in Sharron's case was unlikely. She was only being nice to him. Anything else was off-limits. Unless she was with Anthony. Because *strangers* don't touch. And women were protective that way.

Touching, for guys, was more allowable. Especially with a woman who looked good enough to peek two and three times at. That was another problem for men. They just couldn't seem to keep their greedy paws off of so much tasty candy. The more well-curved and available the women were, the more it tempted guys to just reach out and touch someone, anytime and anyplace, whether they were permitted to or not.

"Damn, Ant! You see that?!" Tone asked his partner. They were heaving his blue tweed sofa up the steps of his new, second-floor duplex apartment on Louisiana Avenue. Tone had found a southside apartment that was walking distance from Ant's place on Nebraska. And he was moving in right away, forcing Ant to take off from work early to rent a truck, because Tone didn't have any credit cards to rent with.

Ant shouted from the front end of the sofa, "Shit, man. Pay attention to what you're doing before you drop this shit on me!"

Tone's eyes were filled with a sexy brown neighbor, walking into the apartment just two doors down from his.

"I can see it now, dawg. I'm gon' *love* living over here!" Tone expressed excitedly as they made their way up the stairs with the sofa.

I can see it, too, Ant thought. *I can see that I'm gonna* hate *it!*

They made it up to the new apartment and gingerly set the sofa down in the living room on a shiny hardwood floor.

"Was your floor this shiny when you first moved in, Ant?"

Ant shook his head and grinned. Tone seemed astonished by his new place. "I guess you don't remember," he commented.

"Naw. I don't remember it being as shiny as *this.* But now you got them oriental rugs everywhere. I think I like this shiny floor better," Tone responded.

"You better buy a good mop then," Ant advised with a chuckle.

"Yeah, I'ma buy a lot of stuff. I can't *wait* to hook this crib up!" Tone was an oversized toddler in a new playground.

"You *better* wait," Ant warned him. "You just *got* that job, man, and until you've had it for at least *four months,* I wouldn't start spending my money too fast." *You shouldn't have even gotten this apartment so soon,* he thought.

"Aw, man, we get overtime up the ass on that job. And you wouldn't believe how many calls we get. I mean, *everybody* need their carpets cleaned. And them fancy cribs gotta keep up their appearances for guests and shit," Tone argued.

"I'm just saying, man. It took me *a while* to hook up *my* apartment. Remember how empty it was for them first five months?" Ant reminded his friend.

Tone blew off his warning and said, "Yeah, well, that was *you,*" before heading back outside to have another look at his sexy brown neighbor. Fortunately, she decided to sit out on her front steps and suck in the cool summer air as the sun traveled westward and slipped out of sight. Tone took the opportunity to admire her. Ant joined him outside a few seconds later.

"Is she tough or what?" Tone asked him, referring to the well-curved neighbor. She appeared to be in her early twenties with poise.

Ant gave her a look and smiled. "Yeah, I'd talk to her. No doubt."

"Well, you got Sharron now, so don't worry about it. I'll do it. You just start me off."

Ant looked at his partner and frowned. "I'm not startin' shit off for you, man. I'm dirty, tired, stinking, and we're finished moving your shit, so I'm gettin' out of here and walking back home. I'll see your ass tomorrow morning when we turn the truck back in. And remember, seven o'clock, *sharp,*" he said, walking off.

Tone grabbed him back. "Come on, man. Let's just walk over there and act like we being good neighbors, and then I'll take it from there."

Ant shook his head and grinned. Tone was apparently too dependent on his partner's social skills.

"Just act like we all in a club and go over there and ask her to dance or something," Ant joked. "We too old for that set-up shit. She knows it, too."

"Aw'ight, aw'ight, this last time, dawg," Tone pleaded.

Ant was still hesitant, so Tone found the heart to go ahead and speak up for himself.

"Excuse me, is this a nice neighborhood around here? I'm just moving in," he said.

Ant frowned at him. "Man, go over there and talk to her like you got some sense."

To his surprise, she responded openly.

"Yeah, it's pretty nice. But it gets boring around here at times, too. There's more people who hang out further up," she said, waving her hand eastward, in the direction of Ant's apartment.

Ant nodded and said, "Yeah, it *is* more people up that way. A bunch of wild-ass kids. I live up on Nebraska," he told her.

"I know," she responded to him.

"You know?" he responded back. *Do I know this girl?* he thought. He tried to focus on whether he knew her or not.

She said, "Yeah, you have a burgundy car, right? With shiny rims and stuff?"

Ant nodded, still trying to figure out who she was. "Yeah. It's cranberry. A seventy-nine Chevy," he told her.

She smiled and said, "My girlfriend used to talk about you washing your car with no shirt on. This was a few years ago. She lives on California."

California was two blocks east of Nebraska.

Not to be outdone, Tone slipped into their cordial conversation and said, "Well, why don't you call your girlfriend up and see what she's doing right now?"

"She *should* just be getting in from work. Hold on. Let me call her and see," she said, getting up to go inside for a phone.

Ant looked at Tone and asked, "What the hell you doin', man?"

"We might be able to get with these girls," Tone answered, cheesing.

"Man, I'm not thinkin' about no damn girls. I'm thinkin' 'bout a hot-ass shower."

"Just talk to her first. You can take a shower and come back."

Ant was still hesitant. "I thought I had *Sharron,* a few minutes ago," he added sarcastically.

"I mean, it ain't like you gotta do shit with this girl, man, just talk to her. Ain't no harm done in that."

Before Ant could say another word, the sexy brown neighbor was back outside with a cordless phone in hand. She was headed in their direction over the small grass lawn.

"He's out here in front of me right now," she was saying over the phone. "You wanna talk to him?"

Ant could not believe it! *Shit!* he told himself. *And her girlfriend's probably the ugly one at that.*

The next thing he knew, he was being handed the phone.

"Hello," he answered.

"Do you even know who this is?" a confident voice asked him through the line.

"Naw. Who is it?"

"Diane."

"Diane?" he repeated. The name didn't ring a bell with him.

She said, "Remember you were outside washing your car a while ago, and you asked a girl with long braids how old she was. And when I said that I was nineteen, you told me to stop lying. *Then* you said that I would break a grown man's heart one day when I got a little older."

Ant began to laugh. "Oohhh, yeah, I remember you. You looked like you was about fifteen."

"I can't *help* how young I look. But I *am* turning twenty-one in October, so I'm *not* some young teenager," she huffed. She sounded headstrong and sexy. From what Ant could remember of her, she was. She was just extra young-looking in the face, which in the long run would be a good thing.

"So what are you trying to say?" he asked her. Language was a loaded gun, especially for people who knew how to use it. Anthony Poole used it well. He wanted Diane to express just how confident she was. Then he could use it against her.

"I'm saying that I'm old enough to handle myself," she told him.

"Well, your girlfriend said that you would come around here if I asked you to. She said you had a crush on me."

"She told you that? Oh my God! What else she tell you?"

"She said you used to fantasize about me," Ant bullshitted. He figured he might as well have a good time with it since Tone had led him right smack into the middle of things.

Tone's new neighbor smiled it off, and did not seem to mind that Ant was making up stories on her. After all, he was just the kind of man her girlfriend Diane would want: crafty and confident in his own right. If he wasn't, Diane would have chewed him up and spit him out anyway.

"So are you staying in the house, or are you coming around here to see me?" he pressed her. He had nothing to lose. Why *not* force the issue?

"All I have to do is put my shoes back on. I can drive around there in five minutes," she responded.

Meanwhile, Tone began a conversation with her friend, who was much less impressed with *him* than Diane was with Ant. She figured that after Ant and Diane were able to go in their own direction, she would politely tell Tone she was uninterested in him.

Ant said, "Aw'ight, well let me see how *grown-up* you are."

Diane laughed at it. "Five minutes," she repeated.

Ant handed the phone back to her girlfriend and thought, *What the hell did I just do that for?* It all happened so fast, he didn't have time to think and slow himself down. Nevertheless, he was curious about her, so he waited anyway. And when Diane drove up in her dark blue Honda Civic and climbed out, he was glad he'd waited. She had done away with the braids and wore her hair in a shoulder-length bob, making her look closer to her age. Her body was much thinner than her girlfriend's, but her brown babydoll face *more* than made up for it!

Damn! Ant thought to himself. Tone thought it, too. It was just Ant's luck, all of his life it seemed, to have a way with pretty women.

"So, do I look my age now, or at least *older?*" she asked him.

Ant nearly swallowed his words. "Ah, yeah, you ah, look your age now. Definitely!"

They all shared a laugh.

"What brings y'all around here?" she asked.

"His friend Tone just moved in," her girlfriend answered. "He was helping him to move, and I noticed him, and we just got to talking, so I called you."

Diane looked them over and smiled. "Both of y'all are sweaty from moving furniture and stuff?"

Ant was still in a minor daze, checking her out. In her neat work clothes, she could even pass for a part-time fashion model.

"I was just about to head back home and take a shower," he responded to her.

Diane smiled, giving her thoughts away *far* too soon. She was fantasizing about his godly brown, car-washing body. Ant read her smile and jumped all over it. Instinctively.

"Then I can change into something nice, spray on something that smells good to you, and just kick it with you for a while, if you can stay out. 'Cause we all gotta go to work in the morning."

"Ain't it the truth," Tone added his two cents, proud of his new employment.

"Why don't you drive him around there, Diane?" her girlfriend commented. She just wanted to get rid of Tone, basically. Diane and Ant could do their own chitchatting in the car.

Ant looked at Tone and couldn't believe his good fortune. *This is crazy! I can't drive around there with her! Or can I?* he thought.

"All right, I can do that," Diane responded.

All eyes turned to Ant, who looked confused. He was the only one who wasn't pleased. *This girl lives right around the corner from me. I can't fuck with her. Or can I?*

"Do you want a ride home?" Diane asked him, grinning. "I won't bite you," she added.

Ant didn't want to seem gun-shy. He finally spoke up and said, "Let's go then."

"Aw'ight, then, Ant. I'll see you when you get back," Tone told him. If he knew his partner as well as he *thought* he did, there was no guarantee that they were coming back.

Ant climbed into the passenger side of Diane's Civic, still thinking how crazy it was to luck up with an unexpected brown beauty queen. Then he decided to get buck wild with it, to find out if he was only dreaming. Guys would do that, roll their dice all the way to the edge to find out if they would be millionaires or broke bums. But since he still had Sharron, waiting in the wings, Ant didn't really care if he lost Diane at the crap tables. He wasn't planning on keeping her anyway. He was just curious to see how far he could go with her.

"You know what apartment I live in?" he asked her.

She didn't want to admit it him. She grinned and said, "Would you hold it against me if I did?"

"Why would I hold it against you?"

"I mean, I don't want you to think that I was *stalking* you or anything."

"Naw, if anything, I would be *flattered,*" he told her.

She didn't admit to anything. At least not verbally. Because she *did* pull up in a parking space behind his car. But that was easy to do since she knew what his car looked like and what block he parked it on.

Then he got cold feet again. *What if Sharron just popped up around here out the blue and caught me?* he asked himself, guilt-ridden. That only made him roll his dice more desperately, expecting to lose. Ant *wanted* to be broke. That way, he could claim that he had tried and failed. Then he could leave empty-handed and regain his real treasure: Sharron.

Ant went for broke and said, "Now, if you decide to come in and wait for me, who's gonna stop you from stripping naked and jumping into the shower with me?" He just *knew* that she would put a stop to it all, sooner or later. He planned on saying anything he could to turn her *off,* and make it easier on himself to get out of a sticky situation.

Diane broke out laughing and said, "I'll stop *myself.*" Yet, she was still willing to wait inside for him instead of in the car, or back at her girlfriend's. How did Ant know? Because she was taking her key out of the ignition and grabbing her pocketbook.

"So, you'll wait for me then?" he asked her, making sure.

She nodded. "Yeah, I don't mind. I'll wait if you want me to."

He looked into her pretty brown face once more, and decided that he did. They climbed out of the car and headed inside. As they ascended the stairway, Ant continued to think how unlikely it was to luck up so good. *Damn! Am I* that *smooth or what?* he thought to himself. He led Diane into his apartment and told her to make herself comfortable on the sofa, where she could watch television or listen to his stereo system.

"Do you want something to drink?" he asked her.

"What do you have?"

"Water. 7Up. Orange juice."

"7Up," she told him.

He went and filled her a large glass of 7Up and made sure to turn the ringer off on his telephone.

"Aw'ight, well, relax right here, and I'll be back out when I'm all washed up," he told her.

"Okay," she said with a grin and a sip of her pop.

Ant went ahead and ran his shower water, still shaking his head concerning his unplanned company. "I don't believe this shit," he mumbled to himself. "And this girl is *fine* as hell!"

He began to take his shower and got anxious. He slipped up and thought with his wrong head. *You got a fine-ass girl waitin' inside of your damn living room for you, and you in here butt naked taking a shower. You didn't even* try *anything with her yet! What the hell is on* your *mind?! If you're gonna get caught in the act, then at least get caught* IN *the act!*

Ant gave himself a quick wash down, wrapped a towel around his waist, slipped on his slippers, and walked back out to his living room to go for it all, while still dripping wet with shower water.

"Are you sure you don't want to join me in a shower?" he asked his company with a ridiculous smile. It was outlandish to even ask. But that's a man for you, rolling his dice *hard!*

Diane looked at him, chuckled in his face, and calmly sat her drink down. She said, "You know what I was just thinking while you were in the shower?"

"Naw. What?"

She shook her head and said, "This is crazy. I don't even know what I'm doing here. I have a boyfriend, you have a girlfriend, and this doesn't even make any sense, Anthony."

It occurred to him at that moment that he hadn't even given her his name. He just assumed that she knew it. And she did.

"How you know I have a girl?" he asked her. *How much does she know about me anyway?* he thought.

"I mean, it's obvious," she answered. "You have everything going for you. Why *wouldn't* you have a girlfriend? Or at *least* one."

It was a crazy situation indeed. The craziness made it more tempting. Ant rationalized that it was such an unbelievable occurrence that it was *meant* to happen. Give a guy an inch, and if he's cunning enough, he'll find a way to stretch a mile out of it.

Ant got slick on her and said, "Well, if you really want to leave me, then I guess that's what you have to do," looking puppy-eyed, wet, and homeless.

Diane read the game and cut him off. "Don't even try that with me. You know this isn't right. It's *not*."

"What's not right? We haven't done anything. We're just talking. Unless you have a guilty conscience about what you *want* to do?"

"What I want to do is leave, because this is not happening."

Ant poised himself. "If you really wanted to leave me, you would have left already."

She said, "I thought about that, but I didn't want to be rude."

"So, you were afraid to even face me when I came back out," he said, working her confidence again.

She smiled it off. "I am *hardly* afraid of you." Then she stood up to head for the door. But on her way to the door, she slipped up and looked at his wet, chocolate brown chest, and got caught staring.

"Do you want to come back again?" he asked her.

"For what?" she asked from the door.

"Because you just looked at me like you were leaving something that you wanted."

She smiled, forcing herself not to be swayed by him.

"You know what . . ." she commented with her palm up in a stop motion. But she couldn't seem to finish her words. Flashing images of his towel dropping off, unleashing all of his brown maleness, stood in her way.

"What? What do I know?" he asked her. "That you don't really want to leave? I mean, you *want* to stay, but now you're acting all nervous about it. I was nervous at first, too."

"Nervous about what?" she asked him. Her shoulder was against the door.

"I was thinking, 'Is she really coming over here? Does she really want to see me?' And then you came. So don't get nervous on me now. You a grown woman, right?"

In the sport of boxing, there was a common thought that if you worked blows to an opponent's body, the hands would eventually fall to where you could work the head and score a knockout punch. But in the sport of women, the pros went about it oppositely. They worked their blows to a woman's head, and when her hands went up in a scramble of confusion, she left her body unprotected and vulnerable for attack.

Don't even listen to him, girl, Diane tried to tell herself. *Just leave!*

He reached out his hand to her, still moist from the shower. "Come here."

She shook it off and said, "No, I have to go."

Ant smiled and asked, "How long are you gonna stand at the door, talking about you're ready to leave when you *know* that you're not."

"I *am* ready to leave," she insisted.

"Go ahead then. And make it fast before you change your mind. Because in a minute, I'm gon' have to turn the lights off and lead you to where you *really* want to go," he told her. By that point, Ant didn't care anymore. He just wanted to get the temptation over with. Leave or stay!

But then she lost track of her words. And before she could react, he gently backed her against the door and wet her lips with his. Then he slid his tongue onto hers. Right when she began to kiss him back, he slipped his tongue away, tickling it down her neck and back up to her ear to whisper.

"Don't you wanna stay? Tell the truth."

No, I can't do that, she told herself. Since Ant could not hear her words, and did not want to, he clicked off the light switch beside her head and guided her hand through his towel. And as he continued to wrestle with her tongue, she caressed his wand.

"Why are you doing this to me?" she asked him, noticeably aroused.

Ant slid his moist hands under her blouse and up to fondle her twins.

"Because you want me to?" he answered her.

And it was the truth. She did. But not right then. She wanted him on *her* terms. At *her* time. Nevertheless, the moment was too powerful for her to deny. Her body told her that it was too *late* to turn away. So when he gently took her by the hand and led her through the darkness to his bedroom, she followed him without any resistance.

"I don't believe I did this," Diane sat up and said out loud, less than an hour later. She sunk her face into her hands, pulling her knees up to her bare chest in shame.

Who you *tellin'*? Ant thought to himself. *I don't believe I did this shit either. And now I gotta get rid of you to call my lady.*

"Do you feel guilty?" Diane asked him.

"Do you?" he asked her back.

Generally, guys felt guilty when they were *caught* doing wrong, and not much beforehand.

Diane looked into Ant's face and said, "Of course I do. I shouldn't have done this."

Ant began to think about Sharron, wondering what she was up to, and how many times she may have called him while he was out with Tone, and then while entertaining himself with unplanned company. When he looked over at his clock, it read 10:49 P.M.

He thought, *Man, I gotta get her the hell out of here so I can make my phone call.*

"So, do you?" Diane asked him again, referring to his feelings of guilt.

In the heat of the moment he said, "I feel guilty that I want you to leave right now." And he *did* feel guilty about that. Because he was tired of having to push women away as soon as the heat had simmered. That was what made him realize how much Sharron meant to him. He wanted to hold her *close* when they were done. Hold her tightly and tell her . . . "I love you, girl. I *love* you!"

Diane got the message and began to gather her things, dressing herself in haste, feeling miserable. Not only because their sex had been too fast and too meaningless, but that she could be discarded so soon after, with not even a hug or a kiss to keep her warm, if just for the short ride home.

"Thanks for nothing," she told him as she left. She said it not bitterly, but as a matter of fact. Ant knew just what she meant. Their sex had been next to nothing. It was only temporary, feeling good while it lasted, and then vanishing into thin air as soon as they were done. Ant sat up in his bed and felt empty all over again. He felt ugly inside. Wasted. Dirty. Dirty all over. The kind of dirt that could not be washed away, but had to be scrubbed from the inside out, and vigorously, until he was all cleaned out, which could take a very long time.

"Damn, man! What the hell is wrong with me?" he mumbled to himself. "Tone did it to me again," he added, starting up with the blame game. Tone had nothing to do with stripping Diane's mind naked, and holding her body hostage to have his way with her. Tone did not have the ability to do that even if he wanted to. Ant had his *own* conscience to deal with. Few humans had enough ice water in their veins to ignore the heat of guilt. That's what lawyers were paid for. But no lawyer could defend a man against his own conscience.

In the dark lonely nights they spent alone, many men *did* feel the guilt of detachment. Yet, the brother in the barbershop was right. Diane *had* to know what she was getting herself into. She could feel it. And she let it happen anyway. It wasn't all *Ant's* fault. Nevertheless, Sharron was right as well, in the sense that Ant had *led* Diane to *believe* it was her decision to stay, when in reality, he had conned her *out* of leaving.

Ant nodded his head, convinced, and made up his mind. "Yup. I might as well settle down with Sharron. I can't take this no more. It's *killin'* me! I knew *damn well* that girl wasn't supposed to be over here tonight! Now I gotta be on the lookout for her whenever I bring Sharron around. *Damn* that was dumb!"

He stood up and walked to his telephone to retrieve his messages and to call Sharron. She had called him and left a message before seven, and there was another hang up closer to ten. He turned his ringer back on and prepared to make his call, surprised to find Tone on the other end of the line as soon as he picked up.

"She still over there, Ant? Did you get with her?" Tone asked him.

Ant thought about it and lied. He didn't need Tone complicating things for him. "Naw, man, she left a while ago. She said she had a boyfriend, I had a girlfriend, and that was about it. But I tried."

"You told her you had a girl?" Tone asked. That wasn't Ant's style.

"Naw, man, I didn't tell her that, she just *assumed* that I did, and I didn't deny it."

"Oh. In that case, it sounds like you didn't really wanna do her."

"Yeah, I was too tired anyway," Ant responded. "So what happened with you and her girlfriend?"

"Who, Debi?"

"That's her name?"

"Yeah, her middle name. She don't like using her first name."

"What is it?"

"She wouldn't even tell me."

Ant shook his head and smiled. *How can* I *have it so good and* Tone *have it so damn bad?* he thought. "I didn't know they knew *my* name," he commented.

Tone said, "Yeah, they knew it. You popular around here and don't even know it."

"Popular for what? I barely even hang out around here."

"Man, you know how it is when you move into a new 'hood and people get to talking about you. I'm about to be popular around here too, soon."

Yeah, popular for what? Ant thought. "Man, we too old for this neighborhood-reputation shit. That's exactly what I'm trying to get away from," he piped.

"Anyway, man, I'm 'bout to roll up a fat one, relax, and think about the possibilities of my new crib," Tone commented.

"You gettin' *high* tonight? Hey, man, we gotta get up early to take that truck back tomorrow morning," Ant complained. "And don't you go back to work?"

"Shit, I'll be aw'ight by then. How long you think this weed lasts?"

Ant said, "You actually gon' light up some weed on your first night in your new apartment?" It was a ridiculous idea.

Tone laughed and said, "Damn right. I *wanted* to get some ass on my first night around here, but that girl started talking some shit about having a busy work schedule and some other shit. Then she started talking about she just came out of a relationship and whatnot. A bunch of bullshit, man. So I said, 'Fuck it then. Let me just leave this damn girl alone.'"

"And now you gon' get high again," Ant reiterated.

"Are you hard at hearing or something? That's what I said." Tone went ahead and took his first toke while still on the phone.

"Don't call me back acting crazy tonight, man. And I'm serious about that shit, too," Ant warned him.

Tone laughed through his marijuana smoke and said, "Don't worry. I won't."

Ant hung up the phone and shook his head. "I really need to stop hangin' out with that boy," he told himself out loud. He got back on the line to call up his "lady."

Her roommate Celena answered.

"Hello, can I speak to Sharron."

"What is this, the hot line for Sharron tonight or something? Who's calling?"

"It's Anthony."

"Oh, how are you doin'?" she responded, changing her tone. That was a good thing. He was finally growing on her. "Sharron's not with you?" she asked him.

"Naw, I was with my boy Tone all night. I had to help him move into his new apartment. I didn't get Sharron's message until late." A lie mixed with the truth was practically bulletproof. It was too hard to pick it apart.

"Well, she didn't leave me any messages, so I don't know *where* she is right now," Celena responded.

Ant didn't like the sound of that at all. "Aw'ight, well, tell her that I called when she gets in."

"Okay. I'll do that," Celena said, hanging up.

That's when Ant's guilty conscience *really* began to play tricks on him. He asked himself, *What did Celena mean by that "hot line for Sharron" shit? What if Sharron just popped up around my block and caught me taking Diane up into the crib or something?* DAMN! *Now she might be out there with another guy somewhere.*

Did men *really* cry inside and in the dark? Definitely! *If I coulda, I shoulda, woulda* was how *men* cried, and usually only *after* they committed their acts of stupidity. Because beforehand, they viewed themselves as invincible. So Ant was crying like a baby, twisting and turning inside with butterflies of a lost opportunity of love.

"And I was just starting to get into this girl," he told himself. "That's just what the hell I get. I probably don't even deserve her.

"DAMN!"

Right as he was about to lose his mind, Sharron saved him with her perfectly timed phone call.

"Are you ready for bed yet?" she asked him. She sounded chipper, too. She wouldn't have sounded that way if she had gone on a date with another man. Or at least from what *Ant* thought he knew about women.

"Naw, why?" he answered excitedly, happy to hear her voice.

"I'm not coming over there or anything," she said with a chuckle. "I was just asking you."

"I wasn't expecting you to come over. I'm just happy to talk to you. I missed you," he told her, sounding like a little boy addressing his mommy.

Sharron stopped laughing and said, "I missed you too."

"I didn't get your message until late," he told her.

"Yeah, Celena told me."

"I was helping Tone move into his new apartment."

"She told me that too."

"I even had to rent a truck for him because he don't have no damn credit."

"That's why you left from work early?" Sharron asked him casually.

"Yeah. You called me at my job?" he responded to her.

"I wanted to get in contact with you so you could go skating with me. Or go *somewhere.* I just didn't feel like being home tonight," she answered. "So I went by myself."

"My bad. I'll make it up to you next time." *And I might as well get used to her tracking me down,* he told himself. *When you hook up with a woman like Sharron, she'll end up knowing everything about you. But that's the way it* should *be in a tight relationship, just like I know everything about my boy Tone, and she knows everything about her girl Celena. Or not* everything, *but more than enough,* he corrected himself.

"So where did Tone move to?" Sharron asked him.

"Right around the corner from me, on Louisiana Avenue. I don't like that shit either. He's too close for comfort." *And so is this girl Diane,* he thought. *I may have to move away from this area.*

Then his other line rang.

"That's probably Tone right now. And I told him not to call me back tonight," Ant informed her. "Hold on for a minute."

He clicked over his line and was immediately bombarded by an angry woman:

"Anthony, this is Debi, Diane's girlfriend on Louisiana. And I just called to say that you're a *fucked-up individual!* She told me what happened. And it didn't even have to go down like that."

"Go down like what?" he asked her, gathering the facts before he could respond accordingly.

"That y'all could just do *whatever,* and then you just kick her out like that. I mean, I'm not saying that it was a good situation to begin with on her part. But God! You could *at least* show a little human courtesy," she told him. And she was right.

"What's her phone number?" he asked.

"Why?"

"So I can call her up and apologize to her," he answered. He wanted to get off the line as quickly as he could to return to Sharron anyway.

Debi agreed to it and gave him the number. When Ant clicked back over to Sharron he felt heavy with increased guilt, knowing that he would have to lie to her.

Did guys pray when they were caught up in jams? Yes, they did. *God, if I get out of this one, I'll never do this shit again. I mean, stuff,* Ant prayed.

"So what did he want?" Sharron asked, referring to his friend Tone, and making it easier for him.

Ant lied and said, "Nothin'. He was just calling me up with the same old nonsense. And he's high now, talking about he thought he heard somebody messing with the truck outside his window. And the paperwork has *my name* on it. So I might have to go back around there and make sure it's still in good shape for when we turn it in tomorrow morning."

Bulletproof again. Another lie mixed with the truth.

Sharron said, "Well, it's been a long day for me, too. I'm going to bed. So do what you have to do, and I'll just talk to you tomorrow."

Perfect! Ant told himself. *Now let me go ahead and tie up these loose ends so I can start off fresh tomorrow morning.*

First he called Diane.

"Can I speak to Diane?"

"Speaking."

"This is Anthony."

"I know," she responded.

"Well, I'm calling to say that I apologize to you for being insensitive tonight. I didn't mean it that way."

She paused. "How *did* you mean it?" she asked him. She even *sounded* hurt. Not tearfully, but angrily.

He said, "Really, we weren't even supposed to be in that situation. Like you said, we both have relationships already. So I meant it like . . . you know, we shouldn't have even been there in the first place."

"Yeah, I understand," she told him. There wasn't much else to say, but Diane held the line, as if she was waiting for something else, a conversation of sorts. Ant knew what *that* meant. She still had feelings for him. Nevertheless, there was nothing he could do about that. He was going back to Sharron. For good! He no longer wanted to juggle extra women. Especially with one who lived so close by him. It was a disaster waiting to happen.

At Diane's hesitation Ant reiterated his reason for calling her. "So I just wanted to let you know that I apologize," he told her again. "I don't want us to become enemies or anything if we don't have to be," he added.

"Especially for when your *girlfriend* comes over again, right?" she hinted.

If he didn't know any better, Ant would have thought that she was trying to pick a fight, just to keep him on the line with her. She would rather have *any* emotion from him than none.

"I mean, what else do you want me to say?" he asked her. "It wasn't like you didn't say and do some things yourself that led us to where we went."

"Don't try to blame this on me," she argued. "You had some things on *your* mind before I even drove over to my girlfriend's block to see you."

Ant got fed up and said, "Look, if you remember correctly, I didn't even know who you *were* when I talked to you on the phone. So how are you gonna tell me what I was thinking? I just wanted to see what you looked like."

"And then once you saw what I *looked like,* you took it to a whole different level. And don't act like you didn't remember me *either,* because you *did* remember me. So don't even try that."

Ant couldn't believe it. He let himself fall right into her trap, having an argument just for the sake of arguing. Because once he hung up that phone, he had it set in *his* mind that he was moving on, and that was that.

"Okay, so how do we end this conversation?" he asked her. He had been on the phone with her longer than he expected already.

"Maybe I don't *want* to end it, just like *you* didn't want me to leave your apartment tonight," she snapped. "Or at least not until after you fucked me."

She surely wasn't letting Ant off the hook as easily as he wanted to be.

He's not gonna get involved with me and just up and walk away like nothing happened, Diane was thinking.

Ant thought, *What the hell have I gotten myself into now? I* swear *I need to stop hanging out with* Tone! *I don't even feel like goin' through this shit with this girl. It's too late at night for this!*

It was close to twelve midnight. Ant had to be up extra early to return the rental truck, and then go back to work at Paul's.

He thought of a different angle and said, "Do you really have a boyfriend? Because if you do, you must not care too much about him. Why are you sitting here arguing with me?"

She said, "What if I don't have a boyfriend anymore? And what if I still wanna be with you?"

Bingo! She'd wanted to express that all along. And Ant was shocked by it. Diane must have really liked him. But it was too damn bad, because he wasn't in the market anymore.

"We can't have it like that," he told her. "Like you said, *I* already have somebody, and *you* already have somebody."

"I mean, it's not like you're *married* or anything. And *I'm* not married. Or *are* you married?" she asked him.

"Okay. What if I *was* married?" he responded, trying anything to do away with her.

"But why would you say you're married if you're not?"

"Because I'm *taken,*" he snapped at her. "You know that already."

"You wasn't *taken* two hours ago!" she countered. "You was still available *then.* And how do I know? Because your ass was all up inside of me!"

Shit, this girl has issues! Ant thought to himself. *She's trippin'!*

Years ago, he would have been smiling his behind off, thrilled with his good work. But on this particular night, he was tempted to scream at the top of his lungs, *LOOK, GIRL, JUST LEAVE ME THE HELL ALONE AND LET ME GO BACK TO MY LADY! IT WAS A MISTAKE! OKAY?! NOW GO FIND YOURSELF SOMEBODY ELSE TO BE WITH!*

Instead, he asked her, "So what do you want to do, come back over here and have me finish off the job? And then fuck you every day until you get tired of it and go out looking for somebody else. Is that what you want? Because I can't give you much more than that."

"Is that how you treat your girlfriend?" she countered. "I want what *she* gets."

Ant lost his cool and shouted, "You can't *have* what she gets! You don't even know how to *get it!*"

Diane was really pushing him to his limit.

She said, "Well, fuck you too, then!" And it was weak. He could tell that she didn't mean it. That changed everything.

Ant stopped himself and began to laugh, remembering how bad *he* was years ago. *This girl thinks she can have her way with anything she wants, just because she's pretty. But I got news for her ass. I've had pretty girls before. And it don't mean* jack *to me!*

"Now I guess you're gonna go ahead and hang up on me, right? Just like *I* would have done when *I* was younger, because you can't have your way," he told her. "Well, let me tell you something. You may *think* that you're grown and all that, but you still have a lot of maturing to do."

"Yeah, whatever," she responded to him. "We'll see how much *maturing* I have to do the next time your *girlfriend* comes around," she warned.

Ant stopped smiling and fell silent. Diane took that for what it meant. She was crossing dangerous ground. You don't mess with the heart of a grown man. They were liable to do very bad things when stressed, especially over issues of the heart. They were liable to respond three times as badly as the average woman. Diane was only bluffing anyway. So she decided to tell him before he threatened to wring her damn neck until she could no longer breathe.

"I was only jokin'," she said. "I wouldn't even do that to you."

"That didn't sound like no damn joke to me," he told her.

She said, "Good. So you think about that the next time you decide to take advantage of somebody."

Trust me! Ant thought to himself. *I already did.*

When he finally hung up the phone, the bone he wanted to pick with Tone for giving Debi his phone number was buried, along with all of his depleted energy from one *very* long night. So he stretched out on his bed, spread-eagle, like Jesus on the cross, and proclaimed, "This is it. From now on, it's just me and Sharron. And my dealings with all these other women out here is over with. Because it's nothin' out there but the same old shit. So from now on . . . I'm retired."

Plans for an immediate and long-term future are nice to have, but the world rarely runs as smoothly as we would all like it to. And we can *say* anything. But actually carrying out what we plan is a whole different story. As we know from popular American athletes, retirement can be an extremely hard thing to do. Many times, help is needed to uphold that decision. Sometimes we receive that help in mysterious ways. So when the month of August rolled around, and all seemed well again for the two lovebirds as they waited in line for popcorn, drinks, and candy at the Northwest Plaza movie theater on a Saturday night, another hurdle was presented in the form of an old temptation. Dana Nicole Simpson.

"Do you know her or something?" Sharron asked Anthony when she noticed the intense stare of a woman who presented a challenge to a browner sister. Because the *lighter* shade of brown, when connected to a pretty face and an all-about-me attitude, was legendary for the heartache of black American men, even as the new millennium approached.

Anthony looked in her direction and said, "Yeah. I know her."

Dana was still with her tall new love, as Ant was with *his* new love. Nevertheless, she was making Sharron feel uncomfortable.

"Well, why is she staring like that?"

Because she always got something up her damn sleeve, Anthony thought, nervous about it himself. He hadn't set eyes on Dana in months. He didn't need to see her when around Sharron either. He cared about Sharron too much to put her in that position. Dating a man known to many women was indeed nerve-racking.

But it was too late for an escape, because Dana had spotted them. And as soon as she got a chance to break away from her man, she walked right in their direction to say what she had on her mind.

"Hey, Anthony. Good to see you." She gave Sharron a nod and smiled at her.

"How you doin'?" Anthony responded, reserved.

"I'm being good. How 'bout you?" she asked him with a lingering grin. When talking about the use of words, Dana could use the fewest and still get her point across.

Anthony nodded, hoping that Sharron didn't hear it the way *he* heard it. "I'm doing all right," he said, anxious to move on.

"Well, I'll see you around," Dana commented. She slid away as quickly as she had arrived, and headed for the ladies' room.

Sharron had a thought to follow her inside and whip something on her just for being a slick-ass. However, women like Dana knew how to say or do just enough to bite and get away with it. Any response to it on Sharron's part would have appeared irrational. But she still had a question or two for Anthony, no matter how much she tried to let the incident slide.

"What did she mean by that?" she asked him.

Of course, he had to play the know-nothing role. "What did she mean by what?"

"'I'm being good. How 'bout you?'" Sharron repeated, word for word. Evidently, she *did* understand that there was an underlying message.

Anthony took a deep breath and decided to use the best policy for a change. The truth. He said, "We used to talk, and we both had other people that we dealt with. But now she's supposed to be committed. So, what she was saying was that she's still committed, and she was basically asking me if *I* was."

Sharron disliked the sister even more. How *dare* she try and keep some kind of connection to Anthony, and do it right there in her face? It made it seem as if she knew Anthony a whole lot more than Sharron did. This woman was somehow closer to him, and could jump back into his life whenever she wanted to. *No woman* liked a competitor having past influence over her man! The conversation was far from over. Anthony would have to explain things from day one with this woman. And as *soon* as the movie ended, too! To make things worse, guess what show Dana and *her* man were there to see? Sharron wanted to change her mind about the film, the time, the theater, or *something*. She just could not set her mind to rest in the presence of the woman until she had enough answers.

She let out a long sigh and forced Anthony to read her concern.

He said, "It's not like that with us anymore."

Sharron took in his comment and asked, "When was the last time you were with her?"

"February fourteenth," he told her.

The truth hurts, but that was what Anthony had decided to give her, complicating everything. Good lies, on the other hand, were much easier to settle obvious disputes. However, Anthony was fed up with the lies. And if he could not tell Sharron the truth, he figured there was no sense in trying to open so much of his soul to her.

Sharron looked into his face and said, "That's Valentine's Day."

"And it was a long time ago, too," he countered.

Sharron waited a minute to see if she could force herself to move on and failed. *Terribly!*

"And you haven't seen her since then?" she asked, feeling more insecure by the minute.

Why the hell am I doing this? she asked herself, as her blood seemed to boil. She wasn't even the jealous and insecure type.

"I can see what kind of night *this* is gonna be," Anthony commented to her.

Sharron nodded, agreeing with him. She was still attempting to calm her nerves. But how could she do it while in the same theater with the woman? She just *couldn't!*

She said, "Would you be upset with me if I wanted to see this movie at another time? I mean, it'll be out for a while, right?"

Anthony smiled at her. "Is she bothering you that much?" he asked. It wasn't as if he didn't feel uncomfortable himself; but what the hell, they weren't even sitting anywhere near Dana and her man. He wouldn't leave an entire theater for her, especially when he was satisfied with who he was with. Nevertheless, Sharron didn't find *herself* satisfied with being around some *mystery* woman until she knew the whole story. And until she knew, she felt a strange distance between herself and her man.

"I really just don't feel comfortable," she answered him. She was ready to stand up and leave immediately.

Anthony could not believe Dana was able to bother Sharron that much. So he obliged, and stood up to leave, planning to get his money back for their wasted tickets.

"I don't believe you did all of this, just because we were in the same movie with them. They're not thinking about *us,*" he complained as soon as they left the theater. Sharron made him feel like a loser. Anthony had always considered *himself* a winner. Most definitely!

Sharron felt guilty about it and was speechless. But once they made it to the car, she was all mouth and ears.

"So tell me about her. What's her name, anyway?"

"What does it matter?" Anthony asked, starting up the ignition. Sharron was beginning to get under his skin, especially since there was nothing going on with him and Dana.

"She made it *sound* like you're still seeing her. 'I'll see you around,'" Sharron mocked, staring at him with plenty of attitude.

"Well, I'm not. And you shouldn't let her get to you like that. This is stupid."

The R & B singer R. Kelly wrote a song called "When a Woman's Fed Up," and he was right, because Sharron seemed to be coming from left field concerning Anthony's past. His past did not seem to have been a problem with her before.

"Just tell me her name then," she requested.

"Her name is Dana," Anthony spat.

Sharron said, "I tell you everything about *guys* that *I've* dated before. So why are *you* having such a problem with *this?*"

"I never asked you about your guys."

"Yes you have."

"Well, I didn't act like *you* when I did."

"Because you had no reason to."

"Are you saying that you had a *reason* to act all crazy, like I'm lying to you about it?"

"Are you?" she asked him.

Anthony hit the roof in the middle of a two-lane street and swerved the car.

"You know what, you have *no fucking idea* how much *shit* I went through for you! And now you gon' sit up in here and talk this shit over some girl I haven't even dealt with since *February*! It's *August* now, Sharron! I didn't even *know you* back in February!"

"I know you better keep your eyes on the road before you kill us. And don't *yell* at me like that *either!"* Sharron warned him.

Anthony was so incensed that he pulled his car into a shopping center parking lot up the road. He looked Sharron in her eyes and asked, "Now, what do you want to say to me?"

Sharron went blank for a second. It was their first major confrontation.

"I just want you to tell me about your relationship with her, that's all."

"Okay, so what do you want to know about it? Let's spit it all out right here, right now," he snapped.

She said, "Well, how long have you known her?"

"For about two years."

"And how long have you been . . . off and on with her?"

"All the way up until February. I guess that's when she met her new man."

"So *she* broke it off?" Sharron questioned.

Anthony thought about it. "We were never like a real couple to begin with."

"You were just intimate with her?"

He nodded. "Yeah. We were fuckin'. Is that what you want to hear?"

"I want to hear the truth."

"Well, that's the truth. Now what else do you want to know, so you can just leave me alone about it?"

Sharron paused and did not want to ask him, but since she thought about it, and they were getting it all out in the open, she decided to ask him anyway.

"Do you still have feelings for her?"

Anthony paused himself. How exactly did he need to put it?

"Not like I have for you," he said.

Wrong answer. The truth hurts.

"Explain that," she told him.

It would have been a hell of a lot easier if he had just said no. Instead, he tried to explain.

"Sometimes you have people in your life who will always be a part of you, but that doesn't mean you don't move on. I'm sure it's the same way with you and some of the guys in *your* life. But I'm into *you* now, and that's all that should matter."

Was he gaming her, and lying to cover it up? Did he still have a secret relationship going on with the woman? Or was he telling the truth? Sharron was still filled with doubt.

"So how am I supposed to feel about that?"

"About what? That she's a part of my past?"

Sharron asked, "What if she calls you up and says that she misses you, and she wants to get back with you? What would you do then?"

"I'd tell her that she can't have it like that," he answered. And he would have.

"Would you fuck her?" Sharron asked him.

That was another question entirely. Why did she have to ask him that?

"No," Anthony answered. The truth was that he wouldn't know until it actually happened.

"You wouldn't?" she asked again, still doubting him.

Anthony looked away, uncertain about it himself. Could *I turn it down?* he thought. *This shit is impossible! I may as well just be a player for life. Dude in the barbershop was right!*

Sharron nodded her head, pissed the hell off that they had come so far and seemingly had gotten nowhere. Because if push came to shove, Anthony would still choose to be intimate with another woman.

"See, this is just what I'm talking about," she said. "That's *exactly* why I didn't feel comfortable in there. You would *still* fuck her."

"I told you that I wouldn't," Anthony responded weakly.

"Yeah, whatever." Sharron was tempted to make him drive her back home. She wanted to get away from him for a while. Not that she still didn't want to be with him. Not that she still didn't care about him. She just felt hopeless. As they say, like a penny with a hole in it. Because no matter what she did, she just couldn't put her faith in a man. He would only ruin it.

Anthony broke their silence and said, "You shouldn't even ask me something like that. I don't ask *you* no shit like that."

"Because guys think it's a given that the woman won't cheat on them."

"No they don't. I know *plenty* of guys who don't trust their women," he countered.

"*I* wouldn't either with guys like *you* around," Sharron spat. And that was low. *Too* low!

"What are you trying to say?" Anthony asked her. "Is that how you feel about me now, like I'm that slimy, to fuck my friend's girl?"

Sharron looked away and didn't answer.

Anthony got low himself and said, "Why are *you* fucking me then? That makes *you* slimy for even dealing with me, if *that's* the case."

"I don't know what I was expecting from you anyway," she grumbled to herself. That's just how pissed off she was.

Anthony looked at her and was ready to throw her ass out of his car! He was really hurt by it. He had gone through all kinds of struggles and sacrifices for her, and she didn't seem to appreciate it. She wanted a perfect damn world; one that he couldn't give her in a thousand years!

"Aw'ight then," he said, restarting his ignition. "Let me just drive you the fuck back home! And then you can do whatever you wanna do, and think whatever the hell you wanna think."

Anthony continued to talk out loud to himself while he drove:

"Change my life around for this shit. For what? Now I see *why* I never did this shit before. It don't fuckin' work!"

"It would work if guys just stopped being such *dogs,*" Sharron responded to him.

"Well, stop *chasin'* dogs then!" Anthony snapped. "You knew what kind of guy I was when you first met me! So if you want a virgin, then you go out and find one! But you didn't *want* no damn virgin!"

"I know you better stop cursing and raising your voice at me!" Sharron shot back.

"Or what?" he dared her.

"Or I'll make you crash this damn car of yours," she threatened.

"Yeah, okay. Do it then," he challenged her, releasing the wheel for her to grab.

"I don't want to," she told him.

"Well, don't talk that shit then!"

"I just want you to stop hollering at me," she responded calmly.

And he did. He calmed down and composed himself. But he couldn't wait to get her out of his car. He still had some old phone numbers of women who were still strung out on him. He planned on *using* those numbers. Immediately!

"Is that how you act when you get upset?" Sharron asked him, concerned. She began to think about a future with him again. Because if he could get that upset about it, then maybe he was telling the truth about his feelings. She even wanted to apologize to him. But not while he was still piping hot. She decided to wait right up until they reached her apartment building to tell him that she still cared about him. She still wanted to be with him, and that she wanted to apologize for jumping to conclusions. She was willing to stick it out with him if he was still willing to stick it out with her. So when Anthony cruised up to the parking lot outside of her apartment, Sharron did not budge from his car.

"Aw'ight, here you go," he told her, waiting for her to leave. He was dead serious about using those old phone numbers, too. However, that wouldn't change anything. He would still feel useless shortly afterward. Useless and alone, like he felt with so many other women.

Sharron placed her hand on his right arm at the wheel and said, "I didn't mean what I said. I don't know what came over me. I guess I just don't want to think about you with any other woman. So I'm sorry that I said all of that."

Anthony remained silent.

"You don't have anything to say?" she asked him.

"Like what?" He was still pouting.

She said, "So, you changed your life around for me? That's what you said earlier." She was flattered by it.

"I was just bullshittin' when I said that," Anthony told her, straight-faced.

Sharron's smile disappeared. "So you didn't mean it?"

He thought about how much he enjoyed her company and said, "Yeah, I meant it. But so what? It's time for you to leave now," he persisted.

If she wants me back, then she's gonna have to act *like it,* he told himself.

"You don't want to come in?" she asked, rubbing his arm with her hand. He still had not bothered to pull away from her.

"Come in for what?"

"To spend the night with me. And we can make our own music," she hinted.

"I'm not a musician. I'm a mechanic," he told her, finally cracking a slight smile.

"Well, I'll let you fix me then. And tighten me up," she said with a grin.

Anthony laughed out loud at that one.

"Tighten you up, hunh?" he repeated.

"Yeah. You got your tools with you?" she teased, referring to prophylactics.

He smiled, catching on, and said, "Maybe, maybe not." He was still playing hard to get with her. *If she wants me back, then she's gonna have to* act *like it.*

"Well, do we need to go and get some?" she asked.

"For what?" He looked around and spotted Celena's black Maxima. "Your roommate's home anyway."

"So? I have my *own* room, with a *door, and* a lock on it."

"You would just lock the door on your roommate and go on about your business?" The idea sounded intriguing to him.

"She did it *many times* to me," Sharron answered. "Not that I *cared* about her business, but still."

"And you want to do it back to her now?"

"No, I wanna do it to you," she responded with a chuckle.

Anthony forgot about how pissed he was and was all for it. He threw his Chevy into park, turned off the ignition, and said, "Come on then."

Sharron said, "Wait a minute. We still have to get you some tools."

"No we don't. I *got* tools," he told her, cheesing.

"So, why did you say that you didn't?"

"Because I was still mad at you."

"And now you're not?"

He said, "I probably wouldn't have been mad at you later on, either. As long as you apologized to me."

She smiled, realizing that guys had feelings too. Then she asked, "What if I *didn't* apologize?" just to see what his response would be.

"You would have *had* to eventually."

"Why?"

"Because if you didn't, that shit you said would have always been on my mind. And it would have gotten in the way of anything else we tried to do."

She nodded her head and understood his concern. "I'm sorry," she told him again, looking into his eyes. "I really didn't mean that."

Anthony broke up the mushy stuff and said, "Aw'ight, well, let's go and make it up then."

Sharron burst out laughing. "Is that what you call it, *'making it up'?"*

"It was *your* idea," he told her. "What do *you* call it?"

"I call it having my man over to spend the night."

"Right after an argument? Well, what if we *didn't* argue?" he asked her.

"If we didn't meet your old *friend* at the movies," she emphasized, "I would have had you over after that. I mean, it *is* Saturday night, and we both have off from work tomorrow."

Anthony smiled and nodded his head. "Aw'ight then. So let's go," he pressed her.

"Oh, now you're all ready to go inside with me because we're going to do the make-up sex thing. But before, you were all pissed off at me and ready to kick me out of the car," Sharron commented.

"If you piss me off like that again, you'll get the same result," Anthony warned her. "And you'll have to apologize to me again to get me to change my mind. And don't go *overboard* with that shit either," he told her. "Because I'm not giving you ten strikes."

"What about when *you* piss *me* off? How many strikes should *I* give *you?*" she asked him curiously.

He grinned and said, "As many as you can handle, I guess. Then *I'll* have to apologize to *you.*"

"But what if it's *beyond* apologies?" she questioned.

Anthony thought about that and said, "*Nothin'* is beyond apologies. I mean, if Jesus Christ can come down here and die on the cross for our sins, then how can *we* not forgive each other?"

Sharron looked into her man's face and smiled with pride.

"I didn't know that you read scripture," she said.

He looked at her and said, "Scripture? I don't read it like that, but I *do* know that nobody in this world is perfect."

With that, Sharron felt more relaxed and confident about Anthony than she *ever* had. She looked into his face and said, "Come on then. Let's go up to my room."

They walked into her apartment with Anthony hot on Sharron's heels, and said, "Hi, Celena."

Celena was painting her nails with undone hair, and looked a complete mess on the living-room sofa. "Damn, girl! You could at least give somebody a *warning* around here!" she screamed, embarrassed.

Anthony smiled and rubbed it in. "Hey, Celena. You look real good tonight."

"Ha, ha, real funny," she told him.

They laughed at her as they entered Sharron's room and shut the door, locking it behind them.

"Nobody wants to see y'all ugly faces anyway!" Celena yelled through the door at them.

Sharron smiled and attacked Anthony's lips with hers, wrapping her arms around his head of low-cut smooth dark hair.

"You forgive me?" she asked him.

He slipped his hands inside her clothes and said, "Yeah, I'm gonna forgive you *real* good."

She let him push her over to the bed, where they fell on top of her stuffed animals.

"Damn. It's pretty crowded in here," Anthony joked.

Sharron reached out with her hands and knocked all of her stuffed animals from the bed.

"Now it's not," she joked back to him.

And they pleased each other desperately, and recklessly, completely naked, and with nothing left to save or hide, until it felt *too* good. Then they were far too gone to stop themselves. They both wanted to feel *how good* it could get, and *how far* they could go when they blasted off together. And when they exploded, they knew that something had gone wrong. The heat of their connecting brown bodies became overwhelming, as though they were both on fire, grabbing and squeezing each other for dear life! But *OOOOOOHHH* it felt so . . . *SWEET!*

Sharron was afraid to even ask it. But she had to.

"Did it come off?"

Anthony was afraid to answer. But he had to.

"I think it did."

And they did . . . nothing about it.

Sharron sighed and said, "I can't even run out to the bathroom because Celena's still out there."

"So what?!" Anthony told her. "This is an emergency."

Sharron said nothing, and didn't budge, afraid to disconnect from the mess they had made of each other. But she *had* to. *He* had to. Yet, neither one of them found the urgency.

"What if I'm pregnant?" she looked up into his eyes and asked him.

"Then I'll be a daddy."

Silence again.

Then Sharron had an impulsive reaction. "Get up!" she told him with a shove to his hips.

"Ahh," he complained squeamishly. She squirmed from beneath him and scrambled to her feet.

Sharron dashed out the door and headed to the bathroom. Fortunately, Celena had gone to her room and didn't see anything. She did, however, hear the slamming of doors and the running of shower water. In the bathtub, Sharron was trying her best to wash it all away, and as quickly as she could to stop herself from becoming a mother before her time, as if water was all that she needed.

"Please don't let this happen," she mumbled to herself as she washed away. When she found the mess of their protection, she felt safer, hoping that it still had done its job.

She sighed and said, "God, please let this work," as if praising a wasted prophylactic. Then she wrapped it up in an excessive amount of toilet tissue to discard it in the trash.

"Don't you have any *shame?*" Celena asked, catching her roommate on the return trip to her room.

Sharron made it back to her door wrapped in a towel. She just smiled at Celena and slipped into her room with Anthony, who had covered up her messy sheets and put his underwear back on.

"Do those condoms have spermicide?" she asked him, searching for the package that it came in.

"Yeah," he answered glumly.

She didn't assess his mood, she was too busy searching for the condom package to make sure.

"What, you don't trust me with that either?" Anthony asked her while she confirmed it.

"I'm not ready to be a mother," she answered. "I'm planning to go back to school for nursing this year. I want to go back to school in September."

Anthony nodded. "That's good. How long will it take you to finish?"

"Two more years," she answered. She expected him to react negatively about it. A lot of guys refused to honor a woman's timetables. She had gone through it all before, just expressing her future plans with them.

"It took me a year to get my mechanic certification," Anthony told her. "And I already knew most of what they were teaching me."

"So my two years doesn't bother you?"

"Naw. As long as you're happy with what you're doing. I like my job, so why wouldn't I want you to like yours?"

"Some guys don't like their women working as much as they do," Sharron stated.

He frowned and said, "My mother's been working all her life. I'm *used* to a workin' woman."

Sharron smiled and jumped back into her bed with him. She thought, *I want him to meet my father.* "Would you go back home to Memphis, Tennessee, with me?" she asked him excitedly.

Anthony grimaced and said, "When?"

"I don't know. In two or three weeks, before the summer is out."

He thought about it. He had vacation time coming, if he wanted to use it. Usually he used a day here and a day there instead of a bunch of them together.

He got curious and asked her, "For how long?"

"Not long. Just for like, two or three days."

"That's all?"

"Yeah."

He didn't see any reason *not* to go. He said, "Aw'ight, just tell me when so I'll know when to take off."

Just like that, he was willing to go. Sharron hadn't been able to convince Celena to visit Memphis for years.

"You think I would leave you if you got pregnant?" Anthony asked her.

Sharron stopped and thought about it. "I didn't say that."

"I mean, I'm just responding to how you acted."

"Well, I don't want to be pregnant right now," she responded.

"Answer my question," he pressed her.

She shrugged her shoulders. "I don't know."

He said, "I thought about it before. And I *wouldn't* leave you."

She sat up and asked, "You thought about gettin' me pregnant?" She said it as if he had set off an alarm.

"I mean, you were the one talkin' about tellin' our kids my lines and stuff. *You* started that," he countered.

"But I didn't mean like, *right now.* I meant in the future, if we were still together."

Anthony nodded, understanding they would have to spend a lot more time together before he could predict anything.

"I understand that," he told her.

Then it was her turn to ask a deep question.

"Have you ever been tested for AIDS?" she asked him.

He looked at her and said, "Damn! One rubber slips off on us and you start asking me if I have AIDS? What the hell is that?"

"I didn't ask you if you had AIDS, I just asked you if you've been *tested* for it."

He calmed himself down and said, "Naw. But I know I ain't got it though. Have *you* been tested?"

"Yeah, for my health insurance with this company through my job," she answered.

"Will you still have it if you stop working there?"

"Yeah. Once you have it, you have it. You just continue to pay your monthly rate, and you can even add your family onto it. You don't have health insurance at your job?"

"I could of had it. They came around asking about it, but you know, I'm healthy."

Sharron shook her head and said, "That's how a lot of people get stuck without it. They think they're so *healthy. Insurance* means that you *insure* yourself for the future."

He nodded and said, "Yeah, you're right. Maybe I'll think about it."

"So you're gonna go home with me?" she asked again, as if reminding him.

He smiled and said, "Yeah. I've never been to Memphis before."

"Well, now you will," she told him with a hug and a kiss. Then she added, "I think I need to get on the pill."

Sharron caught up with Celena that Sunday morning after Anthony had left, and dropped a bomb on her at the kitchen table.

"Anthony's protection came off in me last night. You think I'm pregnant?"

Celena swallowed down her Honeycombs cereal. "Can't you see that I'm eating? What the hell is on your mind?" Then she changed her tone and said, "I told you you needed your own protection. I told you that a *long* time ago. I wouldn't leave everything up to *them.* So when was your last period?" she asked.

"Last week."

Celena nodded. "That's what I thought. So you have a long-ass time to wait then."

"Or I could just get one of those pregnancy tests. But I don't think that I am, though," Sharron said. She felt fairly confident that she was not.

"You have to wait awhile for that pregnancy test thing to work anyway. I mean, this just happened last night, right? Is that why you ran into the bathroom like a damn fool?"

Sharron smiled and nodded. "Yup."

Celena snapped her fingers. "I should have *known* that something was up. You ain't *that* damn bold to be running around here butt naked. I don't care *how* much in love you are. So what did *he* say about it?" she asked.

"I asked him, 'What if I'm pregnant?' He just said, 'I'll be a daddy then.'"

"No he *didn't,*" Celena snapped.

"Yes he did too."

"Was he serious?"

"I guess so."

Celena frowned and said, "*You guess so?* Girl, you better *know* so."

"Well, anyway, I asked him if he would go home to Memphis with me in a couple of weeks, and he said that he would."

Celena didn't like *that* idea so much. Anthony was invading too much of her turf. "I thought *I* was supposed to go with you," she responded.

Sharron sighed and said, "I *knew* you were gonna say that. I've been asking you for *years* to make that trip with me, and you always came up with excuses."

"But I was gonna go *this* time," Celena said.

"Yeah, sure you were."

Celena stopped eating her cereal altogether. "This might be it then. You gon' introduce him to your father and everything."

"Yup. That'll be the test. But Anthony isn't a bad guy or anything, he just had a lot of women in his life."

"Hmmph," Celena huffed. "And *that's* not a bad thing?"

"I mean, it's not as bad as going to jail or being a drug dealer or a woman beater or anything. And a lot of guys *do* grow out of the dog stage you know. I'm sure *our* fathers had *their* dog days when *they* were young, too."

"Not *my* father," Celena said. "He fell for my mom straight out of high school, went to college, and is still with her."

"Well, that's a nice thing," Sharron told her.

"I told my dad he must have been the biggest square in the world," Celena commented.

"Mmm," Sharron grunted, standing up from the kitchen table.

"Anthony and I had an argument over guys being dogs last night, and he broke down and said, 'Well, stop chasin' them then! You knew what kind of guy I was when you met me!'" she said, imitating his intensity.

Celena laughed at it. "So, y'all had an argument? *That's* a first."

Sharron shook her head and smiled. "You just love yourself some drama, don't you? And here you are calling your father a square because he fell in love and stayed dedicated to your mother."

"Different strokes for different folks," Celena said.

"Yeah, and it seems like a lot of *our* strokes are gettin' us into trouble with the wrong men," Sharron responded. She walked away and headed for the telephone.

"If you feel that way, then turn Anthony loose and get back with your sweetheart, Sean Love."

Sharron looked back at her roommate and frowned. "Don't even start it," she said. Sharron had cut the strings from Sean for good, in a short and devastating phone call: *"Look, Sean, I have somebody who is* very *dear to me right now, and I hope and pray that* you *find somebody soon too."*

Celena grinned, remembering the phone call.

"You think he'll ever be friends with you again?" she asked her roommate.

Sharron sighed, tired of even mentioning Sean. "Probably not. But that's life. Things happen like that sometimes," she answered.

"And that married guy? I was *glad* to tell *him* the fuck off for you. He had *nerve!"* Celena huffed.

Sharron banished *both* of those men from her mind and grabbed the phone into her room to call her father. Celena went right back to eating her bowl of Honeycombs cereal.

"Hello, can I speak to a Mr. Robert Francis, please?" Sharron asked over the phone, teasing.

"Hey, puddin'. How are you doing this Sunday?" he responded to her. "I was just thinking about you earlier this morning, and now you're calling me."

"Pudding?" she questioned. "Dad, how come you call me something new every time I talk to you?"

"Because you're something new to me every time you call me," he teased her right back.

"Well, I'll be coming home to visit soon, Daddy. In a couple of weeks," she told him. "And I'm bringing someone with me."

"Celena?" he assumed. He had met Celena twice on trips he had made to St. Louis.

Sharron said, "No. I'm bringing a young man with me. His name is Anthony Poole. And we'll probably stay at a hotel to respect the house."

"Stay at a hotel? Why, *that* would be disrespecting the house. You don't come back and stay at some hotel. You'll be right back in your room here."

Her father had moved into a smaller house after her mom had died. Her mother's family hadn't liked the idea of him selling their hard-earned house. But he had too many painful memories there to stay. He didn't need so much space to continue cleaning anyway.

"Well, I just didn't know how comfortable it would be for us to stay there, Dad. That's all," she explained.

"Nonsense," he told her. "Your boyfriend can sleep on the fold-out couch in the family room. He'll be all right."

Sharron couldn't tell if he was joking or serious. She laughed anyway.

"So, what kind of young man is he?" he asked.

"You'll see," she answered him. "He's a mechanic."

"A mechanic? How old is he again?" Mr. Francis could only picture an old, oily man with missing front teeth and a fetish for young women.

Sharron caught on to his stereotype and said, "He's twenty-seven. All mechanics had to start off sometime, Dad. He's not some old, trifling man."

"Oh, okay. Because I don't want you bringing home anybody who's as old as me. I'd have to pull out my rifle on him."

Sharron laughed and said, "Well, you can keep your rifle in the closet, because that is *not* the case."

"I can't wait to meet him then," he commented. "Is he good-lookin'?"

"Dad?" Sharron snapped, embarrassed. "What does *that* matter?"

"I gotta think about my grandchildren, don't I?"

He was jumping way too far with conclusions.

"Grandchildren? Where'd you get that idea from?" Sharron asked. And maybe he was right if she was pregnant.

"You told me his first and last name," he commented. "That usually *means* something. And Sharron Francis Poole doesn't sound that bad," he added.

She smiled and said, "That's the same thing Celena did, adding his name on to mine. But what if I wasn't planning on doing that when I got married. Would that bother you?" she asked him.

"No," he told her. "That's the way it's been in the past. But so many educated girls are keeping their names now, that I just assumed that you would. You *are* going back to school, aren't you?" he asked.

"I may just be a little old-fashioned then. And yeah, I am going back to school. Starting this fall." She'd informed him of her plans in their last conversation.

"Ain't nothing wrong with being old-fashioned," he told her. "They make the best kind of women. Your mother was old-fashioned. And she believed in family first."

Sharron thought about her parents' relationship and asked her father, "Was Mom the only woman you had in mind to marry?"

"Actually, no. At the time, I was getting serious about your mother, I had two other women I was thinking about. And I went ahead and made the right decision to choose her. A *good* decision."

Sharron smiled, thinking of Anthony's decision to choose *her,* and felt good inside.

"So, men make hard decisions on which woman they want to be with?" she asked rhetorically. She already knew the answer to that; she just wanted to hear her father tell it.

"Of course we do," he answered. "What do you think, we just go out and keep the first woman who bats her eyes at us. That's what's wrong with a lot of these marriages now. You got young people today who don't know the first *thing* about choosing a good mate. And that's the most important choice that you'll ever make in your life! Because you can change a job, or a car, or where you choose to live. But once you marry and start having children with a woman, even if you divorce her, that woman's gonna be the mother of your children. Or at least of *some* of 'em. And then you'll have to tell your children for the rest of their lives, 'Your mother's crazy! I don't know *what* I saw in her!' Or vice versa if you choose the wrong man."

Sharron burst out laughing. Her father was a riot sometimes.

"How is Lucille doing?" she asked about his friend.

"She's hanging on in there with me. I can be hard on her sometimes, you know, because she says I'm set in my ways. So I told her, 'I'm nearly sixty years old now. And if I wasn't set in my ways by now, then I must haven't learned how to live yet.'

"Hell, she's set in her ways, too. And she ain't gettin' no younger," he commented. "She's almost *fifty* herself."

Sharron grinned and shook her head. Men were men, no matter *how* old they were. And they were always complaining about their right to be themselves.

"Well, I just wanted to let you know that I was coming. We didn't want to just pop up on you," Sharron said.

"Bring him on down," her father told her. "And if he ain't right, I just want you to know, baby girl, I'll be sending him back to St. Louis in a box."

Sharron hung up with her father and was tickled by the whole idea of introducing Anthony to him. She hadn't done that since Sean Love, back in high school. Her father was never too cordial to Sean. He said the boy didn't have a proper backbone. He wasn't too sure of himself. Or maybe he was just plain nervous. After all, at six foot two and buffed, Robert Francis was an imposing man. And Sean was taking his daughter out to the prom, hoping to finally score with her.

Sharron thought back to those days and kept right on smiling. But she was older now. She had a *new* man to bring home to Daddy. And she had a feeling that *this* young man had the right kind of "backbone." So she couldn't help but to be a little anxious about her trip back home.

Home was what too many marriage-age black men could rarely call their own. Because too many of them still lived in their *mother's* home, or in temporary apartments, or cold, empty houses that they seldom paid a mortgage for, while claiming to be proud of it. "It ain't much, but it's mine," too many of them bragged. However, Anthony "Tone" Wallace was learning that there was much more to be gained out of available property. He witnessed up close that many *homes* were filled with love, togetherness, warmth, tradition, appreciation, and real family values. And he was beginning to understand the treasure that those homes held, day by day, as he clocked in for work to clean carpets.

"What are you thinking about, man? Why are you so quiet tonight?" Ant asked him. Tone was daydreaming in Ant's car. They were on their way to a warehouse furniture store to continue furnishing Tone's new place.

Tone shook it off and said, "Nothin' really. I'm just thinking about these big-ass houses that we clean every day."

"What about 'em?"

"I'm just saying, man, the people who live in *these* houses . . . they livin' for real. We could put both of the houses we grew up in in theirs, and still have leftover rooms for visitors. Some of these places got like thirty rooms. I walk around in there and get lost and shit," he exaggerated.

Ant laughed and said, "That don't mean they livin' all that better than we are. Some of those rich folks are as miserable as people who live in homeless shelters."

Tone frowned and said, "That's bullshit, man. Who do *you* know that wouldn't wanna live in a big-ass house?"

"I'm not saying that most people wouldn't want to live in one. I'm just saying that it ain't a perfect situation no matter how big or how nice the place may *look.*"

"So if you and Sharron got a place, would you want some small-ass apartment, or a plush-ass crib where your kids could run around and get lost in it?"

Ant shook his head and grinned. Tone failed to get his point, so he tried explaining again.

"What I'm saying is that a good, well-kept house, is a *good,* well-kept house, no matter how small it may seem compared to some of them houses out Richmond Heights or Brentwood or Ladue."

Tone changed the subject. "Yeah, anyway. So when did you say you was goin' out to Memphis with Sharron again?"

"Next week."

He smiled and said, "You got her on the pill now, hunh?"

"It wasn't *my* decision. She decided that on her own," Ant answered him.

"And what would you do if she *was* pregnant?"

Ant looked straight ahead and responded, "I would be a daddy. Just like I told *her.* I'm *raising* my kids. Sharron would be a good mother anyway." *And a good* wife, *too,* he thought.

Tone watched him to see if his expression would change. Once he saw it wouldn't, he said, "I guess you can't deny it no more. She got'chu."

Ant looked over at his partner and smiled. "She's the one."

"She gettin' y'all free or discounted plane tickets to Memphis?" Tone asked. She *did* work at the airport.

Ant said, "Naw."

"Y'all driving or catching the train?"

"She want us to catch the bus."

Tone looked at him and frowned. "*The bus?* What she want to catch the bus for? It's cheaper?"

"Naw, she just said that ah . . . it'll be nice to take a good, long bus ride together."

Ant felt silly about it and started laughing.

Tone smiled at him. He was far too impatient for a long bus ride *anywhere.* He joked, "Come this winter, she gon' have you taking nature hikes with her."

"And have me out in the woods in a damn hut, hunh?" Ant joked back to him.

"I'm serious, man," Tone warned him.

Ant thought about his partner's warning. And why not go on a nature hike? It *was* something different. But he would never tell Tone that, so he smiled it off as they went on about their business. Sharron was starting to be a lot more fun than Tone anyway. Ant would not express *that* to his partner either.

Memphis, Tennessee, wasn't exactly a nature hike, but it sure felt uplifting. Imagine, feeling perfectly at home in another place with someone special. If the connection is right, *everything* becomes enjoyable. Being in the right place with the *wrong* person can be close to torture. As well as being in the *perfect* place alone. You feel like you wasted the experience, wishing you could share it again with someone you enjoyed, like Ant enjoyed Sharron.

"So, you and Tone were laughing at my idea to catch the bus?" Sharron asked. They were headed south on their bus at ten o'clock on a Thursday morning. Who *knows* what they'll talk about on a four-hour bus ride.

Ant had gotten used to telling Sharron things. He felt the comfort with her that a man *should* feel with his woman.

"I could have driven us down here if you wanted to, with only one stop to eat and to use the bathroom," he told her.

"But I didn't want to drive this time. We'll have *plenty* of times to drive. We're always in your car."

"Are you getting tired of my car?"

"No. I just wanted to catch the bus and relax with you without you having to worry about the road and stuff, that's all. Does that make any sense to you?"

Ant nodded, knowing better. "So what you *really* wanted was my undivided attention."

She leaned into him in his seat by the left window and said, "Exactly."

"So your father's supposed to pick us up from the bus stop?"

"Yeah."

"And he's gonna let you use his car so we can hit Memphis?"

Sharron grinned. "Yup. I'll get to drive *you* around for a change."

"I wouldn't know where I was going in Memphis anyway," he told her with a chuckle. "Do they still like Anfernee Hardaway in Memphis?" he asked, referring to the Orlando Magic basketball star out of Memphis State University.

"Of course we do."

"Oh, so it's a *we* situation. You like him, too?"

"Why wouldn't I? I mean, I'm no big basketball fan or anything, but why wouldn't I like somebody who came from Memphis and did something with his life? That's what *I* hope to do. Don't you like ah, what's his name from St. Louis?" she said, trying to remember the basketball star's name.

"Larry Hughes," Ant filled in.

Sharron sucked her teeth and said, "I was just about to say that."

"Sure you were," he teased her.

"So what did you tell your father about me?" he asked curiously. He knew she told her father *something*.

"I told him that you were a mechanic, and he started thinking that you were an old man or something."

Ant laughed and said, "Then what?" There had to be more than that. She was probably just getting started.

"Well, I told him that we would stay at a hotel, and he told me he didn't want me to do that, and that you could sleep on the fold-out couch in the family room."

Ant looked at her and grimaced. "I gotta sleep on the couch?"

"Not if you don't want to. I didn't tell my father that we were definitely staying there."

"How would he feel if we didn't stay?"

She shrugged her shoulders. "I don't know. It depends on how much he likes you," she commented with a grin.

Ant smiled back at her and said, "What if he *doesn't* like me?"

"Then you'll be sleeping at the hotel by yourself," she joked.

Ant chuckled and shook his head. It was all a big setup. "And I don't even have my damn car to drive back home," he said out loud.

Sharron looked at him in shock. "You would leave me here?" she asked.

"*Leave you here?* This is your home. Would you leave *me* at the hotel by myself?" he countered.

"I was only joking about that, Anthony."

"Well, I was only joking too."

She leaned away from him and pouted, "No you weren't. You *would* leave me. Just like a guy."

"What else am I supposed to do if your father don't like me?" he questioned.

"Fight for your woman," Sharron snapped. "You tell him, 'I know you may not like me, sir, but I care a lot about your daughter, and I'm gonna stand right by her *regardless* of how you feel about me!'"

"Would you say that to my mother?" Ant challenged.

Sharron thought about it, caught off guard. "If I had to, I would."

"Yeah, right."

"I would though," she argued.

"You were scared to even *meet* my mother," he reminded her.

"It wasn't that I was scared, I just wasn't expecting it. *You* had time to prepare for meeting my father. You didn't tell me that we were going to see your mother until we were five minutes away."

Ant reflected on Sharron's birthday date and laughed.

"And it *wasn't* funny either," she pouted again.

He looked out of the window as they traveled south and yawned. He had been up late with last-minute packing for their weekend trip, Thursday through Sunday. Sharron had been up late herself, talking to Celena about the visit home with her man, while wondering how her father would receive him. Ant thought about that too. And before they knew it, they had both fallen asleep on the bus and were just ten minutes away from downtown Memphis when they awoke.

"Mmmph, we slept for all that time," Sharron stretched out and grumbled.

"It was better than talking the whole way," Ant teased.

Sharron frowned at him and nudged his shoulder. It had been a peaceful bus ride with no chatty travelers or whining babies on board.

"So this is Memphis," Ant commented. They crossed the Mississippi River and rode into downtown. There was no St. Louis Arch, dome stadium, or as many densely structured hotels and office buildings like there were in St. Louis, but there was an interesting looking pyramid there.

"What is that?"

"That's The Pyramid center," Sharron said. "They have concerts and things there. Like if Whitney Houston or Mariah Carey comes to town. Memphis State plays their big games there, too."

He smiled and joked, "What about the country singers? I thought Memphis, Tennessee, was a country music lovin' town."

Sharron sighed and said, "Here we go with that. I get enough of that from Celena, okay. I don't need *you* doin' it."

"I'm just jokin'."

"That's the same thing that *she* says."

When they reached the bus station, Ant noticed the lost brown faces of several black men who were wandering the downtown streets.

"They have a lot of jobless people down here?" he asked Sharron.

"You know it," she answered. "People who are just happy to get up for another day. But that's not *everybody*," she told him. She didn't want him stereotyping her hometown.

"Of course it's not everybody. I'm just sayin'," he commented as he continued to watch the Memphis streets.

Sharron left the subject alone. She had left home to make sure that she was still motivated to move on with her life, and yet, after her mother died, she ended up lacking motivation anyway. But in September, she was *definitely* going back to school to finish what she had started, earning a college degree and becoming a professional.

They pulled in at the bus terminal and prepared to grab their luggage.

"There's my daddy. Right on time," Sharron said, pointing him out.

Ant looked and spotted a tall black man who was just beginning to gray around the edges of his short, squared afro. Despite his size, he didn't look intimidating at all. He had a soft, compassionate face.

"Hey, baby!" he shouted to his daughter. He greeted her with a hug.

"Hey, Daddy. This is Anthony," Sharron told him, stepping aside for her father to greet her man.

"How are you doing, young man?" Mr. Francis asked with his hand extended.

"I'm doing fine. I'm a little tired, but I guess I'll snap out of that soon," Ant commented.

Mr. Francis nodded. "Yeah, you'll snap out of that. The bus ride did it to you."

"Where's the car, Dad?" Sharron broke in and asked. She was eager to get her luggage in. As with most women, she had *twice* as many bags as Ant had packed.

"I had to park it around the corner. Let me take that from you," her father said, going for her bags. Ant already had her largest bag in hand.

Sharron handed her two smaller bags to her father and followed him to his car with Ant. Her father drove a dark blue Oldsmobile that was fairly new.

He looked at Ant and said, "My daughter tells me that you're an auto mechanic."

Ant nodded. "That's what I do," he responded to him.

Mr. Francis nodded while they loaded the trunk.

"I guess you'll *always* be employed with *that* profession," he commented.

"Or at least until we start driving spacemobiles," Ant joked.

He smiled and said, "We got a long time before that happens."

They walked back to the front end of the car where he told Ant to ride up front.

"What if he doesn't want to ride up front, Daddy?" Sharron said, instigating. She was looking forward to riding up front herself.

"Well, then, he'll speak his own mind," her father answered.

"I'll ride up front," Ant said. "But it looks like Sharron was planning to," he added. She was already standing at the front door.

"She always gets to ride up front," her father snapped. "Get on in the back, girl, so this auto mechanic can see how smooth my car rides."

"He doesn't need to ride up front for that," Sharron argued.

Mr. Francis wanted to test the boy and see what he was made of, but Sharron was getting in the way.

"Okay, well, how 'bout I let *you* drive and then we can both sit in the back?" he suggested.

Sharron sighed and finally conceded. "I'll sit in the back," she huffed.

Ant chuckled at it. Mr. Francis was no cream puff.

"What kind of car do you have?" her father asked Ant up front as soon as they pulled off and into the downtown streets.

"A seventy-nine Chevy."

"What color?"

"Cranberry."

"You fixed it up?"

"You know it."

"With those bouncing hydraulics?" Mr. Francis asked with a grin.

Ant smiled, used to people assuming. "Naw, I don't mess with them. Every old car doesn't have to have that. But I do have a nice steering wheel and a CD stereo system."

"So why did you get an old car; because you know you can fix it up whenever you want to?"

"Not only that, I like the space inside old cars. Them bucket seats and cup holders take away a lot of the comfort inside, *I* think."

"Yeah, I know what you mean. Too many gadgets can take away from the basics of a good ride and a relaxing feel. How long have you been into cars?"

"Since I was a kid. My uncles, older brothers, *and* my father did a lot with cars. So I just picked up on it."

"You already knew that you would be a mechanic from a young age."

"Not really. But I got certified. I have one uncle who is certified, and the rest just know what they're doing from trial and error."

"So, you were the one who took it to that next step?"

"Yeah."

Sharron sighed loudly from the back seat. "Can we stop talking about *cars* for a minute," she asked them jokingly. She was pleased that they were getting along so well, but enough was enough.

"Okay, well, what would you like us to talk about, honey?" her father asked her.

"Anything else."

"Anything like what?"

"Like sports or something," she commented, just for the hell of it.

Her father nodded, looked at Ant, and asked, "How do you think the Rams are gonna do this year?"

Sharron and Ant broke out laughing. Her father had character. Ant didn't find a problem with getting along with him at all. But he sure saw where Sharron got her inquisitiveness from. It ran in the family.

They arrived at a small red brick house on the central west side of Memphis that looked like a peaceful area. The neighborhoods definitely had more space for comfort than in St. Louis. It almost seemed as if the farther south you traveled, the more land you had available between houses.

They unloaded the car and took the luggage into the house, a small well-kept place with nothing fancy. When they finished, Ant looked around and thought, *Now what? I guess I can lay back and rest for a while on the sofa.*

"What do you like to eat?" Mr. Francis asked as soon as Ant sat down and relaxed in the family room.

"Ah, it doesn't really matter to me. As long as it's good food," he joked.

"What does 'good food' mean to you? You know *Sharron* don't cook much. She's been spoiled by too many cooks in her family."

"Daddy!" she hollered, overhearing him from the stairs. She walked back down to join them in the family room and said, "I guess I can't leave you alone for *one minute* with Anthony."

"Well, it's the truth. And honesty is the best policy," her father told her. "Let a man know what he's gettin' into before he gets into it."

"And what about a *man* letting a *woman* know what *she's* gettin' into before *she* gets into it?" his daughter countered.

"I agree with that, too," her father responded. "Your mother let me know what she was thinking every step of the way, and she wanted me to tell her what *I* was thinking. So if you have a man who can't express himself to you, then you don't have a real man."

That comment rang Ant's bell. *If you have a man who can't express himself to you, then you don't have a real man.* It made perfect sense. Just like a man who couldn't defend his family was not a real man. Or a man who could not pay his bills. Or a man who had no mission in life.

"What do you think about that, Anthony?" Mr. Francis turned and asked him.

Ant smiled, and was up for the challenge. "Your daughter *made* me express *myself*. So I guess that's what women need to do. It makes sense to me."

Mr. Francis turned back to his daughter and smiled. "There you go," he told her. "Sounds like you got a real man."

Sharron smiled, feeling all warm inside. She *knew* her father would like him. Ant seemed relaxed around her father as well.

"So, what do you think?" Sharron asked Ant, once they had time alone outside her father's house.

Ant daydreamed about the peace, quiet, and wonder of being with a woman on her turf. He was at her mercy and with no car to get away. Yet, he felt perfectly at home with it. Many *married* men never felt that comfortable!

"What do I think about what?"

"My father."

"What about him?" Sharron was ready to throw a fit when Ant smiled and said, "Naw, he's cool. He's talkative. A lot of older men don't talk that much *to you,* they talk *at you.*"

Sharron smiled and said, "I didn't know you knew the difference."

"Yeah, I know the difference," he said. "My boss talks *to you,* so he finds out what's going on in your life because he cares. But a lot of older guys talk *at you,* and they never hear shit you have to say about yourself. They too busy trying to tell you how *they* think you should live."

Sharron smirked. "Hmmph. You wait until he *really* talks to you."

Ant smiled. "What, he's rough?"

"You'll see."

"Is it true that you can't cook?" he asked.

"Oh, I can cook. I just don't like to do it that much."

Ant looked at her from the cement steps they sat on and said, "I guess I have to accept the fact that you're not a dedicated cook then."

"Just like *I* have to accept the fact that you're not a doctor or a lawyer," Sharron countered.

He looked at her surprised. "You wanted a doctor or a lawyer?"

"No. But a lot of women fantasize about that. And that just gets in the way of them being happy with their man."

"So you won't drop me after you get your nursing degree?" he joked.

"Hell no," she answered. "You know how hard it is to find a man as dedicated to his job and as fun to be with as you are? I wouldn't give you up for the world," she told him. "To hell with a nursing job!"

Ant laughed, knowing how quickly things can change in life. "Yeah right," he told her. "If I told you that I didn't want you to go to nursing school, you'd drop me in a heartbeat."

Sharron said, "No I wouldn't. I'd just ignore you. But why would you tell me that, though?"

"*I* wouldn't. But some men would."

"Why? I just can't understand that," she commented. "If anything, they should be *glad* that I'm making my own money."

"Yeah, and that's the problem. Some guys can't take a woman having her own life. But then they complain when they end up with women who are too dependent on them," he explained.

"What about you?" she asked him.

"I like when a woman has her own life. Because I got other things to do. And if I have a woman who gives me the space that I need while she does her own thing, then I can build up a business without worrying about her ridin' me all the time."

"What, like your own auto repair shop?" Sharron guessed.

"Yeah. Something like that. That's how my boss was able to build up his place. He had a woman who pushed him and allowed him to do what he needed to do."

"You think I'm like that?" she asked him.

"I *know* you are. Otherwise you would have complained already. Because I work late hours sometimes."

"You two ready to eat?" Mr. Francis stepped outside and asked them.

"Yup. Perfect timing, Dad," Sharron told him, standing up. "My stomach was just starting to growl."

"Mine, too," Ant said, standing up to join her.

They all sat at the dinner table and Sharron proceeded to say a quick grace before they ate.

She don't normally pray before she eats, Ant thought to himself. *I guess she's doing this for her father.* He made a note to ask her about that later on. And when she made a run up to her bedroom, Mr. Francis had another minute alone with him.

"So, how many years you think you got left?" he asked across the table.

"How many more *years* I got left?" Ant repeated. *What is he talking about? Did I miss something?* he thought to himself.

"You know, playing the field with different teams and whatnot?"

Ant smiled, understanding what her father meant.

"I'm retired already," he told him.

"Are you sure? You don't lie to yourself, do you?"

"No, sir. I *can't* lie to myself. That's when you're *really* lost."

Mr. Francis nodded. "I'm glad to hear that. And nobody's perfect.

"Now, I'm gonna ask you *another* question before Sharron gets back down here. Do you think you could ever *love* my daughter?" he asked.

An easy question.

"Yes, sir."

"And does she love you?"

"Well, she *acts* like she does, but she never said it to me."

"And do you *act* like you love her?"

Ant thought about it for a minute. He thought about all of the quality time he had spent with her. The pain of lying to her. All of the things he had expressed to her about himself. The thoughts that he had about her. And the retirement of his player lifestyle to maintain what they had together. He said, "Yeah, I guess I do."

Sharron reappeared and interrupted their candid conversation.

"Okay, what were you two talking about?" she asked with a smile. She noticed their hesitancy when she walked back into the room.

"Some things you don't have to know," her father told her. "This here is *man* talk."

"But I'm your daughter," she protested.

"Exactly," he countered.

Ant started to laugh.

"Does that mean you would have *more* to talk to me about if I was a *son?*" Sharron asked her father.

"No, that just means that I have *different* things to talk to you about because you're a *daughter*."

Sharron didn't know how to argue with that. She said, "I see," and sat back down at her seat.

When it got late, her father left them alone to call his own companion and to catch up on things.

"We'll do a lot more tomorrow," Sharron promised Ant. "Let's go to the family room," she told him. She sat their dishes in the kitchen sink and led him to the small, well-kept room with a brown sleeper couch and a 19-inch color television with VCR attached.

"What, you think I was bored?" Ant asked her. He wasn't. "I would have been tired today anyway. I *needed* to chill," he told her.

"Just in case you were, I wanted you to know that."

"Were *you* bored today?" he asked her back.

Sharron smiled and said, "Of course not. What woman would be bored on the first time that her man meets her father?"

They took a seat on the couch, real close to each other.

"So this is a big deal for you?"

"Was it a big deal when you introduced me to your mother?"

Ant smiled.

"All right then," Sharron piped.

"So, I guess I gotta sleep down here on the fold-out bed, right? Because we didn't talk about calling no hotels or nothin' since we been here."

She smiled and asked, "Would you hate me for it?"

He shook his head with a grin. "I'm definitely gonna hate you for this. I came all the way down here to Memphis to sleep on a damn pull-out bed."

"It's not all like that. We'll get a hotel tomorrow night then," she promised.

"And what about the next night?" he asked.

"We'll stay in the hotel for the rest of the weekend. Okay?"

"Yeah, sure."

"Awww, don't be mad at me," she whined, kissing his cheek.

"Stop that before your father comes back," he teased her.

She smirked and went after his neck.

"Now, what are you gonna tell him when this shit gets out of hand?" Ant warned.

"I'll say, 'Daddy, I'm a grown woman now. I'm not a little girl anymore,'" she said.

"If that was the case, I wouldn't have to sleep down *here* while *you* stay up in your room."

Sharron shook her head and leaned away from him. "Is this bothering you that much?"

He smiled. "Naw, I'm just teasing you about it."

"Yes it is," she said to him. "It *is* bothering you. Otherwise, you wouldn't keep talking about it."

Ant was just thinking how quickly he could go from scoring with women, almost at will, to sleeping on the couch. Funny how things change.

"Well, like they say," he commented, "you have to make sacrifices for what you really want in life."

Sharron smiled and said, "You're willing to make sacrifices for me?"

"Are *you* willing to make sacrifices for *me?*" he asked her back.

"Of course I am. What do you want me to sacrifice?"

"Your bed," he joked.

Sharron took it seriously. She said, "All right. I'll sneak back down here when my father goes to sleep."

Ant shook his head and said, "Aw, naw, you not gettin' me embarrassed and shot to death. No way."

"My father's not like that."

"Have you ever been caught with a guy before?"

Sharron frowned and said, "No. I wasn't even *having* sex before I left home. You're the only guy I ever brought back with me."

"You don't know how your father would react then."

"He wouldn't shoot you, Anthony."

"Does he own a gun?"

She smiled again. "He has two guns, a rifle and a thirty-eight."

Ant laughed and said, "You stay in your own room then."

However, once the moon had been shining for hours, and the air was filled with the sound of good sleep, Sharron disobeyed her man *and* her father and snuck down the stairs. Ant didn't need her to. He accepted it. It was a part of life, and a part of growing up, accepting that he couldn't have everything his way. That was a lesson too many young couples had *yet* to learn.

"What are you doing down here, Sharron? I want to live," Ant told her, barely conscious.

"Shhhsssh," she whispered. "Be quiet then."

"I'm all right, though. I don't need you down here," he told her.

"But I *want* to be here."

"Aw'ight. But I'm telling you now. I'm *not* touching you." And he was serious, falling back to sleep on her.

Sharron laid there and stared at him while he slept, thinking again about the irony of *her* life and the songs of Lauryn Hill:

I sometimes watch you in your sleep
excuse me if I get too deep

The Sweetest Thing.

Sweet like the mornings down south, hearing the birds chirp loudly with few cars driving by to disturb the mood, was what it felt like to wake up with your man in your arms and in *your* hometown. What else could a woman ask for? That kind of sweetness you want to protect. Sharron went with the moment in the morning, long before her father was up and about, and whispered, "I love you," into Anthony's ear.

Anthony smiled, hearing for the first time what Sharron had wanted to say to a caring brown man outside of her father for years. He cracked his eyes, just enough to search for *her* ear, and returned the favor. Of course, since he was a man, he had to camouflage it.

"You got me in love with you, too," he whispered back.

What else could a woman ask for? But to keep it home.

"Will you love me tomorrow?" she whispered again.

Anthony smiled at her a second time. "If *you* can, then *I* can," he told her.

"But can you love me as much as I love you?"

He said, "I already do."

And she kissed his cheek with glee and smiled as bright as the sunlight, oblivious to corniness, because the silliness of love was a reality. Ask the couples who have been married for thirty years or more how it felt when *they* first started.

Then Anthony jumped in alarm. "You hear that? Your father's up. Go back to your room before he shoots me."

Sharron shook her head and climbed to her feet. "He's *not* gonna shoot you. We didn't do anything anyway."

"Well, just sneak back up to your room to make sure."

That time, she listened to him and crept back up the stairs to her room.

"What do you two have planned for the day?" Mr. Francis asked them at breakfast. They were having eggs, bacon, grits, wheat toast, and orange juice.

"I'm taking him downtown to Beale Street, Main, and the National Civil Rights Museum," Sharron answered.

Her father nodded and said, "Good. And he can meet Lucille when you two get back."

"How is she getting over here if I have the car? You need me to pick her up?" Sharron asked.

"No. She knows how to catch a cab. You think I go out and get her every time she comes over here?"

Sharron shook her head and said, "Dad! I don't believe you."

He said, "Believe it! Because *I'm* not driving Ms. Daisy."

Anthony sat there and broke out laughing. Watching Sharron's relationship with her father made him realize he could be as straightforward as he wanted with her. She was used to it.

"Are you gonna see your aunts while you're down here?" her father asked her.

Sharron looked and grinned. "Daddy, you know I can't come home without seeing them. How's Mia doing?"

"She's doing better," he answered. "She hasn't tried anything crazy lately. She's just working and trying to take care of those kids. I'm sure she'll be *dying* to see you."

"Please, don't use the word 'dying.' I've had enough of that in my life already," Sharron snapped.

Her father nodded. "Sorry, baby. I know what you mean."

Anthony looked at both of them, dying for an explanation. Sharron planned on giving him one, just as soon as they left that morning.

Before they did, Mr. Francis pulled Anthony aside. "Now, her aunts are the kind of women you *don't* express yourself to. Because the more you say to them, the more they want to know. So, you watch what you say over there. Okay?" he warned with a grin.

Anthony smiled back at him and nodded. "All right. I'll do that."

When he walked out to join Sharron at the car, she smirked. "My father told you to watch out for my aunts, didn't he?"

He shook his head and grinned, feeling like a pawn in the middle of a father-daughter chess game. "If you know already, then why are you asking me?"

"Mmm-hmm," she grunted. "Men!"

"Women!" he shot back.

When they climbed into the car, he asked, "Who is Mia?"

"My first cousin," Sharron answered, guarded.

Anthony sensed the guardedness in her tone and left it alone.

"She tried to commit suicide," Sharron added. "She has three kids, two girls and a boy, all out of wedlock, and none of the fathers do anything for their kids, and my aunt just can't figure out what went wrong with her."

Anthony looked out the window as they headed through the city of Memphis and was silent.

"I know you're probably thinking that I have a lot of baggage in my family, right?" she asked him self-consciously.

"Who doesn't?"

"And it doesn't turn you off?"

Anthony looked at her and said, "Would *you* try to commit suicide?"

Sharron frowned. "No way in the world."

Anthony nodded and thought of an even tougher question. "Have you ever thought about having cancer like your mom?"

A dagger, but it was fair to ask, and meaningful.

"I used to think about that a lot when she died. So I get checked now regularly."

Anthony nodded. "And you're okay?"

She smiled. "Yes, I'm okay. Sometimes I even used to think that my mother stressed herself to death, outside of the breast cancer. She was never satisfied with anything."

"My mom *could* have been satisfied. But my father just wouldn't act right," Anthony added with a chuckle.

Sharron said, "Will you act right with me?"

Another meaningful question.

He smiled at her. "I hope so. That's all I can say. I could ask you the same thing, and what would you say?" he asked her back.

"I'd say that I would do everything in my power to."

He nodded. "It's just one of those things where you can't really predict the future. You just have to live it day by day and find out."

"Well, how come we're able to have same-sex friends for so long?" Sharron questioned. "What's the difference?"

"Sex."

They laughed.

"Is sex that powerful, where two people can totally change opinions about each other?"

Anthony said, "It used to be. But now . . . I just think of it as a part of life, instead of a mission. But when sex is a mission, as soon as you get it, you're ready to move on to the next mission."

"See that? And sex is not 'a mission,' as you call it, with most women. We're more into the man."

"You mean, *the fantasy* of the man," he argued. "That's why I was able to get with so many women. They started making up their own dreams about what they wanted, and I always knew how to take advantage of that. Women need to come back down to earth and stop fantasizing so much."

"Yeah, and then when you come back to earth, you end up with sorry men who don't want to do much with themselves," Sharron countered. "Then you try to motivate them to want more, and they complain about you not accepting them for who they are, and all kinds of other nonsense. So my friend Celena tells them outright, 'If you don't have what it takes, then don't even open up your mouth to me.'"

Anthony shook his head thinking about Dana Nicole Simpson again. "That's a hard way to live, too," he commented.

"Don't I know it. I've seen her going from man to man for years now, like there's no tomorrow. But *I want* a tomorrow. And I want *one* man."

Anthony grinned. "I'm glad you do. Especially if that one man is me."

They shared a smile as they reached the downtown area and parked near the legendary music scene on Beale Street.

"This is Beale Street, a tourist area for music lovers and Memphis's pride and joy," Sharron announced as they walked out onto the lively street of restaurants, music stores, and memorabilia shops.

Anthony looked around at all of the reminders of Elvis Presley and smiled.

"This is where The King lives forever, hunh?"

Sharron frowned and said, "*Elvis* lives forever, *everywhere.* At least in America. They have a statue of him further up the street."

"A *statue?*" Anthony asked her, surprised.

Sharron chuckled. "Yeah, we have a life-size statue of Elvis Presley here."

"And people are not supposed to touch it, right? But they can't help themselves."

"You know it," Sharron told him. "They have a lot of cops who patrol this area though. And they don't play that."

"Yeah, because the entire police force probably has Elvis's whole collection at home."

Sharron playfully pushed him away as they walked. Anthony noticed the brass music notes cemented into the ground that honored legendary singers, like Hollywood did with their stars.

"Lou Rawls," he read one of them. "So they give props to the black singers here, too?" he asked.

Sharron looked at him as if he had lost his marbles. "Are you crazy? You can't celebrate American music without bringing up black people. And B. B. King may not have a statue here like Elvis, but you have to give him respect. And he has just as much stuff on this street."

"B. B. King, hunh? What's his guitar named again?"

Sharron smiled and said, "Lucille. Just like my father's girlfriend's name. At first I didn't like her. I used to call her Lucy."

"*Lucy?* Why didn't you like her? You thought she was taking your father away?"

She nodded, embarrassed by it. "Especially thinking about my mom dying. But then I just had to get over it. At least my father didn't bring her into our same house. He moved into the new one like a year after my mom was buried."

Anthony looked down again and read, "Ike and Tina Turner."

Sharron smiled. "Yeah, they have them, too. And I know, they started off in St. Louis, you don't have to tell me. But Tina *was* born in Tennessee."

He just smiled and kept walking. "I should buy one of these shirts or something," he commented, looking through the shop windows.

"You all need a tour guide?" an idle black man asked them.

"No, we're not tourists. *I* live here," Sharron told him.

"Okay, just checking, sister." He headed by them for the next excited couple.

"That's what you deal with when you come back down to *earth,* Anthony. Men who don't know what to do with themselves."

He shook his head and countered, "That's everywhere. But don't think that the white man doesn't have anything to do with that."

Sharron sighed and looked away for a second before coming back to him. "Here we go with that white man stuff," she commented. "When are we ever going to stop blaming white people for stuff and just get on with our lives?"

"When they stop holding the deck of cards away from us."

"Well, we're gonna have to make our *own* deck then, Anthony."

"They didn't make *their* own deck. They stole it. Then they studied and reproduced it. Now they go around talking about they originated it. And that's with a lot of things they do."

Sharron said, "They *did* originate a lot of things."

"And like you said, so did we," Anthony argued. "Including *rock* music."

Then he smiled at her. He was just pulling her leg. He knew what he had to do, regardless of oppression. He would take care of his own time, space, and destiny.

He said, "Naw, for real, I don't dwell on it. Some people do, some people don't. But I don't *forget* about it either."

"I didn't say to forget about it," Sharron told him. "But if you have your own life to live, what are you gonna do, live your life or use *them* as an excuse *not* to?"

Anthony continued to grin, viewing the other Friday morning tourists, who were mostly white couples and families, along with the police, and the hangers-on, who were mostly black men.

He thought about it and said, "Women don't seem to be as affected by it anyway."

"Yeah, because we know we have to *eat.* But black men would rather starve, beg, and complain about shit."

Sharron was getting a little testy. *I'm tired of hearing all these excuses about* four hundred years ago! she thought. *Are we gonna talk about the white man for another thousand years or what? I mean, when do we ever move on from that?*

Anthony noticed her sour mood and grabbed her by the waist. "You don't have to worry about me. I'm gonna do what I need to do. Okay? I'm just teasing you. I feel the same way you do. It ain't always about race. I tell my boy Tone that all of the time."

"And what does he say?"

"He says, 'That's bullshit. It's *always* about race!'"

They laughed again, right as they made it to Elvis's statue.

"So, here he is," Anthony commented, taking a look. "They got him in full swing and everything. But we have a holiday for Martin Luther King. And now we have a stamp for *Malcolm X* of all people," he said. "I thought white people would *never* give us a stamp of *Malcolm X.*"

That reminded Sharron of the National Civil Rights Museum that she planned to visit with him.

"Actually, we have an entire museum just down the street from here. They still have the room and the cars parked outside where Dr. King was shot."

"You mean assassinated," Anthony corrected her with a grin.

Sharron grinned back and agreed with him. "Okay, assassinated."

"You don't believe he was?" he asked. Anthony did. With all of his heart.

"Yeah, I believe that. I mean, I may not blame white people for *everything,* but I'm not *crazy* either," she told him.

Anthony laughed out loud and said, "Good. Because I can't have a woman who thinks white people can't do any wrong, whether I decide to live my life without blaming them or not."

"Everybody can do wrong. And after visiting this museum, I know they're *far* from being perfect," Sharron responded.

Anthony said, "You needed a museum to teach you that?"

"No. But it just reminds you and puts it all into perspective, so that we *don't forget* as you say."

She led him just a few blocks east to the National Civil Rights Museum and paid the small entrance fee.

"Who's that standing across the street?" Anthony asked as they entered the museum that was modeled after a sixties hotel with two old cars parked out front.

"They've been protesting the museum since it opened up, saying it capitalizes on the tragedy of King's death," she told him.

Anthony nodded, half-agreeing with it. "Everything in America is for sale anyway. Don't they have a holocaust museum for the Jews?"

Sharron looked surprised. "I didn't know you knew about that."

He frowned and said, "What, I can't read and watch news reports? I may not be the smartest guy in the world, but I'm not Gomer Pyle over here either."

"I didn't say that you were."

"Well, stop being surprised by what I know."

She smiled and said, "Gomer Pyle wouldn't be with *me* anyway."

They walked through the first museum room filled with the documented history of scholar, athlete, actor, and singer Paul Robeson. Then they moved along to the second room of college protesters on a North Carolina campus, climbed aboard the bus where Rosa Parks made her historic stand, and walked through southern prison cells where black men either committed suicide *or* were more than likely *hanged* by their bedsheets. Then they eyeballed the intimidating white sheets of Klansmen and viewed the black sanitation workers in their fight, while reading the newspaper articles that were posted to the walls, regarding black men, women, their work, their words, and the lectures that all added to the framework of American history. At the conclusion of their tour, they climbed the stairs to the second floor and took a good long look at the modest hotel room where Dr. Martin Luther King Jr. rested on his last day with the living before being shot and killed on the hotel's balcony.

Sharron looked at her man, who had been surprisingly quiet throughout their tour, and asked him what he felt about the museum.

"It's much bigger inside than it looks from the outside," he commented. "From the outside, it's deceiving."

"They did a good job designing it," Sharron said. "But does it make you want to go after white people?" she asked him. It was *her* turn to play devil's advocate. *She* sure felt like getting some retaliation with white Americans after *she* first walked through the museum.

Anthony shook it off and responded, "Not really. It just makes me understand that I have to keep on working to move ahead. It wouldn't make no sense to go out here and do something stupid. I'd end up arrested, and it wouldn't change a damn thing."

Sharron smiled, thinking, *Now* that's *a black* man*! We can't dwell on the past. We have to keep moving forward. The best that we can do is use the past as fuel for the future.*

After the museum, they walked outside and up to Main Street and rode the twenty-five-cent trolley, jumping off farther up to walk in and out of Memphis's downtown shops.

Anthony looked in the showcase windows at many of the six-button, colorfully striped and tweed suits and laughed.

"What, y'all got the return of the mack down here in Memphis?" he joked.

Sharron smirked and said, "Don't even try it. I saw some of the same kind of suits in stores in St. Louis."

"Yeah, and nobody was wearing them."

"So, you wouldn't wear a six-button, double-breasted, wide-collar suit?" Sharron asked as if she were serious.

Anthony said, "You trippin'. Then on top of that, they got all of them crazy colors: big, thick yellow and orange stripes. You see the kind of outfits I wear. I'm into solids."

"You wouldn't even wear one of these suits if I bought it for you?" Sharron asked, hinting with a smile.

He nodded. "You make sure that you keep your receipt. Because you'll be taking it right back to where you got it.

"What if I bought you an orange sequin dress with both legs hanging out and a big orange bow tie on the shoulder? Would *you* wear *that?*" he asked her.

Sharron broke out laughing. "If we were going to a *costume* party."

"All right then," he told her.

They crossed the street and went into a furniture store just to walk through.

"Damn, look at how big these bedposts are," Anthony said, grabbing ahold of bedposts with knobs the size of soccer balls. "Who would want these giant things on their bed?"

"Evidently, *somebody* thought people would," Sharron told him. "Just like with the six-button suits."

"What kind of bed would you buy for us?" Anthony asked.

"It would be more of a *we* thing, and I probably wouldn't shop here. We just came in here to be nosy."

"Oh, is that why we came in here?"

"Yeah, just to look," Sharron repeated, loud enough for salesmen to overhear her and leave them alone.

"There's no charge for looking," an eager salesmen in a cheap blue tie responded.

Anthony walked over to the sectional sleeper-couch area and sat down.

"I'd buy one of these for my sixty-inch color TV, to watch the World Series, the Super Bowl, the NBA finals, the Final Four, and a couple of X-rated movies," he joked.

Sharron sat down next to him and said, "Yeah, me too. I'd even have some live X-rated dancers so me and my girls could stick money in their jock straps."

Anthony frowned and said, "Not in *my* house you won't. What are you talking about?"

"Well, what's with the 'X-rated movies'?" she countered.

"They're not real people."

"They may as well be."

Anthony smiled and said, "Would you dance naked and put on a show for me then?"

"Would you do it for me?"

"If you didn't tell anybody."

Sharron started to laugh. "Still worried about your rep, hunh?"

"So worried that I would never do somethin' like that."

"I wouldn't either."

Anthony said, "So, we'd be a conservative couple then."

"I guess so. Why, is something wrong with that?"

"I don't know. I mean, I guess it can get boring after a while, you know."

"Well, you find ways to liven it up by going different places and experiencing new things together, not by acting all freaky."

Anthony smiled. "What if you can't just jump up and fly off to Jamaica or somewhere though?"

"There's other things that people can do. Most of the time they just don't try it. Like when you first took me out to watch airplanes. *That* was original."

"No it wasn't. If it was, we would have been the only people there."

"*I* had never been there before, and you had only *thought* about it," Sharron said. "And that's the kind of stuff I'm talking about, like the museum we just went to, and Beale Street, and this whole trip to Memphis," she said. "Do you know that my friend Celena has never come down here with me in what, close to six years since I've known her?"

"Not once?"

"*Not once!* She always had an excuse not to go. So, of course she got jealous when I said that you were going with me this time."

"At least she likes me now," he said.

Sharron thought about her aunts, Miriam and Julianne. How would *they* judge Anthony? How many questions would they ask him? How many questions would they ask *her* about him? And how many assumptions would they make? Frankly, Sharron had a pair of tough aunts. Her mother had been tough herself. Sharron's good nature came from her father. Not that her mother could not be easygoing at times, she just was never fluent with it like Sharron was.

"Are you hungry yet?" she asked Anthony.

"I *been* hungry."

"Why didn't you say something earlier?"

"I figured we'd eat eventually, so I wasn't in no big hurry about it."

"We'll get a big meal at my aunt's house later on, so we don't need to eat that much down here," she told him.

He nodded. "Fine with me. So go get my dinner and I'll be relaxing right here, honey," he joked.

Sharron looked him over and said, "I hope you don't think that's the way it would be with me, because you can get your ass up and get your *own* dinner. I'm not *hardly* going to be the cook *and* the waiter," she snapped.

Anthony laughed and said, "Don't get so touchy about it. I'm only playing with you."

"Yeah, as long as you *know*," she huffed at him, grinning. "And don't think that I'm all up for that Superwoman thing either, because I'll get just like your mom on you," she warned.

Anthony didn't like the sound of that. His mother could be brutally cold sometimes.

Sharron read the panic on his face before he even said anything. "Don't get so touchy about it. I'm only playing with you," she mocked him.

He grinned and said, "That shit wasn't funny."

Sharron stood up and grabbed his hand to pull him along with her. "Come on before we get too comfortable in here and I start wanting my own house right now."

Anthony chuckled real good at that. He had those same thoughts about houses on his mind for weeks. His friend Tone had inspired that thinking with his carpet cleaning job.

"So, when do you think you'll be ready for that big move?" Anthony asked Sharron.

"What big move?"

"Moving into a place of our own."

She looked at him and froze. "You mean before marriage or anything?"

Marriage hadn't crossed his mind as strongly as moving in. Moving in was a lot easier to swallow.

"You don't have to be married to get a nice place together. Because I'm ready to move away from Tone right now," he said to her.

Sharron had to think for a minute. Her friend Celena thought that moving in with a guy was like a cow pumping her own milk for the farmers. *I don't know about all of that,* Sharron assessed to herself.

Anthony snapped her out of it and said, "I got you again, hunh?"

"What, you were only joking about that, too?" Suddenly she wasn't hungry anymore.

"If it makes you that nervous, then yeah."

She sucked her teeth and said, "That's a cop-out. I mean, if that's how you feel, then I have to deal with it. You want us to move in?"

Anthony backed off of the idea. "We may end up doing that, but for now, I guess we're all right where we are. I mean, you're gonna be going to school for nursing soon, and you're gonna need your space to do your thing."

"But if we moved in together, then we wouldn't have to miss each other in the meantime."

Anthony smiled. "I believe that's how it works. Yeah."

Then it wasn't such a bad idea to Sharron. *I really need to think this over,* she pondered, more on the positive side than when she first heard it.

They walked up the street and ate a bite of fried chicken and potato fries before it was time to head over to Sharron's Aunt Miriam's on the far northwest end of Memphis. They arrived and parked outside a much larger brick house than Sharron's father's, with a driveway and a two-car garage.

"So, this is it, hunh?" Anthony asked, grinning.

"What?"

"Your aunts get to rip me apart."

Sharron laughed. "You got your mom to rip *me* apart."

"No I didn't," he told her. "All I did was introduced you to her."

"Yeah, and with no warning. And it was on my birthday at *that.*"

"I guess you can get me back now," he told her.

She shook her head. "My aunts aren't that bad. Just be yourself. You know how to handle women," she advised, grinning.

That's what Anthony was most afraid of, being himself. Players usually were when it came to settling down. And older women generally knew who they were. They had lived long enough to pick up the flirtatious vibes. Sharron knew it too. But she didn't care anymore. She was willing to fight for him if she had to. He was her man regardless. Her visit to her aunt's would be more of an announcement than an interrogation. Anthony had already passed through the only court that really mattered. Sharron's.

"Nice-looking place, too," Anthony said of the five-bedroom house.

"Yeah, my Aunt Miriam and Uncle Che' are doing all right."

"What do they do?"

"They both work for the city government of Memphis."

"They're political people?"

"Not really. They just *work* for the government. I never really even asked what they did. My Uncle Che' does have a law degree."

"His wife runs the show, though, hunh?" Anthony asked teasingly. It seemed as if more emphasis was on her aunts than on her uncles, so he assumed that they were dominant women.

"I guess you can say that," Sharron admitted. "My Uncle Che' doesn't really get excited about much."

"And is your cousin Mia their daughter?"

"Yup. I guess she just didn't get all the attention she needed as their third child. My cousin Che' Junior is doing all right. He's the oldest. And so is my cousin Helen."

"Well, are we going in or what?" Anthony asked. He noticed that they hadn't budged from the car.

Sharron smiled at him and said, "Come on." By that time, it was close to six in the evening.

"I see they drive some nice cars." Anthony noted a white Infiniti and a black Mercedes-Benz parked in front of the garages.

"That's another reason my father had issues with them. We were never into the money like they were."

"I see."

They walked inside and were smacked in the face with a pouring out of love.

"Sharron, baby, look at you!" her aunt gushed with a big hug as soon as she spotted her niece. "You look as good as your mother used to look at your age."

Oh, gee, thanks, Sharron thought sarcastically. That *sure sounded good.*

Anthony stood off to the side, waiting to be introduced, while looking over the elegant home: paintings, small sculptures, vases, and quality furniture.

This is the kind of home that Tone was talking about, he mused. *I wouldn't mind having a crib like this myself. No doubt!*

"This is my Anthony," Sharron said, introducing him to her aunt.

"*Your* Anthony, hunh?" her aunt asked.

Sharron was already protecting her man without even realizing it.

Anthony looked over the full-figured brown woman in her dark blue power suit, and immediately wondered about Sharron ten years down the road.

"How are you doing?" he greeted her.

She asked, "Anthony, are you a real black man or a pretender?"

He looked at Sharron, who looked sternly at her aunt.

Aunt Miriam smiled and added, "Tough question, ain't it? It didn't use to be."

"Well, what's the definition of a 'real black man'?" Sharron asked her.

"Let Anthony answer that," she responded. "And excuse me for asking you, Anthony. But we just had a book club discussion last night, and that was one of the key questions in the book we were reading."

"Did you ask any other men about it?" Anthony quizzed her.

"Well, *my* husband already *knows* that a real black man takes care of family business. I'm just more concerned about asking these *younger* men out here who don't hold up *their* ends of the bargain."

"How is Mia doing?" Sharron interjected. She knew exactly what her aunt was getting at. And she and Mia were two different people.

"You'll see her. I'll let her tell you all about it. She's tired of *me* being in her business anyway. But she's dying to see *you*."

Sharron looked at Anthony and smiled. "So I've heard," she commented.

"So, how long have you two known each other?" her aunt asked.

Anthony smiled, remembering his mother asking Sharron that same question months ago.

"Since the heat of spring?" Sharron answered, no longer ashamed of it.

Miriam raised her brow. "Well, you two *do* know what they say, don't you? The heat cools down after a while. Then what?"

"We strike another match," Sharron countered.

Good answer.

Her aunt smiled and chuckled at her cleverness. "Hmmph. I sure hope you have a lot a matches to strike."

Sharron was ready to go to battle with her aunt but decided not to. *Just let it go,* she told herself. *My Aunt Miriam has* plenty *of reasons to lack faith in a lot of the young black men out here, but much of that has to do with the choices that* we make *as women as well. I could have had Sean Love a long time ago, but I chose to wait for an Anthony Poole. So I'll just have to live with that decision and not complain about it.*

Once they had another minute alone, Anthony said, "Your father wasn't lying when he talked about your aunts."

"My Aunt Julianne is not as bad as Miriam," Sharron told him. "Thank God," she added.

When most of the family arrived for the get-together dinner and Sharron's summer visit home, Anthony found himself in the heat of the discussion while Sharron fought off the wolves. Not that he couldn't represent himself; Sharron just wanted to make certain she did her part to support him. Then there was cousin Mia, who wanted time alone with Sharron, away from her new man and the family so they could catch up on things.

Mia looked healthy, positive, and energetic. She became depressed after her first child and broken heart. She grew more depressed after the second. And by the third time around, she was suicidal.

"So, how is it with him?" she wanted to know, more concerned about Sharron and her man than how her cousin was doing on her own. They were outside on the front patio.

"What do you mean, how is it?" Sharron asked her. She knew good and well what her cousin meant. She meant was it *secure?* Was she *satisfied* with him? Was *he* satisfied with her? Did they really have a chance to make it together? If so, then when was the wedding, and could she be a bridesmaid?

Sharron knew what her cousin wanted to hear. She wanted to hear that a relationship could actually work out for her same-age cousin, who was once extremely close to her. The best of friends and family.

"You know, how does he treat you?" Mia asked again.

"With respect," Sharron answered. *Because he knows that I respect myself,* she wanted to add. She had run her cousin's story through her mind a thousand times and still could not understand it all. Mia had wanted her first love to be a part of her life, so her first son was a given. But when the first daughter came along from a new man, and then another daughter from a third, Sharron had to ask herself, *What the hell is going wrong?* And when it all came out in the attempt of suicide with an overdose of pills, it was obvious that Mia was desperate for love. From anywhere! And from anyone. So she refused to abort her "babies," while her lawyer father fought with all of his power to make sure that she could keep them with mandatory counseling. It was all family history Sharron had tried her best to block out, just in case she too could slip that far into the abyss for love.

"Are y'all gettin' married?" her cousin asked her with all seriousness.

"Why has everyone been assuming marriage tonight?"

"Because you brought him all of the way to Memphis with you. That *must* count for *something!"* Mia countered.

"Well, we haven't even talked about marriage. Not seriously. We just *started* talking about moving in."

"Movin' in? Oh, no, girl, don't do that," Mia warned her. "That's how it all gets started. Then they start taking advantage of the situation. And you can't even get them to come *home* half of the time."

"You're gonna move in together *eventually* if you're getting married," Sharron told her.

"Yeah, but then it's different because you're bonded."

"And you think *that* changes something?"

"It *should.*"

"Well, it *don't.* And if you don't have a bond *before* you get married, then I don't know why so many people *think* that they're gonna have one afterwards. It doesn't work that way. Marriage should be the *icing* on the cake, and not *the* cake."

Mia just stared at her. "You always understood things so much better than I could," she said. Then her head went down. Sharron didn't like the sight of that at all. But what could she say to her cousin? That things would get better? Lift up her head and look forward to the future? You're going to find somebody to love you one day? What could she tell Mia to soothe her pain? Realistically? So she hugged her instead. And hung on to her. Until Mia couldn't take it anymore.

"I know my kids are looking for me in there, Sharron. Let me go and find them. You know, I'm a three-time mother now."

She left Sharron standing outside alone, like so many men had left her.

"Why are you so quiet?" Anthony asked Sharron. They were on their way back to her father's house that night.

She shook her head at the wheel. "I'm just thinking about my cousin."

"Mia?"

"Yeah, man. What do I do about her?"

Anthony looked straight ahead and asked, "What *can* you do?"

"Yeah, like, start her life all over again, right? With a snap of my fingers."

"But that wouldn't be fair to her kids. They're here now. And I hate to say it, because it may not be the thing she wants to hear, but the only thing she can really do is look out for them. And I'm just being real about that," Anthony suggested.

"I know you are," Sharron told him with a hand on his knee. "And you know what, we're supposed to be sleeping at the hotel tonight. I just remembered."

"We don't have to if you don't want to. I mean, it *is* kind of late to be checking into a hotel now, ain't it?"

"No. We can still check into a hotel."

"I just don't want to press the issue. We have to get our stuff from your father's house anyway. By the time we do all of that, we might as well chill there."

Sharron shook her head and made her own decision. "No, we can get that stuff tomorrow morning," she said. And that was that. She headed to a nice Memphis hotel, because she wanted to be close to her man that night, and without any restrictions.

"Daddy," she called from their room on the seventh floor, "I'll be home with your car in the morning."

"Well, where are you?"

"We're at the Radisson downtown."

"The Radisson? Don't you need your change of clothes and your toothbrushes?"

She laughed. "Yeah, I know, Dad. Anthony said that too, but I was too tired to drive home and have to drive back to the hotel. We'll just have to get that stuff in the morning."

"Okay. Well, Lucille was waiting to see Anthony, but she knows I have to go to work tomorrow morning, so she's gone now. I guess she'll meet him when she comes over on Sunday maybe."

"Yeah, Sunday. And we can even go out to get a bite to eat," Sharron suggested.

"It's a deal," her father told her.

When she hung up the phone, she looked over to the bed at Anthony watching cable television, and flung herself on top of him.

"Anthony, this has been a *long* day."

"I know."

"So are you tired?"

"Yeah."

"Really tired?" she asked, undoing his pants.

"Yup," he added with a smile.

"Too tired for a warm bath together?"

He grinned and said, "Not if you can carry me in there. Because I don't even feel like getting up right now."

"I can compromise. Let's just get under the covers then. Are you too tired to do that?"

"Naw," he told her, helping her with his pants.

Sharron stripped them both to their underwear and climbed into the hotel sheets with her man to wrap her arms around him.

"What do you think about my family so far?" she asked him. "Can you deal with us?"

"Why, you think I can't?"

"I'm just asking."

He thought about it and nodded. "Yeah. Family is family."

Then she caressed his tool. "Are you too tired for this?"

He smiled again. "Do I still have to use protection?"

"Of course you do. Let's not get sloppy just because I'm on the pill now. We're not ready to start a family of our own *yet.* Or *are* we?" she asked him.

He said, "I'm ready when you are. But I guess that first we have to figure out all of the arrangements. You know, stuff like, where we would live? How we would separate our bills? How we would watch our kids? And then you have to finish up with your nursing school, and I have to figure out if I want to open up my own shop one day."

Sharron thought about all of that herself. "Sounds like couples have lots of decisions to make before they just up and do things, hunh?"

"I guess so. But we just up and have sex though," he added with a chuckle.

"Maybe we shouldn't even do this then," she suggested, releasing him under the sheets.

Anthony laughed, wanting to smack himself in the mouth for being a smart-ass. "Maybe I shouldn't have said that," he said.

"But it's the truth, though. And it don't make any sense. It *don't*."

"Now you know why men don't like to talk much about this kind of thing. So now I guess we won't have sex tonight," he stated.

"Oh yes we will," Sharron responded to his surprise. "Unless, *you* don't want to."

"You know that won't be the case," he told her.

Sharron asked, "Would you say that we were close to bonding as a couple yet? Because a lot of couples can't seem to do that nowadays. And to be honest with you, it doesn't seem like time matters anymore."

Anthony smiled, thinking of his partner Tone.

"Before we came down here to Memphis, I was kind of unsure about us, you know, how long it would last and stuff. But Tone kept saying from the first time we hooked up at the skating rink that you had my nose open. And at first I was denying it. But the more we hung out with each other, and you kept getting closer to me, it got to the point where I couldn't . . .

"Well, let's just say that, yeah, I feel that we *are* bonding," he answered, cutting himself off from rambling.

"Mmm-hmm," Sharron grumbled at him with a grin. "My father told me what you said, too."

"What I said about what?"

"About retiring," she told him, eye to eye.

Anthony was shocked. "Your father told you I said that?"

"You thought that he wouldn't? He actually sounded proud of you when he said it."

"He did?"

"Yeah."

"I guess I wasn't even thinking about him telling you. You know, with all that *manhood* stuff he was telling me."

"Yeah, but I'm *still* his little girl. Don't forget that."

"Oh, now I *won't*. Believe me," he responded, grinning.

Sharron turned off the television with the remote control and slid her right hand under his T-shirt. "I want your undivided attention again, Mr. Retired," she teased him.

"I'm not retired with you," he told her.

She leaned over and kissed him in the dark. "Good. I don't want you to be." He undid her bra and slid off the rest of their clothes under the sheets.

"Don't forget the condoms," she reminded him.

Anthony chuckled to himself and scrambled for his wallet. And the love they shared got stronger every time, with mind over body, bonding two human souls.

And *bonds* are even tested by the unpredictability of nature. But *real* bonds are strong enough to make it through turbulence. And if not, then how strong was that *bond* to begin with, *if* you even had one?

Less than a week after returning home to St. Louis from visiting Memphis with Sharron, Ant cruised familiar territory on Kingshighway Boulevard on a late Thursday night, singing along with his radio:

Sweet lay-dee
would you bee myy
sweet love for
ah life-time . . .

Oblivious to the activity on the street, while singing to Tyrese's ballad "Sweet Lady," Ant didn't notice his partner Tone scrambling to his car at the red light.

Tone hollered through the window, "Open the door up, man!"

Ant then noticed two guys running behind him, two roughnecks from Tone's mother's neighborhood. Before Ant had a chance to question what was going on, they had all jumped into his car.

"What the hell is this?!" he asked them.

"Drive us the hell out of here, man!" Tone snapped at him.

Ant hesitated.

"Drive the fucking car!" one of Tone's friends hollered from the back seat. A black pistol appeared in his hand, and Ant drove off on instincts, right before he heard the police sirens.

"What did y'all do, man?" he asked his partner.

Tone was silent.

"Just keep driving!" his roughneck friend shouted again from the back. He made sure he kept the gun aimed at Ant's head, too. Ant continued to drive, praying that the police sirens were not after them, and praying as well that he would live to see another day.

"This shit reminds me of *Cooley High,*" the third passenger said from the back seat. He was the comedian of the bunch.

They actually laughed at it, in the heat of a police chase. However, Ant had nothing to laugh about. It wasn't funny to him. None of it!

Tone felt guilty and stopped the silliness as the police made chase. It was poor bad luck for Ant. He was at the wrong place at the wrong time for the wrong friend. So if they made it away from the cops, Tone planned to apologize to him profusely.

I can't believe this fuckin' shit! Ant thought to himself. *I'm gonna kill this nigga! He finally went and did it, didn't he? And he dragged* me *into this crazy shit with him! Just my damn luck! Right when everything was looking beautiful.*

Up ahead, a third police cruiser headed straight for them with two behind.

"Make a right!" the gun holder yelled at Ant.

Ant made the right turn much slower than the gun holder wanted.

"Can you *drive* or what?!" he snapped.

Ant would have rather been stopped. He didn't want to be shot at as some kind of fugitive. And there was no way in the world that he would smash up his car.

"This car is his pride and joy, man," Tone responded to his friend in the back seat.

"Man, fuck this car! I could see if it was a Mercedes," the gun holder countered. "This is just a fixed-up bomb. He can get another one. Get us the hell out of here!"

However, the right turn put them behind a slow-moving truck.

"Shit! Go around 'em!"

Ant had enough of that guy already, but what could he do about it? He tried to drive around the truck and nearly wrecked his car with the oncoming traffic.

BURRNNMP!

Horns blew and tires skidded as Ant saved his car and maneuvered away from an accident and the police in one big yank of the wheel.

"Shit! His ass *can* drive!" the comedian celebrated. He was enjoying the ride as if they were at Six Flags amusement park. Maybe the kid was on drugs.

By the time they traveled up the street and whipped around two corners, Ant came up with a quick suggestion.

"If y'all jump out right here, I can keep driving, and they'll just chase after me."

Tone looked at his partner and said, "That's a good plan." And it *was.* A good plan to get his friend out of Dodge, and an opportunity for *them* to escape as well.

"For what? So he can stop the car as soon as the police catch up to him? They know how many of us it is," the gun holder contested.

Tone argued, "Look, man, if he drives for another two miles with them after him, we in the wind before they know what happened." He even initiated the jump by opening the passenger-side door, sending Ant's heart rate skyrocketing.

Don't fuck up my damn door! he snapped to himself.

"Let's do it, man!" the comedian agreed from the back. And with one last hesitation, the gun holder followed their lead and hopped out of the car behind them. Ant took off up the street and made another right turn, just as the police rounded the corner.

"Now how long do I drive before I give this shit up?" he immediately asked himself. He was relieved that he no longer had a gun to his head and fugitives in his car. He still, however, had police cruisers on his tail: three behind him, and no telling how many on the way for backup.

He thought about his loyalty to Tone, but shook it off. "Fuck that! I'm not going to jail for his ass!"

He made it to Hampton Avenue, a big enough street to be seen by onlookers, and pulled over. Inside the car, he immediately raised his hands to the roof and kept them there as four St. Louis police cruisers surrounded his car.

"Step slowly out of the car," they told him with guns pulled from every angle. Three more cruisers arrived as they shot high beams and flashlights into Ant's Chevy for better vision.

"Where are your friends?"

"I didn't know those guys," Ant told them, stepping away from the car with his hands still up.

"Shit! They jumped!"

Three of the cruisers took off into the street with their sirens blaring. The remaining officers slapped cold, steel handcuffs on Ant's wrists and forcefully brought him to the ground.

"Where did they jump out?" he was asked.

"About four blocks from here. I would have turned myself in then, but I didn't want y'all to shoot me," Ant explained.

"Shoot you for what? You're innocent, right? Stand up," they told them. Some of them were white and some of them were black. But what difference did it make when they had no reason to believe your story?

"You guys had it all planned out, hunh?"

Ant said, "I don't know what you're talking about. They pulled a gun on me at the red light and told me to drive. That's all I know."

"No one asked you if you knew anything."

Shit! Ant thought. *Just stay calm.*

"It sounds like he knows something to me," another officer commented. They searched his car and came up with nothing.

"Let me get this right. They just picked you out at a red light to be the getaway driver? Is that it? Out of a possible ten cars that were at that same intersection?"

"That's what happened," Ant told them straight-faced.

The remaining officers were radioed by the others.

"They got 'em?" the officers reported.

"Well, let's take this one down to join them, and see if he's telling us the truth." They grabbed Ant by the arm and led him to a squad car.

Fuck! he panicked. *How are they gonna act? My story is still true though.* Most *of it. I guess it depends on Tone. Damn! I gotta give his ass a clue or something.*

"I guess if you don't know these guys, we can set you free," the officer teased on the way to the southside precinct. "Then again, you drove a little too well there to be a random carjack."

"I didn't want to wreck my car," Ant commented truthfully.

"Is that your car?"

"I got my registration and insurance on it. I've had it for four years now."

"Is that right?"

Ant's heart was pounding out of his chest! The handcuffs were the worse feeling in the world, pressing into the flesh of his wrists, while bending his arms uncomfortably backwards against the back seat of the cruiser. Handcuffs were not made to be a pleasant experience.

I don't believe *this shit!* he continued to tell himself. *If I get out of this shit here, I will* never *deal with Tone's ass again. And I* mean *that shit!*

"I guess you're the *next* unlucky guy tonight, aren't ya?" the officer continued to tease him. "You got caught. That's *always* unlucky."

They pulled up to the southside precinct, which definitely had more white officers than the other precincts in St. Louis. The fact that it was so close to Ant's job at Paul's Fix It Shop didn't help his nerves much either.

"Well, let's go in here and see if they know you," the officer joked again.

Ant's heart could not beat any faster! You wouldn't know it from the outside. He was too busy thinking about his choice of words in the ensuing interrogation.

All three fugitives were handcuffed and sitting in chairs with their backs up against the wall when Ant walked in on them.

"Hey, guys. Say hi to your friend," the officer addressed them.

Ant looked only at the gun holder, who scowled at him and remained speechless.

"You got nothing at all to say to your friend?" the officer instigated. The other officers watched and listened, planning to interrogate them separately.

"I told you, I don't know anything," Ant repeated.

"You also told us that you don't know *them?*"

The officers watched and waited for everything to unravel. Ant felt more confident about his story by the minute. They were playing right into his hands.

He said, "And I told you I had no choice," and looked away.

The gun holder caught on and said, "Why you lying on us, Ant. You know us, man. It was *your* idea to have us jump out the car and separate."

"Yeah, man," the comedian added. "That was your idea, Ant."

Shit! They know my name.

"So, which one had the gun to your head, Ant? Or did they *all* have a gun?" the officers asked him. "We didn't *find* any guns."

He must have tossed it when they ran, Ant thought.

"I want a lawyer," he said, mimicking a thousand television shows.

"Of course you do," they told him. They began the interrogation process with the gun holder. "Let's see who gets the lawyer first."

They took him into a separate small room where he was joined by a detective. Ironically, the detective was a black man in his midthirties. What a surprise! He was damn good at what he did, too.

"Do you have something to tell me?" he asked, cool, calm, and collected.

"It was all his idea, man. We hop out of the car, and he keeps driving to give us time to get away. We know Ant. He lives around the way. He's Tone's boy."

Guilty, the detective thought. *He's just trying to take everybody down with him.*

Next he brought in Tone.

"Do you have something to tell me?"

Tone shook his head.

"You have nothing at all to tell me, Tone?" the detective asked him again.

Tone just stared at him.

Okay, I have something to work with here, the detective pondered.

"Do you know Ant?" he asked.

"Who's that?" Tone said.

Okay, we have some loyalty here. "Your getaway driver."

Tone shook his head again. "Like he said, he had a gun to his head."

"Your friend Bryant said that Ant was your boy."

"My friend Bryant was the one who held the gun on him."

Hmmm. Interesting. "So where is the gun now?"

"He threw it in the street."

"And what about the house that you robbed? Was Ant in on that?"

Tone frowned and asked, "What house?" *How much did Bryant tell him?* he pondered.

"What were you running from?" the detective asked.

Tone was stuck.

In his silence, the officer added, "By the way, we found the truck you had."

"What truck?"

Guilty.

Then he brought in the comedian, who was considerably younger than the other guys.

"How old are you?" the detective asked him.

"Nineteen."

The brother had pity in his eyes. *Poor kid. Another one bites the dust.*

"You have something you want to tell me?" he asked him.

"I don't think so. *You* have something *you* want to tell *me?*"

The detective shrugged his shoulders. "Maybe. Maybe not. But I *will* tell you this. You're looking at doing anywhere from seven to twenty years of your life for burglary, resisting arrest, carjacking, and assault with a firearm," he ran down to him.

"Assault with a firearm?" the younger fugitive questioned. He was turning twenty in October. Unfortunately, he had picked the wrong company to brainstorm with.

"Ant said that one of you held a gun to his head."

The kid was speechless, but his nervous energy told everything.

"I didn't have no gun, man," he coughed up.

"What about the burglary?"

He paused. "It wasn't my idea. I was just there, man."

Shit! the detective thought to himself. *I pity this fool. He won't last two weeks in prison. Maybe I can try and get his charges dropped down and a sentence of a year or two.*

He saved Ant for last.

"You have something you want to tell me?"

Ant had his story all together. "I was driving home from my girl's house. I had my windows down, blasting music on Kingshighway. I stopped at a red light. These three guys run up to my car and one points a gun at me, talking about 'Open the fuckin' door!' So I panic and let them in. And the guy with the gun gets in the back, and points it right at my head, telling me to drive.

"So I start driving and I hear police cars behind us. Then another police car ends up in front of us, coming from the opposite direction. So he tells me to make a right turn.

"I make a right turn, and a truck is in front of us. He tells me to go around the truck. As soon as I do that, I almost crash my car in traffic, but I made it around anyway, and that's when we separated from the police cars.

"So at that point, I tell them that if they jump out of my car, I'll keep driving and lead the police away from them, so they could get away. And when they agreed to do that and jumped out, I drove to Hampton Avenue because I didn't want no Rodney King shit to happen to me on a small street with no witnesses. Then I stopped the car on Hampton, put my hands up, and let the police catch up to me, so I could tell them what happened."

He looked the detective right in his eyes and said, "And that's what happened."

The detective nodded. *That's a good one,* he mused with a grin. *But how much of it is true? I guess we'll have to find out. That's why I love my job. The intrigue keeps me motivated.*

"That's what happened?" he asked, deadpan.

"That's what happened," Ant repeated.

"So which guy had the gun?"

Ant said, "Sometimes, the guy who talks the most tough talk had the gun. So when you find it, you match up the fingerprints. But I think you already know who had the gun. You talked to everybody before me, right? Who do *you* think had it?"

The detective nodded. *He's smart, too,* he thought. *Do I mix him up with these other guys? . . . Probably not. But just to make sure . . .*

"And what about Tone? Do you know him?"

Ant was stuck for a second by loyalty. His slight pause was enough to give him away. So he told the truth. Painfully! But if it had been a white detective, he would have lied faster than Pinocchio. But a brother? Maybe *he* could understand. Maybe *he* had a friend at one time who went astray.

Ant opened his mouth and said, "You keep trying to . . . be close to somebody. And they just keep doing stuff that make you ask yourself, *'Why?!'* And sometimes you grow up with these people."

He looked into the brother's eyes to make sure he understood him, detective or not.

"So, how much of this story you told me was true?" the brown detective asked him.

Ant thought about that question. Hard! He looked straight ahead with determination and answered, "All of it." He thought, *I love Tone. He's my boy and all. But I'm* not *going to jail with his ass!*

The detective *did* understand. Perfectly. He stood up and told Ant, "I'll see what I can do," before he walked out to rejoin the other officers.

"So, what do you think, Scott?" he was asked.

He said, "Let's book them all, but keep the driver separated. We already know that he was not at the scene of the burglary. In the meantime, let's see if we can come up with this gun."

In the meantime, the black detective hoped that Ant would learn a valuable lesson concerning his choice of friends. The bail was set at one thousand dollars, and Ant would spend his first night behind bars. He could call his lawyer or a loved one to gather his bail money in the morning.

Ant couldn't believe it!

"You're holding me?" he asked, surprised, as they led him away.

"What did you think, that we would let you go?" an officer teased him.

Ant looked around for the detective, thinking of betrayal. *That motherfucker!* he thought. "I'm innocent, man," he said out loud.

The detective reappeared from an office and pulled him aside.

"Here's the deal," he said. "I'll check out all of the facts, and if everything is what you say it is, then you'll have nothing to worry about. So make sure you have a phone number for whoever you need to call in the morning to make bail."

"A thousand dollars?" Ant repeated incredulously.

"Don't worry, you'll get it all back. Have your family call a bondsman if you don't have it."

He had it all right. But how would he get it out of the bank? He *definitely* wasn't calling his mother. His brothers, father, uncles, and cousins were not too fond of precincts and jail cells either. And what about his car?

"What about my car?" he asked.

"It's being impounded. You'll have to pick it up when you get out."

"They won't mess with it, will they? That's my car, man."

The detective smiled. "I would be more worried about my choice of *friends* than my car. You think about that tonight."

The four brown suspects were shipped by three separate cars to a nearby holding facility, and booked for the night inside tiny, lifeless, gray brick cells. Ant was put into a room alone, where he was nearly in tears from fear, anger, hurt, betrayal, and confusion about everything he *thought* he knew. He also knew that he wouldn't call his mother in the morning when they allowed him his phone call. He *couldn't* call her. Because he had no faith in her to understand his situation. *Her* faith had been lost somewhere, like *his* faith had been lost on his friend Tone.

The time seemed to stand still and fade away, becoming meaningless, as Ant tried to imagine what sleep would feel like in jail. Because instead of sleeping, he paced the hard, cement floor.

"Hey, Ant?" Tone called from the cell beside his. "My bad, man. I'm sorry."

Bryant sucked his teeth from inside the cell with Tone. "You sound like a bitch."

His comedian sidekick laughed at it, as though a jail cell was just another experience in growing up.

Tone ignored them and begged his partner for forgiveness.

"This shit won't stick, man. I promise you," he said.

Ant had no words for him. He continued to pace his cell like a caged tiger.

Fuck that motherfucker! FUCK HIM! he snapped.

Bryant laughed out loud. "Ant ain't forgivin' you. You gotta be crazy. He goin' to jail now. I'ma make sure of it.

"I told y'all that running shit wasn't gon' work," he reminded them. "What you thought, we was gon' get a taxi home?"

The comedian continued to laugh, as the other inmates began to complain.

"Some people are trying to *sleep* over here!" a deep voice commented from across the hall.

"You should have thought about that shit before your ass got locked up," Bryant responded to him.

"Okay. I'll see you tomorrow then, motherfucker," the inmate promised.

"Yeah, *see me* then." Bryant wasn't all that big, but he sure *talked* a tough game.

Tone ignored them all and said, "Ant, when you get out of here, man, and you go back to your girl, you stay wit' her, dawg. And make a family or something . . . I mean . . . I wish *I* had somebody to love."

His words were the last spoken before a long silence. Not one inmate there had anything negative to say about it. They *all* wanted somebody to love. And somebody to love them back. *For life!*

That was the trick for Ant. He began to think of Sharron, wondering if he would lose her if he called and asked to borrow a thousand dollars to bail him out of jail. He wondered if *she* would understand. Or would he be another disappointment in her life of many disappointments. Another tragedy, in her life of many tragedies.

Damn! he thought to himself. *Would she still like me if I called her tomorrow and told her that I was in jail? . . . Would she still love me? And would she put up a thousand dollars to get me the hell out of here? I mean, it's not like I'm guilty of anything. I'm no damn criminal! She should* know *that by now! Or should she?*

He sat up for half the night in jail, pondering his many questions until the sun rose, a sun that he could not even see while locked away inside the pale, dark emptiness of a jail cell.

Would Sharron come to her man's rescue in the morning? Good question. Would you? . . . Well, Celena wouldn't. She'd let him rot and smell his own stench until it drove him insane. Because if he was unfortunate enough to go to jail, then he was *also* unfortunate enough to lose her good graces, and stand punishment for the same crime twice. The crime of imperfection. And when it rained, it poured. So with hard-edged women like Celena Myers and Mrs. Poole, an imperfect man had better buy himself an oversize umbrella, or face being left out and soaking wet in the rain.

But Sharron, as we now know, was a different kind of woman. She had the heart of the old school, to love a man to her death. And the steel of the new school to ask him *everything* about their future together without flinching, to do away with the destructiveness of assumptions. Nevertheless, was four months of knowledge on a man enough to go on?

When Anthony's phone call arrived at Sharron's apartment that Friday morning, Celena, on a day off from work, answered his call.

The operator announced, "You have a collect call from—Anthony—from the St. Louis Holding Facility. Will you accept the charges?"

Celena cringed and hesitated. *St. Louis* Holding *Facility?* she thought. *Like in* jail? "Yes, I accept the charges," she agreed. Then she called Sharron from the bathroom. "Sharron, you have an important phone call this morning."

"From my father?" Sharron guessed, half dressed and still combing her hair.

Celena handed her roommate the phone and waited for her to find out on her own.

"Hello."

"Good morning," Anthony answered, clearing the lump from his throat.

"Hey," Sharron chirped, smiling. She was happy to hear from him. "What, you're calling to drive me to work today?" she teased. Unless he *was* calling for that.

"Ahh, naw," he answered her. "I'm calling with some bad news."

"You crashed your car this morning?" she asked in a panic, knowing how much his '79 Chevy meant to him.

Celena began to smile, expecting a knockout punch. Sharron was only making the situation worse with her guessing.

"It's worse than that," Anthony told her.

"You ran somebody over?"

Celena laughed out loud. *This is gonna be* good! she thought to herself. *She doesn't even have a* clue! *She just* swore *that her man was so damned* perfect! *But now she'll know. And boy am I glad I didn't have to work today!*

Sharron turned and faced Celena, wondering what the hell was so funny.

Anthony finally told her, "Sharron, I'm in jail. But I'm out of here as soon as somebody can bail me out with a thousand dollars. I got it in the bank, so if you use yours, I can give it back to you today. But if not, I may need you to call a bondsman, and tell him I got the money in the bank."

Sharron faced Celena again and was absolutely *pissed* at her! *She knew where he was calling from! This was all a damn* game *to her! All she wants to do is* prove *that no man is right!*

She took the phone into the bathroom and closed the door before speaking another word.

"What did you do?" she asked, heart racing. She could even feel a minor headache coming on. Or was that from the hair comb? She was due for a perm that week before she started school again. And she *did* have a thousand dollars to bail Anthony out with. She had saved money so she could finish her training without having to work desperate hours to pay her bills. Her father had offered to help out as well.

Anthony said, "I'll tell you about it when we're face to face. But I'm innocent. I was just at the wrong place at the wrong damn time."

"Last night?"

"Yeah. After I left your apartment."

"Well, where did you go?"

"I was going home. But I'll tell you about it," he repeated, trying to keep his conversation to a minimum. He noticed her hesitation and said, "I had nobody else to call, Sharron."

"What about your brothers?" she asked him. She didn't mean to distance herself from him. The question just slipped out of her mouth.

"Or my father, or my cousins?" he asked her sarcastically. "Or even my mother, right? *She'd* understand," he added.

Sharron poised herself and questioned, *Why me?*

Anthony felt guilty about it, because he knew she had the money to do it with. And at that particular time in his life, she happened to be the closest to him. It was natural to call her. But as he continued to think about it, he could not help predicting her feelings of being used. He found himself at a woman's mercy when it counted the most: for his freedom. How strong was his game now? And how strong was Sharron's dedication to their future? *If* they still had one.

"You know . . ." Sharron uttered. She couldn't finish her sentence or even *think* straight.

He said, "I understand how you feel." Since he knew that he was innocent, he took a chance with their lives and called her to the plate. "If you don't feel that you want to deal with this, then call my mother and tell her I'm at the St. Louis Holding Facility, and I need a thousand dollars to make bail."

Sharron heard him but remained speechless, thinking a thousand thoughts. *I've only known him for four months. And why do I feel like he's a con man now? He even spent the night in my father's* house *for God's sake!*

She shook her head against the phone and mumbled, "I just can't believe this."

But she *had* to. Anthony couldn't tell her much over the phone. He tried to make her understand anyway, through selective words.

"I can't believe this either," he said. "But I'm alive. I could have been shot in the head last night. I told them all of the details already. That's probably why my bail is only a thousand dollars. They know I'm innocent. This is just a technicality."

"Then how can they keep you then?" Sharron wanted to know.

"I don't know, Sharron. Let's call a lawyer and ask *him,"* he said, growing frustrated. Who *wouldn't* feel frustrated from a holding facility? "I've never been here before. I just want to get out of here. I have a thousand dollars in the bank."

Do you really? Sharron thought. She knew her thoughts were wrong. She had just told Anthony that she loved him less than a week ago. Now she questioned everything. But he had given her *reason* to. He was in *jail!*

"How long do you have to get the money?" she asked him. She pondered the idea of getting him out, getting her money back, and letting him go his own way. Damn, love was painful!

"I think the judge has to have it by five o'clock or something, but I'm not sure." And he wasn't sure. It wasn't as if he was a veteran of the criminal court policies. Anthony hadn't even been cited for driving violations. He loved his car too much to speed or to miss stop signs and red lights.

"What time is it now?" she asked him.

"It's nine thirty-seven," he answered her, looking up at a clock on the wall. Clocks were extremely noticeable in prison. Time meant everything. Everything and nothing at all.

Sharron paused, and decided that she would do it. She couldn't walk away from what they were building together on a "technicality."

"Let me finish getting dressed," she told him. "I'll have to call in to work, and tell them that I'll be late."

"Oh my God!" Anthony responded, relieved. "Thank you, Sharron. And I'll give it right back to you."

You better! she thought. *I have to use that money for school.*

"How long do you think it will take you?" he asked her.

"I don't know how far this place is. I'll have to get a taxi. But first I have to go to my bank and get the money, right?" she asked.

"Yeah, you right. That sounds like about . . . two hours," he told her. Realistically, he was thinking closer to three hours, but he wanted to force the issue.

Sharron caught on to his urgency and held her tongue. *I'll get there when I* get *there,* she thought.

Their good-bye was an awkward one.

"Well, I guess I'll see you soon then," he said.

"Yeah, I guess so," Sharron grumbled in response.

"Okay then," Anthony countered, upbeat, to inject some life into her somber mood. He just wanted to see her face and have his freedom. He realized that it was tough on her. However, the bottom line was getting him out. Then he could tell her everything she needed to know. Surely she wouldn't drop him before hearing an explanation.

They hung up the phone on borrowed time, both wondering how long they had left together. Sharron would overlook this *one* incident, *if* Anthony was innocent of what they were holding him for. She was only petrified at having to go through reccurrences of various natures with him. But that was life. Shit happens, and you deal with it.

Anthony honestly couldn't blame Sharron if she decided to cut him loose. Maybe it just wasn't meant to be. Then again, maybe his impossible situation was just what he needed to see how much Sharron believed in him. Not that he would ever *plan* something like bail money to do the trick. However, that was the situation they were stuck with.

As soon as Sharron stepped out of the bathroom, Celena asked, "You're not going to go and bail him out are you? Girl, this is the biggest *hint* in the world for you. And if you can't see that, then you make Helen Keller look like an eye doctor."

Sharron gave Celena the meanest look in the world and snapped, "Leave me the hell alone right now! Okay? Because I *don't* appreciate your *bullshit!*"

Celena was ready to jump in and make her point concerning untrustworthy men, but Sharron didn't give her a chance. She slammed her bedroom door in her roommate's face and continued with her business.

If that girl bothers me today, I swear to God, *I will* hurt *her! And she* will *find out that I can fight!* Sharron thought as she jammed on the rest of her clothes, still with half-combed hair.

"She thinks everything is a *fuckin'* game!" she mumbled. "Just because *she* can't find nobody. That's *her* damn problem! She ain't *perfect* either!" Sharron continued to snap. It was a good thing Celena was in her room and out of sight when Sharron walked out to the front door, because she just may have started something wild, something she did not have time to finish that morning.

Sharron was so hot that she walked out to catch a bus on Olive Boulevard instead of waiting for a taxi like she had planned. And while she sat there, riding the bus to her bank, she thought about turning right around and going back in to work. To hell with Anthony Poole! To hell with Celena Myers! And to hell with love! So when she arrived at Kingshighway, and was right up the street from her bank, she was confused and walking in circles. Then she stopped and stood there in the middle of the sidewalk and sunshine while St. Louis pedestrians made their way around her.

Should I really go and get him? Is he worth all of this stress? Maybe Celena is *right. That's why I want to beat her ass right now, because the* truth *hurts. Black men ain't worth a* damn! *Maybe I should have stayed with Sean after all. This is just what I get!* she mused.

A thousand dollars for a young black man was the issue. Ten big-faced Benjamins, fresh out of the mint. But was he worth it? And in the long run, would he end up as a big waste of her time and effort?

Sharron stood motionless on the sidewalk, contemplating everything. Then she had flashbacks of when she had first met Anthony, right there on Kingshighway Boulevard, cruising up beside her in his old-school ride:

Hey, miss?

She found herself remembering that first look at his confident brown face, and his blue denim work clothes, with his right arm and hand relaxing against the length of the passenger door.

You wanna make a trade with me?

Then he sat there and waited for her to respond, as all kinds of confusing thoughts ran through her mind concerning his sudden proposition.

A trade? Trade for what? she was asking him again in her mind's eye.

His classic line vibrated its way down from her head to her toes, and slipped into her soul. Not because of the line itself, but because of the young man she had grown to love *behind* the line.

A piece of me for a piece of you.

And she still wanted that piece. Bit by bit. Until she could no longer have it. Until she could no longer take it. Or until it was no longer available to her.

A thousand dollars was a small price to pay to fill up the emptiness she would feel in her heart if she did not at least *try* to take that chance on long-lasting love. She had to at least *try* to hold on and see if Anthony could be true. She couldn't allow him to just slip away from her palms like sand in the wind. Somebody *had* to hold on. Somebody *had* to try and make it last. Somebody *had* to stop the madness! Because the madness of easy separations had only increased the *hunger* for love, while *decreasing* all of the *faith* that it took to make love a reality. And somebody *had* to have *faith,* and let *faith* lead the way!

So Sharron sucked up all of her doubts and realized the most valid mission in life: to love somebody so bad until it hurt *not* to. She gathered her leg strength and her heart together and made that walk to the bank to withdraw a thousand dollars in big bills.

But if I lack love, I have nothing at all, she told herself while waiting in line for their money. Because she saw it as a chance for *both* of them. After all, bailing a man out of jail was no small thing. Unless, of course, he made a habit out of it. Yet, she had to give Anthony that opportunity to prove himself.

When she felt the money in her hands, she couldn't *wait* to arrive at the St. Louis Holding Facility and get her man, ignoring everyone. Their chance at love was between *him* and *her* and *not* the world. It was none of their damn business! Including the taxi driver who looked at her funny when she told him her destination.

She arrived at the gates and barbed-wire fencing that surrounded the gray brick building of the St. Louis Holding Facility and paid her fare. Then she climbed out of the taxi and took a deep breath.

"I got your back, baby. I got your back," she mumbled to herself, approaching the front door and slipping in. Everything else was a blur. She told them who she was there for. She gave them the bail money. She signed some paperwork. And she waited on a small, wooden bench for what seemed like an hour.

Anthony walked out and stood before her with his things. Sharron looked into his eyes and *knew* that she had made the right decision, because his eyes were filled with her, like two reflecting mirrors, filled with warmth, appreciation, commitment, and real love.

Anthony didn't even speak to her. They didn't *need* any words. He grabbed Sharron into him and hugged her with everything he had, over seven hundred minutes of anticipation since the hour that he was arrested. And Sharron held on to him with twenty-four years of desire to love a brown man for as long as she could breathe.

"Let's get out of here," he told her, breaking away softly and leading her to the front door. When they made it back outside to the sunshine, Anthony looked into Sharron's eyes and told her, "You know I owe you for this."

She countered, "I don't *want* you to *owe* me. I want you to *love* me. The right way. By never doing anything that would break us apart. And by never giving up on us."

He held her hands right there outside the St. Louis Holding Facility's barbed-wire gates, a free man, and committed himself to his woman with a slow nod. "All right then. I'll do that. I'll love you the right way. Forever, girl. 'Cause you're my lady. No doubt!

"You looked out for me. So I gotta look out for you," he said. "And not just because you bailed me out. But because I *want* to. And I love you."

She smiled and squeezed his hands tightly in hers. "I love you, too," she told him. "And not because you're driving me crazy. But because I *believe* in you. And I believe in *us.*"

Everybody in the world wants to be in love with *somebody*. However, too many of us have lost focus on what it takes to *stay* there. So after the attractions to the faces, hair, skin, eyes, and bodies of our potential mates, we must then evaluate their intelligence, creativity, spirit, self-respect, and economic stature. Economically speaking in terms of human progression, and not simply capital gains. Like the age-old invention of the wheel, relationships based on love were *meant* to roll forward. Sometimes they roll backwards before finding their way, but they were *never* meant to stand still, idling, and rotting away. And in their forward roll, they grow stronger.

So by the time Anthony and Sharron arrived at the impound lot and paid the necessary charges to reclaim his car, he had told her everything about the night before, and Sharron was satisfied in putting her worries to rest.

"We'll go straight to my bank after this," Anthony promised her. He was thoroughly inspecting his car on hands and knees, searching bumper to bumper and underneath.

"There's no damages on her," the impounder addressed Anthony during his inspection. He was a burly man in a tight gray shirt, appearing to hold his stomach up from the pull of gravity.

Anthony ignored the man and continued to look for the faintest scratch on his Chevy, failing to find any. He rose to his feet and nodded, pleased with the results of his search. Then he opened the passenger-side door for his "lady."

The burly man asked him, "Is everything all right by you?" He knew that it would be. He had done a thorough job with the car.

"Yeah, it's good," Anthony mumbled to him. He just wanted to drive his car the hell out of there, and forget about the entire nightmare.

Sharron smiled at him when he slid behind the wheel.

"You really love this car, don't you?"

Anthony frowned and said, "I just don't trust these impounds. They don't give a fuck about your car. All they care about is the money they charge you to get it back from 'em."

Sharron just shook her head and strapped herself in as they drove through more barbed-wire gates and hit the free roads of St. Louis. And as she looked back, she pondered the regularity of so many brown-skinned American men, locked behind similar gates in correctional facilities all across the country.

"What did you feel like while you were in there?" she asked him. "It just seems like those places are magnets for black men. Why is that?" she asked rhetorically. She had a few obvious reasons behind it, but the racism game was getting *very old.*

Anthony looked straight ahead, well on his way to his downtown bank office, and answered, "Too many of 'em have nothing to do with their lives . . . and nothing to look forward to to keep them out of there." Then he looked at Sharron and smiled. "And women like you to *bail* them out."

She grinned at it, but thought too much to laugh. "So, what happens to your friend Tone?"

Anthony shrugged his shoulders. "There's nothing I can do about that now. All I can do is *hope* that he makes out all right. Because *I'm* not going to jail. They know I'm innocent. So after the court date . . . I guess I'll just see him when he gets out."

Sharron looked surprised. "You mean, you wouldn't go and visit him?" she asked curiously. Anthony would have surely wanted someone to visit *him.*

He chuckled at it. "It's fucked up, ain't it? But after last night, I don't want to be nowhere *near* jail! I mean, I can still write to him. But visits?" He shook his head. "I don't know if I can do it."

Good! Sharron thought to herself. Not to disrespect the love that Anthony had for his boy, it was just that jail was no place for a sane man to feel an affinity to. And boy did she feel good about his response to that! Because *some* men took macho loyalties to the point of ridiculousness.

They arrived at Anthony's bank downtown, and he hopped out to run inside with the engine still running.

"I'll be right back out with your money," he told Sharron with a proud smile. It felt good to him to be able to give his word and to *stand* by it!

Sharron sat still inside the car, smiling from ear to ear, and was moved by that herself.

I got a good man, she told herself. *He actually* does *what he* says *he's going to do.* In an era of love where black men increasingly dropped the ball, Anthony Poole's sure hands were indeed treasures to behold. But when he made it back to the car, his hands were empty.

He sat back down in his driver seat and sulked. "You know what they told me in there? They said I can't get my money out today," he said, looking straight into Sharron's face.

"Why not?" she asked him.

"Something about my funds not being available."

"Well, when will they *be* available?"

"They told me like in four days. They said a couple of my check deposits bounced."

"So, you had about a thousand dollars on the nose? How much *could* you take out?" she asked him.

Anthony read the panic in her face and began to laugh. "Naw, I'm just bullshittin'," he told her. "I got the money." He dug inside his pants and pulled out a white envelope filled with ten one-hundred-dollar bills, to replace what Sharron had withdrawn from *her* bank earlier.

She shook her head and grinned, counting her money as they pulled away.

"What were you about to say to me? 'You're a *lying* asshole!'" he mocked her, assuming.

Sharron continued to smile and didn't answer.

"My girl Celena told me not to bail you out this morning," she confided in him instead.

Anthony looked over at her, then back to the road, and was noticeably upset by it.

"Are you glad you didn't listen to her?" he asked.

Sharron glued her eyes to him and nodded. "You *know* I am. I don't let her control my life. She didn't even tell me where you were calling from. I was thinking about moving out after she did that."

Anthony looked at her with determination and said, "I'm serious about that, Sharron. I think it's about that time for me. Especially after *this* shit! I *need* somebody to come home to. God was giving me a message, and I'm *damn sure* listening to him!" he joked. But he was dead serious.

Sharron laughed out loud. "I'm serious about it, too," she said. "But a lot of people say that moving in can spoil the relationship."

Anthony held his tongue on it for a minute. Then he asked her, "You believe that?"

She answered, "I don't know. I never did it before."

"Did it spoil your relationship with Celena?" He thought better of that question and said, "Well, maybe I should take that back."

"Yeah," Sharron agreed with a nod. "Because she gets on my nerves a lot. But I guess it just takes getting used to."

"Everything takes getting used to," Anthony told her.

Sharron broke from their conversation and asked, "Where are we going?"

They were heading north on Route 70.

"I'm taking you to work," he told her.

"Don't *you* have to be to work too?"

Anthony said sternly, "Look, don't worry about *me.* I'll make up something. But after what *you* went through to get me out, I'm driving you to work. Are you straight with that?" he asked her.

Sharron smiled that easy smile of hers again. "Yeah, I'm straight."

"Good. But I ain't in no hurry to get you there either," he told her, placing his right hand on her left knee. He squeezed it and drove no faster than fifty miles an hour in the slow lane.

Sharron Francis continued to smile, feeling like a queen in her chariot. Then she undid her seat belt and slid over next to her king to lay her head against his strong shoulder, confident that they had tomorrow, and next week, and next year.

And as they cruised north on Route 70 toward the airport, well below the speed limit, they both looked ahead to holding each other after work that night and making love . . . *sweet* love, like it *should* be . . . in St. Louis . . . and everywhere else in the world.

Acknowledgments

PEACE & LOVE to Pamela Artis who is still hanging in there and helping me to organize and edit new and improved material. She's like the Energizer Bunny; keeps reading and reading (smile). Let's outlast all of the competition, Pam. I have about eight more books waiting in the wings for you. To Tierney Davis and Walter "Rap" Pearson for my St. Louis research. And to Sister Jamilah Nasheed for inviting me out to St. Louis in 1997 when I first came up with the idea.

Peace & Love to my uncle Joseph McLaurin, the creative force and passionate Web master behind *www.OmarTyree.com.* Two thousand hits per month ain't too shabby for an author who's never been on many national television shows. What will happen to our #1 author's Web site if I do hit national TV? BOOM! We blow up! So keep the new ideas rolling out strong, Joe.

Peace & Love to my aunts: Shelly, Gina, Tuta, Dee Dee, Shirley, Hazel, Florence, Stella (RIP), Anita, Burlie, Eltie, Jaycina, Greta, Bert, Sharon, Linda, Rudy, and Eassie (RIP). My sisters: Dee Dee, Darlene, Cydnee, Paula, and Kate. My cousins: Donna Jean, Claranell, Mamie, Estelle, Hodgie, Theresa, Cassandra, Liz, June, Adrienne, Priscilla, Nettie, Penny, Hellen, Jackie, Judy, Ashley, Quanie, Sabrina,

Diane, Robin, Paula, Lauri, Sherri, Dawn, Sebrena, Angel, Lisa, Tina, Tiffany B., Tiffany F., Monique, Rasheeda, Kieara, Sharisse, Shanae, Squirt, Ki-Ki, and Boo-Boo. My nieces: Deanna, Dominique, and Amani. Also family: Joy, Bernadette, Evelyn, and Helena. And my wife's girls: Dawn, Nadeje, Kai, Ashleigh, Monique, Pascha, Octavia, Toby, and the twins, Amina and Ayesha.

My grandmothers: Mert (RIP), Betty (RIP), Gerri, Dorothy, and Frances Clarke. My mother-in-law Donna. And my six godmothers: Peaches, Linda, Donna, Ruth, Mariam, and Ellen. Keep looking after me for my mom, you guys. Much respect!

Peace & Love to my agent, Denise Stinson. We have a big contract year coming up. Let 'em know, Denise, "Omar Tyree is *loaded* with new book ideas and *definitely* here to stay! But he wants people to *know* that he's here! So put the cheese on the table and switch on the high beams!"

R-E-S-P-E-C-T! Assertive marketing is the key to the castle! Let's just *DO IT!*

Peace & Love to my fourth new editor at Simon & Schuster, Geoffrey Kloske. Thanks a million for introducing me to the head honchos up at the office on Sixth Avenue. Now they can place my face of charm, intelligence, determination, and commitment to my name. I'm no spoiled artist over here. I'm a *thinker* and a *doer!* So support the man with the plans and commit to a golden future.

Peace & Love to Georgia's Brown Restaurant in Washington, D.C., for letting me snap that handsome back jacket photo at your place on 17th and K Streets, Northwest. And thanks to my main man Daniel McNeill for all of the photo shots you continue to snap of me.

Peace & Love to new friends: Bernard Love for turning up the heat in Kansas City (MO) with "The Breakfast Brothers." Anthony Weatherly in Chester (PA). Brother Malik and "The Home Team" in Los Angeles (CA) for turning me on to the West Side. Teresa and Antoine for making me feel at home in St. Louis (MO). Traci L. McKinley and Sister Garbo in Little Rock (AR). Melissa Lee for hooking me up in Trenton (NJ) through Wendy "What" Williams and crew. Lisa Evers for hooking me up on the "Street Soldiers" of New York (NY) side of things. And Sherry McGee for blowing up the book market in Detroit (MI). Also to Raynelle Wiggins (DE), Deborah Ramcheran (PA), Tanya Moss (NY), and "Zee" (GA)—keep writing your hearts out, sisters. *Sweet St. Louis* is for *all* of you who search for love! Maybe us hardheaded men will finally understand one day that love is a blessing and not a curse.

To Tulsa University, Temple, NYU, Lincoln, Pennsylvania, Delaware, Bowie State, Del. State, Del. Tech., College of Staten Island, and Wesley College for inviting me to educate your campus population on the issues of my novels. Or at least those who came out to hear my loud behind speak (smile). Ask them what they learned. Ask them if Omar knows what he's talking about. Ask them if they'd invite me back again. . . . *Definitely!*

To the magazines and newspapers that gave me love: *News Dimensions* (DC), *The News Journal* (DE), *The New York Daily News* (NY), *Black Issues Book Review* (VA), *Dialogue* (DC), *Mosaic* (NY), *Grace* (TN), *Upscale* (GA), *Philadelphia Tribune,* (PA), *Philadelphia Daily News* (PA), *RapPages* (CA), *The Daily Press* (VA), *The Oakland Press* (CA), *The Black Suburban Journal* (DE), *Harlem Overheard* (NY), and *San Francisco BayView* (CA).

Last but not least, and in alphabetical order—DRUM ROLL PLEASE—I'd like to give a special thanks to all of the book clubs and literary groups who have supported my mission to uplift the mind state of the people: African-American Literary Book Club (NC), African-American Literary Forum (GA), African-American Sisters Club (NY), Afro-American Reading Book Club (SC), Agape Reading Club (NY), The African-American Authors' Network (OH), The AKAs (USA), Baltimore Reads (MD), Black Author's Literary Cruise Konnection (NC & GA), Black Expressions Book Club (KS), Black Literary Sisters (VA), Black Men Advocating Reading (GA), Black Women's Literary Guild (MA), Books For Us (GA), Borders Reading Group (NJ), The Black Bookworms (TX), BrainStorm, The Book Club (GA), The Black Library (MA), The Busara Nayo Bookclub (PA), Campbell's Theories Book Club (MD), DeBose Music, Film & Books (PA), Diva's Book Club (DC), Doubleday Book Club (IN), Drum & Spear Books (DC), The Deltas (USA) EZ Street Online Book Club (DC), Go On Girl #3 (NJ), Houston African-American Writers' Society (TX), The Imani Book Club

(CA), Kindred Spirits Book Club (CA), Literary Expressions (FPO, AP), Literary Speaking Book Club (MD), Mahogany Cafe Book Club (OH), Moonstone Inc. (PA), Msichana Rafiki Literary Club (NJ), The Next Phase African-American Women Book Club (TX), Onyx Book Club (GA), PageTurners Book Club (MD), Phyre & Eyce (PA), A Reading Circle of Friends (DC), Sibanye, Inc. (MD), Sistahs With a Vision (NJ), Sisterhood Book Club (TX), Sister 2 Sister (MA), Sister Circle Book Club (CA), Sister Friends Book Club (DC), Sisters & Brothers of Hotlanta (GA & DE), Sisters Searching For Knowledge (TN), Sisters With Books (WI), Soul Sisters Book Club (TX), The Saturday Afternoon Book Club (MD), The Shaw Literary Group (NY), Tenaj's Books (FL), Tennessee State Book Club (TN), Thee Writa's Block (PA), United Brothers & Sisters Communications Network (VA), and all other supporters that I'm unaware of. Let me know for next time!

"I'm still standing, Mom! The well is drying up in the industry, just like I knew it would, but your boy is just getting started. So stay tuned and watch me continue to shine! Whoooweee! Look out above!"

Omar Rashad Tyree

About the Author

OMAR TYREE is an acclaimed author, journalist, lecturer and poet. His books include *Flyy Girl, A Do Right Man, Capital City, Battle Zone,* and *Single Mom.* He lives in New Castle, Delaware.

To learn more about Omar Tyree, you can view his Web site at www.OmarTyree.com, send an e-mail to Omar8Tyree@aol.com, or write to MARS Productions, P.O. Box 12814, Wilmington, DE 19850.